# NEAR + FAR

### STORIES *of the*
### NEAR FUTURE *and the* FAR

## Cat Rambo

Hydra HH House

# Near + Far

Copyright © 2012 by Cat Rambo

978-0-9848301-4-5 (print)
978-0-9848301-5-2 (ebook)
Library of Congress Control Number: 2012943112

Hydra House
1122 E Pike St. #1451
Seattle, WA 98122
*http://www.hydrahousebooks.com/*

Cover art by Sean Counley
*http://www.seancounley.com/*

Cover design by Tod McCoy

Illustrations by Mark Tripp
*http://www.spiderpig.com/*

Text design by Vicki Saunders

## PRAISE FOR NEAR + FAR

Five reasons to read Cat Rambo:
#1:  If you like stories about strange places and strange creatures
#2:  If you like stories that leave you yourself feeling a little strange
#3:  If you like a good love story
#4:  especially one with talking cats, deadly mermaids, mind-altering technologies, live coats, detachable limbs, gorgeous descriptions and great leaps of imagination, wit and power
#5:  plus travel through space and time
Then this is the book for you.

### *Karen Joy Fowler*

Cat Rambo's futures are complex, and often dissonant and eerie—they evoke the familiar in their careful world-building, intricate detail and recognizable characters, while simultaneously constructing futures flavored with the strange. Her futures are often unsettling, but never so simple as to be dystopic; her stories inhabit complex, ambiguous worlds. Her simultaneously familiar and unfamiliar settings sharpen her portrayals of human relationships. By recasting core experiences against disjunctive backgrounds, she causes the reader to appreciate them anew. People are always at the center: they fall away from each other, cope with betrayals, seek connections. While the inner eye marvels at her immersive images, the body resonates with the subtle, deft emotions imbued in her characters. Cat Rambo's finest stories shimmer in the memory like the lights of the Aurora Borealis: vivid and eerily illuminating.

### *Rachel Swirsky*

Cat Rambo's stories never go where you expect them to. They twist and turn and end up in strange places—sometimes very strange indeed. Both the stories set on the Earth we know (or think we know) and those set far away will surprise and delight you.

**Nancy Kress**

Cat Rambo's newest collection shows two sides of her fiction. Powerful prose, coupled with telling details. Not only does the collection flip, physically, it will also turn you on your head. Read with caution: these stories are only safe in small doses.

**Mary Robinette Kowal**

Near + Far is a survey of the terrain of Cat Rambo's imagination, ranging from small fantasies of the moment to vest pocket planetary romances. She tends to the quiet, internal, disturbing reflection, far more Bradbury than Heinlein. Moving, thought-provoking literature in nicely comestible chunks.

**Jay Lake**

An exemplary short story collection in both senses of the term— excellent and also a model of what the range of the career of a speculative short story writer should be, and these days unfortunately so rarely is. Wide in its subject matter from the immediate future to the wide open spaces, deep in its psychological characterization when that is the central point, speculatively amusing when it isn't, well-realized almost all of the time, and always entertaining.

**Norman Spinrad**

# Near + Contents

# Introduction

IF YOU'RE HOLDING THE PHYSICAL COPY OF THIS BOOK, YOU'RE seeing the outgrowth of my theory regarding how electronic publishing will affect books. The book is more than a delivery mechanism for text: it should feel nice in your hands if we've done everything right. You can flip it to find a second set of stories, which I find downright cool. Attention's been paid to the art, both exterior and interior, and we've proofread the heck out of it, so there should be very few typos to distract the reader. It's an object that can be prized in its own right.

This is how, I think, physical books may survive, as objects that are aesthetically pleasing or entertaining in their own right, and which add something to the text they hold. Look at Subterranean Press' strategy of making beautiful, collectible books: I've got more than a few of those on my shelves and I'll keep buying them periodically, despite the fact that I do most of my reading now on the Kindle. That's the kind of book we've tried to put together.

If you're reading this electronically, we've tried to make the most of that as well. You'll find there's an accompanying mobile device app (or will be, Goddess willing, by the time this comes out) that lets you access extra material, including audio recordings of several stories.

I am incredibly pleased with this book. It's allowed me to work with some of my very favorite people, and particular shouts should go out to: Tod McCoy, without whom this book would not have been possible; Vicki Saunders, for incredible design skills and meticulous work; Mark Tripp, for allowing me to use some of the art he's been showing me for over a decade; Sean Counley, for his gorgeous cover art; Jo Molnar, who kindly pruned typos and corrected embarrassing misspellings; and Wayne Rambo, who provided support, encouragement, and occasional nagging. You guys rock, and you rock hard.

The stories themselves come from close to a decade of writing. Sometimes when you're writing, you feel you're leveled up, that you've moved through some plateau and jumped to a new degree of skill. Some of these stories are ones that let me know I'd leveled up. I hope you enjoy them all.

# THE MERMAIDS SINGING, EACH TO EACH

 NIKO LEANED BEHIND ME IN THE CABIN, raising his voice to be heard over the roar of engine and water. "When you Choose, which is it going to be? Boy or girl?"

I would have answered, if I thought it really mattered to him. But we were off shore by then, headed for the Lump, and he was just making conversation, knowing how long it would take us to get there. He didn't care whether I'd be male or female, I'd still be his pal Lolo. I could feel the boat listening, but she knew I didn't want her talking, that I'd turn her off if she went too far.

So I kept steering the *Mary Magdalena* and said I didn't know, and it didn't matter, unless we did manage to cash in on the Lump before the corp-strippers got there. After that we were silent again, and everything was just the engine rumble moving up through my feet. Jorge Felipe turned over in the hammock we'd managed to fit into the cabin, hammering the nails into the paneling to hang the hooks. He let out something that was either snore or fart or maybe both.

Jorge Felipe was the one who had found out about the Lump. It was four or five kilometers across, the guy who'd spotted it said. Four or five kilometers of prime debris floating in the ocean, bits of old plastic and wood and Dios knew what else, collected by the currents, amassed in a single spot. All salvageable, worth five new cents a pound. Within a week, the corp-stripper boats would be out there, disassembling it and shoveling all that money into company machines, company mouths.

But we were going to get there first, carve off a chunk, enough to pay us all off. I wanted to be able to Choose, and I couldn't do that until I could pay the medical bill. Niko said he wasn't saving for anything, but really he was—there'd be enough money that he could relax for a month and not worry about feeding his mother and his extended family.

Jorge Felipe just wanted out of Santo Nuevo. Any way he could escape our village was fine with him, and the first step was affording a ticket. He wanted to be out before storm season hit, when we'd all be living on whatever we could manage until a new crop of tourists bloomed in the spring.

Winter was lean times. Jorge Felipe, for all his placid snoring right now, was feeling desperation's bite. That's why he was willing to cut me in, in exchange for use of the *Mary Magdalena*. Most of the time he didn't have much to say to me. I gave him the creeps, I knew. He'd told Niko in order to have him tell me. But he didn't have any other friends with boats capable of going out to carve off a chunk of the Lump and bring it in for salvage. On my side of things, I thought he was petty and mean and dangerous. But he knew the Lump's coordinates.

I tilted my head, listened to the engines, checking the rhythms to make sure everything was smooth. The familiar stutter of the fan from behind me was nothing to worry about, or the way the water pump coughed when it first switched on. I knew all of *Mary Magdalena*'s sounds. She's old, but she works, and between the hydro-engines and the solar panels, she manages to get along.

Sometimes I used to imagine crashing her on a reef and swimming away, leaving her to be covered with birdshit and seaweed, her voice pleading, as long as the batteries held out. Sometimes I used to imagine taking one of the little cutting lasers, chopping away everything but her defenseless brainbox, deep in the planking below the cabin, then severing its inputs one by one, leaving her alone. Sometimes I imagined worse things.

I inherited her from my uncle Fortunato. My uncle loved his boat like a woman, and she'd do things for him, stretch out the last bit of fuel, turn just a bit sharper, that she wouldn't do for me or anyone else. An abandoned woman now, pining for a lover who'd moved on.

2

I could have the AI stripped down and retooled, re-imprint her, but I'd lose all her knowledge. Her ability to recognize me.

I'd left the cabin the way my uncle had it: his baseball cap hanging on the peg beside the doorway, his pin-up photos shellacked onto the paneling. Sometimes I thought about painting over the photos. But they reminded me of my uncle, reminded me not to forgive him. You would have thought they would have been enough, but maybe they just egged him on. Some people claim that's how it goes with porn, more and more until a man can't control himself.

I can't say my experience has confirmed this.

Uncle Fortunato left me the *Mary Magdalena* from guilt, guilt about what he'd done, guilt that his niece had decided to go sexless, to put away all of that rather than live with being female. I was the first in the village to opt for the Choice, but not the first in the world by a long shot. It was fashionable by then, and a lot of celebrities were having it done to their children for "therapeutic reasons." My grandmother, Mama Fig, said it was unnatural and against the Church's law, and every priest in the islands came and talked to me. But they didn't change my mind. There was a program funding it for survivors of sexual assault. That's how I got it paid for, even though I wouldn't tell them who did it.

I couldn't have him punished. If they'd put him away, my grandmother would have lost her only means of support. But I could take myself out of his grasp by making myself unfuckable. Neuter. Neuter until I wanted to claim a gender. They didn't tell me, though, that getting in was free, but getting out would cost. Cost a lot.

When I first heard he'd left the boat to me, I didn't want her. I let her sit for two weeks gathering barnacles at dock before I went down.

I wouldn't have ever gone, but the winter was driving me crazy. No work to be found, nothing to do but sit home with my grandmother and listen to her worry about her old friends' children and her favorite soap opera's plotlines.

When I did go to the *Mary Magdalena*, she didn't speak until I came aboard. First I stood and looked at her. She's not much, all told: boxy, thirty years out of date, a dumbboat once, tweaked into this century.

I used to imagine pouring acid on her deck, seeing it eat away at the wood with a hiss and sizzle.

# Near +

As I made my way up the gangplank, I could feel that easy sway beneath my feet. There's nothing like being on a boat, and I closed my eyes just to feel the vertigo underfoot like a familiar friend's hand on my elbow.

I used to imagine her torn apart by magnets, the bolts flying outward like being dismantled in a cartoon.

"Laura," a speaker said, as though I hadn't been gone for six years, as though she'd seen me every day in between. "Laura, where is your uncle?"

I used to imagine her disintegrated, torn apart into silent atoms.

"It's not Laura anymore," I said. "It's Lolo. I'm gender neutral."

"I don't understand," she said.

"You've got a Net connection," I said. "Search around on "gender neutral" and "biomod operation.""

I wasn't sure if the pause that came after that was for dramatic effect or whether she really was having trouble understanding the search parameters. Then she said, "Ah, I see. When did you do that?"

"Six years ago."

"Where is your uncle?"

"Dead," I said flatly. I hoped that machine intelligences could hurt and so I twisted the knife as far as I could. "Stabbed in a bar fight."

Her voice always had the same flat affect, but I imagined/hoped I could hear sorrow and panic underneath. "Who owns me now?"

"I do. Just as long as it takes me to sell you."

"You can't, Laura."

"Lolo. And I can."

"The licenses to operate—the tourism, the sport-fishing, even the courier license—they won't transfer to a new owner. They won't pay much for a boat they can't use."

"Oh, I don't know," I said. "You'd fetch a decent amount as scrap."

She paused again. "Keep me going, Lolo, and you can take in enough to keep yourself and Mama Fig afloat. Your uncle had ferrying contracts, and every season is good for at least a couple of trips with very cheap or eccentric tourists."

She had grace enough not to push beyond that. I didn't have much choice, and it was the only way to support my grandmother and myself month to month. With the *Mary Magdalena*, I was better off

4

than Niko or Jorge Felipe by far. I could afford the occasional new shirt or record, rather than something scavenged.

At the end of a year, we'd reached an agreement. Most of the time now, the boat knew better than to talk to me. She could have been with me everywhere. Button mikes gleamed along the front railing, in the john, even in the little lifeboat that hugged the side. But she stayed silent except in the cabin, where she would tell me depths, weather, water temperature. I told her which way to go. Businesslike and impersonal.

Niko went out on deck. I didn't blame him. It was too warm in the cabin. I knew the *Mary Magdalena* would alert me if there was any trouble, but I liked to keep an eye on things.

Jorge Felipe stirred, stuck his head out over the hammock's edge. His dark hair extended in all directions, like broken broom straws.

"Morning yet?" he rasped.

"Couple more hours."

"Where's Niko?"

"Went to smoke."

He grunted. "Shit, it's hot in here," he said. He swung his legs out from under the blanket's basket-weave, thumped onto the floor. "We got soup left?"

"Thermos in the cupboard."

Behind me the microwave beeped out protests as he thumbed its controls. The display was a steady, grainy green, showing me the surface far below the boat. Drifts and ridges. They said you could spot a wreck by the unnatural straightness of a line, the oddness of a corner. Unlikely, but it had been heard of, in that friend-of-a-cousin-of-a-neighbor's sort of way.

"Heat me one," I said.

"Soup or coffee?"

"Coffee," I said, and he clanked another mug into the microwave.

Niko came into the doorway. "Mermaids out there," he said. "Be careful if you swim."

Jorge Felipe handed me my mug, so hot it almost bit into my skin as I cupped it.

"Fucking mermaids," he said. "I hate them even worse than sharks. One tangled with my sister, almost killed her."

"Everyone on the island's tangled with your sister. I'm getting coffee and going back out," Niko said, and did.

Jorge Felipe watched him go. "He's fucking obsessed with those mermaids."

Mermaids. Back before I was born, there were more tourists. There's always tourists now, but not quite as many. Some of them came here specifically, even, for the beaches. Or for the cheap black-market bio-science. And one black-market bio-scientist specialized in making mermaids out of them.

They paid a lot for it, I guess. A moddie body that they could go swimming in, pretend like they were always sea creatures. It was very popular one year, Mama Fig said.

But the scientist, he wasn't that good, or that thorough. Or maybe he didn't understand all the implications of the DNA he was using. Some people said he did it deliberately.

Because mermaids lay eggs, hundreds at a time, at least that kind did. And the natural-born ones, they didn't have human minds guiding them. They were like sharks—they ate, they killed, they ate. Most of the original human mermaids had gotten out when they found out that the seas were full of chemicals, or that instead of whale songs down there, they heard submarine sonar and boat signals. When the last few discovered that they were spawning whether they liked it or not, they got out too. Supposedly one or two stayed, and now they live in the sea with their children, twice as mean as any of them.

After a while, I said, "Watch the display for me" and went up on deck. The sun was rising, slivers of gold and pink and blue in the east. It played over the gouges in the *Mary Magdalena*'s railing where I'd picked at it with a knife, like smallpox marks along the boat's face.

Niko was watching the water. Light danced over it, intense and dazzling. Spray rode the wind, stinging the eyes. I licked salt from my drying lips.

"Where are you seeing them?" I asked.

He pointed, but I didn't see anything at first. It took several moments to spot a flick of fins, the intercepted shadow as a wave rose and fell.

"You see them out this deep all the time," I said. Niko hadn't been

6

out on the boat much. He got nauseous anywhere out past ten meters, but Jorge Felipe had enlisted him to coax me into cooperating, had supplied him with fancy anti-nausea patches. I looked sideways. One glistened like a chalky gill on the side of his neck.

"Yeah?" he said, staring at the water. He wasn't watching me, so I looked at his face, trying to commit the details to memory. Trying to imagine him as a photograph. His jaw was a smooth line, shadowed with stubble. The hairs in front of his ears tangled in curls, started to corkscrew, blunted by sleep. He had long eyelashes, longer than mine. The sun tilted further up and the dazzle of light grew brighter, till it made my eyes hurt.

"Put on a hat," I said to Niko. "Going to be hot and bad today."

He nodded but stayed where he was. I started to say more, but shrugged and went back in. It was all the same to me. Still, when I saw his straw hat on the floor, I nudged it over to Jorge Felipe and said, "Take this out to Niko when you go."

Looking out over the railing, I spotted the three corp ships long before we got to the Lump. For a moment I wondered why they were so spread out, and then I realized the Lump's size. It was huge—kilometers wide. The ships were gathered around it, and their buzz boats were resting, wings spread out to recharge the solar panels.

They must have seen us around the same time. A buzz boat folded its wings, shadows spider-webbed with silver, and approached us. As it neared, I saw the Novagen logo on its side, on its occupant's mirrored helmet.

"This is claimed salvage," the logo-ed loudspeaker said.

I cupped my hands to shout back, "Salvage's not claimed till you've got tethers on it. Unless you're pulling in the whole thing, we've got a right to chew on it, too."

"Claimed salvage," the pilot repeated. He looked the *Mary Magdalena* up and down and curled his lip. Most of the time I liked her shitty, rundown look, but pride bristled briefly. "You want to be careful, kid. Accidents happen out here when freelancers get in the way."

I knew they did. Corp ships liked to sink the competition, and they had a dozen different underhanded ways to do it.

Jorge Felipe said at my elbow, "Gonna let them chase us off?"

"No," I said, but I nodded at the pilot and said, "*Mary Magdalena*, back us off."

We moved round to the other side.

"What are you going to do?" Niko asked.

"We're going to cut the engines and let the currents creating the Lump pull us into it," I said. "They're watching for engine activity. After it gets dark, they won't notice us cutting. In the meantime, we'll act like we're fishing. Not even act, really."

We broke out fishing gear. The mermaids had deserted us, and I hoped to find a decent school of something, bottom-feeders at least. But the murk around the Lump was lifeless. Plastic tendrils waved like uneasy weed, gobbling our hooks till the rods bent and bowed with each wave.

I wanted the corp ships to see our lines. Every hour, a buzz boat would whoosh by, going between two of the larger ships.

When the sun went down, I went below deck. The others followed. I studied the weather readout on the main console's scratched metal flank.

It took longer than I thought, though. By the time we'd managed to cut our chunk free with the little lasers, draining the batteries, the sun was rising. Today was cloudier, and I blessed the fog. It'd make us harder to spot.

We worked like demons, throwing out hooks, cutting lumps free, tossing them into the cargo net. We looked for good stuff, electronics with precious metals that might be salvaged, good glass, bits of memorabilia that would sell on the Internet. Shellfish—we'd feed ourselves for a week out of this if nothing else. Two small yellow ducks bobbed in the wake of a bottle's wire lacing. I picked them up, stuck them in my pocket.

"What was that?" Jorge Felipe at my elbow.

"What was what?" I started hauling in orange netting fringed with dead seaweed.

"What did you stick in your pocket?" His eyes tightened with suspicion.

I fished the ducks out of my pocket, held them out. "You want one?"

He paused, glancing at my pocket.

8

"Do you want to stick your hand in?" I said. I cocked my hip towards him. He was pissing me off.

He flushed. "No. Just remember—we split it all. You remember that."

"I will."

There's an eagle, native to the islands. We call them brown-wings. Last year I'd seen Jorge Felipe dealing with docked tourists, holding one.

"Want to buy a bird?" he asked, sitting in his canoe looking up at the tan and gold and money-colored boat. He held it up.

"That's an endangered species, son," one tourist said. His face, sun-reddened, was getting redder.

Jorge looked at him, his eyes flat and expressionless. Then he reached out with the bird, pushed its head underwater for a moment, pulled it out squawking and thrashing.

The woman screeched. "Make him stop!"

"Want to buy a bird?" Jorge Felipe repeated.

They couldn't throw him money fast enough. He let the brown-wing go and it flew away. He bought us all drinks that night, even me, but I kept seeing that flat look in his eyes. It made me wonder what would have happened if they'd refused.

By the time the buzz boats noticed us, we were underway. They could see what we had in tow and I had the *Mary Magdalena* monitoring their radio chatter.

But what I hoped was exactly what happened. We were small fry. We had a chunk bigger than I'd dared think, but that wasn't even a thousandth of what they were chewing down. They could afford to let a few scavengers bite.

All right, I thought, and told the *Mary Magdalena* to set a course for home. The worst was over.

I didn't realize how wrong I was.

Niko squatted on his heels near the engines, watching the play of sunlight over the trash caught in the haul net. It darkened the water, but you could barely see it, see bits of plastic and bottles and seawrack submerged underneath the surface like an unspoken thought.

I went to my knees beside him. "What's up?"

He stared at the water like he was waiting for it to tell him something.

"It's quiet," he said.

Jorge Felipe was atop of the cabin, playing his plastic accordion. His heels, black with dirt, were hooked under the rungs of the ladder. I'd let the plastic fray there, and bits bristled and splayed like an old toothbrush. His music echoed out across the water for kilometers, the only sound other than splash or mermaid whistle.

"Quiet," I said, somewhere between statement and question.

"Gives you time to think."

"Think about what?"

"I was born not too far from here." He stared at the twitch and pluck in the sun-splattered water.

"Yeah?"

He turned to look at me. His eyes were chocolate and beer and cinnamon. "My mother said my dad was one of them."

I frowned. "One of what?"

"A mermaid."

I had to laugh. "She was pulling your leg. Mermaids can't fuck humans."

"Before he went into the water, idiot."

"Huh," I said. "And when he came out?"

"She said he never came out."

"So you think he's still there? Man, all those rich folks, once they learned that the water stank and glared, they gave up that life. If he didn't come out, he's dead."

I was watching the trash close to us when I saw what had sparked this thought. The mermaids were back. They moved along the net's edge. It shuddered as they tugged at it.

"What are they doing?" I asked.

"Picking at it," Niko said. "I've been watching. They pick bits off. What for, I don't know."

"We didn't see them around the Lump. Why now?"

Niko shrugged. "Maybe all that trash is too toxic for them. Maybe that's why we didn't see any fish near it either. Here it's smaller. Tolerable."

Jorge Felipe slid onto his heels on the deck.

"We need to drive them off," he said, frowning at our payload.

"No," Niko protested. "There's just a few. They're picking off the loose stuff that makes extra drag, anyhow. Might even speed us up."

Jorge Felipe gave him a calculating look. The look he'd given the tourist. But all he said was, "All right. That changes, let me know."

He walked away. We stood there, listening to the singing of the mermaids.

I thought about reaching out to take Niko's hand, but what would it have accomplished? And what if he pulled away? Eventually I went back in to check our course.

By evening, the mermaids were so thick that I could see our own Lump shrinking, dissolving like a tablet in water.

Jorge Felipe came out with his gun.

"No!" Niko said.

Jorge Felipe smiled. "If you don't want me to shoot them, Niko, then they're taking it off your share. You agree it's mine, and I won't touch a scale."

"All right."

"That's not fair," I objected. "He worked as hard as us pulling it in."

Jorge Felipe aimed the gun at the water.

"It's okay," Niko told me.

I thought to myself that I'd split my share with him. I wouldn't have enough for the Choice, but I'd be halfway. And Niko would owe me. That wouldn't be a bad thing.

I knew what Choice I'd make. Niko liked boys. I liked Niko. A simple equation. That's what the Choice is supposed to let you do. Pick the sex you want, when you want it. Not have it forced on you when you're not ready.

The *Mary Magdalena* sees everything that goes on within range of her deck cameras. It shouldn't have surprised me when I went back into the cabin and she said, "You like Niko, don't you?"

"Shut up," I said. I watched the display. The mermaids wavered on it like fleshy shadows.

"I don't trust Jorge Felipe."

"Neither do I. I still want you to shut up."

"Lolo," she said. "Will you ever forgive me for what happened?"

I reached over and switched her voice off.

Still, it surprised me when Jorge Felipe made his move. I'd switched on auto-pilot, decided to nap in the hammock. I woke up to find him fumbling through my clothes.

"What you pick up, huh? What did you grab and stick away?" he hissed. His breath stank of old coffee and cigarettes and the tang of metal.

"I didn't find anything," I said, pushing him away.

"It's true what they say, eh? No cock, no cunt." His fingers rummaged.

I tried to shout but his other hand was over my mouth.

"We all want this money, eh?" he said. "But I need it. You can keep on being all freaky, mooning after Niko. And he can keep on his own loser path. Me, I'm getting out of here. But I figure you, you don't want to be messed with. Your share, or I'm fucking you up worse than you are already."

If I hadn't turned off her voice, the *Mary Magdalena* would have warned me. But she hadn't warned me before.

"Are you going to be good?" Jorge Felipe asked. I nodded. He released my mouth.

"No one's going to sail with you, ever again."

He laughed. "World's a whoooooole lot bigger than this, freaky chicoca. Money's going to buy me a ticket out."

I remembered the gun. How far would he go? "All right," I said. My mouth tasted like the tobacco stains on his fingers.

His lips were hot on my ear. "Okay then, chicoca. Stay nice and I'll be nice."

I heard the door open and close as he left. Shaking, I untangled myself from the hammock and went to the steering console. I turned on the Mary Magdalena's voice.

"You can't trust him," she said.

I laughed, panic's edge in my voice. "No shit. Is there anyone I can trust?"

If she'd been a human, she might have said "me."

Being a machine, she knew better. There was just silence.

When I was little, I loved the *Mary Magdalena*. I loved being aboard her. I imagined she was my mother, that when Mami had died, she'd chosen not to go to heaven, had put her soul in the boat to look after me.

I loved my uncle too. He let me steer the boat, sitting on his lap, let me run around the deck checking lines and making sure the tack was clean, let me fish for sharks and rays. One time, coming home under the General Domingo Bridge, he pointed.

At first it looked as though huge brown bubbles were coming up through the water. Then I realized it was rays, maybe a hundred, moving through the waves.

Going somewhere, I don't know where.

He waited until I was thirteen. I don't know why. I was as skinny and unformed that birthday as I had been the last day I was twelve. He took me out on the *Mary Magdalena* and waited until we were far out at sea.

He raped me. When he was done, he said if I reported it, he'd be put in jail. My grandmother would have no one to support her.

I applied for Free Agency the next day. I went to the clinic and told them what had been done. That it had been a stranger and that I wanted to become Ungendered. They tried to talk me out of it. They're legally obliged to, but I was adamant. So they did it, and for a few years I lived on the streets. Until they came and told me my uncle was dead. The *Mary Magdalena*, who had remained silent, was mine.

I could hear Jorge Felipe out on the deck, playing his accordion again. I wondered what Niko was doing. Watching the water.

"I don't know what to do," I said to myself. But the boat responded. "You can't trust him."

"Tell me something I don't know," I said.

On the display, the mermaids' fuzzy shadows intersected the garbage's dim line. I wondered what they wanted, what they did with the plastic and cloth they pulled from us. I couldn't imagine that anyone kept anything, deep in the sea, beyond the water in their gills and the blood in their veins.

When Jorge Felipe went in to make coffee, I squatted beside Niko.

He was watching the mermaids still. I said, urgently, "Niko, Jorge Felipe may try something before we land. He wants your share and mine. He'd like the boat, too. He's a greedy bastard."

Niko stared into the water. "Do you think my dad's out there?"

"Are you high?"

His pupils were big as flounders. There was a mug on the deck beside him. "Did Jorge Felipe bring that to you?"

"Yeah," he said. He reached for it, but I threw the rest overboard.

"Get hold of yourself, Niko," I said. "It could be life or death. We've got sixteen hours to go. He won't try until we're a few hours out. He's lazy."

I couldn't tell whether or not I'd gotten through. His cheeks were angry from the sun. I went inside and grabbed my uncle's old baseball hat, and took it out to him. He was dangling an arm over the side. I grabbed him, pulled him back.

"You're going to get bit or dragged over," I said. "Do you understand me?"

Jorge Felipe grinned out of the cabin. "Having a good time there, Niko? You wanna go visit dad, go splashy splashy?" He wiggled his fingers at Niko.

"Don't say that!" I said. "Don't listen to him, Niko."

Something flapped in the water behind us and we all turned. A huge mermaid, half out of the water, pulling itself onto the trash's mass. I couldn't tell what it was trying to do—grab something? Mate with it?

The gun went off. The mermaid fell back as Niko yelled like he'd been shot. I turned, seeing the gun leveling on Niko, unable to do anything as it barked. He jerked, falling backward into the cargo net's morass.

His hands beat the water like dying birds. Something pulled him under, maybe the mermaids, maybe just the net's drag.

I tried to grab him, but Jorge Felipe's hand was in my collar pulling me back with a painful blow to my throat. The hurt doubled me over, grabbing for breath through the bruise's blaze.

"Too bad about Niko," Jorge Felipe said. "But I need you to keep piloting. Go inside and stay out of trouble." He pushed me towards the cabin and I stumbled into it, out of the wind and the sound of the water.

I stood, trying to catch my breath, my hands on the panels. I wondered if Niko had drowned quickly. I wondered if that was how Jorge Felipe intended to kill me. All around, the boat hummed and growled, mechanical sounds that had once felt as safe as being inside my mother's womb.

I waited for her to say something, anything. Was she waiting for me to ask her help? Or did she know there was nothing she could do?

Underneath the hum, I could hear the mermaids singing, a whine that echoed through the metal, crept into the *Mary Magdalena*'s habitual drone.

When I said, "How much farther?" she didn't pretend she didn't understand the question.

"Fifteen hours, twenty minutes."

"Any weapons on board I don't know about?" I pictured my uncle having something, anything. A harpoon gun or a shark knife. Something wicked and deadly and masculine.

But she answered, "No." The same flat voice she always used.

I could have wept then, but that was girlish. I was beyond that. I was the master of the *Mary Magdalena*. I would kill Jorge Felipe somehow, and avenge my friend.

How, I didn't know.

Outside splashing, something caught in the netting. I pushed my way out the door as Jorge Felipe stared down into the water. I shoved my way past him, unsure for a moment whether or not he'd hinder me. Then his hands were beside me, helping me pull a gasping Niko onto the boat.

"Welcome back, man," he said as Niko doubled over on hands and knees, spewing water and bile across the decking.

For a moment I thought, of course, everything would be fine. He'd reconsidered killing us. We'd pull into port, sell the cargo, give him the money and go our separate ways.

I saw him guessing at my thoughts. All he did was rest his hand on his gun and smile at me. He could see the fear come back, and it made him smile harder.

Behind me, Niko gasped and sputtered. There was another sound beside the hiss and slap of the waves. *Mary Magdalena*, whispering, whispering. What was she saying to him? What was going on in his head, what had he seen in his time underwater? Had the mermaids come and stared in his face, their eyes as blank as winter, his father there, driven mad by solipsism and sea song, looking at his son with no thoughts in his head at all?

I stood, Jorge Felipe looking at me. If I locked myself in the cabin, how long would it take him to break in? But he gestured me away as I stepped towards the door.

"Not now," he said, and the regret in his tone was, I thought, for the time he'd have to spend at the wheel, awake, more than anything else.

She was whispering, still whispering, to Niko. Why hadn't she warned me? She must have known what was brewing like a storm beneath the horizon. I couldn't have been the first.

I started to turn to Jorge Felipe, *Mary Magdalena*'s voice buzzing under my nerves like a bad light bulb. Then weight shifting on the deck, Niko's footsteps squelching forward as he grabbed at Jorge Felipe, backpedaling until they fell together over the side in a boil of netting and mermaids.

~⌀

In a fairytale, the mermaids would have brought Niko back to the surface while they held Jorge Felipe down below, gnawing at him with their sharp parrot beaks. In some stories, dolphins rescued drowning sailors, back when dolphins were still alive. And whales spoke to the fishing boats they swam beside, underneath clear-skied stars, in waters where no mermaids sang.

But instead no one surfaced. I turned the boat in great circles, spinning the cargo net over and over again. Finally I told the *Mary Magdalena* to take us home. It had started to rain, the sullen sodden rain that means winter is at elbow's length.

I took the yellow ducks out of my pocket and put them on the console. What did Jorge Felipe think I'd found? I stared at the display and the slow shift and fuzz of the earth's bones, far below the cold water.

"What did you tell Niko?" I asked.

"I told him that his father would be killed if he didn't defend him from Jorge Felipe. And I activated my ultrasonics. They acted on his nervous system."

16

I shuddered. "That's what I felt as well?"

"There should be no lasting effects."

"Thanks," I said. I stirred three sugar packets and powdered cream into my coffee. It was almost too hot to drink when it came out of the microwave, but I cupped it in my fingers, grateful for its heat.

I could have slept. But every time I laid down in the hammock, I smelled Jorge Felipe, and thought I heard him climbing out of the water.

Finally I went out and watched the water behind us. The *Mary Magdalena* played the radio for me, a soft salsa beat with no words I could understand. It began to rain, and I heard the sound of raindrops on the decking beside me, pattering on the plastic sheeting I drew over my head.

By the time I arrived back in port, the mermaids had plucked away all but a few tangles of seaweed from the netting. I'd be lucky to net the cost of a cup of coffee, let alone cover the fuel I'd used. Never mind. A few more seasons and I'd have the money I needed, if I was careful. If there were no disasters.

Neither body was there in the net. Perhaps Niko's father had reclaimed him.

The wind and rain almost knocked me off the deck as I stared into the water. The green netting writhed like barely visible guilt in the darkness.

The *Mary Magdalena* called after me, as she had not dared in years. "Sleep well, Lolo. My regards to Grandma Fig."

I stopped and half turned. I could barely see her lines through the driving rain.

Sometimes I used to imagine setting her on fire. Sometimes I used to imagine taking her out to a rift and drilling holes in the hull. Sometimes I used to imagine her smashed by waves, or an earthquake, or a great red bull stamping through the streets.

But the winter was long, and it would be lonely sitting at home with my grandmother. Lonelier than time at sea with her, haunted by the mermaids' music.

"Good night, *Mary Magdalena*," I said.

# Near +

## Afternotes

*The title of the story, which most fellow English majors and poets will recognize, is taken from T.S. Eliot's* The Love Song of J. Alfred Prufrock, *a poem I love enough to have completely committed to memory at a stage in my life when my memory was less prone to lapses. The inspiration for the story itself, though, was a book I've always greatly admired, Ernest Hemingway's* The Old Man and the Sea. *When I sat down to write the story, I had in my head that I'd do an updated version of someone who finds something with the potential to lift them out of their troubles, only to see it vanish, bit by bit.*

*Katherine Sparrow, both a terrific writer and fellow Clarion West student, had recently posted online a news story about giant floating garbage masses. I'd also been thinking about feral mermaids when someone mentioned to me what a glut of mermaid stories they'd been getting lately. When I threw all that together, this story emerged.*

*The core of the story shifted in the writing of it to center on the relationship between Lolo and Mary Magdalena, becoming a story of coming to terms with and forgiving betrayal. The setting is an unidentified island with a Hispanic culture, whose main source of income is tourists.*

*Lolo's decision to become ungendered is one some reviewers have criticized. But the fact that bodies will become more malleable, more self-defined in the future, is a theme that fascinates me, and one that will be increasingly resonant with our day to day lives as we move into an age of electromagnetically-configured tattoos, of changeable hair color and lips and eyes and limbs.*

*I was happy with how this story turned out, and it sold to the first person that looked at it, Sean Wallace, who bought it for Clarkesworld, which is always pleasant. I count it a success because when I ran into one of my writing heroes, she specifically mentioned reading and enjoying this story. That's awfully nice when it happens, and other people liked it enough for it to get some nice mentions here and there.*

# PEACHES OF IMMORTALITY

DECADES LATER THE MUSIC WAS WHAT REALLY tipped Glen off. He heard a song on the radio, a brand new release, and remembered the day he'd first heard it, twenty years earlier.

Everything began to fall together then. Or maybe that was when it really started to shatter.

There were four of them in high school. Glen wasn't one of the quartet. Instead, it was Fred Lipton and his gang.

But you could have said that of any of them. Derek Cho and his gang. Penelope Nantes and her gang. Casey Lucas and her gang. Casey Lucas, Barbie-blond, eyebrows as fine and wispy as fledgling feathers. Graceful Casey, but smart, too, planning on becoming a journalist, colleges salivating at the prospect.

Shiny happy careers lined up before all four. Glen's post-high school future was murkier. He was a D&D player and artist, trying not to be thought the only queer in a Catholic school while not above exploiting his sensitive side to get girls, a pursuit that beguiled him more than studying.

Casey hadn't yielded to his best brooding looks. He suspected she thought herself above him, but the heat in the way she looked at him egged him on.

Once she'd laid her hand on his arm to steady herself, a delicious trusting pressure, and ever since then he'd always stood as close to her as possible.

So—it was perhaps not *entirely* a surprise when she invited him to the loft.

"What for?"

"We like to play music," she said. "We're pretty good, even. Come and listen to us." She laid her hand on his, this time not to catch herself, but to snare him. He turned into his locker to hide his sudden erection.

"All right," he said, half over his shoulder.

He'd found a magazine a few weeks ago while in the library that advised boys to play it cool at first. He didn't want to play it cool, though. He wanted to turn and look into her blue eyes and lean close enough to smell the perfume she wore, a lemon and musk scent unlike any other girl's perfume.

The Lipton's house was within walking distance, but Casey gave him a ride over, along with Danny and Penelope. They knew who he was—their entire class was a few hundred kids, and only the most aloof didn't know the names of the rest. They creaked up the stairs and into the loft, a high-ceilinged, drafty space smelling in equal measures of marijuana and incense.

Fred was there, along with Jenny, a girl from the Social Studies class Fred and Glen shared, and another boy, Alf Reidle, who looked up as Casey entered and tried to catch her eye. Unsuccessful, he settled back like the others. The pellets in his grimy beanbag chair scrunched and rescrunched as he passed around an enormous bong with layers of skull-shaped bubblers in the stem.

Casey swung open the door of an old-fashioned refrigerator and gestured. Glen stared in. It was stocked with soda and beer, an emphasis on the latter. Casey took one. He hesitated. Beer made him sleepy and stupid. It might make him say or do something dumb around Casey.

"What's the matter, worried the folks will smell it when you get home?" Fred sneered.

The door banged open and Derek barged in, grabbing the bong, discarding his jacket, a bustle that allowed Glen to grab a soda and settle in his own beanbag.

"We're all here," Fred said. He slapped Jenny's thigh jocularly and stood up. "Let's play."

The four of them sang. It was November, 1980, and they began with some of the most popular songs of the day: "Another One Bites the Dust," "It's Still Rock & Roll to Me," Dan Fogelberg's "Longer"—songs overplayed on the radio, almost perfect renditions, note for note. They all played instruments, and sometimes between songs they'd trade off according to some system Glen didn't understand, some combination of challenge and self-declaration. The boys strutted and pranced like TV tough guys. Derek's snarl like dark, bitter honey; Fred's voice husky and sincere. The girls' voices seemed interchangeable at first, but Glen began to pick out nuances. Casey's was lower, more syrupy; Penelope's edged with crystal.

Like Glen, Jenny and Alf were onlookers, sitting on the beanbags, watching the enchanted four play.

Then they switched to other things, music that seemed all new. Often they resorted to the synthesizer in the corner for beats and effects: ethereal glass flutes or tiger yodels or a rhythmic sandpaper rasp, magnified a thousand times, almost painful underneath the screamed defiance of the song.

As they changed instruments after something that somehow seemed more disco than disco could ever be, Glen leaned over and touched Casey's elbow.

"Who wrote these?" he said.

She paused. She was rising from the drums, still breathing hard from playing the last song.

The moment stretched longer than it should have. He found her looking at him with an inability to answer the question, a lack of preparation that surprised him.

"We all do," Fred said. "Someone comes up with an idea and we all contribute. We like to improvise." He began a bouncy beat, staring at Glen. "Here's one I like from U2, 'Still Haven't Found What I'm Looking For.'"

They joined in. The words flowed along, strangely ominous. Fred's speculative black eyes watched Glen as though assessing his reaction to each chord.

"I haven't heard of them," Jenny said. "Did they just release an album?"

Casey broke off playing. "Our friend Ana's visiting," she said, warning in her tone. Derek nodded as though in confirmation. Glen didn't know what they were talking about.

"It doesn't matter," Fred said. He waved a lazy hand at the bong and shrugged. "We can play anything we like. We're all just a bunch of stoned zombies."

Penelope picked out the first few bars of a Beatles song, "Yesterday," and Derek half-laughed. He picked up the bass and they launched into a version that was somehow campy and mocking one moment, and heartbreakingly sincere the next. Tears welled in Glen's eyes as Casey sang, and he swallowed hard. Looking up, he saw Alf watching him with a frown on his face.

He could have listened all afternoon, all evening, long into the morning hours. But they could not play that long. All too soon, they were putting down their instruments, exchanging wry smiles as Alf and Jenny and Glen applauded.

"What do you call your band?" Jenny asked.

Derek shrugged. "We don't really have a name," he said. He was a skinny Asian boy who kept a proprietary hand on Penelope at all times. "I call it the Peaches of Immortality, but you can call it anything you like."

"That's a pretty name," Jenny said. "Where's it from?"

"In Chinese legend, the gods eat them and become immortal," Derek said. "My grandfather believed in them. He was an alchemist back in China. I remember him telling me stories about them when I was just a little kid."

Alf departed after a whispered, angry conversation with Casey in the corner. She shrugged off questions and settled into the beanbag next to Glen.

They smoked more pot and drank more beer and watched a movie on the dilapidated VCR in the corner.

"My folks like to get the latest thing, so they let me have this," Fred explained. Glen thought that Fred had one of the luckiest existences possible: permissive parents, beer and technology, cool friends, the brains to get through classes while seeming to coast, bored and above it all. He sighed.

"What's wrong?" Casey breathed in his ear. She leaned over from her beanbag, half settling on his. He wondered if he could slide an arm around her. How would she react? Maybe best not to.

But the article had said *be bold.*

His arm raised and curled around her shoulders as though by itself. She rested against him, and he could feel her warmth like a burning coal along his side. He could smell her perfume.

It made it hard to focus on the film, even more than the pot. He couldn't make out the plot, but gathered that it was a love story, lovers separated by fate and meeting each other by chance at intervals through the years, never at the right time.

Casey nudged him. "This is my favorite part."

The lovers in a garden.

*Him to her: We only meet when we're tangled with others, it seems.*
*Her to him: Someday we'll meet at the right time.*
*He takes her hand, moonlight silhouetting them, a cut paper portrait.*
*His voice lowers. Till then, a kiss to dream about, he says.*

The inevitable clinch. It seemed cliché and sappy to Glen. The sort of thing girls liked, he supposed.

Casey's perfume filled his senses, and he was focused on the soft, round breast pressed against his side. He held still, as though afraid of frightening her, breathing in a mix of smoke and happiness.

But the next day at school, Casey was distant again. He saw her in the corridors, but she didn't look at him.

Fred clued him in when he caught Glen waiting near her locker.

"Don't let Brad Effer catch you," he said.

Brad was captain of the football team, a hearty, handsome hunk with a touch of the bully about him.

"What?" Glen stammered.

"She's dating him now. You'll have to wait for your chance."

Disappointment engulfed Glen, shading the hall a few colors darker. But he tried to keep it off his face, conscious of the odd avidity with which Fred watched him. He muttered something and turned away.

High school passed like high school. He never got that close to Casey again. She flitted from boyfriend to boyfriend, but by the time he was aware she'd left one, she'd already be with someone else. Once, for three days, it was Alf. Then they broke up, leaving him red-eyed and ragged.

Most of the kids watched the four of them, knew what they were doing (which instantly became cool, whether it was bowling or wearing baseball hats), but didn't socialize with them. It was as though the rest of the school provided a backdrop, scenery against which their stories played out.

He wasn't sure what most of the teachers thought of them, but Mr. Laskowski warned him at one point when he caught Glen trying a cigarette—some girls liked the taste, and it never hurt to have a touch of bad boy about you—in the school parking lot.

"Don't become like Lipton or Cho," he said. "They're just treading water, waiting to get through high school. Missing out on some of their best years. You can do better than that. You're a decent artist when you work at it."

Glen thought later, years later, that perhaps every high school had them. The boys and girls who ruled the school, whose favor or lack thereof could shape a lesser kid's personal existence. He thought, though, that usually everything after high school was uphill for them, that they would never achieve their glory days again.

But it wasn't so for the Peaches. Fred started a software company halfway through his time at Harvard that made him a millionaire by the day he graduated. Penelope's novel made the bestseller list, somehow expressing the zeitgeist in a way that had every young adult in America clutching a copy. Derek was rumored to have gone to work for a government think-tank.

Casey went to journalism school. Her lively, informal prose led her to television journalism, where her looks and personable delivery netted her an early morning show.

It surprised him that they hadn't kept up with the music. They'd been so *good*. But nothing of it, as though, ascending to college, they'd abandoned their adolescent passion.

Life overtook Glen. He forgot about them for the most part. He met a woman, Eloise, in grad school and married her. They had no children, but had successful careers.

He still drew sometimes, although only for himself; he never showed the pictures to anyone. Complex landscapes with machinery buried underneath, showing through like a skeleton, gears gleaming in the rent of a tree's bark, screws bolting a clump of grass to the sidewalk.

Periodically he remembered that music. He'd hear something on the radio, some new release, and he'd think that it reminded him of a song played in the echoing loft. They had moved effortlessly from one style to another, sometimes a hard driving metal beat that had acquired a gritty edge, an undertone of concrete and late night steel, then bubblegum as vacuous and sweet as cotton candy, singing it, half-laughing all the while.

When he ran into Casey, he knew her immediately, despite the decade and a half since he'd last seen her. He could tell she knew him from the way her eyes widened, even though she tried to play it off as though she didn't. He bought her a Frappuccino and they caught up.

As he might have expected, the four of *them* had stayed in touch with each other. Fred had been off in Tibet, she said, and added, "Studying some sort of transcendental stuff." Penelope had recently approached Casey about a film project.

"A chance to break into films." Casey's dimples were still deep enough to lose your heart in. "It's very kind of her, to give me that."

Something odd about her tone. Perhaps she and Penelope had had a falling out? Glen thought better of questioning it, not wanting to bring up a potentially upsetting topic.

"I bet the others would like to see you," she said. "Fred's got a box at the baseball stadium, and we're all going there next Saturday."

His wife would be out of town. There was no reason to say no.

At the game, deferential ushers showed them down a hallway to the luxury box. Again, a fridge full of beers, but this time wine and champagne as well, and harder stuff, all dispensed by a bartender with teeth as white as his apron.

No one seemed surprised by Glen's appearance after all this time. In fact, Fred said, "I was just wondering when we'd see you again."

Glen accepted a Heineken from the bartender and settled down to nurse it. The seats were covered with soft red velvet, clean and fresh. The rug underfoot was sculpted with deep swirls. Penelope and Derek were in a corner, arguing in low whispers. Penelope looked unhappy. Dark rings splayed themselves underneath her eyes.

The rest of them played "Whatever Happened To." Time had not dealt well with most of their classmates: several suicides, a public and inadvertent outing that destroyed a political career, multiple scandals (one involving a teacher).

"What about Alf?" Glen said.

A silence fell on the room like a curtain. Even Penelope and Derek glanced over from their argument.

"He jumped off a building," Fred said. "Isn't that right, Casey?"

Glen was uncertain whether or not to laugh. Fred's tone implied he should; Casey's angry face said he shouldn't.

"We don't talk about Alf," she said briefly.

After the game, they went back to Fred's loft, this time a place of exposed brick and floor-to-ceiling windows and stainless steel appliances and an enormous balcony somehow joined onto the side of the building. Casey followed him out onto it. She laid her hand over his. Her perfume hadn't changed after all these years.

He closed his eyes, inhaling. The sounds of the street floated up, cars and shouts, and distant rap music. He could feel her next to him. When he opened his eyes again, the light dazzled him.

"I've always liked you, you know that, don't you?" she said.

He flashed on moonlight and a grainy screen. "I have a wife," he blurted out.

"It's like high school again," she said. "Never the right time. Maybe someday we'll meet when the moment's ripe."

He wanted her, she wanted him, but thoughts of Eloise fettered him. "Give me something to remember," he said. "Something to fantasize about till then."

Years of longing pressed his mouth to hers.

When he woke the next morning, his lips felt bruised and raw. He stared into the mirror, wondering what to tell—if to tell—Eloise. He didn't want to leave her, he realized. He was done with fantasies, illusions. They had built a good life together, one that outweighed any castle in the air.

Something about Casey made him wary. He'd sensed it before, first in girls and then in women—ones who thought themselves in total control of the relationship. Sometimes arrogance, sometimes just a deep belief in the power of pussy. Casey thought she had him sewed up, and that set him on edge.

Making coffee, he glanced out the window. Rain. But he'd left his hat at Fred's loft. When he called, Fred said sure, come over and get it.

He took a cab, thinking about Casey, going over and over the memory of the kiss on the balcony, the way she had looked at him when he'd stammered goodnight. She burned in his mind. He felt himself fluttering too close. Eloise, think of Eloise, of the comfortable house and the deck they liked to sit out on and read to each other. Eloise understood him, and liked him more than he liked himself, truth be told. Was the same true of Casey? Was she amusing herself with another three-day wonder like Alf, or was she in it for the long haul?

He complimented Fred on the loft again. Fred was blue-striped bath-robed, barefoot, and sleepy-haired.

"The place is all right," Fred said with a twist of his lips. "The view is nice, anyway. Have you seen Casey's place?"

Embarrassment struck Glen. What was Fred implying?

"No," he said.

"Not yet, eh?" Fred said.

"What do you mean?"

Fred looked at him, surprised. "She wants you. You can tell that, certainly."

"Yes," he said. The wonder of it fluttered in his chest. He added, "But I'm married, I told her that."

"Ah, a touch of frustration to up the tension. Well played."

Glen had the sensation of treading water far out of his depth. "I don't ... "

Fred said, "Do you love your wife?"

"Beyond any question," Glen replied without hesitating.

"How sad." Fred shoved the hat towards Glen and gestured at the door.

Glen resisted. "What do you mean by that?"

"Things have a way of working out for Casey," Fred said.

Two weeks later, Eloise was hit by a car that jumped the curb when its gas pedal got stuck.

She had been on her way to the hardware store to get a washer to fix a leaky faucet. Glen's first thought upon hearing the news was ridiculous irritation, a petty infant whimper regarding who would take care of small house repairs now.

Then the news hit him.

The bottom dropped out of his world. Shattered. He could feel himself flying in all directions, out of control. Helpless to control the explosion that tore him apart.

Casey wasn't at the funeral, but Fred was.

"A real shame," he said.

Glen fumbled for the unthinkable. "Fred ... you said ... did Casey have something to do with this?"

Fred studied his face. That same old avidity, a greedy hummingbird sipping at Glen's emotions. "How could she have?"

"I don't know ... all of you four ... everything seems so golden for you," he said helplessly.

Fred grinned. "Oh, does it seem odd? Are you waking up, zombie boy? Or is this all just part of her overall game? I thought she had this one refined by now, but she's never been finished working on you. What's the appeal, I wonder? All that shaggy poetic charm, with your hipster beard and earnest look and outlet jeans?"

Other people in the funeral crowd were watching. Glen leaned into Fred and said, low and fierce as he could manage, "I don't know

28

what you mean, but I will, I promise you that."

Fred laughed.

"What about the music?" Glen said.

He'd scored a hit, he could tell. Fred took in a breath, released it. Said, "I don't know what you mean." He wheeled and walked away.

The house was empty without Eloise. He lived on Ritz crackers and KFC. He left the radio, the television on, tried to keep sound going in the empty rooms, but inevitably it all died away into grayness.

He turned the music up on his headphones, introspective Bach cello suites, complicated as crossword puzzles. He scoured the Internet, hometown paper microfiches, talked to old neighbors, every source he could find. Looking for anything about the four. Anything and everything.

Their existence had been charmed, he discovered. Parents had died early, leaving two in the care of permissive guardians. Fred's parents had been wealthy and aloof, Penelope's wealthy and extremely attached. He remembered they'd given her a baby-blue Mustang convertible for her sixteenth birthday, remembered seeing them all jammed into the car, Penelope at the wheel, Derek beside her, Casey next to Fred in the back seat.

All of them were only children.

Their teachers agreed that they got the grades they wanted to, but that sometimes they seemed to be doing the minimum. All spoke of their "independent" manner, and there were some disciplinary incidents.

Derek had given him a business card. When Glen called, he agreed to meet in a coffee shop. It was a rainy day, flickering between misty and a harder torrent as though unable to decide. A strong wind pushed the rain under passing umbrellas; they tilted to combat it. One blew inside out and fluttered past, its owner struggling to reverse it.

"Whatever happened to the Peaches of Immortality?" Glen said.

Derek froze for a second before saying, "What?"

Glen pressed. "Your band from high school. I always remembered hearing you play. You guys could have gone professional."

But for some reason, Derek relaxed. "That's a shitty life, really," he said. "Being famous is overrated." He said it with authority, and Glen wondered what Derek had done in the intervening years.

So it wasn't the music. But something about what he had said.

Standing out on the curb, he checked his theory. "The peaches of immortality," he said, testing it.

Derek stared at the street, expressionless.

"What does it mean, Derek? What are the peaches of immortality?"

Derek sighed. "Oh, it's this one," he said, abstractly. "Why bother? But okay. The peaches of immortality? Think of them as something a thinker stumbled upon, and gave to a couple of friends. Not immortality, not really. But something like it. A chance to live forever, certainly, but not really forever, to loop back through one's life over and over again."

"That sounds horrible," Glen said.

Derek fixed him with a hawk-like eye. "Do you really think so?" he said. "Really? A chance to go back and fix mistakes, to nudge destiny so it gives you all it can?"

The cab pulled up, splashing Glen but not Derek, who was sheltered by a trash can.

"I need to talk to you about this some more," Glen said. "Where can I reach you?"

Derek shook his head. "I'll call you in a couple of weeks. I don't have much time left with Penelope, I want to spend as much of it as possible with her."

"Is she ill?" She had looked fine, if subdued, at the baseball game.

"She commits suicide this month," Derek said. "Usually after the 15th, never before the 12th." He swung the cab door and hopped in, rolled away. The puddle surged at Glen, infiltrating his shoes with a wash of cold water.

Glen was at his favorite restaurant, an Italian place named Tropea. It had been a favorite for him and Eloise, and he hadn't dared come back until then.

He saw a profile, a fall of golden hair across the restaurant. Despite everything, his heart surged.

He forced himself to look away. This was all part of the ... plan?

Scheme? Machinations? He absorbed himself in picking his bread roll apart into shreds.

A presence beside him. Familiar perfume: lemon, musk. He looked up and was lost. Her dress was pleated silk, a blue that echoed her eyes. Had they been that blue in high school?

She said, "Glen, I don't know what to say, I was so sorry to hear about Eloise."

He lowered his gaze again as though fighting off tears. "Thank you, Casey. If you don't mind ... "

He let that trail off. After a beat too long, she said, "Oh, you want to be alone. My apologies, Glen. I'll catch you another time."

And she would, he knew. Somehow she'd show up, checking to see if the hooks she had planted in him years ago were still firmly set. When she was ready, she'd collect him.

Derek called, mumbling into the phone.

"I can't hear you," Glen said. "What is all that noise?"

"I'm near construction," he said. "Look, this line isn't safe, not really. Not like anything is safe, but come down and meet me here?"

*Here* was a diner, red paper placemats and the smell of coffee and burned toast. Glen slid into the booth across from Derek, who looked as though he hadn't slept or shaved in several days. His eyes were red-rimmed, and the flesh of his face hung loosely.

"I'm sorry about Penelope," Glen said.

Derek shrugged, curling his fingers around his coffee cup as though cradling it against harm. "It happens."

"How does it happen?" Glen said. "How do you keep going back in time?"

Derek stared into the curling steam of his coffee. "Once upon a time, there was a smart little Asian kid," he said. "A hyperachiever, whose grandfather spent his life trying to achieve immortality. To find the peaches of immortality. And so his grandson decided to do the same, through a combination of a bunch of things you don't have jack shit chance of understanding, involving the basic way the universe works and he learned that you could project your consciousness back through time and relive your life. Not only that, but you could shape events through concentration and purposeful thought. And he grabbed a couple of friends, friends who had also been unloved nerds in high school and then gone on to become nerdy losers, and said, how about we give this thing a shot?"

"How do you control it?" Glen said.

Derek sighed, a long exhalation as though his soul were trying to escape. "Fred's got it," he said. "He stole it from me a long time ago. Now I'm just a hamster like you. A hamster with a nicer wheel, maybe, but a hamster nonetheless. Do you really think we haven't had this conversation before?"

"How many times?" Glen asked.

"Forty, maybe fifty? Whenever Casey picks up with you again."

The number staggered Glen. Then he thought of something even more staggering.

"How many times have you done this?" he asked.

Derek shrugged. "Hundreds. I'm pretty sure we haven't topped a thousand yet. Who knows? It's a game now. Fred and Casey figure out what we score points on this time, and here we go again."

When Glen arrived home, Casey was sitting jack-knifed on his door-step. She didn't look the way he usually pictured her, put together as carefully as a fashion model, every glossy hair in careful position. Instead she wore an old sweatshirt and no makeup. She'd been cry-ing. Rain glittered on her hair.

"What did they tell you?" she demanded. "Those fuckers, don't you know—all they want is to keep us apart!"

He regarded her warily, even though his heart ached at the sound of tears in her voice. Had she killed Eloise? Was any of this true, or was he going mad in some complicated, paranoid way, driven insane by the stress of his wife's death?

"Let's go inside and dry you off," he said.

But even muffled by a towel, the question emerged again. "What did they *tell* you?"

"That you all keep living the same life over and over again," he said.

She tossed the towel on the sofa and combed her fingers through her hair. "Not the same life," she said. "We change it each time."

"How?"

"When you're a baby, at first, you're half there and half not. You can shape things." She shrugged.

"Shape them?"

"Steer them one way or another. Money's easy after college—you can play the stock market, but high school's harder to change. But enough work and you can change your family, the circumstances you're born under—not outright change, but you can push them one way or another."

"Like eliminating a potential sibling," he said.

"That was just a coincidence," she said. "Do you really think we'd kill people? Even knowing that they're still alive in another time-line? How ruthless do you think we are?"

"Ruthless enough when it comes to getting what you want," he said. "How hard was it to 'shape' Eloise's death?"

"I would never ... " she said, but broke off at his look. "Oh, god, this one's falling all apart. Why are you so difficult? I thought if I just set things up in high school but didn't follow through, you'd be so ready now."

He stared at her. "Do I count for extra points in this game you're all playing? Do you allot so much per personal victory? What about the rules, how do you set them all up ahead of time?"

"Before we die, we manage it," she said. "We have to all stay in touch to make sure, and Penny's been opting out for a while, but that just means we tell her what her goals are." She smiled. It was a mean smile.

"Who decides the goals?"

"Whoever won last time, of course," she said with a touch of sullenness at his obtuseness.

"Get out," he said. He couldn't stand being in the same room with her anymore. She made his skin crawl. How many times had she seduced his other selves?

But she came toward him, pleading. "We can still recover this game, you know. And this time, this time you caught on ... " She broke off.

"Caught on? What do you mean?"

She lowered her eyes. "We call them zombies, all the people we shape. They're so slow to catch on. Most of them never do. But now you're awake and not a zombie anymore. You can become one of us. You and I can be together over and over again."

Over and over again, repeating their lives.

"I'd sooner die," he said.

"All right," she said. "I'll go now."

But over her shoulder she said, "You'd sooner die this time. But I can keep on trying."

When he got to Fred's, he half expected Casey to be there before him, but she was not in evidence when Fred opened the door. Glen pushed past him.

"Very abrupt and angry," Fred drawled. "Oh my, did she actually overplay and wake you up? We used to be so careful about that sort of thing."

"That's why you don't play the music anymore," he said. "But why play it in high school?"

Fred flopped onto the couch. "Dude, do you *remember* high school?" he said. "It's boring as shit. Why not be rock stars for a bit? Get people stoned, they don't remember what they heard. Particularly when they won't hear it again for a while. It's an indulgence."

"What did Casey mean about Ana visiting, all those years ago?"

Fred laughed. "That's how we used to warn each other if we got too anachronistic. It was hard keeping all of that straight at first. We got better at it."

"So you go back and engage in some juvenile dream of being a high school rock star?" Glen snorted.

For the first time, Fred lost his condescending calm. "We've been *actual* rock stars," he said. "Did that a couple of times. It's overrated. Too many people following you around all the time." He smiled, "But just think, in another world, Peaches of Immortality hit the Billboard charts seventeen weeks in a row."

"I want you to take me out of this game," Glen said. "Leave me alone from now on."

Fred said, surprised, "You won't be joining us? It's a rare honor.

Only two people have made it, Penny and Casey. Casey took to it a lot better though."

"Join you?" Glen said incredulously. "In your egocentric merry-go-round?"

"The alternative is to die, knowing that's it," Fred said. "You may relish the idea, but by the time I'm geriatric, I find myself looking forward to all that crazy kid energy again. It's even better when you really appreciate what you have." He stood. "Look, I'll show you something."

He went to the wall and took down the picture, an enormous Ansel Adams print. Behind it was a safe. The tumblers clicked as he worked the lock and took out ...

... how to describe the Peaches of Immortality? They were made of light, golden light, intersecting, clustered spheres that shone from within. They filled Fred's hands with their glow.

"How do they ... " Glen stammered.

Fred laughed. "How do they work? What do you think, I'm like some comic book villain, to reveal everything?"

"Well, but how would it work if I wanted to join you?" Glen said. His eyes drank in the sight of the object in Fred's hands. Something about its lines made him feel safe, and happy, and as though the world were filled with perfection. It was infinitely seductive.

He wrenched his gaze from it, stared out at the stone railing of the balcony where he had kissed Casey. It seemed like years ago, but it had only been a few months. He wondered what time felt like to them, after they'd lived it over and over. He thought that boredom must be a constant slow rasp, wearing against nerve and resolve. But perhaps he was underestimating the wonders of rearranging your own life.

He heard the peaches jingle as Fred turned them in his hands, a distant sound like fairy bells, like enchantment.

"The music's the only real moments you have left, isn't it?" he said.

Fred's voice was strained. "You have no idea what it's like, zombie."

"You hate me for being what you think you are," Glen said. "Someone helpless in the face of the Universe. Aren't you, in the end? Either you keep reliving your lives, or you die. Why won't you let Penny opt out?"

"She makes the game more interesting."

"And the game is all you have."

"It's all we ever need."

"Maybe," Glen said. "But it seems ... a little masturbatory."

The peaches jingled again as Fred set them down. They sounded like far away rain on crystal spires. Tears welled in Glen's eyes at the sound.

"You've surprised me once or twice this time," Fred said. "Are you really waking up or are we going to end, as we always do, with you giving in and going back to sleep? If you're serious this time, close your eyes. The peaches will set you up."

"Set me up?" It made no sense, but he closed his eyes.

Like being in a dark room, putting a hand out, encountering a surface. Biting on tinfoil and feeling it like sparks inside your skull. An internal organ that had never twinged before, but now twisted with gut-wrenching intensity. Electric eels along his spine, sharp pink then soothing gold, and ...

Click.

Everything aligned.

He could sense Fred's mind, and the minds of the others, sensing him in the time loop, in the peaches. Casey with a touch of anger, as though Fred had won. Fred, reckoning points on an intricate, abacus-like structure. Derek, despair and contempt at everything, including himself. Penny, absence and presence at the same time, a hole in such a particular shape that it could only be her.

And beyond that, the feel of the possibilities, the tiny shifts that resulted in a different configuration for one's life—not too far off course, but there were a surprising number of ways one could shift things, he was somehow told.

Fred, triumphant, flashing Casey a string of numbers and symbols, an intricate score, even as Glen reached out and grabbed the structure with his mind, wrapping tendrils of thought sinewy as muscle around it, and *pulled and pushed* at the same time.

A noise as high-pitched as pain shrilled from the peaches, and he felt it flay at the inside of his thoughts, more piercing than shame or grief or heartbreak. In the real world, he was falling forward, he could tell, but he flickered back and forth between the physical and mental landscape, stomach-jarring shudders of reality, falling forward on the golden object, tangling it with his head and arms, feeling the light sink into the side of his head, eclipsing the world, taking it apart. Far beyond himself, he could feel all the lives that had been contained in the loop, the lives lived over and over again, variations and repetitions, held by the peaches of immortality, escaping, slipping away like fish through a net, and his mind was the peaches and the peaches were his mind and they were taking each other apart and everything was being released and his last thought, confused and full of light, was *oh the peaches are sweet.*

## *Afternotes*

*This story came from one of those thought chains we all engage in—what might we have done if we'd been able to change some life decisions? It's one of those obsessive games we play over and over in our heads, and so many speculative fiction stories center around time travelers going back and manipulating the past with their knowledge. What would happen if you were able to do it, time and time again? Would it, in the end, become as meaningless as it seems to have for Fred and the others?*

*Another influence that shaped it is Fritz Leiber's novel,* The Sinful Ones, *which also appeared under the title,* You're All Alone, *and in which some people are more awake than others and able to exist outside of the daily life that everyone else grinds through. Leiber says: "What if the whole world were like a waxworks museum? In motion, of course, like clockworks, but utterly mindless, purposeless, mechanical. What if he, a wax figure like the others, had suddenly come alive and stepped out of his place, and the whole show was going on without him, because it was just a machines and didn't care or know whether he was there or not?"*

*The idea terrified me. It still does.*

*The story was submitted to* Lightspeed Magazine, *but editor John Joseph Adams felt it was more fantasy than SF, and the story ended up in* Lightspeed's *companion publication at the time,* Fantasy Magazine, *under the title, "The Immortality Game." As the former fiction editor of* Fantasy, *I was glad to have a story in there before the publication was merged into* Lightspeed.

# CLOSE YOUR EYES

THE STORY MIGHT BEGIN LIKE THIS: "Thank you for bringing me some water," Lewis said as Amber neared the kitchen table. "Thank you for working to pay the rent on our house, because otherwise we wouldn't have access to the water that comes free with it."

"Fuck you," Amber said. She was tired of this tune, tired of its tension clamping down on her neck muscles, gripping like lightning-laden wire along her inner arms.

This morning Lewis wore an unexpected, Dr. Seuss-bright tie, along with the usual plain white shirt and stiff new jeans. The cat strode across the fabric, peppermint-striped hat tilted, infinitely more carefree than her younger brother. Lewis folded his fingers, thumbs pressed together, pointed towards himself.

"No, I mean it," Lewis said. "Thank you."

She thumped the glass down near his elbow, settled to sprinkle salt substitute over her own microwaved sausage-in-an-egg-in-a-biscuit. Lewis had the same, plus a paper cup holding a dozen horse-sized pills, and two glasses of oily liquid.

After three bites of sausage, he methodically downed the pills, first using the vitamin-ade, then the water. He did it with a frown, looking into the distance as though examining himself in the bathroom mirror while shaving.

Was she supposed to ask why he was wearing a tie? What sort of scheme was he involved with now? How much of her money or energy or patience or love would it consume?

She was never sure how much of his hostility was humor, but the majority was genuine rancor at being unemployed, dependent on her.

"I'm staying late at the hospital after my treatment this afternoon," Lewis said. "Using the spare time you so generously provide me with to read to children. I'm sure you'll agree it's a valuable use of my time, a contribution to society that you're sponsoring."

She wavered between opting to swat back the hostility or ignore his tone. She didn't want to fight. "What are you reading to them?"

He gestured at the tie. "This sort of thing."

"What time should I take you?"

"More shining generosity on your part. Don't worry, I'm keeping track. I'll figure out how to pay you back. Eventually. A little before two."

"What kids are you reading to?"

"The fatalities," he said. "Who better? The ones that aren't going to make it."

Like him, Plague-touched. The rare genetically gifted ones that could survive its ravages, though not neurologically intact, knowing that they had a few years left.

That too is another way the story might begin, Lewis and Amber listening to the doctor explain how long Lewis might live, given the right care and treatment: one to five years. And how long he would live without it: less than a year.

Amber watching a cloudy sky outside the window, ashy as Lewis's face. He kept looking at her as though to judge her reaction. Dependency shaded by years of sibling rivalry and affection. Amber seeing Lewis as though through a window. Seeing too little time left with her brother.

And also too long, too long to dedicate herself to him, putting aside everything but her work, in order to support him, like some nun in a solitary abbey. One to five years of watching over him. One to five years of driving him to his hospital appointments, one to five years of seeing the hospital, becoming familiar with its corridors, knowing where every bathroom, every drinking fountain, every vending machine, every waiting lounge was.

"Enjoy reading to the kids," Amber said as she pulled up to the curb. "I think it's a nice gesture."

Lewis had been silent during the car ride, even when she tried to bait conversation with conservative talk radio.

"What time should I pick you up?" she said.

"7:00."

"That late?"

"Can you do it or not? I can take a taxi if I need to."

And be stiff and terrified all through the ride that one of his fits come, without her to coax him back away from unbending panic, with a driver who wouldn't know what to do with a hyperventilating, shaking passenger.

She could let him do it, but she'd sit there waiting, anxious, unable to work, until he came home.

"I can do it," she said.

He stepped out, thin and frail with recent body loss. Almost time for another trip to Sears, he'd dropped another pants size. The tie flashed in the sunlight.

He walked away.

The air was full of cottonwood that spring, riding the air like memories of ash. Last year Mount Rainier had rumbled, as though announcing Lewis's diagnosis, sent out a cloud that had coated the countryside for miles. Even now, traces of it lingered on roofs and rocks. Like everyone else, she had mason jars filled with the silky ash, so unsettlingly smooth to the touch.

Time and solitude in which to work. She ascended to her attic studio, settled like a weary bird into the papa-san chair, queued up Kay Gardner, Bach cello suites, then Beatles and Will Flirt For Fairy Fruit on the music player, pulled over her graphic tablet, and began to sketch.

When work was going well, it *flowed*, a narrow river into which she could submerge herself, almost forgetting to breathe, feeling colors, lines move through her, coming from her lungs and heart and brain, coiling together before racing through her stylus point onto the computer, words and pictures becoming the Land of Everkind, its citizens the people of Leaf and Flower, and the talking animals that helped and hampered them.

She had been working on them for two decades now. Characters as familiar to her as Lewis: Mrs. Mountebank and her be-ribboned head;

the Whistling Gypsy; the Turtle-headed Woman; the Count of Cube; Pepperjill's Magic Monkey troupe; the Tango Gotango Gotengo.

Some parents thought the books too dark. The characters too raw, too savage. But that was what children liked. The monster under the bed. The touch of fear at their heels. Mrs. Mountebank's dark-windowed wagon; the magic monkeys' pointed teeth.

A new character was coming to her. She could feel it fluttering at her mind's edges. She sat still for a half hour, trying to will it closer. It stayed out of reach, as it had for months now.

She drew herself, Lewis on the pad, drew them looking at each other. Similar features. Lewis was skinnier, but not by much. Staring, caught.
*Trapped.*

She wiped the image away, let a story distract her. Caught herself moments after seven. She'd be ten minutes late. Not inexcusable, but he wouldn't excuse it. And she'd wasted valuable alone time on reading! She raced down the steps to the car with an angry clatter of keys.

She pulled into a waiting space in front of the hospital lobby. Lewis was staring at his watch. Her dashboard read 7:13.

He attacked, vicious as a wasp, as soon as he entered. "Glad you could spare time to pick me up."

"Lewis, sorry, I lost track," she said.

"Beggars can't be choosers," he said. Brittle, icy-edged in a way that sometimes signaled a fit's imminence, sometimes just a tantrum. "Perhaps you would be so kind as to stop at the drug store? I have some things to get. Wait in the car if you want."

He knew she'd opt for that.

After ten minutes she raised her head in time to see Lewis exiting the drugstore.

She readied her keys but saw him turn into the craft store that was next door.

What was he doing?

She waited.

The store was busy. A few dozen people came and went through the double glass doors before Lewis exited, carrying a plastic bag. Stems protruded from the opening, brown and knobby. Dried flowers?

He dumped his purchases in the back seat. She smelled eucalyptus. His look dared her to ask.

Whatever it was, he'd tell her in time.

The car chimed reproof as she started it, flashing an indicator for Lewis's missing seatbelt. As always, she thumbed it off, rather than argue with him.

"How was reading to the kids?" she asked.

"Fine," he said. "Good kids. Most of them."

"Not all of them?" she said, surprised.

"Think being close to dying makes somebody automatically good?" he said.

He pressed his fingers to the ledge where door met window, marched his hand along, middle finger become a head half raised.

When they were little, Amber eight to Lewis's three, they had pretended their hands were animals that explored the tops of the sofa and walked like tightrope dancers along the playpen's high wire.

The memory made her smile.

"People just become more of whatever they were to begin with," Lewis said. "Concentrated. Much more so." Malicious smile. "Like ever so much more grateful to you, darling Amber."

Plucking away her expression like a spider web.

Lewis read to the children every Tuesday and Thursday. He continued to be inexplicably late. He couldn't be reading to children for five hours.

Might he be dating someone?

Imagine if someone else took him on, drove him from place to place, paid for the medicine that kept him alive for the perhaps four years (but who knew what might happen, how that statistic might stretch with medical advances) he had left. It would be as sudden, as welcome as a fairy godmother granting a wish, removing the responsibility for Lewis from her life.

What would it be like if someone else—perhaps a nurse with excellent health insurance, susceptible to wounded bird sorts—took that on?

Extracting the hospital newsletter from the mail one morning, she looked through the list of classes and discussion groups: *Social Networking for Seniors*; *Health Insurance Basics*; *Applying for Disability*

*Benefits*; *Journaling for Beginners*; *Intensive Journaling*; *Extreme Journaling*; *Alcoholics Anonymous*; *Sexoholics Anonymous*; *Netheads Anonymous*; *Strength Training and You*; *Ornithology for Your Window Feeder*; *How to Live Without Salt*; *You and Your Colon*; *Learning to Trust Doctors*; *Making a Living Will*; *Vegan Cooking*.

*Practical Shamanism*.

She'd smelled sage and lavender wafting from his room. New habits: an odd gesture with his hands before and after eating, a phrase said under his breath. A scuttle of unintelligible words, like a tinny echo of a prayer in foreign movie. Sitting by himself staring at plants in the garden.

What could it be other than *Practical Shamanism*?

She stuffed the brochure in the recycling bin, as though it might tip him off that she'd been snooping. Give him something new to reproach her with.

She didn't want to ask him directly. She wasn't sure what to make of the concept of shamanism, or even where it fit into the world of the New Agey.

What else could she do but search on the Internet, making mental notes, bookmarking as she hopped from page to page?

A range of beliefs. Tarot and divinatory dreams. The healing properties of tourmaline and snowflake obsidian. The ability to enter other dimensions. *Healers and renders of the soul*, one website read. Animal or spirit guides.

She pushed her chair back and stretched. Wondered which of her characters would be her spirit guide. She loved them all. Maybe Mrs. Mountebank and the Whistling Gypsy a trifle more. Only a trifle. And they weren't animals.

What was Lewis' spirit guide? A snake, a wasp? Something more terrifying? She could not imagine it benign.

But Lewis seemed happier, less snappy. Perhaps she could relax. Never entirely, though. She'd been ambushed too often.

*From The Annals of Everkind:*

LILY THE TURTLE-HEADED WOMAN:

*Something's coming, sure as shooting stars.*

# Near +

*Mr. Wiggly:*
  *Baa!*
*LtThW:*
  *No, I mean it. A chancy sort of thing, and lunatic as the moon's frown.*

Lewis flipping through TV channels. The trees rattled their fingers on the dark window, swished their leaves against the glass as though asking to come in.

"They're called Dhami," he said.

"Who?"

"The shamans in the school of teaching I'm studying." He smirked. "Now you'll tell me how nice it is I'm doing something outside the house."

"I didn't know you were interested in shamanism," she said. She could see, given the list of other groups, why he might have chosen it.

His tone altered, slipped out of its usual snakeskin coated form. Became more sincere. "They teach what might happen after death. How you can prepare."

The honesty stunned her. The first moment like this they'd had, since he'd become a nuisance. A nuisance but also something she loved fiercely, had missed like a lost forearm ever since he'd withdrawn from her.

She groped for words like someone trying not to scare an exotic, unimaginable bird, phoenix or quetzalcoatl. If the shamanism class had taught him this, she was all for it.

"What are you learning?"

But the moment had passed, sudden as a cloud's shadow slipping away.

He folded his arms. "I'm going in Sunday mornings as well, for a drumming workshop at the coffeehouse."

Did she need to stay and wait, in case he needed her? She could take her pad and wait in the car. He shook his head in answer.

"Some nurses from the hospital are attending too. They know what to do." He sneered. "It'll get me out of the house, I knew you'd approve. You can make more of your little books."

44

That stung enough that she retreated to her workshop. She took her buzzer. It would alert her if he fell prey to a fit.

She curled in the chair. How had she come up with Everkind? Stories she wrote as a child, crude wish-fulfillment, a kingdom of magical ponies battling a villain called Brutescruel. She'd drawn them whenever she could.

Eventually she added more characters, made more and more sophisticated stories. She listened to concepts, dramatic tension, denouement, foreshadowing, in a creative writing class, and found them familiar, like learning a language you knew as a child. *Find your voice*, one teacher kept saying, but she had already found hers.

The stories had possessed her. They emerged beneath her pen, flowed like a fountain. Even when she'd graduated and gone to work as a graphic designer, she'd still drawn them. An art director who liked to mentor had sent one off to a publishing company.

The rest was history. The Everkind graphic novels, her "little books," might not be wildly popular, but they did provide enough to pay the rent and for the medicines that ate up four fifths of her income. He knew as well as she did that she could be living much better. His illness was responsible for the shabby but clean house that they lived in, the ten-year-old car she drove.

Downstairs, Lewis moved about, restless, turning to a nature show on the TV, then talk radio, the kitchen mini-TV sending out the ping of a bat, a crowd's roar. Battling soundtracks. The inevitable precursor to a fit.

She was downstairs before the device in her pocket buzzed.

He lay on the floor, shuddering for breath. She thumbed the hypo-spray, pressed it into his forearm. He moved from side to side, helpless, staring up. She looked away, didn't meet his eyes. Her fingers rested on his inner arm, letting his pulse race against her fingers, agonized, slowing at an imperceptible rate.

Her hand drooped like a sad little animal.

She wanted him to live.

She wanted, more than anything else in the world, for him to die.

Pain and hate and despair twisted his face.

Twisted her heart.

A childhood memory:

They'd insisted on going by themselves through the fun house, twelve-year-old Amber, seven-year-old Lewis.

Amber knew it a terrible mistake the moment the cart jolted forward into darkness. Bones and red cloth and LED-lit eyes swooped at her. Lewis screamed. She flinched into him and put her arm around him.

"Close your eyes," she said. "Nothing can hurt you if your eyes are closed." She did the same.

There were noises, of course, shrieks and cackles. Twice string brushed over her face. Lewis clutched her; she held onto his reassuring presence. The cart shuddered and tilted, ascended an incline. Doors swung open. Sunlight flooded around them, almost blinding them.

The second floor balcony track led along a ledge before returning to the funhouse. Amber could see her father and mother in the crowd below. They waved up, smiling.

Lewis screamed, trying to climb out onto the balcony. She held onto him, terrified he'd be caught in the machinery. She was the only thing protecting him. Anger flashed through her. Why had her parents left her with this terrible responsibility?

"Close your eyes. Close your eyes," she repeated.

They returned to darkness and clamor.

Afterwards they emerged, shaken and hand in hand, to eat hot dogs and throw up without preamble. Their displeased parents took them home.

In later years, they were uneasy allies. Sometimes they stole toys or candy from each other's rooms. Other times generosity moved them. Lewis made Amber an elaborate Christmas crèche in his art class that was still a treasured decoration in her study. She spent a month making him a dollhouse/space station in which his Star Trek figurines and her Barbies played.

Coming into the kitchen, she saw him with saltshaker raised over the pot bubbling on the flat stove surface.

"Don't put that in," she said. And exasperated, "For Pete's sake, you know I have to watch that for my blood pressure."

He shrugged. "Guess I forgot. I don't have to watch that sort of thing."

He picked up his socks and jacket after himself, as though he had more energy. The lines around his eyes plumped out. He was nicer.

He still smelled of sage and lavender, and now other things, musk and sweet-amber and something with an odd metallic edge. Still muttered almost beyond her hearing, a phrase that sounded like calling for an errant dog.

Did she trust Lewis? No. And disliked herself for not being able to go that far. When had she gone so cynical, so cold?

She kept waiting. Had a character ever taken such an agonizingly long time to come to her before? She wondered what a shaman would suggest. How to invoke it.

What had she ever known of this unseen world that Lewis dabbled in? Once, when she was eight or nine, she'd been upstairs, standing near the head of the staircase, when she'd heard a woman's voice shout, "Help me, someone help me." It had been so real, so close that she'd called out to her parents.

But there were no alarms from neighboring houses. Her father convinced her that she must have heard something from the downstairs television. For years after, thoughts of that woman obsessed her. She imagined her trapped, buried underground. Attacked. Lost. Alone. That mysterious figure became a motif in Everkind, was rescued in three separate episodes, once by Mrs. Mountebank, twice by the Whistling Gypsy.

In the current storyline, she was under siege again.

*From The Annals of Everkind:*

*MRS. MOUNTEBANK:*
*Sometimes you must waltz, even with Madness in his best ball gown.*
*THE WHISTLING GYPSY:*
*I never thought I'd hear you say such a thing, Madam!*
*MRS. MOUNTEBANK:*
*These things are the very bones and sinew of our world, if not the ichorous blood itself.*
*THE WHISTLING GYPSY:*
*Words were ever things of madness.*

47

Exhibit A:

Pulling up to get him, she'd seen a mousy woman trying to talk to him. Trying to chat him up. Lewis stared straight ahead, ignoring her. The woman faltered, tried again, glanced at the sound of wheels pulling up, walked away slump-shouldered as Lewis got into the car.

"Who was that?" Amber asked.

"No one," he said.

"Is she from your Shamanism group?"

"No, it's men only."

"It looked as though she wanted to start a conversation with you."

"Shall we begin the conversation about how important it is to build friendships? Let me cut to the chase—I'll be dead. It won't matter."

She refused to speak again, turned on the radio, let his jeers contend with a right-wing talk show discussing Mars' drain on the global economy, commercials selling gold and colon remedies, a tuna fish selling car insurance.

"All right," he shouted over the last. "We'll play it your way. I'm sorry."

Exhibit B:

Too unspeakable to be mentioned.

Exhibit C:

Was it something she could point to, or rather a series of things? The way her alarm clock turned itself on, on the days when she could have slept in, or how it went off twice at 3:00 am, a time she knew she hadn't set it for? Dogshit smeared inside her Crocs; her favorite zinnias blackened and drooping after he'd spent an afternoon contemplating them.

But still. Face to face, it was so much better that she thought she could endure this covert war for now.

After all, it was true. He would die and move on. All she had to do was outwait him.

A precious whole day to herself, to go into the city and talk to her editor. The nurse-aide arrived at 8; Amber was gone by 8:05.

"You need something new," the editor said over lunch, tender mussels and saffron pasta and a wine like the end of summer. "How long has it been since you introduced any new characters? It used to be one—sometimes two—per book."

Had it been that long? Was that why she found the latest one's imminence such a maddening itch?

"I'm working on a new one right now," she said.

"What is it?"

"It's still coalescing," she said, seized with fear that discussing it too much would drive the new character away, back into the darkness outside Everkind's bright borders.

The editor knew her well enough to shut up at that, to direct her attention to concerns of a possible change in paper, and where the e-rights might be picked up. It was delightful to eat and not worry about Lewis, to pretend that she was unencumbered by him.

Riding down in the elevator, laden with several advance proofs, she could feel the elevator moving downward. It made her feel vertiginous, as though she was plunging, rocketing into some unknown.

She leaned against the wall, its metal surface slick against her fingertips. The elevator was still plunging, still giving way under her feet. On and on. A dizzy reel, while the world whirled away. Amber was dizzy-dumb, and the fluorescent lights buzzed as though voicing her panic. She wanted to spread her arms, her wings and swoop upward. Escape this trap.

Would they die when they hit the bottom? Of course they would. Would she throw up before they hit or would it be quick enough to spare her that?

But no. The elevator was slowing, moving back to a normal speed. Water from a street vendor chased the taste of almost vomit from her mouth.

She was determined, though. This would be her day. Tomorrow, when she took Lewis to the hospital, she'd stop in and find out what the dizzy spell might mean. Maybe nothing more than too much food.

She went shopping, found two tailored blouses, a pair of shoes that were comfortable, strolled through a Picasso exhibit, then a set of smaller galleries.

She could feel the new character, so close she could almost glimpse it in the crowd, following at her heels. She practiced the things she might have said to it if it showed up at her elbow, the pictures she might have pointed out to it: a serigraph of Tinkertoys in bright primaries; a skull and feather fan; a distorted face floating in an abandoned hubcap, broad-stroked in acrylic paint.

She looked up. Reflected in the glass of the frame. Hawk or woman? The menacing curve of its beak. A flower-pupiled eye, cherry and amber.

She spun.

Gone.

Breathlessness seized her. She stood in the middle of the crowd, half-expecting the dizziness to attack her again. It passed. The noise of the crowd eddying around her pressed in on her ears. She need solitude, craved it.

She could not coax the vision back, but still—close. At the botanical garden, she sketched birds: starlings managing to be glossy and shabby all at once; rusty finches; a fat seagull; a smugly stupid robin; pigeon after pigeon after pigeon. None seemed right, but she lost herself in the detailing of lines forming each feather's vane: rachis and barb, plumy tufts of afterfeathers.

When she returned, she was still giddy with the pleasure of the drawing. The nurse-aide's scowl ripped the mood away.

"Don't call our agency again," he said.

"Did he have a fit?"

"Yes. It was after that. Client was inexcusably rude. I'm blacklisting you."

Not the first time. But she had thought Lewis' recent good mood might extend to interacting with other people.

He slouched on the divan, watching a feed of some event in a garden, people planting a tiny tree in a circle of cameras and tulips. Tired and drawn, hunched over himself.

"What happened?" she asked.

"The usual," he said. "You living don't understand."

"We living?" she asked, incredulous.

He looked up. His lips firmed. "It's what we call you. We who are about to die." He saluted her.

"Lewis, I didn't cause any of this. Can't you cut me some slack?"

"It is the nature of the wild bird to hate its cage," he said.

"What does that mean? How are you analogous to a singing bird?"

"I didn't say singing," he said. "I am a representative of the wild world, though. A dimension that you can't touch or comprehend."

"You never even went to summer camp," she said. "The closest you've ever come to the wild world is grilling in the park."

He snarled at her, his face so distorted with fury that it drove her a step back. "I can be anything I want to be!"

"Of course you can," she said.

"Don't fucking *humor* me!" He plunged his face into the side of the couch. Rope-skinny arms covered his head. "Just go the fuck away!"

She did.

Was he going crazy? She couldn't imagine the pressure of having Death a constant presence at your elbow. Had he become more himself, as he had said? Had he always been this mean at the core, just hid it better before?

He'd been in her study.

Nothing she could point to at first. Then she noticed the shelf where she kept her knick-knacks, inspirational objects, remembrances. The crèche Lewis had made her in childhood was off to one side.

The figures had been smashed, reduced to terra cotta shards.

She touched one little heap. The sheep, with its spiral curls signifying wool and funny, lopsided expression. A version of it was a frequent visitor in her novels. Mr. Wiggly.

The fragments were beyond reassembly, almost pulverized. She swept them into a shoe box, closed the lid on it. Shoved it in the bottom of a cupboard.

She rearranged her shelf to compensate for the absence. She touched a sheaf of feathers clustered in a vase. Eagle or hawk, she wasn't sure which. Gathered by a lake one morning at summer camp, long ago. They ruffled against her fingertips, soft comfort.

The loss hurt.

The intrusion into her workspace, always off-limits in unspoken terms, hurt even more.

Middle of the night; waking.

Something, someone stood there in the bedroom in the darkness. But she knew the door was locked, she did that habitually, couldn't sleep if she knew it was open.

Moonlight sliced across the carpet. Was she dreaming?

Something *breathed* immediately next to her ear.

She couldn't move.

Surely this *was* nightmare. All she had to do was force herself awake.

The brass-framed bed creaked and tilted as it settled onto the mattress beside her. She smelled musk and smoke.

*Force* herself awake.

Weight, so great it *hurt*, even more than the pinprick of claws, settled onto her shoulders, directly on the joints.

Another massive weight on her hip.

The ashtray reek of its breath, stink-fumbling at her lips.

*Force herself awake.*

She managed to pull her hands under it, shove it away by digging her thumbs into the pits directly behind its forelimbs.

*She wasn't dreaming. Her eyes were open.*

She was frozen. She remembered being told what to do when attacked by a brown bear. Kick and punch and drive it away. If she was dreaming, couldn't she drive it into that shape, fight it off?

It had seemed impossible, the idea of a human fighting off a bear, but people had, the instructor said. People had done stranger, more valiant things.

It bore down on her. Claws drove into her side.

She dug her thumbs as deep and hard as possible with a wild shriek like an eagle's squawk.

It roared and tried to pull away from her. She let herself be drawn up, used the momentum to swing her feet under herself, clamber back away and over to the bed lamp, all in the space of one terrified breath.

Screamed, "Help me, someone please help me." Heard it go ringing down the corridors of time.

*Wake.*

Clicked the light on.

*Nothing.*

Her room, ordinary, bedclothes askew, laundry hamper, paperback straddle-backed on the bedside table. Beige carpet. The sound of her heartbeat, hammer-blasting in her chest, her throat, her ears.

She paused. Surely the commotion would have drawn Lewis. He was the lightest of sleepers.

Only silence from the rest of the house.

She crept down the hall in bare feet, paused outside his door. Her arm was sore, pain biting at it whenever she moved.

Only the sound of his breathing inside. Nothing else. She waited. She had read you could tell when someone woke up, that no one could control the pattern of their breathing from sleeping to waking. But the sounds continued, deep regular inhalations, rhythmic as a saw blade in action.

Faking? Or exhausted by his day, by the draining effects of his disease?

In the bathroom she avoided looking in the mirror as she dabbed at the edges of the wound with a washcloth, then covered them with Neosporin and a gauze bandage.

*What had happened?*

But that was not the real question.

Her mind crept around and around the real question.

*How had Lewis managed it?*

Because Occam's razor, the simplest explanation—who hated her, who wanted to harm her?

*Only Lewis.*

Back in her room, she left the light on.

Somehow she slept.

And dreamed. Child-Lewis, standing beside Child-Amber, hands intertwined, his voice chirping, "What's up, sis?" Love between them like a knotted rope.

Her arm around him, protecting him. "Close your eyes."

*How could it be any other way?*

At 5:30, she rose and did her morning run, steadfastly not thinking of the creature and showered while avoiding its shadow. It came at her in snatches of memory, so vivid she could smell its breath, fetid as old meat, feel the way its claws thudded into her flesh.

The water streamed down and down around the raw blotches along her arm. She looked at her flesh and felt herself shaking again.

Steadying herself, *what would Mrs. Mountebank do? Well, then, do it.* She picked dried blood from along the edges of the wound.

She should have had stitches. It was not too late. Maybe when she dropped Lewis off at the hospital.

In front of her bedroom door, she stopped. Three claw marks across it like a sign. Had they been there before? She hadn't looked.

Beside her, Lewis. "What's up, sis?"

She looked from him to the marks.

He must be pretending not to see them. Just looked at her with a half-smile.

Not Child-Lewis. Something else. Someone else. Someone born of despair and hate and desperation.

Her brother was gone. When had he vanished? Why hadn't she noticed?

Somehow she managed to pretend too. She'd make him wonder. Maybe think she had some plan up her sleeve. Or that she thought it was still a dream. She pretended. She dressed, ate breakfast, took him to an early appointment.

"Seven," he said curtly as he left the car, not even bothering to feign courtesy or curiosity about the stiff way she held herself.

*Till seven. Hours in which to figure out what to do.*

She was just about to pull away from the curb when someone tapped on the window. She rolled it down.

Ginger-haired, balding. His sleeves rolled down to expose his burly forearms. Tattoos covered the left, an intricate black and white pattern of tribal thorns around crossed daggers. He smelled of cigarette smoke and sweat.

She disliked him immediately.

But his voice was unexpectedly soft-spoken as he introduced himself as the Practical Shamanism group leader, Sam Mintie. He'd seen her waiting to pick up Lewis, he said, half-apologizing for invading her privacy, imposing himself.

"Lewis is having a hard time with some of the class concepts," he said. "Actually, some of the other members want me to kick him out of the group. Particularly Mrs. Oates."

Her cheeks burned. What horrible things had Lewis said, to make the entire group want him to go? She could only guess.

"Mrs. Oates? But Lewis said the group was men only."

Sam shook his head. "No. Perhaps he wanted to make sure you didn't check it out."

54

That made sense. Lewis didn't like sharing anymore.

"What concepts is he having trouble with?"

He hesitated. "It'll take a while. Do you have time to go get coffee?"

"Give me the short version and I'll decide."

His eyes were blue and watery. "He thinks he's a dark shaman—or can become one—and that to do so, he needs to kill you."

"Get in the car," she said.

At the coffee shop, she asked, "Why me? He'd have an easier time luring in some homeless guy or something."

"Because you're his closest blood," he said. "To move with ease in other dimensions, he has to symbolically cut ties with this one."

"He's got it all worked out, doesn't he?" she said.

"He does."

"Lewis said people become more like themselves as they get closer to death," she said.

Sam shook his head. "Really? I don't think so. You get more distanced, maybe, but not in a bad way. You know the saying, don't sweat the small stuff? You learn how to do that."

But this, this wasn't small stuff.

"So what is Lewis doing to symbolically cut ties with this one?"

Sam looked down at the table. His voice was low, forcing her to lean in.

"I'm sure you've noticed he's been especially mean, perhaps downright nasty to you lately. Maybe destroyed something that had personal significance for both of you."

"Lewis has always has his sharp side."

"He is very ... talented."

The hesitation pulled her even closer. "More talented than any of the rest of the group?"

"More talented than any of the rest of the group could ever dream to be."

"How?"

Sam shrugged. "Some mutation from the Plague? Or a genetic quirk? The right stars? But it seems to follow its own mythology. I've listened to Lewis expound on it at length."

"How does his being nasty fit in?"

"He must renounce you, as the representative of his ties to this world. First by not being emotionally attached."

"And then?"

"After he's killed you symbolically, he must do it physically."

"And how much of all of this bullshit of Lewis's do you believe?"

He didn't hesitate this time. "All of it. We don't need more dark shamans in this world."

At no point did she think, "I'm going crazy." Or even, "Perhaps this is *still* a dream." She thought it should have astonished her more. Shaken her world. It was surprisingly easy to change the laws in your head, or twist them to allow certain loopholes, it seemed.

Had she believed, in some corner of her mind, in this sort of thing all along? She had always despised superstition. It was appalling to think she'd secretly been a believer in the bogeyman under the bed.

*There had to be a rational explanation.*

At some point she'd have to sit down and think out all the implications. Now wasn't the time.

"What have you seen?" she asked. Had he also woken to find something settling onto his bed, heard its harsh erratic breathing?

"I saw a shape hovering around him when he spoke of it," he said. "Everyone did. The room seemed to grow dark. Poor Mrs. Oates nearly had a heart attack." His voice trailed off before he half-whispered, "Everyone wants magic. But to see it in action ... that was too much. Afterward everything seemed new, as though the world had been stripped of its skin. Too much to bear."

"So what can I do?"

He recovered himself. "He's made his own mythology, combined it with bits of H.P. Lovecraft and horror movies, but it has its own laws, ways it works, I presume. If I understand it right, it will be no problem thwarting him, so long as he hasn't made the first attack yet."

She rolled up her sleeve to show the bandages from last night. "Too late for that."

His fingertips hovered above the wound as though testing the air around it. "So strong," he said. His eyes were wide as he shook his head, pushing his chair away from the table.

"Where are you going?"

"I can't help you," he said. "This is all outside my experience." He fished through his pockets, took out a crumpled feather. He handed to her, "I wish I could pretend this would be of help. Maybe you can believe in it more strongly than I ever could."

"But you're a shaman."

"I wish I was. I've pretended all my life," he said. "Closed my eyes and willed my spirit animal near. And then, with only a few little scraps, I see your brother accomplish what I've dreamed all my life. I saw his animal and it terrified me, but it thrilled me too. But I know in my heart that nothing I can do will stand against it. I'm sorry."

She gaped after him as he walked out. The feather rocked on the table, caught by the shifting air as the door closed behind him.

This wasn't how it was supposed to work. He was intended to be the *deus ex machina*, the source of wisdom that would tell her how to defeat the evil Lewis had summoned.

When life started to act like fiction, you expected it to follow fiction's patterns. If there was no happy ending, how would you know when the story was done?

She could flee, leave the city, go into hiding somewhere. But who was to say he couldn't send his creature after her, that it couldn't track her down no matter where she went? She fingered the edge of the table as though testing its solidity while her mind raced. She couldn't deal with this. It was impossible. It was asking too much.

Could she confront Lewis? Could she bring him to his senses, let him see this wasn't what civilized people did, moving outside the laws of reality?

That was what she would do, over food that night.

She left the useless feather there beside her half-empty coffee cup.

But in the reality of kitchen, the smell of lemon-scented dish soap, the sunlight streaming in the windows, Formica countertop under her fingers, she couldn't think where to start. She moved methodically from stove to table, setting up dinner. Hamburgers sizzled with senseless abandon. Broccoli melted under fierce steam.

*Dessert? What best expressed "Happy Day That I Learned My Brother Is a Supervillain Planning on Killing Me?" Chocolate lava cake? Bombe Alaska? Some flaming dish?*

When he entered the room, she froze like a wary animal. But he didn't seem to notice.

"Smells delicious!" he said with a wide smile. He spread the napkin in his lap with a flourish. "Food like this, it's worth living for, don't you think?"

Their gazes met and locked. She felt herself pressing against a door, trying to find the handle, trying to open it. Her mouth cracked, trying to smile, trying to say anything ordinary, but only a hollow croak escaped.

"You don't look so good," Lewis said. His gaze traveled over her outfit. "It's pretty warm for long sleeves, isn't it? Are you feeling okay?"

She could almost hear the beast's breath.

In the window glass, a flash of copper feathers, the glint of a predatory eye. It struck along her nerves, a sudden intuition, and she smiled.

"Bad dreams, that's all," she said. She turned back to the stove, pretended she was busy ladling out soup. She tossed over her shoulder, "Dreams can't hurt anyone, after all."

Uncertainty flickered in his eyes. "Well," he said, taking a spoonful of soup. "Sure. Dreams."

Years of bluffing him, of not betraying how much a blow had hurt, steadied her. She could act as though she wasn't afraid. And that made her less afraid, somehow.

Still, after he went to bed, she stayed up, saying she wanted to work on a sketch.

Up in her chair, she leaned over the graphic pad. It was very close, so very close.

"Come in," she said, and began to draw.

*From The Annals of Everkind:*
MRS. MOUNTEBANK:
   *It comes!*
THE TANGO GOTANGO GOTENGO:
   *Whose side is it on?*
MRS. MOUNTEBANK:
   *There's no telling. Pray that it's ours.*

It was her best work. She didn't know how suitable for children it was, this one, but children liked a touch of darkness, after all—look at

*Charlie and the Chocolate Factory*, the gruesome ends of the children there. Would children like this new character, the Madhawk?

It came in a swirl of feathers and talons; it came as swiftly as pulling the string that dissolves a tangle and lets the lines sweep free. It was graceful and deadly, and it rode the winds high above Everkind, feared but loved at the same time.

It came as suddenly as a battle trumpet shrilling, and its claws were sharp, sharp enough to defeat anything. Sharp enough to defeat fear and despair.

Sharp enough to leave Lewis in a tangle of red in his sheets, the dissipating smell of ash and smoke around him as his creature dissolved beneath the Madhawk's fierce attack.

Afterward.

## Ending #1:

When Sam knocked on her door, he didn't say anything about Lewis' death. He had shown up at the funeral with the rest of the Practical Shamanism group. She didn't know whether they had come to express their condolences or to make sure that Lewis was really dead.

*Perhaps a mixture of both.*

Sam was easy to talk to, though, about things other than Lewis. He loved her books, it turned out, and had dabbled in writing himself, just long enough to appreciate it. They went out to coffee.

Then dinner, then a movie, then other things.

The Madhawk was very popular, it turned out. Everything she touched turned to gold from then on. Sam read each new book with wonder and appreciation. The perfect reader.

Of course he was in love with her.

Of course she fell in love with him.

She kept Lewis's ashes on the mantel. The criminal who had broken into the house, inexplicably killed an already dying man, was never caught.

It was a good life.

## Ending #2:

Of course the Madhawk came to her once it was done with Lewis. Roused to blood, it could not relent until its maker was gone, until she had raised her wrists one last time to let its talons slash across the surface and set the crimson floodgates free.

When she had breathed her last, shuddering gasp, wondering what they would make of her stories now, the Madhawk stayed for a few moments, as long as it took for her to leave the world and enter its dimension. It plucked a strand of her hair, and carried it back to begin building its nest.

Its chicks were strong. It was a good life.

## *Afternotes*

*I avoid horror movies in the theater because I get far too wrapped up in them and have been known to scream at tense moments. Hence, we watch them at home. After watching the truly dreadful movie "Paranormal Activity," I was thinking about how to make it the movie scarier and ended up coming up with this story as well as making sure I couldn't sleep that night. Some of Lewis and Amber's childhood is the one I shared with my brother Lowell, but he is not a shaman and resembles Lewis in no other way.*

*The Madhawk also owes a certain amount to the Bird in a Heinlein story, "The Unpleasant Profession of Jonathan Hoag," whose disturbing, reality-isn't-exactly-what-you-think quality always unsettled me (now that I think about it, it's much the same terror as that evoked by the Leiber novel I talked about in another of these notes) and which I ran across as a teenager in the collection by the same name.*

*But more than anything, the story's origin lies in thinking about both sides of the caretaker role and the fierce resentment that may arise on the part of the person being taken care of. That's what lies at the heart of Lewis' transformation, and I don't know that there's any way Amber could have staved it off.*

*The story's also got a metafictional side that some readers like and which drives some others nuts. All I can say about that is forgive me. John Barth's influence as a teacher pops out at odd times and this was one.*

*The piece originally appeared in Apex Digest, under editor Lynne M. Thomas.*

# THERAPY BUDDHA

THE OFFICE'S NEW WORK-FROM-HOME POLICY had its advantages, but housekeeping service wasn't one of them. Even though he was escaping the smog-laden outside air, Lyle's apartment smelled too-lived in, filled with the odor of ancient take-out, unwashed clothing, and dead house plants.

"I should clean this place up," he said. He thought about hanging up his damp windbreaker, but shrugged it off to toss it over a chair. He dumped his bag on the dining nook table as he edged his way past.

When he thumbed the frame, the metallic square lit with the evening news logo, four stories ribboned and scrolling across it. All showed scrambles of military activity, puffs of bomb smoke, a scattered flash of gun fire, muted and surreal, before they combined into a single burger commercial.

From behind him, the device on the table said, "You seem to use the word 'should' a lot. Do you attribute a particular meaning to that word?"

Lyle scrounged through the refrigerator, pulling out a plastic meal bag to throw in the microwave. Coming back to the coffee table, he said, "I suppose I say 'should' when I really mean 'don't want to do.'"

The Therapy Buddha sat cross-legged, three feet tall and made of soft plastic. It was bright green.

Its calm, big-cheeked face said, "How do you feel about that?" The sound emanated from a speaker that glinted dentally between unmoving lips, like a slanted front tooth.

"Yeah, whatever, toy. TV on." He retrieved his meal and slumped into the couch to flip through channels on the wall screen.

"A broken mirror never reflects again," the Buddha said. "Fallen flowers do not return to their branches."

"What the hell does that mean?"

"Zen koans are sayings that challenge habitual thought processes. For another Zen koan, say 'Koan, please.'"

He did not reply. The Buddha sat, silent and immobile. His co-workers had bought it for him on his fortieth birthday, wrapped in sheets of bright pink bubble wrap.

"Gives pop therapy a whole new meaning." Scott laughed and almost patted him on the back. The voice-activated Buddha was a rip-off of a Sony model, but the imitation was very good except for the wrong color.

The party had been a typical office gathering—sheet cake from the corner grocery store with bright red, slightly crooked lettering reading "Happy 40th Lyle!" over white frosting. Everyone stood around and made small talk. He chatted with Scott and the latest intern.

"What do you think of your new surroundings?" Scott asked the intern. He was in full charm mode, relic of his days selling Christian comedy albums.

She was busty and blonde, wearing green-striped overalls that matched the beads in her hair. Her tenure in the office was sixteen hours, as of that afternoon. "I've never worked in a data-selling corporation before," she admitted. "This is my first time working since college."

"You didn't work in high school?" Scott said. "A shame—I think it really builds character. What did you do instead?"

"I was on the swim team," she said. Lyle imagined her briefly in a tank suit, her long hair tied back.

"Sports are good," Scott said. "I worked in my dad's store, making deliveries. What about you, Lyle?"

"I farmed gold in an online game and sold it."

"Every geek's dream job. But how can there be actual money in that?"

"It paid for college," he said. "I didn't really have the grades for a scholarship. Real jobs pay better, though, particularly since they now outsource a lot of gold grinding to Thailand and China."

Scott nodded, looking interested in a way that Lyle knew was forced. The intern didn't bother to conceal her boredom. Beads clicking together as she moved, she went to take another sliver of cake. Scott and Lyle stood staring after her.

"She'll last, what, two weeks?" Scott said. "Someone will want coffee and she'll get huffy and leave."

"If that long."

"How are you liking working from home?"

When the memo had come down from the home office—to decrease costs, remote logins, etc.—Scott had been one of the first proclaiming the glories of the new policy, but every time Lyle made his way into the office to check-in or for functions like this, he found Scott there.

"It's all right," he said. "But a little isolated. How about you?"

"Sometimes it just seems like I can get a lot more done here, you know what I mean?"

Lyle shrugged. "Not really." Most of his work consisted of surfing the trade nets to find places looking for batches of data of the kind he could deliver. Sometimes he looked for new products and then pitched his dataherd to their marketers, pointing out the markets they reflected and the insights they provided, depending on how he grouped them. A data herder needed agility of mind, the ability to see opportunities and seize them quickly.

The coffee shop down the street was wider than his apartment, so he usually took his datapad down there. If he got there early, he could find a spot near the window, overlooking Lake Washington. A latte and a croissant's worth of lunch bought him at least an hour uninterrupted before the servers started cleaning his space too obviously, edging him out. He liked to watch the sailboats on the water, and the little red water scooters, shaped like dragons, that had been rare last year and this year were everywhere.

His fingers danced over the keys as he performed his yearly evaluation of the demographics of his dataherd. As expected, they'd scattered even more geographically, and a few more had married than had divorced. Overall, wages were down. Outside the sky was pinkish and cloudy as dying water, reflected in the metallic sides of the hot dog vendor's cart, steaming as he pushed it along.

Lyle frowned as numbers flowed across his pad in response to his query. The dataherd was trending towards a particularly unprofitable sector—he could no longer mine them for singles data. That had been coming for a while. He'd foreseen it five years ago, but didn't like it nonetheless. He drank the rest of his latte in quick gulps, not tasting it, watching the vendor negotiate with a dragon boat, the rider struggling to pass her credit card across the vendor's beam to be read before it signaled with a green light and the hot dog was passed down. She wore a white face mask, as did the vendor and the others on the street. A bad day for breathing, the morning news had said.

Waving cheerfully, rider and boat made their way back into deeper water, circling the tour boat cruising along the waterfront. Lyle gathered up his pad and put his own mask on to go home.

"The trick is figuring out a way to pitch them," he said to the Buddha. He'd left earlier than he'd meant to, rehearsing this conversation in his mind. It startled him to realize that he had been looking forward to talking to an inanimate object.

"Why is it a trick?"

"Because it's creating something where it didn't exist before. The demographic of people who eat chocolate in the bathtub, or whatever else you can claim them to be representative of, that someone can aim a product at. It's a knack."

"How do you feel about that?"

"I have to go into the office," he said. "It's a bad sign when I'm having conversations with a toy."

The plaza office was much the same as always. Downtown Seattle always struck him as waiting to become the stage setting for a post-apocalyptic film, its workers and visitors white and blue-masked zombies, a few with brighter faces yet, tie-dyed or stamped with bright yellow ducks and green frogs.

Scott poked his head into the cubicle. "Hey buddy, nice to see you for a change."

"We're supposed to be working from home," Lyle said.

"Well, sure," Scott said. "Sitting around doing datasorts in your bathrobe, who wouldn't like that? But I don't think it's a cost-cutting measure. They're seeing what deadwood they can drop." He grinned mirthlessly. "I've been coming in doing alternative training," he said. "It's good to be agile, employment wise. My cousin worked for a mall corp for forty years, then they cut her loose. Now she's a virtual clerk."

"What world?"

"Second Life, tends a music store. Sits there at the computer all day waiting to give shoppers the human touch."

"Ah yeah. Two of my herd did that a couple of weeks ago," he said. "And one's a virtual taxi-driver. Robots control the driving, she just gives clients human interaction and thanks them when the card is billed."

"Sign of downward social mobility!" Scott said, and laughed. "I'm sure you have other opportunities by the binload."

"I'm thinking about recruiting some new people into the herd to up their marketability," he said.

"Almost too late for this graduation."

"Graduation?"

"They do it by year now. For the cost of a few trinkets, you can sign up a thousand or so college kids. They'll fill out any amount of forms for a coffee chip or an mp3 download. Go look on the internal website, there's a list of promotional items you can request."

"That intern quit yet?"

"Last week. Did I call it or what? Mahalia asked her to pick up soda for the office weekender, and she posted a five screen goodbye e-mail to the rest of us, citing a lack of respect for her as a person. You should have gotten it."

"There's so much e-mail that I delete anything that goes to the office at large."

"That may not be the best strategy."

"It's worked well for eight years so far," Lyle said and went home.

"I don't really feel connected to anyone," he said to the Buddha. He'd moved it to the bookshelf so it could see more of the room. He sat on the couch with his back turned to the television, arguing with the Buddha. Behind him, the screen showed troops marching past an indiscriminate jungle backdrop.

"How does that make you feel?"

"Disconnected," he said, then laughed. "Yeah, whatever." He unrolled his datapad and traced his herd's purchases for the evening, managing to assemble a subset into an infochunk on movie-going trends. He shot it off to the studio markets and waited for usage fees.

Checking prices, he noticed a high profile survey on medicinal teas. It was easy to request coupons for free samples to be sent to his dataherd. He could check the results and peddle the infochunk to the company in a week or so.

"I will tell you a koan," the Buddha said. "The monk Bazan was walking through the marketplace one day, and heard a customer say to the butcher, 'Give me your best piece of meat.' The butcher replied, 'Everything in my shop is the best. There is no piece of meat that is not the best.'"

He stared at it, nonplussed. What sort of reply did it expect?

"For another Zen koan, say 'Koan, please.'"

"The thing," he said to the Buddha, picking up the conversation again. "The thing is this. What right do I have to capitalize on the members of my dataherd?"

"Do you take responsibility for that?" the Buddha asked.

"Their clickprints are changing," he said.

"What are their clickprints?"

"Their web usage patterns, their search keywords, their purchases, how they look at sites. And I make it change—two weeks from now, some of them will have shifted to tea drinkers. Because of me. I manipulate their lives so I can harvest their data."

"How does that make you feel?"

"They're growing away from me," he said. "Ten of them died last month in the war. Now I'm down to 4527. Soon I won't even have a sellable herd."

"Would you like another koan?"

"Should I just give them their freedom, cut them loose?" he said. "Someone else can collect their data. Or reassemble them. I don't know what I'd do otherwise, though. I can stay free in a hostel, maybe, but food isn't free."

"You seem to use the word 'freedom' a lot. Do you find that word significant?"

"It's what I want to do," he said. "You're right. I use it because I'm thinking about it. It's the answer, otherwise I wouldn't be fixed on it like that."

His fingers danced over the keys as he released their contracts. Maybe someone else would pick them up, but he hoped not. They should lead lives undirected by advertising, make their own choices. Like the choice he had just made.

"I don't want to get that list of high schools after all," he said to Scott.

"It doesn't matter," Scott said. "Didn't you get the memo? They're going to be making dataherds assignable at the corporate level. Everyone belongs to a corp anyhow. You won't be able to recruit anymore. Your old herd just skyrocketed in price, buddy. You can form your own agency."

He stared at Scott. "What? I cut them all loose last night. Erased all the data from my infocloud."

Scott stared back. "You really did it, buddy? Jesus, why?"

"The Buddha told me to do it."

"That doll we bought you at the office party? You are shitting me, right?"

He stared at Scott, stricken, and finally Scott patted his shoulder. "There's a lot of careers out there," he said, avoiding Lyle's eyes. "Lots of possibilities. My mom makes a decent living selling antique food."

"Antique food?"

"Things like Space Bars and Twinkies. There's quite a market in them. She buys and sells them. You should see her apartment. Let's go talk to her."

But Scott's mother, Mrs. Laurelman, wasn't much consolation.

"It's hard work, what I do," she said. "I have agents that monitor some online auctions for me, but there's also a lot of leg work. I wouldn't recommend getting into anything like it."

"I'd thought he could sell music, he likes music," Scott said.

"What sort of music?" She looked at Lyle. He sat next to an

enormous stack of pink pastry boxes.

"Oh, all sorts," he said. "I doubt that's what I'd get into, anyhow."

"If you can find a hot fad, you can make a quick buck," she said. "I watch to see if any nostalgic foods are mentioned on videocasts, and if so, I buy up any surplus quickly."

He looked at the package next to his foot. It showed two zebras dancing with each other, their stripes rose and sky blue. The lettering was Arabic.

"What are these?"

"Some sesame treat that got mentioned on a soap opera," she said. "Makes enough to buy groceries for another week."

"Don't you have a corporation plan?"

Her face purpled. "Get out!"

Steve hustled him out, apologetic. "She has a medical condition that kept her from getting health care, that's why she does the buying and selling. She's on base minimum, gets a little help with groceries, but mainly she relies on not going for meds."

Lyle wondered what her demographic was, whose herd she belonged to. The apartment had been too hot, and he felt flushed and sweaty. His garment clung moistly to his skin.

Steve punched his shoulder. "Go home and take a load off," he said.

"Yeah. Yeah." He swung aboard the bus at the corner and went to the monomall before home.

"Good evening," he said to the Buddha as he entered the apartment. He hung up his jacket with careful, deliberate motions, looking at the way the fabric gleamed in the florescent lights. His head still buzzed with an angry whirl of thoughts, words colliding unintelligibly.

"How are you?" the Buddha asked.

He took a breath. "I'm fine, how are you?"

"What did you do today?"

"Why would you care?" he said.

"Are you aware that you are answering questions with questions?"

"It's a game," he said. "We used to play it in Improv Club, back in high school. Oh, wait. You don't have a high school to remember. Mine was a misery. Like my life."

"Why do you think your life is miserable?"

"Why wouldn't I? Oh, there I am going with the questions again, aren't I?"

It was silent.

"Have I hit a new trigger?" he said. "Are you not talking in order to see what I will say to you?"

"What do you want to say to me?" it asked.

He went over and picked it up to stare into the bland green features.

"You betrayed me," he said. "Do you understand what that means?"

"Why do you think you were betrayed?"

He set it down as carefully as a baby.

"You could have told me, and you didn't," he said.

"This unit is not intended to be a fortune-telling device."

"Aren't you? Aren't you supposed to be the random voice of the Universe, addressing me through the luck of the draw and the forces of serendipity?"

"Would you like to hear a koan?"

"No. No koans. I'm done with all that. I don't have anything left. I might as well commit suicide," he said.

It spoke in a different voice. "Alert. Spoken keywords have triggered emergency routines in this unit. If you do not wish to have medical attention summoned, count to ten and backward within one minute."

"Fuck you," he said.

"If you do not wish to have medical attention summoned, count to ten and backward within thirty seconds."

Medical attention would cost an arm and a leg. At the last possible second, he spat out, "One-two-three-four-five-six-seven-eight-nine-ten-nine-eight-seven-six-five-four-three-two-one."

"Transmission aborted," the Buddha said.

He stared at it.

"I'm going out to interact with some real people," he said. And then, "Christ, why am I telling *you* that?"

Steve called while he was coming out of the movie, which had been something about cavemen and mammoths, frothy with laughter, something he hadn't understood at all. He paused to take the call, shielding his ear while the other moviegoers eddied past him.

"It's not as though they depicted Neanderthals correctly," he heard one boy say to another. In his head, Steve's voice said. "Lyle, you there?"

"I'm here."

"Listen, there was this study, you know, one of those market studies, for a tea, some sort of tea that was supposed to make you immune to colds, do you know the one I mean?"

"Yeah, I know the one. I signed my herd up for it, one of the last things I did with them."

Silence from Steve.

"You know what I'd really like to see, I'd like to see magicians," another movie-goer said. Their friend nodded, passing Lyle, and said "Yeah, and a really good bass line."

Steve said, "Well, that's unfortunate."

"Why, what's happened?"

"Turns out they'd modified the recipe, did some sort of cuts with the vitamins, and about a quarter of the people who've drunk it have total liver shutdown. You didn't drink any of it, did you?"

"No," he said.

"Well, there's a plus. But I got to warn you, buddy, they're going to be coming after you with lawyers and maybe even jail-time. It's looking pretty bad. And when the cops see you cut your herd loose, they're going to think there was some reason. Like you knew ahead of time."

He was numb. He couldn't hear anything from the people moving around him. It was all just a high-pitched whine in his head.

"Can I come talk to you?" he asked desperately.

Steve's voice came from far away, hesitant. "Well, buddy, you see. It's just that I don't want them to think—bad timing right now, I think. Maybe in a few days?"

He fumbled with the plastic bag in his pocket, taking out a pill bottle. Thumbing off the lid, he drank the tiny pills, each as big as a bird's eye, down as though they were liquid.

"Go ahead," he said, swallowing. "It'll be too long before they get here for you to save me. I should have known better than trust my life to you. I should have known that an object couldn't be my friend."

"If you do not wish to have medical attention summoned, count to ten and backward within thirty seconds."

They looked at each other in silence.

"If you do not wish to have medical attention summoned, count to ten and backward within ten seconds. Nine. Eight. Seven. Six. Five. Four. Three. Two. One."

The Buddha gave out a shrill squeal, before saying "Information transmitted."

Lyle sat down, staring at his feet, looking puzzled. He made as though to speak, then shook his head twice and slumped back into the couch. His legs shot forward in a flurry of spasms, kicking the table before he bucked the sofa over backwards. The Buddha shuddered sideways.

The paramedics came through the doorway thirteen minutes later. Lyle lay on the floor, staring upward, body tangled in the constraints of the tiny space between sofa and table. Across the room lay the Buddha, staring across the carpet, its face turned to him, no meaning written there.

### *Afternotes*

*I'm fascinated by what we project onto things around us, by how we can imagine that objects are somehow animate, and this story is about that. You may remember ELIZA, a computer program that was a "virtual psychiatrist" intended to simulate talking to an actual person, created by Joe Weizenbaum. Surprisingly, many people who talked with Eliza felt a strong emotional connection, to the point where Weizenbaum felt compelled to write about the social dangers of AI, saying that it was "obscene" to use it in clinical sitations.*

*Lyle is lonely and desperate for connection. Like any of us, when it's not forthcoming, he supplies it himself, and the story tries to talk about why that might become problematic.*

*The story itself originally appeared in 2020 Visions, edited by Rick Novy, which is why there's a joke about Neanderthals in there as a tribute to Rick's novel* Neanderthal Swan Song. *My favorite part is the antique food dealer, truth be told, but some of Lyle's office existence may have been drawn from my experiences with corporate life at Microsoft.*

# Ms. Liberty
# gets a Haircut

THE SUPERHEROES SIT IN A BACK BOOTH AT Barnaby's Ye Olde Tavern and Pizza. It's not the usual sort of superhero hangout and they'll probably never eat here again. They've had four autograph requests: two from customers, one from their waitress, and one from the manager, who also insisted on taking their picture with his cell phone.

It's a shame that they won't be coming back, Ms. Liberty thinks. The cheese pizza is hot and greasy, the sensation of consuming it agreeable. It's enjoyable, even, to sit around talking about the world, bullshitting and comparing stories and wishes and pet peeves.

"You know what I hate?" she says, pouring more beer. "The porn star superheroes. And nine times out of ten, they're female."

"Yeah, I know what you mean," Dr. Zenith Arcane says. "Names like Pussy Whip and BangAGang."

"And Cocktail."

"Goddess, yes. Cocktail." They swap wry smiles.

X, the superhero without a shape, shaves away pizza triangles, slurps down high-octane root beer. Ms. Liberty and Kilroy are splitting a pitcher and well on their way to ordering a second. Alphane Moon Bass. Most places don't have it.

Dr. Arcane eyes X and Ms. Liberty. She says, "Must be nice to be able to eat like that." She's got a watery salad and a glass of apple juice in front of her. She doesn't usually complain. But lately she's been downright snippy.

72

"I need to remind you about your hair," Dr. Arcane continues. "It's so early eighties."

Ms. Liberty's hair falls in frosted blonde waves, a mane, unexpected against the strict lines of her red, white, and blue jumpsuit. She touches a tendril at her shoulder.

"Are you her parent now?" Kilroy says, pouring herself another foamy mug. "By the sands of Barsoom, back off, good doctor!"

The children two booths down gasp in horror and delight as X changes shape while still eating. Now she's a wall-eyed, dome-shaped creature, purple in hue.

"A ghost from Pac-Man," Dr. Arcane tells X. "Celebrating the cultural patriarchy. Embrace your chains!" She takes a sip of apple juice.

"Did something crawl up your supernaturally sensitive ass?" Ms. Liberty asks.

"Don't piss me off," Dr. Arcane says. "Nobody likes me when I'm pissed off."

Ms. Liberty takes another pizza slice, eats it in five quick bites. She knows why she likes eating. It's not about the fuel. Anything will do for that. (Literally.) It's her programming that makes her enjoy the sensation of something in her mouth. And elsewhere. She can achieve orgasm in 3.2 seconds by saying a trigger phrase.

She really hates her creators for it. It's distracting. It's dehumanizing. It's objectifying. She understands the intent behind it, to have her engage in enthusiastic, frequent sex, hopefully with them. She doesn't understand, though, why they chose to then give her free will, to force her to perpetually struggle between that pull and the business of being a patriotic superhero, a cybernetic woman: super strong, super fast, super durable.

Even now she feels the firmness of the bench under her ass, the smoothness of the table's wood against her forearms. She glares at Dr. Arcane.

"What. Is. Bugging. You?" she says, spitting out each word like a bullet.

"We don't have the right dynamic."

"What?"

"The four of us—you a cyborg, X a genetically constructed being, alien Kilroy from four galaxies away, and myself, a pan-dimensional sorceress—"

"Sorcerer."

"Magic-user. At any rate, we need some more human people. To add a few more facets to our toolbox."

"You mean interview some new members?"

"An open call for facets, yes."

Ms. Liberty eats another piece, exploring the hot rush of grease, the intensity of cheese and tomato and basil. New members. It's not a bad idea.

The interviews are held in the Kiwanis hall. Ms. Liberty, X, Dr. Arcane, and Kilroy go through their clipboards while two dozen candidates wait out in the hall.

"If you're going to be our leader, you need to look like you haven't time-travelled here from the 20th century," Dr. Arcane grumbles to Ms. Liberty. "You may have been built with the blueprints from the Stepford wives, but you don't have to keep looking like one."

"It's a little late to be thinking of that," Ms. Liberty says. Her internal chronometer says 14:59:05. At 15:00:00, she'll signal Kilroy to open the door.

Dr. Arcane says something under her breath, glances back down at the clipboard. "What sort of grrl-power frenzy name is Zanycat?" she asks.

Zanycat, as it turns out, is a super-scientist's kid sister, pockets full of gadgets, gizmos, gee-whizzeries. She demonstrates flips, moves through martial arts moves like a ballerina on crack, and does quadratic equations in her head. She's a keeper, all right, although she's very young. Her certificate pronounces her barely at the legal age to be a sidekick: fifteen.

Pink Pantomime, a former reality-show star turned hero, doesn't do much for anyone but X.

Kilroy and Zenith like Bulla the Strong Woman, but her powers are too close to Ms. Liberty's.

Rocketwoman is vague about her origin; perhaps she's a villain gone good? Her armor is like something from the cover of a 40s SF magazine, but bubble-gum pink, teal blue, like a child's toy. Her gun is similarly shaped: it shoots out concentric rings of brilliant yellow energy that contract around a target.

They have gone through twenty-two candidates, making notes, asking questions. The twenty-third arrives, dressed in black and steel.

Dr. Arcane dates women by preference but believes that everyone exists on a continuum of bisexuality. She has slept with demons, mermaids, aliens, shape-shifters, ghosts, the thoughts of gods (and goddesses), robots, and super-models. But she has never seen anything like the sexuality of the woman who steps forward next: the Sphinx. She smells of sweet amber and smoke, her accent is sibilant and smouldering.

Ms. Liberty does not date, has not slept with anyone since discovering how thoroughly her sexuality is hard-wired. The resultant level of frustration, constant as a cheese grater on her nerves, is preferable to knowing that she's giving in to their design. But she also has never seen anything like the Sphinx, her languid power, her lithe curves, her eyebrows like ebony intimations.

Kilroy couldn't care less. X just sings of carrots.

According to the Sphinx's resume, she's a computer hacker and ninja-type. Competent and low-key. She doesn't talk much, despite their best attempts to draw her out.

At one point she looks up, meets Ms. Liberty's eyes. They stare at each other as though hypnotized, but it is impossible to tell what the Sphinx is thinking.

Less so with Ms. Liberty, who goes beet red and looks away.

"Why an all-woman superhero group?" the Sphinx asks.

"Why not?" Dr. Arcane says even as Ms. Liberty replies, "That was somewhat accidental. X and I both wanted to leave our old group and we knew Kilroy was looking for work. X and Dr. Arcane were old friends."

"Is it a political statement?"

"It's like this," Ms. Liberty says. "One of the reasons we left the Superb Squadron, X and I, was because we were the only females on there and we were getting harassed. I'm sure there are good guys out there, who would make a swell addition to our team. Maybe we'll explore that somewhere down the line. But for now, it's more comfortable to be all women."

The Sphinx nods. She and Ms. Liberty exchange looks again. Ms. Liberty imagines the Sphinx as the heroine of a comic book, a solitary wanderer, aloof and sexy and unpartnered.

"Get a haircut," Dr. Arcane tells Ms. Liberty on the way out of the hall.

"Stop nagging me. Why should I be judged on my appearance?"

Dr. Arcane pauses, considers this. "Valid point," she admits. "But here it's not about the group's appearance. It's about getting you laid."

"Artificial beings don't need to get laid," Ms. Liberty says.

"The hell they don't," Zenith retorts.

In the end they take on three provisional members: Rocketwoman, the Sphinx, and Zanycat. Three months trial membership, no health coverage until that period is past, but they'll be on the accidental damage rider as of tomorrow. Rocketwoman tells them all to call her Charisse, but everyone keeps forgetting, and the Sphinx and Zanycat prefer their hero names.

"What's the name of the group going to be?" Zanycat asks.

"We haven't been able to agree on one yet," Dr. Arcane admits.

"What are the candidates?"

"A corporate logo, Freedom Flight, an unpronounceable symbol, and Gaia's Legion."

X projects the symbol in turquoise Lucida Sans on her flank, bats cow-lashed eyes enticingly at Zanycat.

"A friend told me fast food companies are looking to sponsor teams, and there's good money in it," Kilroy says.

Arcane shakes her head. "We don't need to worry about that. I'm independently wealthy."

"*You* don't need to worry about that, you mean," Kilroy says. "Some of us are trying to make a living, put aside a little for retirement. Or a ticket back home."

"We need some sort of name for press releases, at least," the Sphinx says. They all stare at her.

"Press releases?" Dr. Arcane says incredulously.

"We need name recognition," the Sphinx insists.

"We need a fluid interpersonal dynamic!" Dr. Arcane shoots back.

"Actually, what we need is training that allows us to respond efficiently and effectively to threats," Ms. Liberty says. She adds, "In my opinion."

"How about a working title?"

"Like what?"

"Female Force?"

"UGH. Just call us Labia Legion and shoot us in the collective forehead."

The Sphinx and Ms. Liberty are sharing breakfast, the two of them up earlier than the rest for a change.

"I have a question," the Sphinx says.

"Go ahead." Ms. Liberty butters her waffle.

"Are we even really an all-female group?"

"What do you mean?"

"Well, Zenith, Charisse, Zanycat, myself for sure. But Kilroy's an alien—do they even have genders like ours?"

"She lays eggs, I believe, but she's been pretty cagy about it."

"And X—well, X is a construct. Not even built to be female, she apparently just decided it—but based on what? Attitude? Self-identification? Class? Power relationship to her creator?"

Ms. Liberty has had *this* conversation before, in the Superb Squadron headquarters.

"If she says she is, who am I to say no?" she says.

"That brings us to you," the Sphinx says.

Ms. Liberty says, "If I say I am, who are you to say no?"

"You're a construct too."

"Constructed to be female."

"Something you could change or reject as easily as throwing a switch."

Ms. Liberty says, "I have to be something more than superhuman. I'm female."

The Sphinx shrugs, drains the last of her coffee, slides from her chair.

"Going on patrol," she says.

Zanycat finds Zenith Arcane in the library, slouched over a couch reading, with three cats laid at intervals along her body. The group has been using Arcane's Manhattan brownstone, which is much much larger on the inside than on the outside, to the point where Zanycat has taken to spending mornings exploring the wings and passages, trying to map them on graph paper. She intends to ask Dr. Arcane about that, but she finds the older mage intimidating.

Right now, though, she has a different question, and Zenith seems like the best to tackle on the subject.

"So what *is* X?" she asks.

Dr. Arcane slides her reading glasses up her nose and closes her book. She gathers herself up, displacing the cats, and regards Zanycat. She steeples her fingers in front of herself in a professorial fashion.

"What categories do you want me to use?" she says.

"Is X an alien? A human? A manifestation of some cosmic force?"

"Ah. She was created by a human scientist who died when she was only a few years old. He kept her entertained with television and the Internet, so she tends to draw on pop culture forms."

"What's her real form?"

"She doesn't have one."

"Doesn't have one? How can that be?"

"I've known her for a few decades now, and I've yet to see her repeat a shape," Dr. Arcane said.

"Then how do you know she's a she? She doesn't just take on female shapes. I saw her do Invader Zim this morning."

Dr. Arcane beams as though a prize student has just won a scholarship. "Excellent question! Because she identifies as such."

"She said so?"

Arcane nods.

Zanycat presses further. "How do she and Ms. Liberty know each other?"

"From Superb Squadron. Ms. Liberty had been a member for a couple of years when X joined. She had been a member of the Howl, the shapeshifter group before then, but she was just a little too non-traditional for them."

"Aren't they villains?"

"You're thinking of the Pack. They're all shapeshifters as well."

"How many shapeshifter groups are there?"

"Four," Dr. Arcane says with the immediate decisiveness of someone who knows every facet of the supernatural world. This is her main power in fact. Not that she can do that much, magically, but that she knows everyone, can connect you to a source on ancient Atlantean texts or a circle of star worshippers or even the Darkness That Crawls on the Edge of the Universe. "The Howl, the Pack, the Changing—which is a loose affiliation of generally good to neutral supernatural beings—and Clockwork Flight, which has a lycanthrope as a leader."

Zanycat makes a face and Dr. Arcane laughs. "What?" she says.

"There's too much to learn about all of this," Zanycat says.

"That's okay," Dr. Arcane tells her. "Most of the time you can go by your instincts."

Ms. Liberty has never talked about why she left the Superb Squadron before. She and the Sphinx stand side by side, watching an alleyway where giant radioactive battery-powered centipedes are emerging. Ms. Liberty says, out of the blue, "You know what bugged me? X always made it clear she thought of herself as she, but they couldn't take that at face value. They called her it, or that thing. And I thought—how far away is being female from being an it? And so I left, even though I forfeited most of my pension."

The Sphinx says, "Do you and X—"

She pauses, as though trying to pick the next word. Ms. Liberty suddenly realizes what she's going to say and says, "No! Nothing like that. We're friends."

The Sphinx looks at her. Ms. Liberty's heart is racing. A person doesn't ask another person that sort of question unless another sort of question is on that person's mind.

Twin menaces, Prince Torpitude and Princess Lethargia, rampage through downtown, smashing store windows, taking whatever pleases them, draping themselves with sapphire bracelets, fur stoles, shoving iPods and bars of shea butter soap in their pockets.

# Near +

Everyone acquits themselves well. Kilroy shadowwalks behind the duo, distracts them while Rocketwoman swoops in and Ms. Liberty comes at them, Zanycat cartwheeling after, from the opposite side. The Sphinx cuts off their communication gear, keeps them from calling for back-up. Within twenty minutes they're contained and the cops are processing them with shots of hyper-tranquilizer and ferro-concrete bonds.

No press shows up, except for a blogger who interviews them, takes a couple of pictures with his pen-camera.

"What's the name of the group?" he asks, glancing around.

"It's unidentified," Zanycat says in a shy whisper, and he peers towards her, says, "Unidentified, all right. And your name?" Behind her, Dr. Arcane hears Rocketwoman give out a gasp, a happy little fangirl gasp that takes Arcane a moment to process.

He punches info into his Blackberry, takes a few more pictures of the scene of the struggle, and interviews two bystanders.

Ms. Liberty thinks later that she shouldn't be surprised when the post appears calling them the Unidentified.

"It's not a terrible name," Dr. Arcane argues.

"It sounds like a Latin American human rights movement," Ms. Liberty snaps.

X shrugs and moonwalks down the wall. She wears a purple beret and angel wings—no one is quite sure what the shape is, including Dr. Arcane, until Zanycat identifies it as pulled from a recent Barbie video game.

"What do you think, Rocketwoman?" Dr. Arcane says, rounding on her. "How's it stack up for you?"

"It's fine," Rocketwoman stammers.

Dr. Arcane steps closer, "But how's it stack up against whatever we end up with?" she pursues, and is rewarded by seeing Charisse pale. "A-HA, I knew it!" She thumps her fist into her palm triumphantly.

"Knew what?" Kilroy asks.

"She's from the future."

They all turn and stare at Rocketwomen. Time traveling is the most illegal thing there is; there are corps of cops from a dozen cultures that will track a time-fugitive down.

Rocketwoman raises her chin, stares at them squarely. "I don't care," she says, "it's better than going back." Another realization hits Dr. Arcane.

"Goddess," she says, "not just any time-line but one of the Infernos at the end of Time, is that it?"

"I don't know," Rocketwoman says. Everyone can tell she's flickering between relief at finally being able to talk about it and worry that someone's going to come find her.

Dr. Arcane is unstoppable. "And what was our name, in the history books you studied?"

"The Unidentified," Rocketwoman admits.

Dr. Arcane's stare sweeps the room, nails each of them with its significance. "Ladies and ladies," she says, "I think we have a name."

It's hard to argue with that, although X wistfully expresses her symbol a few more times before Ms. Liberty finally tells her to give it up.

Ms. Liberty has taken a front bedroom for her own. It's not that she really sleeps: she can activate a program that is intended to be a simulacrum of sleep, which her creators assure her is far better than the real thing, but it has a disturbing slant towards erotic fantasies that makes her leave it off.

She doesn't sleep. Instead she writes. Romance novels. It's how she keeps herself able to buy cybernetic parts that are very expensive indeed. Let's not even talk about the cost or possibility of upgrades to her very specialized system. Her creators are gone, blown up long ago under highly suspicious circumstances, and she's never been able to track down the malefactor who carried out the deed.

Why romances? There's something about the formulaic quality of the series she likes. She writes for Shadow Press's superhero line, amuses herself by writing in the men of Superb Squadron, one by one, as bad lovers and evildoers. She has little fear they'll ever read one and recognize themselves. She also writes superhero regencies, daring women scientists and explorers, steam-driven plots to blow up royalty, Napoleonic spies and ancient supernatural crystals quarried by emerald-eyed dwarves from the earth's heart.

She works on one now, pausing on the love scene. She writes a kiss, a caress, and stops. She thinks of the feel of lips on her own skin and gives way to the urge to trigger her programming, leaning over the desk, feeling orgasms race along her artificially enhanced nerves.

She touches her face, feels the tears there.

Downstairs in the Danger Room, she works through drills, smashes fast and hard into punching bags, dodges through closing barriers, jump and leaps and stretches herself until she is sore.

The door whispers open and the Sphinx enters. Without a word, she joins the practice.

Is Ms. Liberty showing off or trying to escape? She moves in a blur, demonically fast, she moves like a fluid machine come from the end of Time, she moves like nothing she's ever seen, forging her own identity moment by moment. And feels the Sphinx's skin, inches from her own, fever warm, an almost-touch, an almost-whisper.

"Is this the thing," Ms. Liberty says to the Sphinx, "that it matters because you will only sleep with females?"

"I will only sleep with someone," the Sphinx says, twisting, turning, cartwheeling, "who knows who they are."

Ms. Liberty's arms fall around the other woman, who is iron and velvet in her embrace. Then Ms. Liberty pushes away, stammers something incoherent, and rushes from the room.

The Sphinx looks after her, waits for hours in the room, gives up the vigil as dawn breaks. Several stories above, Ms. Liberty saves the twenty thousand words she's written, a love scene so tender that readers will weep when they read it, weep just as she does, saving the file for the last time before sending it to her editor.

Ms. Liberty lets X cook her dinner. This is a mistake for most beings. X has flexible and fairly wide definitions of "food," and she has no discernible theory of spices. But for a cybernetic body, fuel is fuel, and sensation is sensation. There are no unpleasant physical sensations for Ms. Liberty. All she has to do is make a simple modification, performed by mentally saying certain integer sets.

She knows that she can do the same with her emotions. She could make loneliness bliss, frustration as satisfying as completing a deadline. But would she be the same person if she did that? Is she a person? Or just a set of desires?

She eats chili and bread sandwiches, washes them down with a glass of steaming strawberry-beef tea. X has produced candies studded with dangerous looking sugar shards colored orange and blue and yellow and green. Inside each is a flake of something: rust, brine, coal, alderwood.

Ms. Liberty eats them meditatively, letting the flavors evoke memories.

Rust for the first day she met X, when they fought against the Robotic Empress. Brine for the Merboy and his sad fate. Coal for the day they fought the anti-Claus and gave each other gifts. Alderwood has no memory attached and it scents her mouth, acts as a mental palate cleanser. She goes upstairs and writes five chapters set in Egypt, and a heroine in love with the dusky native guide. At midnight she eats the chocolate-flavored flatbread X slides under the door and writes another 2,000 words before lying down to recharge and perform routine mental maintenance.

She pushes herself into sleep as smoothly as a drawer closing. Her last thought is: is she a superhero or just programmed that way?

They fight Electromargarine, the psychedelic supervillain.

A band of intergalactic pirates.

Super-intelligent orcas from the beginning of time.

The actual Labia League, which turns out to be supervillains who refer to themselves as supervillainesses.

Alternate universe versions of themselves.

A brainwashed set of superheroes.

A man claiming to speak for Mars.

A woman claiming to speak for Venus.

A dog claiming to speak for the star Sirius.

And all the time, Ms. Liberty keeps looking at the Sphinx and seeing her look back.

Dr. Arcane has her own set of preoccupations. There's Zanycat's hero-worship, Kilroy's chemical dependency, and whatever guilt rides Rocketwoman. Zenith suspects the last is some death. She tries to figure out *who*, tries to observe where Rocketwoman's eyes linger, which conversations shade her voice with regret (all of them, which is a little ominous), how she looks when reading the morning newspaper.

Dr. Arcane catches her in the hallway, hisses in her ear, "Listen, Charisse, I need for you to tell me who dies. If it's me, I won't be angry, I just want to get my affairs in order."

"I can't tell you," Rocketwoman says. She looks away, avoids Zenith's eyes.

Zenith snarls with frustration, She doesn't like not knowing, it's the one thing in all the world that can make her truly angry.

Plus all that stuff about the sanctity of the timeline that time-travelers spill out is hooey. You can alter time, and many people have. If it was as fragile as all that, you'd have reality as full of holes as Brussels lace. No, when you change time you just split the timeline, create an alternate universe. The unhappy future still remains, but at least it's got (if you've done it right) a happy twin to balance it out. This is, in fact, why most travelers appear and Zenith is sure that Charisse is no exception. She's here to change *something*. She's just not saying what.

They fight something huge and big and terrifying. That's par for the course. That's what superheroes do, whether they're programmed by three almost-adolescents in lab coats or by centuries of a culture's honor code or by some childhood incident that set them forever on this stark path.

Dr. Arcane fights because she likes the world.

Rocketwoman fights because she's seen the future.

X fights because her friends are fighting.

Zanycat fights because it's what her family does.

Kilroy fights because there's nothing better to do until she gets to return home.

The Sphinx fights because she doesn't want to be a supervillain.

Ms. Liberty thinks she fights for all these reasons. None of these reasons. She fights because someone wanted a sexy version of Captain America. Because someone thought the country was worth having someone else fight for. Because a woman looks sexy in spandex facing down a flame-fisted villain.

Because she doesn't know what else she should be doing.

Because her instincts say it's the right thing to do.

Ms. Liberty finishes her novel, sends it off, starts another about a bluestocking who collects pepper mills and preaches Marxism to the masses. She spends a lot of time pacing, a lot of time thinking.

X has discovered paint-by-numbers kits and is filling the rooms with paintings of landscapes and kittens, looking somewhat surreal because she changes the numbers all around.

Zanycat is about to graduate high school and has been scarce. Next year she'll be attending City College, just a few blocks away, and they all wonder what it will be like. Zenith remembers being student and superhero—it's hard to do unless you're well-organized.

Kilroy has joined AA and apologized to several villains she damaged unnecessarily while fighting intoxicated. Before each meal, she insists on praying, but she prays to her own, alien god, and an intolerant streak has evidenced. She's apparently a fundamentalist of her own kind and believes the Earth will vanish in a puff of cinders and ash when the End Times come. That's why she's been working so hard to acquire money to get off-world, lest she be caught in the devastation.

Ms. Liberty goes to Reede and Mode to find fabric for a new costume. There's a limited range to the fabrics—not much call for high-end fashion in super-science, but she comes across a silvery gray that looks good. She finds blue piping for the wrists and neck, not because she wants the echo of red, white, and blue, but because she likes blue and always has. And it makes her eyes pop. The super-robots take her measurements. They'll whip it up while she runs her next errand.

There are some places that are neutral territory for superheroes and villains. A few bars, for example, and most churches. And this hair salon, high atop the Flatiron Building. Arch rivals may face down there and simply step aside to let the other have first crack at the latest *Vogue Rogue*.

"My friends keep trying to push me to try something different, Makaila," she tells the hairdresser.

"Do you want to try something different?" the hairdresser demands, putting her hands on her hips. She has attitude, cultivates it, orders around these beings who could swat her like a fly, drain her soul, impale her with ice and kill her a thousand other ways, as though they were small children. And they enjoy it, they sink into the cushioned chairs and tell her their woes as she uses imaginarium-reinforced blades to snip away at super-durable hair, self-mending plastic. Usually she just trims split ends.

Ms. Liberty looks at the tri-fold mirror and three of her look back. She thinks that this is the first time she's decided to alter herself, step away from the original design. She thinks of it as modernization—a few decades of crimefighting can date you, after all.

Here's the question, she thinks. Does she want to be a *pretty* superhero? Is that what being a superhero means to her?

And here's another question: what is a superhero's romance? She's been writing them as though they were any other love story, writ a bit larger, with a few more cataclysms and laser-guns in the background. Girl meets boy, there's a complication, then she gets her man. But what does the superwoman do after she's got him? Does she settle down to raise supertots or do they team up to fight crime? Can you have your cake and eat it too, as Marie Antoinette, the Queen of Crime, would insist?

Her makers thought sex was a worthy goal, a prime motivator. And instead all they'd done was make her start to question her body. And now she was questioning her own mind the same way, wondering if she wanted love or sex, and what the difference was.

Her three faces stare and stare from the mirror and she hesitates, conscious of the waiting Makaila. Finally, she says, "I want it short and easy to take care of" and leans back in the chair.

They fight:
Shadow elementals.
A team of super-scientists.
A group of sub-humans.
A cluster of supra-humans.
Ms. Liberty's creators in zombie form.
A villain who will not reveal her name.
The hounds of the Lord of the Maze of Death.
A rock band.

A paranoid galaxy.

A paranoid galaxy's child.

A paranoid galaxy's child's clone.

A witch.

And in the end, everything turns out fine, except for the hovering death that Rocketwoman still watches for, that Dr Arcane still watches her watching for. The Sphinx and Ms. Liberty do go to bed together, after issues and problems and misunderstandings, and at that point we fade to black and a few last words from our sponsor, along with X in the shape of a giant candy bar.

"Every woman knows she's a woman," Ms. Liberty says. "She's a woman. And every hero is a hero. They're a hero. That's who they are."

## *Afternotes*

*This story uses characters from a novel I wrote in grad school, The Furies. Unfortunately the book was lost somewhere along the way to today, and all I've got are the chapters that went into my thesis. Those characters themselves were based on characters I'd run in several superhero roleplaying games (primarily the Champions system). I hope to recreate the novel at some point but this story is a very truncated version of some of its events.*

*The title itself was inspired by F. Scott Fitzgerald's "Bernice Bobs Her Hair" although the subject matter is more than a little different. I'm fascinated by superheroes, and a sucker for any fiction that contains them. And half the fun of writing superhero fiction is coming up with the names.*

*The story begins in Barnaby's Pizza, an establishment in South Bend, Indiana, where my gaming group ate an awful lot of meals over the years.*

# 10 New Metaphors for Cyberspace

### 1. My Grandmother's Kitchen

Databases hang like commemorative plates on the HTML wall, advertisement gilt gleaming on their edges except for the General Patton limited edition, which holds a gunmetal trim of spiky security. Search engines purr like appliances, popping up results while a dishwasher chugs in censorship, scrubbing its links clean of revolutionary references. Underfoot, carpet flickers, old e-mail messages woven into the warp and weft of its threads, scattered with cookie crumbs. Every week there's garbage collection, hexagonal bins full of old files wheeled to the curb, ready to be collected.

### 2. The Garden of Eden

Infomercial butterflies flutter here and there, obscuring knowledge or distorting it through the stained glass shimmer of their wings. Applets dangle from the trees and there are animals everywhere, rabbits quick as web-services and lions protecting copyrights, birds weaving nests of random statistics. Somewhere in the verdant, glassy grass an ASP slithers like a virus, whispering forbidden, encrypted words.

### 3. A Crazy Quilt

Embroideries of data links elaborate each patch, signaling its access type with their pattern, cross-stitch for unimpeded access near French knots of one-time passwords. The fabric tells the access fee, public denims and burlap against slicker subsidized sites made of mercerized cotton or flashy R-rated satin.

Punch through the folds to the infrastructure built of bed linens, layers of uncountable threads, a wooly blanket of processes scratchy to the touch.

## 4. Minkler's Hardware Store, ca. 1980

Here in this room, high ceilinged and sporting a fan whispering daily headlines as it spins above the clerk named Archie, the minutiae are kept, shining bolts and nuts and washers and nails and screws in tiny partitioned drawers. The system jolts with a database's corruption, and silvery data spills in a spray across the wood-grained floor, whose whorls and burls tell the story of the Net's history.

## 5. A Flaming Cave

Flickers of every color, great leaping pyres and half seen shimmers betraying the movements of others in the data stream. See how hotly that corporate database shines? Touch it and you'll be burned, consumed within your mind like a phoenix.

## 6. A Medieval Village

Perhaps it's more like a Disney conception of a medieval village: the rustic inn with a McDonald's logo that serves as main access for the neighborhood, a baudy wench wearing a corporate slogan across her cleavage, the coachman outside a financial access point winking sly stock tips. Teams of white Percheons pull wagonloads of integers, lumbering by in an instant that seems slower than molasses.

## 7. A 12 Year Old Girl's Closet

Oh, pink, pink, relentless pink! Spangles of information everywhere, Hello Kitty stickers sponsored by Sanrio and Sony, poster blogs depicting the latest American Idol, fuzzy spam filters full of lint and bubble gum integers. Each drawer opens with its own perfume, lemon for media biographies, cinnamon for the cooking network, cedar sawdust for history and, hidden beneath the bed, the heavy musk and patchouli of porn.

## 8. A Mall Pet Store

Normal, for the most part, except for the startling way the aquariums float loose and drift around the store. Data fish move from one domain's tank to another, intermingling, frilled fans of checksums becoming tattered as they corrupt each others' integrity. To buy the data, you must purchase a container—anti-virus bubbler optional.

## 9. A Grandfather Clock

Hear the hour chiming? Each time zone perceives it differently, the boom of PST, the bang of Eastern Standard. Tap a numbered sector of its face and the area expands, letting you drill down through history. Somewhere a hacker mouse runs up and down the shiny wood, pursued by software with a carving knife.

## 10. The Junkyard

This is where the abandoned data goes to die and in its rot, daisies of projected theories and Tetris-variants spring up, nourishing themselves on nitrogen-rich bytes of information. That rusted, useless car was once Google's pride, but now they're elsewhere in a cybernetic demolition derby, creating new colossal wrecks to host more flowers and hybrid metaphors.

### *Afternotes*

*After hearing William Gibson speak, I started thinking about cyberspace and how his vision of it has affected speculative literature. It made me wonder what other metaphors might be used for it, since it seemed like everyone else had adopted his and let it shape their perception. Different metaphors might lead to an entirely different definition of cyberspace, and so I tried to come up with interesting ones. As a former network security expert, I may have had too much fun writing it, as is often the case with list pieces.*

*Many figures are drawn from my life. I grew up within walking distance of Minkler's Hardware. The fish store is the one in Scottsdale Mall, circa 70s, South Bend, Indiana. My grandmother's kitchen was hung with commemorative plates, which I now own in turn.*

*This piece originally appeared in* Abyss & Apex, *under editor Wendy S. Delmater.*

# Memories of Moments, Bright as Falling Stars

 THE ORANGE BOXES LAY SCATTERED LIKE LEAVES across the med complex's rear loading dock, and my first thought was "Jackpot." It'd been hard to get in over the razor wire fence, but I had my good reinforced gloves, and we'd be long gone before anyone noticed the snipped wires.

But when we slunk along under the overhanging eaves, close enough to open the packages, it turned out to be just a bunch of memory, next to impossible to sell. Old unused stuff, maybe there'd been an upgrade or a recall. It was thicker than most memory, shaped like a thin wire.

So after we'd filled our pockets, poked around to find anything else lootable, and slid out smooth and nice before the cops could arrive, we found a quiet spot, got a little stoned, and I did Grizz's back before she did mine. I wiped her skin down with an alcohol swab and drew the pattern on her back with a felt-tip pen. It came from me in one thought, surged up somewhere at the base of my spine and flowed from my fingertips through the ink. Spanning her entire back, it crossed shoulder to shoulder.

I leaned back to check my handiwork.

"How does it look?" she said.

"Like a big double spiral." The maze of ink rolled across her dark olive skin's surface. A series of skin cancers marked the swell of one buttock, the squalmous patches sliding under her baggy cargo pants. She sat almost shivering on a pile of pallets. We were at the recycling yard's edge. This section, out of the wind between two warehouses, was rarely visited and made a good place to sit and smoke or fuck or upgrade.

I uncoiled a strand of memory and set to work, pressing it on the skin. I could see her shudder as the cold bond with her flesh took place. The wire glinted gold and purple, its surface set with an oily sheen. Here and there sections had gone bad and dulled to concrete gray, tinting the surrounding skin yellow.

She shrugged her shirt back over her skinny torso. Her breasts gleamed in the early spring's evening light before disappearing under the slick white fabric. Reaching for her jacket, she wiggled her arms snakelike down the sleeves, flipping her shoulders underneath.

"Is it hooked in okay?" I asked.

She shrugged. "Won't know until I try to download something."

"Got plans for it?"

"I can think of things," she said. "Shall I do you now, Jonny?"

"Yeah." I discarded my jacket and t-shirt, and leaned forward over the pallet while she applied the alcohol in cool swipes. The wind hit the liquid as it touched my skin and reduced it to chill nothingness. She drew a long swoop across my back.

"What pattern are you making?"

"Trying to do the same thing you did on mine." The slow circles grew like one wing, then another, on my shoulder blades. She paused, before she began laying in the memory.

I don't know that you could call it pain but it's close. At the moment a biobit makes its way into your own system, it's as though the point of impact was exquisitely sensitive, and somewhere micrometers away, someone was doing something inconceivable to it.

"Tomorrow are the Exams," she said. "Could see what I could download for that."

I started to turn my head to look at her, but just then she laid down a curve of ice with a single motion. My jaw clenched.

"And?" was all I managed.

"One of us placed in a decent job would be a good thing."

She laid more memory before she said "Two of us placed in one would be better."

"Might end up separated."

"Would it matter, a six-month, maybe a year or two, before we could work out a transfer?"

**92**

I would have shrugged but instead sat still. "So you want to take that memory and jack in facts so you can pass the Exams and become an upstanding citizen?"

She ignored my tone. "Even a little edge would help. Mainly executables, some sorting routines. Maybe a couple high power searches so I can extrapolate answers I can't find."

The last of the memory felt like fire and ice as it seeped into my skin. She'd never mentioned the Exams in the two years we'd been together.

You're not supposed to be able to emancipate until you're sixteen, but Grizz and I both left a few years early. My family had too many kids as it was and ended up getting caught in a squatter sweep. I came home and found the place packed up and vacant. The deli owner downstairs let me sleep in his back room for the first few months, sort of like an extra burglar alarm, but then he caught me stealing food and gave me the boot. After that, I made enough to eat by running errands for the block, and alternated between three or four sleeping spots I'd discovered on rooftops; while they're less sheltered, fewer punks or crazies make the effort to come up there and mess with you.

Once I hooked up with Grizz, life got a little easier—I had someone to watch my back without it costing me a favor.

We went around to Ajah's, hoping to catch him in one of his moods when he gets drunk on homemade booze and cooks enormous meals. Luck was with us—he was just finishing a curried mushroom omelet. It smelled like heaven.

Three other people sat around his battered kitchen table, watching him work at the stove. Two I didn't know; the third was Lorelei. She gave me a long slow sleepy smile and Grizz and I nodded back at her.

Ajah turned at our entrance and waved us in with his spatula. His jowls surged with a grin.

"Jonny and Grizz, sit down, sit down," he said. "There is coffee." He signaled and one of the no-names, a short black man, grabbed us mugs, filled them full, and pushed them to us as we slid into chairs. I mingled mine with thin and brackish milk while Grizz sprinkled sweet into hers. The drink was bitter and hot, and chased the recycling yard's lingering chill from my bones. I could still feel the new memory on my skin, cold coils against my t-shirt's thin paper, so old its surface had fuzzed to velvet.

Ajah worked at the poultry factory so he always had eggs and chicken meat. Sometimes they were surplus, sometimes stuff the factory couldn't sell. He'd worked out a deal with a guy in a fungi factory, so he always had mushrooms too. Brown rice and spices stretched it all out until Ajah could afford to feed a kitchen's worth of people at every meal. They brought him what they could to swap, but usually long after the fact of their faces at his table.

Lorelei being here meant she must be down on her luck. As were we—the shelter we'd been counting on for the past year had gone broke, shut down for lack of funds, despite countless neighborhood fundraisers. No one had the script to spare for charity.

Two grocery sacks filled with greenery sat on one counter. Someone had been dumpster diving, I figured, and brought their spoils to eke out the communal meal. A third sack was filled with apples and browned bananas, and I could feel my mouth watering at the thought.

"I'm Jonny," I offered, glancing around the table. "She's Grizz."

"Ajax," said the black man.

"Mick," muttered the other stranger, a scruffy brown-haired kid. He wore a ragged poncho and his hair fell in slow dreads.

"You know me," Lorelei said.

Conversation faded and we listened to the oily sizzle of mushrooms frying on the stovetop and the refrigerator's hum against the background of city noise and traffic clamor. The still in the corner, full of rotten fruit and potatoes, burped once in counterpoint.

"What's the news?" Ajah asked, ladling rice and mushrooms bound together with curry and egg onto plates and sliding them onto the table towards Lorelei and Grizz. Ajax, Mick, and I eyed them as they started eating, leaving the question to us.

"Not much," I said.

"Found a place to live yet?"

"Jesus, gossip travels fast. How did you hear about the shelter?"

"Beccalu came by and said she was heading to her cousin in Scranton. You two have people to stay with?"

I shook my head as Grizz kept eating. "No one I've thought of yet.

We need to head to the library tonight, though, figured we'd doss in the subway station there for a few hours, keep moving along for naps till it's morning. It's Exams tomorrow."

"I know," Ajah said. "Look, why don't you stay here tonight? The couch folds out."

I was surprised; I'd never heard Ajah make anyone an offer like that.

"The Exams are your big chance. Get a good night's sleep and make the most of them. Face them fully charged."

I rolled my eyes. "For what? Like there's a chance." But he and Grizz ignored me.

"We need to make a library run still," she said.

"Yeah, yeah, that's fine. I'm up till midnight, maybe later," Ajah told her.

Despite my doubts, relief seeped into my bones. We'd been given a night's respite, and who knew what would happen after the Exams? "Thanks, Ajah," I said, and he grunted acknowledgement as he slid a plate before me.

The portabella bits had been browned in curry powder and oil, and the eggs were fresh and good. Grizz ate methodically, scraping her plate free, but she looked up to catch my eye and gave me a heartfelt smile, rare on her square set face.

As her gaze swung back to her plate, my glance tangled with Lorelei's. I could not read her expression.

Lorelei and I used to pal around before Grizz and I met up. She and I grew up next to each other, and it's hard not to know someone intimately when you've shared hour after hour channel surfing while one mother or the other went out on work or errands. We suffered through the same street bullies and uninterested teachers. She was the first girl I ever kissed. You don't forget that.

But I knew I wanted Grizz for keeps the first moment I saw her. She came swaggering into the shelter wearing a rabbit fur jacket and pseudo-leather pants. She'd been tricking in a swank bar, but then someone snatched all her hard-earned cash. So there she was, with a bruise on her face and a cracked wrist, but still holding herself hard and arrogant and the only person in the world who could glimpse the softness underneath was me, it seemed like. So I sauntered up, invited her outside for a smoke, and then within a half hour, we were pressed against the wall together, my hands up her shirt like I'd never touched tit before, feeling her firm little nipples against the skin of my palms.

It's been her and me ever since. As far as I'm concerned, it'll always be that way.

~☙

After eating, we helped wash dishes before heading to the library. We had to wait a half hour for a terminal to free. Finally a man gathered his tablet and stood, stretching his shoulders.

"I'll wait," I said, and gestured Grizz forward.

She nodded and went forward to slide her hand into the log-in gloves. Within a moment, her eyes had the glassy stare that means the meat's occupant is elsewhere.

I looked around. Chairs and desks dotted the place, all of them occupied. I went outside to the parking garage for a smoke.

Daylight had fled. At the structure's edge, where the street was dimly visible, I panhandled a dozen people before I found one willing to admit to smoking. I lit the cigarette, a Marlboro Brute, and leaned back against the wall, which was patchworked with graffiti layers. Maybe by the time I was done, a booth would have opened up. It was getting late, after all.

I closed my eyes as the nicotine rush hit me. Footsteps came across the cement floor towards me. I opened my eyes.

It was Lorelei. She wore a slick bright red jacket and lipstick to match over short skirt and chunky boots. Silver hoops all along each ear's edge, graduated to match her narrowing cartilage. She looked good. Very good.

"Nice night, ain't it?" she said as she moved to lean on the wall beside me. "Gimme."

I passed the smoke over and she took a drag.

"Want to try something to make the nice night even nicer?" she asked, smiling as she leaned back to return the cigarette.

"Meaning?"

"It's good stuff." She fished in the jacket before holding out the lighter and one-hitter. The end was packed with gray lintish dust. "Never had better."

I took the pipe and sparked it. The blue smoke rushed into my lungs like a fist, like a physical jolt and the world dropped half an inch beneath my feet. Everything was tinged with colors, an iridescence like gasoline on a rain puddle. I was standing there with Lorelei and at the same time I was on a vast dark plain, feeling the world teeter and slip.

Lorelei watched me. On the side of her face was a new tattoo, a black floral design.

"What's that?" I asked. I raised my hand, my fingers dripping colored fire and sparks. The drug curled and coiled through my veins, and I could feel my heart racing.

"Maps," she said. "Executable that interfaces with a global database. Got a GPS here." She tapped a purple faceted gleam on one earlobe. "Drop me anywhere in the world, I'll know where I am."

"Looks awful big to be a simple database interface."

She shrugged, and took the pipe back. She tapped out the ashes with care before she tamped a new pinch of greenish leaf into the mouth. "Controls the GPS too, and some other crap."

An expensive toy, but one that would qualify her for all sorts of delivery jobs. But she must be broke, to show up at Ajah's, I thought. It didn't make sense.

"How're things?" I asked.

Her shoulders twitched into another sullen shrug. "Got some deals in the works. Just a matter of time before something plays out."

I glanced back at the library door. "I should go in, I'm waiting on a machine to clear."

The drug still held me hard, and every moment was crystal clear as she raised her hand to stroke along my jaw. "I miss you sometimes, Jonny," she said, sounding out of breath.

I didn't want to piss her off, so I used a move that's worked before. Catching her hand, I turned it palm down and pressed my lips against the knuckles before dropping it and taking a step backward.

"See you around," I said.

She didn't say anything back, just stood there looking at me as I turned and walked away.

When I tried to log in, the drug prevented it. Every attempt shuddered and screeched along my nerves, so painful it brought tears to my eyes. But I kept trying and trying. A few cubicles down, I could see Grizz's back, hunched over her terminal, every particle intent. Learning. Preparing.

I stared at the screen, which showed the library logo and the welcome menu, all options grayed out, and cursed Lorelei and myself. Mostly myself. After an hour of pretending to work, I slipped away.

Another hour later, Grizz found me outside smoking. Good timing, too. I was on my fourth bummed cigarette, and starting to wonder when a guard would show to jolly me along on my way.

She looked happy, as animated as Grizz gets, which isn't much.

"You get what you wanted?" I asked.

"Got a bunch of stuff," she said. "Plant stuff."

Grizz likes plants, I know. At the shelter, she tended the windowsills full of discarded cacti and spider plants. But I hadn't known she was thinking about that for a career.

"That memory's something, isn't it?" she said. "I downloaded a weather predictor that monitors the whole planet, some biology databases, some specialized ones, some basic gardening routines, and a lot of stuff on orchids."

"Orchids?"

"I've always liked orchids. I've still got plenty of room, too. What about you?"

"Mine's not so good," I lied. "It didn't hold much at all."

Her gaze flickered up to mine, touched with worry. Her eyes narrowed.

"What are you on?" she asked. "Your pupils are big as my fist."

"Dunno the name."

"Where'd you score it?"

"Lorelei swung by, turned me on."

Silence settled between us like a curtain as Grizz's expression flattened.

"It's not like that," I finally said, unable to bear the lack of talk.

"Not like what?"

"She just came through and glimpsed me."

"She knew you would be here because we mentioned it at dinner. She still wants you back."

"Grizz, I haven't been with her for two years. Give it a rest."

"I will. But she won't." She pulled away and made for the exit, her lips pressed together and grim. I followed at a distance all forty blocks to Ajah's.

In the morning, we showered together to avoid slamming Ajah's water bill too hard. Grizz kept her eyes turned away from mine, rubbing shampoo into her hair.

I ran my fingertips along the spirals on her back. "This is different," I said. Under my fingertips, the wire had knobbed up and thickened, although it still gave easily with the shift of muscles in her back. The gray patches were gone, and a uniform sheen played across the surface.

"Does it feel different?" I asked.

She shrugged. "Not really."

"Do you remember the brand name on the boxes? We could look it up on the Net later on."

"Carpa-something. I don't know. It looked bleeding edge and you never know what's up with that."

"Why do you think they threw it out?" I wanted to keep her talking to me.

She turned to face me with a mute shrug, closing her eyes and tilting her head back to let the water run over her long black hair. Her delicate eyebrows were like pen strokes capping the swell of her eyes beneath the thin-veined lids.

I tangled my fingers in her hair, helping free it so the water would wash away all the shampoo. Muddy green eyes opened to regard me.

"Going to sit out the exams?" she asked.

Saying nothing, I shook my head. We both knew I didn't have a chance.

The Exams were the freak show I expected. Rich people buy mods and make them unnoticeable, plant them in a gut or hollow out a leg. This level, people want to make sure you know what they got. Wal-Mart memory spikes blossomed like cartoon hair from one girl's scalp, colored sunshine yellow, but most had chosen bracelets, jelly purple and red, covering their forearms. One kid had scales, but they looked like a home job, and judging from the way he worried at them with his fingernails, they felt like it too.

You take the Exams at sixteen and most of the time they tell you you're the dregs, just like everyone else, but sometimes your mods and someone's listing match up and you find yourself with a chance. The more mods you have, the more likely it is. So the kids with parents who can afford to hop them up with database links or bio-mods that let them do something specialized, they're the ones getting the jobs.

Usually your family's there to wish you luck. Mine wasn't, of course. And Grizz never said anything about her home life. The only times I've asked, she shut me down quick. Which makes me think it was bad, real bad, because Grizz doesn't pull punches.

You could tell who expected to make it and who was going through the motions. Grizz marched up to her test machine like she was going to kick its ass three times around the block. I slid into my seat and waited for instructions.

You see vidplots this time of year circling around the Exams. Someone gets placed in the wrong job—wacky! Two people get switched by accident—hilarious! Someone cheats someone out of their job but ultimately gets served—heartwarming and reassuring!

In the programs, though, all you see is a quick shot of the person at the Exams. They don't tell you that you'll sit there for three hours while they analyze and explore your wetware, and then another two for the memory and experience tap.

And after all that, you won't know for days.

Grizz wouldn't say anything about how she thought she'd done—she was afraid of jinxing it, I think, plus she was still pissed at me about the Lorelei business.

I could tell as soon as we walked out, though, she was happy. I walked her back to Ajah's and said I was heading down to the court to see if our forms had come in. She nodded and headed inside. It was a gray morning. But nice—some sunlight filtered down through the brown haze that sat way up in the sky for once.

The smoke-eater trees along the street gleamed bright green and down near the trunks sat clumps of pale-blue flowers, most of them coming into their prime, although a few were browned and curling. I could feel all that memory on my back, lying across my shoulder blades and I found myself Capturing.

I'd only heard it described before—most people don't have the focus or the memory to do it more than a split-second. But I opened to every detail: the watery sepia sunlight and the shimmer playing over the feathers of the two starlings on a branch near me. The cars whispering across the street and two sirens battling it out, probably bound for St. Joe Emergency Services. The colors, oh, the colors passing by, smears of blue and brown and red flashes like song. The smell of the exhaust and dust mingled with a whiff of Mexican spices from the Taco Bell three doors down. Every detail crystal clear and recorded.

I dropped out of it, feeling my whole body shaking, spasms of warring tension and relief like hands gripping my arms and legs.

I tried to bring it back, tried to make the world go super sharp again, but it wouldn't cooperate. I stood there with jaw and fists clenched, trying to force it, but nothing happened.

Within three days, Grizz had heard. A year of training at the Desmond Horticultural Institute, then a three year internship at the State Gardens in Washington. Student housing all four years, which meant I wouldn't be going along.

At first we fought about it. I figured it was a no-brainer—go there jobless or stick here where I had contacts, friends ready with a handout or a few days work. But once Grizz had been there a while, she insisted, she'd be able to scrounge me something so I could move closer.

Ajah's girlfriend, Suzanne, got her set up with a better wardrobe and a suitcase from the used clothing store she ran. I bought her new shoes, black leather boots with silver grommets, solid and efficient looking.

"What are you going to do without me?" she asked.

"I've gotten by before," I said. "You work hard for us, get somewhere.

Five years down the line, who knows?"

It was a stupid, facile answer, but we both pretended it was meaningful.

And we did stay in touch, chatted back and forth in IMs. She was working hard, liked her classmates. She read this and that and the other thing. They kept telling her how well she was doing.

Unwritten in her messages was the question: What are you doing with it, with the memory?

Because certainly it was doing the same thing on her body as it was on mine: thickening like scars healing in reverse, bulky layers of skin-like substance building over each other. In Ajah's bathroom mirror, I could see the skin purpling like bruises around the layers. My sole consolation was Capturing; extended effort had paid off and I could summon the experience longer now, perhaps ten seconds all together. I kept working at it; Captured pieces sell well in upscale markets if you can get a name for yourself.

And I had the advantage of being able to do it as often as I liked, although each time still left me feeling wrung out and weak. I kept trying to Capture and never hit the memory's end; the only limits were my strained senses. My eyes took on a perpetual dazzled squint as though holy light surrounded everything around me.

I never told Grizz though. Nor about the fact that every time I went to jack into the Net, the drug got between me and the interface. I was glad I hadn't seen Lorelei—I was starting to wonder if she'd given it to me deliberately. It scared me. I lost myself in Capturing more and more. I started delivering packages for Ajah and Susanne, and laid aside enough cash to buy a simple editing package for it.

Editing is internal work, so you can do it dozing on a park bench if you've got the mental room to spread out and take a look at the big picture. I did. What I wanted to do was start selling clips on the channels. It'd take a while though, I could tell, and I was still working out how I'd upload it, given the problems jacking in. I figured at some point I'd burn it off to flash memory and then use an all-accessible terminal, with keyboard and mouse. In the meantime I caged what meals I could, slept on a round of couches, and showed up at Ajah's often.

Sometimes after a meal, he'd roll out the still on its mismatched castors, and we'd strain its milky contents in order to drink them. He and I would sit near the window, passing the bottle back and forth.

Early on into Grizz's apprenticeship, he asked me about the memory. He said "That med complex near the dock, the one that went bust a few months ago, did you guys ever score out of there? I know that was in your turf."

"Went in one time and scored a little crap but not much." Our hands were both touching the bottle as I took it from him. I added, "Nothing but some old memory," and felt the bottle twitch in his sudden anguished grip.

"What did you do with it?" he asked, watching me pour.

"We used it. How do you think she did so well on the Exams?"

"But you didn't," he said, confused.

"Well, Grizz isn't a moron, and I am, which would account for it."

He grunted and took the bottle back.

"If I'd taken stuff from there," he said. "I'd just not mention it to anyone ever. There have been some nasty customers asking around about it."

I went to visit Grizz a few weeks later; her roommate was out of town for the weekend. We ate in the cafeteria off her meal card: more food than I'd seen in a long time, and then went back to her room and stripped naked to lie in each other's arms.

We could have been there hours, but eventually we got hungry and went back to the cafeteria. The rest of the weekend was the same progression, repeated multiple times, up until Sunday afternoon, and the consequent tearful, snuffling goodbye. I'd never seen Grizz act sentimental before; it didn't suit her.

"You need to do something," she said, looking strained.

"Other than planning on riding your gravy train?"

"It's not that, Jonny, and you know it."

I could have told her then about the Capturing, but I was annoyed. Let her think me just another peon, living off dole and scavenging. Fine by me.

The wall phone rang, and she broke off staring at me to answer it.

"Hello," she said. "Hello?" She shrugged and hung it up. "Nothing but breathing. Fuckazoid pervs."

"Get much of that?"

"Every once in a while," she said. "Some of the other students don't like Dregs. Afraid I might stink up the classroom."

It irritated me that she'd said how much she liked it and now was asking for sympathy, as though her life was worse than mine. So I left it there and made my goodbye. She clung to the doorframe, staring after me.

It wasn't as though I had much to leave behind; it was perhaps my mind's sullen statement, forgetting my jacket. I got four blocks away, then jogged back, ran up the stairs. Knocked on the door and found silence, so I slipped the lock and went in.

By then ... by then she was dead, and they had already left her. The memory was stripped from her skin, leaving ragged, oozing marks. Her throat had been cut with callous efficiency.

I stood there for at least ten minutes, just breathing. There was no chance she was not dead. The world was shaking me by the shoulders and all I did was stand there, Capturing, longer than I had ever managed before. Every detail, every dust mote riding the air, the smell of the musty carpeting and a quarrel next door over a student named Dian.

I didn't stick around to talk to the cops. I knew the roommate would be there soon to call it in. I might have passed her in the downstairs lobby: a thin Eurasian woman with a scar riding her face like an emotion.

When I got to Ajah's, they'd been there as well. He'd taken a while to die, and they had paid him with leisure, leisure to contemplate what they were doing to him. But he was unmistakably dead.

They had caught him in the preparations for a meal; a block of white chicken meat, sized and shaped like a brick lay on the cutting board, his good, all-purpose knife next to it. "Man just needs one good knife for everything," he used to say. A bowl of breadcrumbs and an egg container sat near the chicken.

Someone knocked on the door behind me, and opened it even as

I turned. It was Lorelei, still well-heeled and clean. Her bosses must be paying well.

"Jonny," she said. She didn't even look at Ajah's body. Unsurprised. "Is it true?"

"Is what true?"

"They said he gave up a name, just one, but when I heard the name, I knew there had to be two."

"What was the name?"

She chuckled. "You know already, I think. Grizz."

"Because of the memory?"

"It's more than memory. It grows as you add to it. Self-perpetuating. New tech—very special. Very expensive."

"We found it in the garbage!"

She laughed. "You've done it yourself, I know. What's the best way to steal from work?"

"Stick it in the trash and pick it up later," I realized.

She nodded, "But when two streets come along, and take it first, you're out of luck." Her smile was cold. "So then you ask around, send a few people to track it."

"Did you mean to poison the Net for me? Was that part of it?"

"You mean you haven't found the cure yet?" she said. "Play around with folk remedies. It'll come to you. But no. I was angry and figured I'd fuck you over the way you did me."

"Do they know my name?"

She smiled in silence at me.

"Answer me, you cunt," I said. Three steps forward and I was in her face.

She backed up towards the door, still smiling.

The knife was in easy reach. I stabbed her once, then again. And again. Capturing every moment, letting it sear itself into the memory, and I swear it went hot as the bytes of experience wrote themselves along my back.

"They don't . . ." she started to say, then choked and fell forward, her head flopping to one side in time with the knife blows. She almost fell on me, but I pushed her away. Her wallet held black market script, and plenty of it, along with some credit cards. I didn't see any salvageable mods. The GPS's purple glimmer tempted me, but they can backtrack those. I didn't want anything traceable.

All the time that I rifled through her belongings, feeling the dead weight she had become, I played the memory back of the forward lurch, the head flop and twist, again, again, her eyes going dull and glassy. The thoughts seared on my back as though it were on fire, but I kept on recording it, longer and more intense than I ever had before.

She was right about the folk remedies; feverfew and Valerian made the drug relax its hold and let me slide back into cyberspace. I've published a few pieces: a spring day with pigeons, an experimental subway ride, a sunset over the river. Pretty stuff, where I can find it. It seems scarce.

One reviewer called me a brave new talent; another easy and glib. The sales are still slow, but they'll get better. My latest show is called "Memories of Moments, Bright as Falling Stars"—all stuff on the beach at dawn, the gulls walking back and forth at the waves' edge and the foam clinging to the wet sand before it's blown away by the wind.

I don't use the Captures of Grizz's body or Lorelei's death in my art, but I replay them often, obsessively. Sitting on the toilet, showering, eating, walking—Capturing other things is the only way I have to escape them.

Between the royalties and Suzanne's continued employment though, I do well enough. She's moved into Ajah's place, and I've taken the room behind the clothing store where she used to live. I cook what I can there, small and tasteless meals, and watch the memories in my head.

Memories of moments, as bright as falling stars.

## Afternotes

The story started for me with a vision of Grizz and Jonny putting the memory wire on each other. From there, I tried to build a world that paid attention to class dynamics—in a system where money buys you the augmentations necessary to move ahead in the system, what happens when someone gets augmentation that they weren't supposed to have? It drives me a little nuts when speculative fiction doesn't acknowledge issues of class, and so here, as with other stories, I've tried to think about where the money in the society lies and what effect that has.

This piece originally appeared in Talebones, edited by Patrick Swenson, with an absolutely beautiful illustration by Ben Baldwin that really showed he'd read the story. It's always such an odd delight to have someone else illustrate your work, and I took great pleasure in his lovely artwork.

# REALFUR

You MAY REMEMBER THE AD CAMPAIGNS, which they yanked hastily just as the trial began: a shot of a woman, damask skin and midnight hair, her back turned, against a red-draped background.

As the commercial begins, she has apparently just stepped naked from a fur coat, which lies pooled in silvery-gray folds around her feet. Looking over her shoulder with a Mona Lisa smile, she dips and extends her hands to the fur, which surges upward to meet her touch. Like a cloak of furry snakes, it slides over her exquisite form, and she turns as it extends over her torso. Skin flashes, tantalizing, before the fur curves over it. So cool, so clean, so seductive.

"I believe," she informs us with a touch of hauteur, "in being pampered." She slides a palm along the fur, stroking it.

The fur lengthens as her hand passes over it, extending to calf-length. Her sculpted chin brushes along the fur collar and the subtle soft gray darkens at the touch, like a monochromatic blush. Lifting her face, she gives the camera an orgasmic smile.

"Don't you deserve something real? RealFur. Because there's no luxury like life around you."

Scrolled across her belly: http://www.noluxurylikelife.com.

The Yahoo Most-Mailed Photo of the Day featured her standing with the coat sliding slowly off her. Most of the media furor was manufactured, sponsored advertising hype: few people could afford the coats at 10k a pop.

But Larry always had to have the latest thing for Libby. And because they had a two for one deal, he bought me, her sister, one as well.

At the time I lived in the back of the house, where I had my own little studio apartment, bathroom and kitchenette. Most of the time I was home with Libby; sometimes I went out running errands or working with one of the foundations that sometimes call me in. I'm a CPA, the sort you hire when everything else has failed, or if there are mysterious gaps in the database that need to be reconciled. I could afford my own place easily but this way I felt like part of the family. Larry hinted that he wouldn't mind me out, but he also liked the money I bring in—the way I covered half the mortgage on his lakeside house. That was us, the New American Family.

The package arrived in a big brown truck, two large boxes labeled REALFUR™, which I signed for. They were addressed to Larry, so I left them in the hallway and went in to find Libby in the living room, staring out at the water.

I've always hated that room. It's the Land of Exotic Knickknacks, souvenirs from Thailand, Bali, Australia, Japan, Switzerland, all over the world. Larry's sole decorating criterion was that it not be American-made, and every time Libby suggested it might be updated, he'd whine ferociously until she abandoned the thought.

"Larry got some packages," I said.

She pulled her attention back from the water and looked at me. "What sort?"

"Looks like two RealFurs."

"What? Those cost an arm and a leg."

I shrugged. "Latest thing," I said, my tone noncommittal.

She went into the hallway and looked at the boxes. Even the outside packaging was distinctive: glossy plastic coating with a metallic sheen, the logo like a sleek animal sprawled across the surface.

"I'm opening them," she said. "Well, one at least."

The kitchen knife whispered through brightly colored packing tape. The Styrofoam pellets inside were the same color as the label.

"Nice packaging," I said, peering over her shoulder.

"Piss off," she said. "How much do you think he spent on this?"

"There's the bill of lading." I pointed.

She snatched it up and unfolded it. "Two for one deal," she said.

"What's the description?"

"Basic RealFur (lilac) and Basic RealFur (pink). Two complimentary feeding stations. Two manuals and certificates of ownership."

I pulled out the silvery sack. "Do you think this is RealFur (lilac) or RealFur (pink)?"

"There's only one way to find out."

The knife spoke again, and fur spilled out in lavish warmth. As the air struck it, it stirred, and Libby stepped back.

"Pink, evidently," I said.

She knelt and stretched a hand out to it. It rolled forward and rose to meet her touch like a cat arching its back into a caress.

"So soft," she said.

It crept forward to nuzzle her ankles.

"Will it become a coat now, I wonder?"

"I think it's waiting to be asked," I said, watching it.

She reached her hands down and it flowed upward and along her shoulders. Her eyes closed, focusing on the sensation.

"It's warm," she said a little breathlessly.

I paged through the manual. "It cleans itself through an electrostatic charge," I read. "You set the feeding station up in a corner of the closet you'll be keeping it in."

"Won't that smell?"

"It says it lives off protein molecules."

"That's pretty meaningless. What sort?"

"Doesn't say."

She stroked her bare forearm along the fur, eyes dreamy.

"It's like being hugged," she said. "So soft, so warm."

I found her that night asleep in front of CNN, the coat wrapped around her like a blanket. I shook her awake and left it there on the couch as I walked her off to bed. When I returned it came willing into my arms, soft and warm, stirring against my skin as though scenting it. As instructed, I laid it on the floor on the closet where its feeding station had been placed. They must have figured everyone who can afford one has a walk-in closet, I thought, amused.

Back in my own rooms, I opened the package to extract RealFur (lilac). Libby had claimed the pink without wanting to see this, but I thought I had gotten the better part of the deal. The subtle coloring enchanted me as it shaded to a deeper hue at the touch of my hands. I fell asleep with it layered around me like a cloak of feathers.

Every night that week I heard the rain, the delicious warmth of the RealFur around me in bed. Early every morning it released me to steal out and curl briefly around the rod of the feeding station, and then return to me, bright with heat and a little restive. I grew accustomed to that familiar warmth, the weight of the thick fur along my side.

Over the next few weeks, we took our coats with us everywhere. No matter where we were in the house, they would be nearby or even at hand, coiled around our shoulders like companioning arms, or spread beneath us to shield us from the cold floor while we watched TV during the long hours while Larry was away at work. He laughed about it at first, but he took to hanging the coat up downstairs before coming to bed. He started turning the heat higher in the house as well; he and Libby followed each other from room to room, adjusting the thermostats.

I slept with mine each night. I kept my window open and listened to the rain, nestled in its warm embrace.

He offered to get her a kitten, but she said no.

"Are you offering to clean its litter box for me as well?" she asked, and he hemmed and hawed as she chuckled.

"Get me tickets to the Ballet instead." She wore the RealFur to it, and I wore mine. In the lobby, friends swarmed around us, caressing the coats. We had dressed to match them; Libby wore a shell pink dress and shaggy ivory boots, while I dressed in a more sedate eggplant-colored pantsuit.

My friend Margery fingered the cuff, pinching the soft flesh between her fingers. The coat stirred and I pulled away.

"Doesn't it like being touched?" she asked.

I ran my hand along the front lapel and felt the swathe stir in the wake of my touch. "There are too many people here, it's making it nervous," I said. I made my way to a quieter part of the room and watched the two of them from a distance.

Larry kept one hand slid through the crook of Libby's elbow, his fingers intertwined with hers. He looked around, smiling and nodding to as many people as possible, while Libby focused all of her attention on each person as they spoke to her, leaving out the rest of the world. The fur framed her face. Mine settled in heavy warmth along my shoulders and pulsed slowly along my thighs, subtly nudging them apart.

Outside, the air was cold and crisp before we slid into the taxi back to Redmond. My coat cocooned me, smoothing itself out to catch any gaps.

"Well," said Larry, leaning forward to adjust the car's heating upward. "You two were certainly the belles of the ball with your furs."

"I love mine," Libby said dutifully. "Thank you again."

I kept quiet, pretending to be asleep. We were crossing the bridge across Lake Washington, and the Seattle lights glittered and guttered on the dark water.

Though I love her, I'd be the first to admit that my sister Libby is a flake. She reads her horoscope and watches for signs of it in her day; she believes in aromatherapy and Rainbow Paths. And I think it's one of the reasons Larry was attracted to her in the first place, that delicate nuance of belief he could mock in public and take comfort from in private. He insisted that she not work, but made sure to mention it around friends. He laughed at her for talking to her plants, but at the same time sang the praises of her vegetables to guests.

She named her RealFur Petunia. It gave Larry plenty of fodder.

"It's just a coat," he said. "You don't name your underwear, for Christ's sake."

She stroked the RealFur.

"It's Petunia," she said. "The Findhorns think you should name everything, even your appliances. We could name the refrigerator."

Larry marched through the kitchen, naming the appliances: "Freezy! Heaty! Washy! Blendy!" He turned, pointing at her where she stood with the fur wrapped around her. "Coatie!"

"Petunia," she said.

"It's ridiculous."

"It keeps me company."

He lapsed into silence, looking at her. I was unsure whether to turn away and let them fight or not. They had argued about his hours all through the previous evening. She wanted time; he had none to give her.

"Would you give it up," he said very quietly, "if I stayed home more?"

She stroked the collar. "Find out."

But his hours didn't change—if anything, they grew longer. He was on the fast track, and pausing would have ended in his sliding off.

"Explain it to her, Pol," he begged me one night. "Tell her about the payoff."

"Are you planning on spending every day of your golden years in Barbados?" I asked. "When do you know you have enough?"

He paced the kitchen. I was chopping vegetables to make potato soup. In the corner, my coat was draped over a chair. I noticed Larry avoided its proximity.

"I want to have enough to know I won't want for anything when I'm old," he said.

"Want as in hunger for, or want as in 'Hey, that would be nice to have in blue too?'"

He frowned at me. "I need this," he said. "I can't have kids."

"What does that have to do with the price of eggs?"

"What?"

"It's an old saying. What does you not having kids have to do with anything?"

He gestured, vague and uncertain.

"Tell her," he said.

"And what do you want from her?"

"To give that thing up."

I turned and looked at my coat. "Thing?"

"I know you like yours, Pol. I'm not trying to interfere with you and it. But you don't like men or women, as far as I can tell, so you might as well have something. Maybe she could give it to you."

"Go away." My knife sliced across the onions, cutting them into perfect translucent arcs.

"Just talk to her."

"I said go away!"

The onion smell hung heavy on my hands, so I washed and dried them before picking up the coat. I slung it around my shoulders and passed my cheek along it.

Libby sat in a rocking chair near the living room window, wrapped in pale pink fur. The sky was gray with rain, and whitecaps scudded on the lake.

I went to stand by her, and tendrils of our coats reached out to each other, tangled like intimate snakes. I wound my fingers through her long hair.

"He wants you to get rid of it."

"I know."

"He'll just keep on pushing."

"I know that too, Pol." She leaned her head against my hip. The room was dimly lit from the hallway light. Our coats undulated against each other.

Later, I realized that he must have planned it in advance—why else would he have had the can of gasoline already there? He poured it over the coat and for the first time I heard it make a sound, an ultrasonic keen that brought Libby towel-wrapped from her bath.

My own coat pulled me along to the scene of the crime.

He interposed his body between her and the coat, and flicked his lighter. He threw it with a twist of his wrist and the RealFur screamed again as it erupted in flames, writhing on the tiled floor, leaving greasy black marks in an accusing calligraphy.

I couldn't tell if mine was pulling me forward or back; it convulsed on my shoulders.

"I had a hard day at the office," he said. He had an arm wrapped firmly around Libby, holding her in place as she keened, as she hunched forward in vain. The coat spasmed, thick black smoke snaking from it. The smell was terrible. "A man needs to blow off a little steam."

She struck at him, but he held her wrist with an indulgent strength. My coat moved me forward, towards him, and he half-turned, still holding onto Libby by the wrist.

114

It slid from my shoulders and slithered up his legs with a terrible, sinuous speed. He was enveloped in pale lilac fur, a bag of it, stumbling around the kitchen trying to free himself.

After five minutes, the bag slumped to its knees; at the eight minute mark it fell over entirely. At ten, it slid from him and crept towards me. I gathered it in my arms. Petunia smoldered on the floor.

The police have not outright accused Libby or I of engineering the RealFur's act. By the time they got there, we had hidden it in the garden shed. They found it, of course, and took it into custody. They will not say what will happen to it, but the possibility of destroying it has been mentioned. They let me go visit it at one point and take it its feeding station; it lapped about me in velvety, inarticulate warmth as my tears fell on its blanched fur.

Libby would not come in with me, but waited outside in the car.

"How is it?" she asked, starting the car.

"Fine. Very pale."

She nodded.

We drove away into the silvery gray rain, its tendrils creeping along the windshield. I blew my nose and looked forward, unable to make out more than a glimmer of lights through my tears.

## Afternotes

*This early piece originally appeared in* Serpentarius, *and again deals with the relationship between person and object, as well as a marriage coming apart at the seams. It was written in 2004, before attending Clarion West, but I've resisted the urge to make it more complicated.*

*I'm tactilely-oriented, and I think having a RealFur would be akin to seventh heaven. Can't you feel if you think about it, a heavy, soft warmth draping around your shoulders?*

# NOT WAVING, BUT DROWNING

CURLED ON THE LEATHER COUCH, JAMIE TRIED to pick a stubborn bit of popcorn kernel from between her teeth, worrying at it with a fingernail. On the TV, a talk show host quizzed a guest resembling a small willow tree. Yet another alien, visiting Earth. She'd taken him/her/it around the city last week.

"We need to talk," Emilio said.

The popcorn was wedged to the point of pain between a side molar and gum. She stared at him. His tone sent a panicky thrill down her spine.

"I've decided to join the PsyKorps," he said. "I haven't had luck getting any other job, and they say I'm qualified. They say one human out of a thousand has the physiology to accept a shunt, and I have it."

"I make enough money for us," she said in protest. PsyKorps? It was unthinkable. He'd become someone capable of riffling through a person's thoughts, picking through their innermost being. "You don't need to sell your soul to the government. My guide job gives us food and a roof over our heads."

More than that, if truth be told. Aliens paid well.

"PsyKorps does good work," he said. "Keeps the airplanes able to fly, for one. Catches criminals. Monitors events of state and provides absolute security where needed."

"God knows what else," she said. She would have said, "You can't," would have asked, "Does this mean you're leaving me?" but the look in his eyes forestalled her. She tried again to unwedge the popcorn, bowing her head so her bangs fell forward, obscuring

116

the tears welling in her eyes.

He had made up his mind, she could tell, and was prepared to resist any argument. Why bother?

∼☙

After lovemaking that night, he stroked her hair tenderly, still struggling to control his breath. Once the gesture would have suffused her with love, left her sodden as a sponge with helpless emotion.

But now the touch roused a terrible impatience in her. He had caused the pain that led her here, curled in her bed around the embryo of his decision. It felt as though she had fallen in battle. Her enemy knelt beside her, inexplicably tender and remorseful.

*All's fair in love and war,* she thought, one of those cynical-edged observations, brittle as old paper, that had swirled through her mind since Emilio's revelation of his decision.

She pushed away, went into the bathroom to splash cold water on her burning cheekbones, driving away the heat of tears.

When she came back, Emilio was sprawled on the bed, comfortable as a sleeping cat. Light laddered across his body from the streetlight outside the blind. A car screeched past on the street. The area they lived in was respectable, but just barely, and bordered a more dangerous neighborhood. It was what they could afford, if they wanted this much space. If their income doubled, they could move someplace nice, Greenwood maybe or Queen Anne.

In three months Emilio would be a fully active Psi. In three months they'd know whether or not they could stand it, a Psi and a normal living together. Others before them had tried. All had failed. Living with someone who could read your mind when you couldn't reciprocate—it would be like being a rat in a cage, an experimental animal. What lay on the other side of that line? She couldn't imagine it.

Their marriage was a patchwork of threadbare compromise, but she'd thought it was a partnership. Was there some point at which he'd agreed?

He snored and stretched out in his sleep when she nudged him.

She wanted to shake him awake and say, "Can't we go back to the way things were, where I told you about my day and the extraterrestrials I dealt with? Sure, I always saw the envy in your eyes, but there was no *need* for it. I'd share it with you, share every scrap of it. If I could,

I'd remote you, let you be the one walking among godlike creatures with just my voice whispering in your ear. I'd ghost for you, become a shadow of my former self. I would have done that willingly. Instead, you cut out my heart without asking, you tore it away and never consulted me, just made it collateral damage, an accident of your own quest."

It was the last realization that pissed her off. She'd been reduced to a peripheral, an odd accessory to his life while on her part, he'd been the piston to her pump. Now she felt as though she couldn't function anymore, as though an integral part had been teleported away, its means of abduction unfathomable.

She hugged the pain to her as though it might fill that void. It was the only thing she could think of, now that he'd gone away, leaving his body behind to let her know what she'd miss.

"I want to go over what the process will be like," Emilio said during dinner. "So you know what to expect."

Jamie'd been too exhausted to cook. It felt as though the day had passed in one weary, numb blur. She'd ordered pizza. It sat on the kitchen table between them, a circle of congealing grease studded with pepperoni wheels.

*Why bother*, she thought, but she nodded.

"The shunt won't immediately work," he said. "I'll have to train myself to focus and hear thoughts. They said I could practice with you, would you be up for that?"

He beamed at her, pleased to have figured out a way to involve her in the process that would subtract him from her existence. But she couldn't think of how to put that without feeling as though she were raining on his parade.

"Okay," she said, and put a smile on her lips to match his. She wasn't sure if it fooled him or not.

Aside from that, they didn't talk about it.

It wasn't that it wasn't on her mind constantly. When she woke it was her first thought, and it chased her, circling like the shadow of a shark, into the murky depths of her dreams. She felt submerged, awash, only her arms above the surface to try to signal. Not waving, drowning.

Sometimes she wanted to talk about it, but she was afraid of what he'd say. She was afraid it'd only make him move faster. She had always disliked the inertia of action that sometimes surrounded him. It reminded her unpleasantly of the laissez faire attitude her father had taken to so many things when she was growing up.

But now she prized that quality, thinking that where her words couldn't prevent him, perhaps that force could.

But it didn't.

A handbook arrived from the PsyKorps Institute, mental exercises Emilio was supposed to work on before the shunt was installed, to prepare him for its use. She flipped through it. *Envision water,* it said. *Imagine a pool that is deep and clear. Sunlight plays on the water's surface. Watch the patterns that the light creates.*

She closed her eyes and tried to see the pool. But there was only darkness behind her eyes, flecks and freckles of light that seeped below her lashes, the imaginary light that one sees in a darkened room, the hallucinations of luminescence that trail one when half asleep, like ancient acid dreams.

Emilio kept a notebook, as the handbook suggested, detailing his moods and the influences that might affect them: sleep and food and sex, and a précis of the day's activities. He wouldn't watch TV with her, saying that he didn't want those patterns imprinted on his mind. He shied away from music as well, and kept his laptop closed.

He went for long walks in the park near them. He invited her to accompany him, but she declined after the first one. She could tell he wanted to walk in silence, but to her the silence ate away at their relationship, with the sureness of waves eroding a shoreline, erasing its contour grain by relentless grain.

While he was gone, she lost herself in videos, long painful love stories that made her go into the shower and cry, hot water washing away her tears. These bouts left her feeling ragged as a torn towel, fragile and frayed. She would not show this side to him, she kept it shelled inside like an unhatched chick. He would see and despise it soon enough.

She thought to herself that marriage depended on the ability to lie about little things, about daily farts and other human matters. Perhaps it was the lies that kept us human, kept us from being forced to judge publicly, to confront the things that would tear us apart.

The day of the shunt's installation, Emilio rose and sipped some water. They had forbidden him any food the night before. She'd contemplated fixing his favorite meal: steak au poivre, and broccoli with a cheese sauce, and cherry pudding for dessert. *Too obvious.*

She drove him to the hospital.

"You don't need to stay," he said. "If you want to just take the car, go shopping, come back in three hours. They say that's how long it'll be until I'm done."

She knew all that. He'd explained it to her several times. But she nodded, smiled and waved goodbye to him as he passed through the hallway. He never looked back at her. She stood there with her glassy smile, watching him go until he was gone. She settled into the orchid-scented waiting room with her paperback.

Trying to read was a futile enterprise, though. The words crawled and slithered along the page like recalcitrant insects, persistently worming outside of meaning. She looked at the page. Three chapters in and she still had no idea what was happening. She didn't want to read any further. A traditional love story might make her cry. She did that a lot nowadays.

To pass the time, she walked the corridors, sniffing the changes in the air. A redolence of diapers rode the nursery floor, while a lounge on the seventh floor smelled of talcum and old age, elderly people enjoying the sunlight that streamed in through the plate glass windows framing Mount Rainier.

Several times nurses or interns asked if they could help her, but each time she shook her head and moved on, trying to look as though she knew where she was going.

When she stepped into the operating room theater where a cluster of medical students sat, she paused, trying to see if the body lying on the table was Emilio. She couldn't tell. Several figures blocked her sight of what might or might not be her husband. She settled into a stiff-backed chair, careful not to sit too close to anyone who might ask why she was there.

The students ignored her, though. They chattered among themselves, gossip about Susan pursuing Lee, whose gender was unspecified. Someone said something about paying attention, and a dark-haired girl scoffed.

"Like we haven't already seen this in first year!" she said. "This may be the only West Coast hospital installing psychic shunts, but that only gets tired after a while. It's a simple process, one that any of us could do in our sleep."

Jamie hoped that her husband's doctor wasn't asleep. Or maybe he or she would be, and they'd make a mistake, fail to install the shunt correctly.

Across the way, someone raised their head, looked directly at her. They wore an operating mask, but underneath that was a PsyKorps uniform. Someone watching to make sure that nothing went wrong. Someone who could read her mind already. Terror seized her. They'd tell him. They'd tell him all her doubts and fears and despairs, and he'd know she'd been lying the last few months, pretending to be happy for him.

But they lowered their head and went back to watching what was happening. Emilio lay on the table. She could see the hawkish curve of his nose. His face looked vulnerable but serene, surrounded by white draping.

Afterwards, he came out in a wheel chair (standard procedure, he said) pushed by a candy striper. She helped him into the passenger side of the car and drove him home.

She couldn't help but ask, "How do you feel?"

He was silent for a moment, his gaze turned inward, as though he was assessing each cranny and crook of his mind, to see what slithered or shone there. "I feel all right," he said finally. "My head's a little sore, but there's not as much pain as you would expect."

"Not sensing thoughts yet?"

"That won't happen until at least tomorrow. There's a self-dissolving seal over it, to let me come into it slowly." He frowned as though already reading her mind. "Are you okay? I know this is hard on you. You've never liked hospitals."

How like him, to take her pain and make it something habitual and thoughtless and reflexive. "You've never liked hospitals." *I've never liked things that took you away from me,* she thought, *you turd.*

*Remember that woman at work that had the crush on you? You thought it was funny, but I was ready to go down and punch her out. You never understood that, never understood how much it hurt that you'd been flirting with her. Leading her on. Encouraging her. Were you secretly hoping she'd make a pass, flatter you, make you feel desirable in a way that apparently I can't? You are desired,* she thought. *But I want you in a way that you can't give me.*

That evening, sitting out on the deck, he said, "I need you to help me practice."

*Nice to hear you say you need me.* She flinched internally. What would it be like when he could hear those thoughts? *It would be a disaster.* But she said, "What do you want me to do?"

"I need to practice receiving," he said. "What I want you to do is focus your thoughts at me, make them easier to hear. Imagine it's a word, an object in the shape of a word—don't tell me what it is. Think of yourself throwing it at me."

She thrust the word *hello* at him, imagined herself clubbing him over the head with it. She thought he jumped a little in his seat, but he smiled. "Hello!" he said. "That was your word, wasn't it? I heard it in my head."

"What does that mean, that you heard it rather than saw it?" she asked, curious.

"There are three main sensory modes," he said. "Well, two important ones and a lesser one that they haven't explored more. People tend to think in terms of what they can see or hear or feel."

"Feel? How would that work?"

"I'm not really sure," he said. "But when I'm thinking I hear it as a voice in my head, so it makes sense that I'd perceive your thought that way as well. Let's try again!"

Each time she imagined herself pushing the word towards him, while shouting it somehow into the void. She tried simple words, then harder ones, *fortitude* and *visceral*. He perceived them all.

The shunt worked.

"What's the next step?" she asked. Despite herself, she had gotten caught up in his excitement.

"Later, we'll try some sentences," he said. The effort was telling on him. His face was drawn and gray as a migraine sufferer's. "Let me rest a little, then we'll go out to dinner and celebrate."

At the seafood restaurant, they ran into their friends Betta and Tim. Would Emilio tell them, she wondered. They were staunch liberals, and she'd never heard them refer to the PsyKorps with anything but disdain.

He said nothing about it as they exchanged small talk. Finally Jamie said, "Tell them your big news, Emilio." She felt a mean thrill at the frown that crossed his face.

"Finally found employment," he said.

"That's great," Betta said. She had worked with him at a start-up that had gone under years before, but they'd maintained the friendship. "Where at?"

"PsyKorps," he said.

Betta didn't even flinch. "What, working with their IT staff? Bleeding edge tech over there."

"In more ways than one, eh?" Tim said. "I hope they're paying well."

"I'm becoming an agent," Emilio said. His tone was polite and distant. Jamie could see the danger signals in the crinkling of his eyes. He was furious, and growing stiffer and more polite the angrier he got.

There was a pause as the other couple processed this.

"Oh," Betta said. "Well, that should be interesting, shouldn't it?" She stepped a pace away from the table. "Tim, we really need to get going. Call me sometime, Jamie!" She fluttered her fingers in farewell and dismissal. Jamie suspected Betta wouldn't be returning the call.

Emilio waited until their meal had appeared and the waiter had checked to make sure they didn't need anything else.

"Why did you do that?" he asked.

She bit the tip off a breadstick, contemplating him. "It didn't cross my mind that you'd try to hide it," she lied. "What's the point of that? People will find out, and if it's after you've kept it from them, they'll feel angry. Betrayed."

"We're supposed to keep a low profile," he said. "Not draw attention to ourselves."

"So no one will know mindreaders are walking among them," she said.

"Is that how you feel about the Korps? Snoops and spies?"

"It's how you used to talk about them too," she said.

He crumpled the napkin in his hand, clutching it as though it held the temper he was struggling to contain. "Can't you just support me in this?"

"I could have," she said. "You never offered me the chance to."

"Do you want a divorce?"

The answer was too complicated for her to express. No, she wanted things to go back to the way they had been. She didn't want this world where he could hear what she was thinking. She took all her rage and fury, hurled it at him, and was rewarded to see him pull back as though she'd punched him in the gut.

"How did that sound?" she said with a nasty sneer. She pushed her plate towards the table's center and stood, taking up her coat and purse.

"We have to talk about this," he said. "It can't just live in silence any more. What it means for you."

"Talk about it?" she said. She laughed. "That's two-way communication. Wait another week and you'll be able to pull it from my mind."

"Is that what this is all about?" he said. How could he look so stupid and bewildered? "Is there something you don't want me to know? Have you been keeping some secret from me?" She could see him chewing over the possibilities: adultery, alcoholism, some mental illness hiding in her ancestral closet.

"Nothing like that," she said.

"Then what?"

She couldn't answer through the tears choking her.

She walked out of the restaurant with Emilio scrambling to pay the bill and catch up. She didn't want to strand him, so she walked a block over to the bus stop, and left him with the car.

If he had come after her, she had resolved that she would not go with him. He wanted to be independent of her? Well, that cut both ways.

She rode the bus home, staring out the window and contemplating her solitary reflection. When she came in, he was sitting in the living room in the dark. The window let the moonlight in, making his face a gleaming mask, tilted slightly down as he stared at his clasped hands.

She paused, wondering if he would call to her. He didn't. She took a shower and went to bed. An hour or two later, he crawled in beside her. She moved over, let him share the warmth of the flannel sheets. He pulled her close, cuddled her into him, let their warmth seep together.

He rested his chin on her hair, not speaking, just brushing his fingers back and forth along her arm. It was one of his signals that he'd like sex, and she hesitated, not sure whether or not to give in. Would it solve anything? Would it make things worse?

In the end she reached back, let her fingers stray over the curve of his side as well.

When she came, he was staring into her eyes. She shuddered and laughed and gasped. "What?" she said.

It struck her. He was trying to sense her emotions, trying to feel what she had felt at the moment of orgasm. An experiment, to see how much he could perceive. Indignation filled her in a flash and she pulled away.

"What did I do?" he asked.

She thought-screamed at him. *Snoop! Spy!*

He didn't deny it, just flushed a little.

"I want you to be happy," he said. "Now I can tell when you really are."

She thought about pills. And booze. She bought a couple of joints and smoked them, sitting out on the deck watching the shadows among the blackberry vines. A warm haze suffused her and she let herself slip away into that fog. But when Emilio came home and found her there, all her anxieties reasserted themselves and the comfortable stupor yanked away as though she had been doused with cold water.

He didn't say anything, just took the roach and inhaled the last smoke from it. She wondered what the PsyKorps thought of drugs, even legal ones such as booze and weed. It didn't seem as though they would help you much in envisioning a clear pool.

Emilio stood. She could feel how much he wanted and dreaded talking to her.

"They want me to stay there for training next week," he said.

"Stay there? As in overnight?"

"Yes. They want us getting to know each other and doing some team exercises."

"Well, that should be interesting," she said.

"Will you be all right if I go? You seem so fragile lately."

*Fragile*, she thought. *Smashable. But already smashed. Maybe the only way to make something non-breakable was to break it. A very Zen approach.*

"I'm not fragile," she said. If he thought her fragile, wouldn't he be in even more of a hurry to get rid of her? She'd read an article the day before that had said when people developed cancer, women had a much higher chance of their partners leaving. She'd thought another of those uncontrollable thoughts, *yep, he'd be out the door like a shot.*

Could she blame him for it, really? You go through childhood thinking they're promising you your soul mate will come along eventually. And then you find yourself, after a lot of trouble and discouragement, with someone who you think might fit the bill, only to discover that they're as broken as you are. Marriages were work, but no one ever told you all that.

She was trying to figure out where she fit into his new life, and the fear was that there was no niche for her. And he didn't care about that, or if he did, he'd factored it in and it didn't outweigh the other considerations. Nor did any of her good intentions.

No, she couldn't stand it. And he knew that no marriage had survived this, and he'd accepted that. It wasn't that he was stupid, or overly optimistic. It was that the dissolution of the marriage, the strong and almost certain possibility that it would be destroyed, didn't matter enough to make him reconsider.

Could he even go back, at this point? He'd signed papers. They'd given him training and installed a very expensive piece of equipment in his head. He was committed.

The Korps hadn't even bothered to talk to her about the transition, she realized. They'd written her off without even thinking about it. She wondered if that was one of the things Emilio and the other new agents would bond with during their training, commiserating with each other about their ambitions and the partners who had tried to drag them away from it.

He stood watching her, and she wondered how much of her inner turmoil he could perceive. Either more than either of them thought, or more probably the question showed in her eyes, because he said impatiently, "It's not like that, Jamie. It takes effort to read someone. I will never read you unless you ask me to."

"You can control it that well?" she said.

"Why do you think they give us all this training? They don't want rogue psis running all over the place giving them a bad name, you know that as well as I do. They had to struggle hard enough just to get the airport screening process in place. Everyone screamed about privacy laws. Remember that show, I can't remember the name, about the PsyKorps hunting down rogues? Lasted a season, but it showcased all the anxieties pretty well."

He leaned back on the railing, regarding her. "Believe me, I understand," he said. "But we can get through this, Jamie."

"When no one else has?"

He caught her hand. "No one else is us. No one else loves each other the way we do."

Despite the wariness that barb-wired her, she could not help but be warmed by the emotion in his voice.

But was it real?

She kept watching him, waiting for the moment he would get inside her head. Early in their marriage, he had asked, "What are you thinking?" so many times, checking her state, his state. He wouldn't be able to avoid it. Curiosity would force his hand.

But he didn't seem to notice. He practiced every day, asked her to help him, and she did, thinking word after word, then phrase after phrase. He drove himself hard, would not stop until he was shaking with weariness.

He gave her some of the money from the Korps for household expenses, and she put it away. She wondered what he was doing with the rest of it. Building himself an escape fund, money so he could leave when he was ready?

She had thought it would be a revelation when he gave himself away, but it was nothing more than her thinking that she needed salt and looking up to find him handing her the shaker.

He paled. "I'm sorry, you were thinking loudly," he said.

"You couldn't help yourself, could you?" she asked, her voice and heart cold. "Must have been asking for it, on some subconscious level *I* don't have access to."

"You don't need to worry," he said. "Listen, Jamie, we're all broken inside. We've all got bits that we want to keep hidden. Look, every time I find something out, I'll tell you something in exchange. I picked my nose when I was little, did I tell you that? A nun at school shamed me out of it."

But she had stood, was walking out of the room. He followed her, proffering more secrets: the roommate he'd been attracted to in college, his hatred of his mother's pressures to succeed, the time he'd taken money from the store he worked in.

"It's not that," she said, packing her bags. "Or maybe it is, I don't know." She looked tired and broken to him, and he felt a wash of guilt and shame over how he'd treated her, but he couldn't make her perceive it, no matter what he said or did.

Emilio watched from the doorway as Jamie marched away, suitcase in hand. A fine mist filled the air, glistened like a greasy sheen on the back of her unhatted head. She'd said she'd get the rest of her belongings later.

He stood there with his fists braced against the doorway, watching till she was gone, broadcasting *guilt* and *shame* and *sorrow*, but there was no one around to hear him at all.

### Afternotes

*Writers mine our own lives for material and this story is one of those. I don't think any married person escapes marital stress. This story, as with a number of others in Near + Far, came out of a rough patch in my own.*

*It owes its title to the eminently quotable Stevie Smith poem by the same name, and the lines "I was much further out than you thought/ And not waving but drowning." The lines sum up a certain interior desperation that I strongly identified with at the time.*

*This story originally appeared in* Redstone Science Fiction *and was selected by editor Michael Ray.*

# VOCOBOX™

EVER SINCE MY HUSBAND installed a Vocobox ™ in our cat in a failed experiment, he (the cat, not my husband) stands outside the closed bedroom door in the mornings, calling. The intelligence update was partially successful, but the only word the cat has learned is its own name, Raven, which he uses to convey everything. I hear him when I wake up, the sound muted by the wooden door between us.

"Raven. Raven. Raven." Beside me, Lloyd murmurs something and turns over, tugging the sheet away, the cold whispering me further awake. When I go out to feed the cat, his voice lowers as he twines around my ankles, words lapsing into purrs. He butts against my legs with an insistent anxiety, waiting for the dish to be filled. "Raven. Raven." Kibble poured, I move to make our own breakfast, turning on the coffee maker and listening to its preparatory burble.

"I don't know what I expected," my husband mutters as he drinks his coffee in hasty gulps. "That cat was never very smart for a cat." He glares at Raven as though blaming him for the failures of the world at large. The Vocobox ™ is his own invention; his company hopes to market it this fall, and a promotion may hinge upon it. The last laurels my husband won are wearing thin; if the Vocobox ™ is a success, he'll be able to rest a while longer.

But when he first proposed installing it in the cat, he didn't say it was still experimental. "The kids are gone, and you need some company," he'd said. "The cat loves you best anyhow; now you can talk to him, and he'll talk back." He gave me a slight smirk and a raised eyebrow that implied that without him I'd be a dotty old cat lady, living in a studio apartment that smelled of pee and old newspapers.

"I'll be late again tonight," he tells me now. "And when I'm concentrating, I've found leaving my cell off helps. If you need something, just leave a message. Or call the service, that's what we pay them for." He's out the front door before I can reply.

Every morning seems the same nowadays. My husband's heels, exiting. The immaculate lawn outside. On Thursdays, the housekeeping service remotely activates the grass cutting robot. I see it out there, sweeping through the fresh spring grass that never grows high enough to hide it. A plastic sheep, six inches tall, sits atop its round metal case, someone's idea of creative marketing. But the robot is done within the hour and then things are the same again. Back in the box.

I go into the living room, activate the wall viewer, and lose myself in reality television, where everyone has eventful lives. Soon Raven curls up on my lap. "Raven," he murmurs, and begins to purr.

The mouths of the people on the screen move, but the words that come out are meaningless, so I hit the mute button. Now the figures collide and dance on the screen; every life is more interesting than my own.

At noon, I push the cat off my lap and have a sandwich; at dinner time a hot meal appears in the oven. I take it out myself, pour a glass of Chardonnay, take the bottle to the table with me. When did I become this boring person? At college, I studied music, was going to sing opera. I sang in a few productions, fell in love, became a trophy wife, and produced two perfect trophy children who are out there now, perpetuating the cycle. All those voice lessons wasted.

On the EBay channel that night I look for a hobby. There's knitting, gardening, glass-blowing, quilling ... too many to choose from. I remember quilling from my daughter's Bluebird days. We curled bits of paper, glued them down in decorative patterns on tiny wooden boxes. What was the point? I drink a little more wine before I go to sleep.

When he comes to bed, my husband snuggles up, strokes my arm. He murmurs something inaudible, the tone conveying affection. This only happens when he feels guilty. From the recently showered smell of him, I know what he feels guilty about. This must be an assistant I haven't met yet.

When I don't speak, he says, "What's the matter, cat got your voice box?" He chortles to himself at his clever joke before he lapses into sleep, not pursuing my silence. Out in the living room, I hear the cat wandering. "Raven."

"You're like a cliché," my husband says at breakfast. "Desperate housewife. Can't you find something to do?"

The cat's attention swivels between us, his green eyes wide and pellucid with curiosity. "Raven?" he says in an interrogative tone.

I watch my husband's heels, the door closing behind them, the deliberately good-humored but loud click, once again.

"Raven," the cat says as it looks up at me, its voice shaded with defiance.

"Dora," I say to the cat. I'm tired and sore as though I'd been beaten. The room wavers with warmth and weariness.

"Raven."

"Dora."

"Raven."

"Dora."

I can't help but laugh as he watches my face, but he is not amused as I am; his tail lashes from side to side although every other inch of him is still.

Online, I look at the ads. Nannies, housekeepers, maids...I am a cliché. I embrace my inanity. Desperate housewife indeed, being cheated on by an aging husband who isn't even clever enough to conceal it. This is my reality. But if I explain it, I start the avalanche down into divorce. I'll end up living in a box on the street, while my husband will remarry, keep living in this expensive, well-tended compound. I've seen it happen to other women.

"Raven," the cat says with tender grace, interposing himself in front of the monitor. Facing me, he puts his forehead against the top of my chest, pressing firmly. "Raven," he whispers.

Sunday, while my husband's out playing golf, the phone keeps ringing. "Caller's name undisclosed," the display says. And when I pick it up, there is only silence on the other end. The third time I say, "He's out playing golf and has his cell phone turned off, because it distracts him. Call back this evening." and hang up.

He scuttles out in the evening after another of the calls, saying he needs to go into work, oversee a test run. Later that night, he curls against me, smelling of fresh soap. Outside the door, Raven is calling.

"Another cat would take the implant better," my husband says. "I'll get a kitten and we'll try that."

"No," I tell him. "He's too old to get used to a new kitten in the house. It will just upset him."

"I'm trying to do something nice for you."

"Buy the other woman a kitten," I say, even as dire predictions scream through my mind, commanding me to silence. "Buy her dozens. I'm sticking with this one."

He rolls over, stunned and quiet. For the rest of the night, I lie there. Outside, the night continues, limitless. I pass the time imagining what I will do. Nannying is, I hear, pleasant work. I'll sing the babies lullabies.

He's silent in the morning as well. In the light of day as we sit facing each other across the table, I reach down to extend my hand to the cat, who arches his back and rubs against my fingertips.

"We need to talk," Lloyd finally demands.

"Dora," I say.

"What?"

"Dora. Dora, Dora." I rise to my feet and stand glaring at him. If I had a tail, it would lash back and forth like an annoyed snake, but all my energy is focused on speaking to my husband.

"Is that supposed to be funny?"

"Dora. Dora. Dora." I almost sob the words out, as emotions clutch at my throat insistently, trying to mute me, but I force the words past the block, out into the open air. We stand like boxers, facing each other in the squareness of the ring.

Lloyd moves to the door, almost backing away. His eyes are fixed on my lips; every time I say my name, his expression flickers, as though the word has surprised him anew.

"We can talk about this later," he says. The door closes behind him with a click of finality.

What can I do? I settle on the couch and the cat leaps up to claim my lap, butts his head against my chin. He lapses into loud purrs, so loud I can feel the vibration against my chest, quivering like unspoken words. He doesn't say anything, but I know exactly what he means.

## Afternotes

*This story was one of my first speculative fiction publications, and led to my first reading at Seattle area science fiction convention Norwescon. It grew out of a joke about a cat's intelligence and what one would say if actually given a voice.*

*While the plot is straightforward and the ending uncomplicated, I'm fond of the relationship between Dora and her cat. I've included it in tribute to my own, dearly-loved cat, whose name is also Raven and who definitely appears in these pages.*

*This piece originally appeared in* Twisted Cat Tales, *edited by Esther Schrader.*

# Long Enough and Just So Long

I'D NEVER WANTED TO GO TO EARTH UNTIL THE doctor told me I couldn't, that my bones were too brittle. After that, it wasn't an obsession, just an edge to my days.

Otherwise, my life's good.

I run a courier ship between Earth, Luna, the space stations, Mars, and the Inner Gate. You need as little mass as possible to run a snipship, and due to what that doctor called my defects, I'm one of the smallest, fastest. Good pay, and most of the time I'm low-g, which is easiest on me.

Freetime I slum around Luna, where my best girlfriend Pippi lives. Or she and I go prospecting out in the shadow of the Gate, like the dozens of other crazies, hoping to stumble on an alien artifact, make us all rich. Not too impossible a dream, though. It's happened before.

I had a permanent cradle walker left at Luna, that's how much time I spent there. Pippi worked as a sportscaster for the biggest Moon channel, MBSA. Her name's not really Pippi, but she had orange braids and long legs and freckles everywhere, so what else could everyone call her?

I'm used to my name getting distorted. My parents named me Podkayne after a girl in an old story about Mars. It becomes Poddy and Special K, usually Kayne.

In college, though, they called me the Gimp. Most of the time it was affectionate. Pippi was my roommate, there from day one. She had eight siblings, ranging from twelve years to three months. A roomie with lower limb reduction syndrome didn't faze her. I'd come in with a chip pre-loaded on my shoulder, but I relaxed after a couple of weeks.

Pippi was borderline Aspie, called it like it was, which caused her enough troubles on her own. You had to explain to her why you were angry or sad or whatever, but once she knew what was going on, she knew what sounds to make.

The Aspiness makes her an excellent sportscaster. She knows every sports score for the last half century, and a lot of pre-Net stuff too. You can't come up with a trivia question that's lunar sports-related that she can't answer. That was the only thing she really got passionate about, and in a way that charmed the camera.

We never hooked up. Both of us were wired straight. Pippi had a regular friend named Trevor who was usually away on business trips. I paid for it or went virtual every once in a while, and left things at that.

We were both enjoying sunlight at our favorite park, two blocks away from Pippi's apartment complex. Sitting beside a sculpture there I've always loved, spindly rails of color tumbling taller than me like animation lines, edges glinting pink and blue and purple. The smell of tomato and basil and sage filled the air.

Pippi had her face turned up to the light, soaking in the warmth. She had been indulging in tanners again. Her orange shirt and shorts were vibrant against the expanse of her brown skin.

I was more cautious. I don't want skin tumors later on, so I keep a gauzy over-shirt and hat about me. Silvery sleeves to deflect the light were set over my arms, strapped into the walker's maneuvering legs. Underneath the sleeves, mercurial light played over my skin.

We both saw him when he entered the park: tourist-new, still dressed in arrival shorts and paper shirt with "Be nice, I'm a newbie" printed on the back, which guaranteed him a 10% discount at any participating business.

Pippi squinted over. "Is that ... "

I followed her gaze. Dark glasses gave me the advantage. "Yep. It's an AI."

"Not just any AI, though," she said, eyes watering. "Unless I'm wrong?"

"Nope, it's a sexbot," I said.

It was just after what the newsies were calling the Sexbot Scandal, when that Senator was caught traveling with an AI and had used the momentary notoriety to call for AI rights. Now the Senator's 'droid and several others of its kind had bought themselves free. I'd seen an interview with one while trapped in line picking up Chinese takeout the night before. Its plans for the next year were to travel with its friend, another of the bots. Wink wink, nudge nudge.

The oldest human urge: Curiosity about who or what each other was fucking.

He had the white plastic skin most AIs were affecting that year. On his head a slouched wool hat like a noir detective's.

He looked up and saw us looking at him. He froze as though his battery had been removed. Then he moved again, almost impatient, flinging an arm up as though against us, although I realized a second later that it shielded his eyes from the dazzle of sunlight off the sculpture. Trapezoids of colored light danced over his tunic, glittered on the lenses that were his eyes.

Pippi waved.

He stepped backwards, ducked into the tunnel.

Of course we went in pursuit.

He took the West tunnel. Moving fast, dodging between walkers moving between stations, grabbing handholds to hurl himself along. It wasn't hard to follow him—I'm small, and mostly muscular in the chest and shoulders, so I can rocket along as far as anyone from handhold to handhold. Pippi slowed me down, kept hissing at me to wait up for her.

We emerged in the most touristy of plazas, the complex of malls near the big hotels, the public gardens. I thought I'd seen the flicker of his tunic, his hat's crumpled feather, as he ducked into the Thai garden.

The dome overhead admitted unadulterated sunlight. There were parrot flowers and bua pood, a waterfall, and a grove full of gibbons, safely behind mesh. Trails led off to discreet clothing and lifestyle boutiques, a restaurant, and a walkway to the next mall. I saw his hat bob through its glass confines and elbowed Pippi, pointing.

She said, "He could be going anywhere from there. There's a tube stop in the middle of the mall."

"Where would a sexbot go?"

"Do you think he's for hire?" she said.

The interview had said only a few sexbots had chosen to keep their professions. Most of the others had made enough to fund other careers. Many had become solo-miners or explorer pilots.

"It can't be the first time he's been asked the question," Pippi said.

I hesitated. I could talk her into asking. Could machines feel embarrassment? What was the etiquette of communication? Was a sexbot, like a human, capable of being flattered by a flirtatious or even directly admiring question?

Gibbons hooted overhead. A long-billed bird clung upside down to the other side of the mesh. If we stayed here much longer, we'd have a park fee added to our monthly taxes. Two parks in a single day was way too extravagant.

We went home.

I had a run to the Gate the next morning, so I got up early, let myself out. Took the West tunnel to the tube stop. Grabbed a mushroom roll on the way and ate it on the platform, peering into shop windows at orange and blue scarves and fake ferns and a whole window wall's worth of animate Muffs, the latest wearable animals. The sign said they lived off air impurities. They had no eyes, which to some people made them cute, I guess, but to me just looked sad.

Tourists going past in bright shirts and arcs of perfect white teeth. Demi-gods, powered by cash.

A feather reflected in the window. Behind me stood the sexbot.

This time I followed at a distance. Got in the train car at the opposite end, but kept an eye on him. Luckily for me he was getting out at the port. I don't know what I would have done if it'd looked as though he was going further.

Maybe followed him.

Why? I don't know. There was something charming about the way he held himself. And I was curious—who wouldn't be?—about the experience of someone *made* for sex, someone for whom sex was his entire rationale for existence. What would it have been like for him (it?) awakening to that?

The port platform straddled the Dundee cliffs, overlooking the Sea of Tranquility. He was there at that flickering curtain of energy and I remembered what it did to constructs—shorted them out, wiped them clean. He had his hand outstretched, and I'm the last to deny anyone their choices, but even so I shouted, "Hey."

He turned, his hand dropping.

I caught up to him. I was in the cradle walker because I was being lazy that day. I could see him taking it in, the metal spidering my lower body, the bulge where my flesh ended, where legs might have been on someone else, the nubs of my left hand—two but as useful as three of your fingers, I swear.

I said, "Want to get a cup of tea and talk about it?"

So cliché, like something you might have seen in a cheap-D. But he said, "Okay," and his voice sounded as sincere as a mechanical voice can.

The café was half-deserted, just a couple of kids drinking coffee near the main window. We were between main shifts, and I was late for my pick-up, but I thumbed a don't-bother-me code, knowing I was one of the most reliable usually. They'd curse me but let it slide.

It's weird, talking to a mechanical. Half the time your mind's supplying all the little body movements, so you feel like you're talking to a person. Then half the time you've got a self-conscious feeling, like you were talking to your toaster in front of your grandmother.

Maybe it was just as strange for him. There's a lot of Gimps up here— lower gravity has its advantages, and in a lot of spaces, like my rig, the less your mass the better. Plus times are lean—less elective surgery. Here he was in the land of the unbeautiful, the people who didn't care as much about their appearance. Strange, when he was beautiful in every single inch, every graceful, economical move.

We didn't say a word about any of that.

I told him the best places to sightsee, and where he could take tours. I thought maybe he had some advantages—did he need to breathe, after all? Could he walk Outside just as he was?

The big casinos are worth seeing, particularly Atlantis and Spin City. I sketched out a map on my cell and shot it to him.

"Where do you like to go?" he said.

I'm not much for shopping, and I said so. I liked to take the mega-rail between Luna and the Cluster—cheap and you could stare out the window at the landscape.

"Let's do that," he said.

The Cluster used to be a fundamentalist-founded station that ended up selling its space to private concerns in order to fund itself. The remnants of the church were there. They ran the greenhouses that grew food for Luna, where most of the water got processed too. The stuff at the market there was always fresh and good and cheaper than in stores.

A jazz club had bought space, and a tiny government office matched its grander counterpart in Luna. And there was Xanadu, which was a co-op of five wealthy families. Along with a scattering of individuals who dealt in rare or hand-crafted goods.

There was always music there, and it had enough reputation for being dangerous that all but a few tourists steered clear.

His name was Star. He would be alright with me. I knew enough to keep him safe.

We ate berries and sat beside rippling water. He told me about Earth—never about the people, but the landscape. Trees, pines and sycamores and madrona, maples and honey locusts and cedar. He talked about cliffs that were bound with color: yellows and reds and deep browns. Everything grew there, it seemed.

He talked about rain, about slow gray clouds and tearing nor'easters. Rain drumming on a tin roof versus its sound on slate. Fine spring mist and the hot rain that fell during drought, coin-sized and evaporating too quickly. Rain on sand, echoed by waves. Thunderheads, gathering themselves over the ocean. He had lived beside the sea for a few years, he said.

I wondered who he had lived with.

So much was unsaid. It was like a cloud in the room. We relaxed despite it.

He didn't know where he was staying. He had no luggage. I approved of that. I stick to plas-wear and carry no souvenirs other than the rooms inside my head. Even my ship, where I spend more time than anywhere else, is unpersonalized. I liked it that way.

I was staying with Pippi. Star had money, or so he said, and asked where a clean hotel was. I steered him to Blizz, which caters to the Gate regulars, and went back to Pippi's.

She was surprised to see me. I hadn't felt like going out on a trip, I said, and offered to take her out to dinner.

All the time we were eating sweet potato fries and tempeh steaks, I tried to figure out how to tell her about Star.

I don't know what kept me from just blurting it out. That was usually the level we communicated at. Straightforward and without pretense.

I felt like a shit keeping quiet. Eventually it would come out and the longer it took, the worse it would be.

I wasn't prepared to see him at the door the next day.

Pippi answered the door. "Bless you, my dear little friend!" she shouted over her shoulder.

"What?" I scooted back in my chair, glimpsed his hat.

"You got me a present!" She reached out her hands, "Come in, come in."

Her place is tiny. Three of us made it feel crowded. We stood around the table, bumping it with our hips.

"How much do you cost?" Pippi asked Star.

He looked at me. "I don't do that anymore."

"Then why are you here?"

"I came to see Podkayne."

Pippi was unembarrassed. She shrugged and said, "Okay."

He wanted advice about buying into the colony, where to pick a spot. I made him buy me lunch in return for my advice, and we took Pippi along since she knew better than I where the good deals were.

"Over there in Cluster, someone told me a month or two ago," she said. "He was saying the Church is going to sell off more space, and it's going to get gentrified. It's a long ways off though, over an hour by tram." She licked barbecue sauce off her fingers. Star pushed a wipe across the table towards her.

"I don't think he likes me much," she said to me, later.

"I don't think he likes humans much," I said. "He makes allowances, but I think he'd be just as happy dealing with mechanicals only."

"Not many mechs up here," she said.

"Why?" I said. "You'd think it would be ideal for them. No rust. Less dirt. Fewer pollutants in the air."

"It would make sense," she said. "What does it say about us, we're so crazy we pick a place even mechanicals don't want to live?"

Maybe ten thousand on the face of the moon. The space stations ranged in size from a few hundred to a few thousand. Twenty thousand on the surface of Mars. I didn't go back there much, even though it was where I had grown up, after my parents died in a crash. Maybe two or three thousand existing around the bounty of the Gate, another hundred pilots and vagabonds and Parasite-ridden.

The few, the proud, the crazy.

Why had Star chosen to come up here?

I asked.

He said, "There's too many living things on the planet."

"Why not Mars? It's enough people to qualify as civilization."

"They're spread out and it's dusty. Here it's clean."

"You like the sterility up here," I said. "Then why think about living over in the Cluster? It's the most organic spot on the moon."

His face never smiled, just tilted from one degree to another. "It's a controlled organic."

"But what do you want to do?"

"Live," he said. "By myself, with a few friends." He nodded toward me. "According to my own devices."

"What about sex?" I blurted out.

He froze like a stuck strut's shadow. "I beg your pardon?"

"I'm sorry," I said. "I didn't mean to intrude. It's just that I was somewhat interested, but only if you were."

141

He shook his head, mere centimeters of rejection. "I'm afraid not."

Words I'd heard before. Including what he said next. "We can be friends, though."

"He's not interested," I told Pippi.

"Screw him," she said. "Let's go play Sex Rangers."

We climbed into the virtual suits and tapped in. I found someone interested in fooling around on a rocky shore, underneath fuzzy pines. The suit's as good as sex, any day—releases all the tensions you need released, in my opinion—and a lot cleaner.

Afterwards we logged out and ate pizza and watched a deck about boxing. Pippi said the guy had an 87 percent chance of winning (he did), 54 percent chance by knock-out (he did not).

"I asked Star to come mining with us," I said to her when we were getting ready for bed. I took the couch; she had a fold-down bunk.

"You did what?"

"He'll be an extra pair of eyes. Not like he'll take up oxygen."

She paused. "Fair enough."

He was good enough at spotting. He learned the difference between ice and metal fast enough to satisfy impatient Pippi, who hated explaining things. I focused on getting us close to the debris that swirled in and out of the Gate. You never knew what you might find. One guy picked up a device that fueled a company in food replication and yielded over forty patents. One pilot found a singing harp. Another the greasy lump that ended up becoming snipship fuel.

You never knew.

Pippi and I had a routine. Star didn't intrude on it much, went to the secondary display and focused on looking for mineral spikes.

Usually we chatted back and forth. There, Star was an intrusive, if silent, presence. Pippi ended up thumbing on the usual newschat channel. Nothing much. An outbreak on Mars, but small and well-contained. An ambassador stricken but rallying in order to continue his mission through the Gate. How much he looked forward to being the fifth human through the interstellar passage that allowed us access to the wild and varied universe. How much he looked forward to opening new trade channels.

Who knew what he might find out there?

"What's this?" Star said.

From afar just a glitter. Then, closer, a silver-sided chest, the size of a foot locker but covered with golden triangles. An odd, glittery powder encrusted the hinges and catch as it spun in space.

We brought it in.

Pippi's gloved hand reached to undo the latch. I waited, holding my breath.

Nothing hissed out. A glass sphere inside, clouded with bubbles and occlusions. As Pippi slipped it out of the gray material surrounding it, we could see oily liquid filling it.

"Could be useless," Pippi said, her voice unhappy. "Plenty of stories like that before."

"Could be beaucoup bucks," I pointed out.

"Of course," Pippi said, her voice loud and angry, "it's the time you bring someone along, to split it three ways, that we actually hit a lode."

"I don't want any claim," Star said.

Flummoxed, I stared at him. What must it be like, to have enough to not need more, to have just that one extra layer against yourself and poverty? My parents had left me enough to buy my snipship, but all my capital was tied up in that rig.

"I just wanted the company," he said. "I thought it would be interesting."

"Fucking tourist," Pippi said. "Want to watch the monkeys dance? We'll kiss for another five grand."

He backed up, raising his hands. His feet clattered on the deck. Before he had moved quietly. Did he choose to make that sound to remind us he was a machine?

"Thought we'd just love to take the walking vibrator on tour?" Pippi said. When he remained silent, she turned on me. "See, it doesn't have anything to say to that."

"He," he said.

"He? What makes you a he, that you've got a sticky-out bit? I bet you've got a sticky-in bit or two as well." She laughed. Meanness skewed her face.

"Enough," I said. "Let's tag the find, in our names, Pippi."

She dropped back. I clung to the rigging, started to thumb in figures. She pushed forward. "Let me, it's faster." Fingers clicking, she muttered under her breath, "Get us all home quicker that way."

I took over after she'd tagged the spot and put the coordinates in. I was trying not to be angry. Hope mellowed out some of the harsh emotion. It could be a significant find. It was nice of Star to give up his claim.

Back in the ship bay, the lights laddered his face till he looked like a decoration. Pippi was strapping our find into a jitney.

"Why not a place where there's rain?" I said.

"That could only be Earth," he said. "Do you know the worst thing about rain there?"

"What?"

Pippi tied a rope into place, tested it with a quick tug, glanced over her shoulder at us.

"Rain there has gotten so acidic that if I stand out in it I have to come in and shower after a few minutes. It damages my outer skin."

I tried to picture the cold, then acid burn. Luna was better.

"I'm sorry about Pippi."

She honked the horn.

"Go ahead. I'm taking the tram over to the Cluster," he said.

I hesitated. "Meet me later?"

"I'll call you."

He didn't, of course. We cashed in the case—a lump sum from a company's R&D division that doubled our incomes and then some.

I texted him, "Come celebrate with us, we're dockside and buying dumplings." But he didn't reply until three days later. "Sorry, things got busy. Bought house. Come out and see it."

"When?"

"Tomorrow morning. I'll make you breakfast."

I left in the morning before Pippi was awake.

His place was swank, built into a cliff-side, with a spectacular view of the endless white plains below. He made me waffles with real maple syrup. He was an amazing cook. I said so.

"I was programmed that way," he said, and made a sound that was sort of a laugh.

The sexbots—all of the AIs struggling for emancipation lately—had had to demonstrate empathy and creativity. I wondered what that had been like.

He was standing uncomfortably close. I leaned forward to make it even closer, thinking he'd draw back.

He didn't.

"I'm programmed a certain way," he said.

"How is that?"

"I want to please you. But at the same time I know it's just the way I'm programmed."

"It can't be something more than that?" My arm was pressed against his surface. It was warm and yielding as flesh. I couldn't have told the difference.

He pulled away. I bit my lip in frustration, but I liked him enough to be civilized.

I drank the last of my coffee. Real Blue Mountain blend. He kept his kitchen well stocked for human visitors—who did he hope would stop in?

As it turns out, Pippi. Next time I came through on a quick flight (I might be rich, but who was I to turn down fast and easy money?), she told me how he'd fed her.

"Pasta," she said, rolling the words out. "And wine, and little fish, from Earth. And afterwards something sweet to drink."

She said they'd fucked. I believed her. It wouldn't be her style to lie. It would never occur to her.

So I did and said I'd fucked him too. She didn't respond, not right off the bat, but I caught her looking at me oddly by the time I said toodle-oo and went off to sleep in my ship.

It wasn't the first time I'd slept in there, not by a long shot.

I wished them both happiness, I supposed.

Still, two weeks later, I came in response to Pippi's panicked call. He was going back to Earth, she said.

We both showed up at the farewell hall. He was standing with a tall blonde woman, Earth-fat. Star slipped away from her, came over with a bearing jaunty and happy, his polished face expressionless as always.

"Who is that?" Pippi said.

"A journalist. She's going to help me tell my story, back on Earth."

"I see," Pippi said. She and I both surveyed the woman, who pretended not to notice us. Her manicured hand waved a porter over to take her luggage aboard, the hard-shelled cases the same color as her belt.

Pippi said, "Is this because you don't want to fuck me any longer? You said you liked it, making me feel good. We don't have to do that. We can do whatever you like, as long as you stay."

He averted his face, looking at the ship. "That's not it."

"Then what?"

"I want to go back to the rain."

"Earth's acid rain?" I said. "The rain that will destroy you?"

Now he was looking at neither of us.

"What about your place?" Pippi said.

"You can have it," he said. "It never felt like home."

"Will anyplace?" I asked. "Anywhere?"

"When I'm telling my story, it feels like home," he said. "I see myself on the camera and I belong in the world. That's what I need to do."

"Good luck," I said. What else could I say?

Pippi and I walked away through the terminal. There were tourists all around us, going home, after they'd played exotic for a few days, experienced zero-grav and sky-diving and painted their faces in order to play glide-ball and eaten our food and drunk our wine and now were going home to the rain.

We didn't look at each other. I didn't know how long Star's shadow would lie between us. Maybe years. Maybe just long enough for sunlight to glint on forgotten metal, out there in the sky. Maybe long enough and just so long.

## *Afternotes*

*A central source of inspiration for this piece was a combination of Robert A. Heinlein's* Podkayne of Mars *and "The Menace From Earth"—indeed, the plot is shamelessly stolen from the latter, mainly because that story always infuriated me with its assumptions about teen-age girls. It was originally written for a contest focusing on disabilities in science fiction, but Sean Wallace snagged it after taking an early look.*

*The title is taken from a favorite e.e. cummings poem, "as freedom is a breakfastfood."*

*The story appeared in* Lightspeed Magazine, *edited by John Joseph Adams, the same year the story "Amid the Words of War", which is included in* + Far.

# LEGENDS OF THE GONE

 Y NEIGHBOR MAKES ROBOTIC CATS.
Perhaps cyborg cats would be a better term, since they're an amalgam of metal and plastic parts he took from Microsoft Research Labs a few blocks away, and fur and flesh from the home kit he used to clone his own cat, a one-eyed, lop-jawed male.

His creations haunt our landscape of condominiums and ruin. They ratchet and swivel their way through the desiccated cedar bushes after the squirrels and Stellar's Jays they cannot catch. There are three of them so far.

He offered to make one for me, in return for my picking up his supplies each week, but I declined and said it was no trouble. He is elderly, and his two false legs make it difficult to travel. As the youngest man in the complex, I felt obliged to help him out.

He thanked me. His immense cat rubbed against his legs, watching its two descendents out in the parking lot, circling each other on the cracked asphalt. Up on a telephone pole leaning at an angle, victim of a windstorm ten years past, three crows sat at angles and cawed in slanted commentary. We stood with our arms folded, men discussing the world as it faded around us.

"I'm going to make a kitten next," he said.

"A kitten?"

"Yep. I'll make the brain pan small. Juice it up a bit."

"Juice it up how?"

He squinted at me. At one point he worked for a large company, and the habit of secrecy has stuck with him. I half expected him to say, "Have you signed an NDA?" He hawked and spat instead.

"There's chemicals," he said.

"I think it's a bad idea, Joe."

"Why?"

The two Frankenstein cats traced slow loops around each other. They purred and spat, confused by their own proximity, caught between longing and antipathy.

"Just do," I said.

"The ladies might like 'em."

"Maybe."

"Yer gal might like one."

"Celeste? Yeah, she might. I dunno."

"Always seems such a sad girl. A kitten would cheer her up."

"We're all sad, Joe. We're living at the end of the world."

He squinted up at the immaculate, cloudless sky, then looked back at the cats grooming themselves. "Least we're living," he said.

"Do you ever think about what might have happened to them?"

"Ain't like wondering will make us find out any sooner."

We turned to look at the parking lot. Past it lay the cabana and boat docks, the wood long since fallen into decay, overgrown with water lilies except where we had cut them back to keep the fish pens clear. Two golden eagles circled the lake in slow loops and a heron worked its way along the shore.

"I guess it won't," I said. "Still."

"I ain't saying it wouldn't be nice to know."

He named the first robotic cat Gaston Le Deux, after its progenitor. Its skeleton, supplemented with outside struts and ribs made from red plastic, gave it a macabre toy's appearance. It had something wrong with its ears, which stayed in the same position always, never flicking back or forward in the subtle language cats employ. This stillness gave it an uncanny appearance, dead but blinking.

The second was covered with fur but had steel paws that clicked awkwardly when it walked. Joe christened it Pierre, but another neighbor, Sally, started calling it Patches when some of its fur fell off.

The third he called Heracles and refused to divulge the name's origin.

"If you have to ask!' he would say, blue-veined hand fluttering outward like a broken-winged sparrow. "Well, then." Then he'd subside into silence.

Heracles was the most monstrous looking; the cloned fur had grown awry and clumped in angry black bristles. Like the other two, it was neuter, unsexed. The construction-surplus orange hue of its eyes proved their artificial nature. It was nowhere to be seen at the moment; it spent its time skulking in the dry juniper bushes.

Today's clear sky meant everyone would have their curtains closed tight against the ultraviolet. I checked my truck to see if the windmill had generated enough juice for me to go to the market. We were close enough to walk, but in these unrelenting days, I wanted to stay out of the sun. Skin cancer brewed along my forearms. No sense in making it worse. The battery had charged, so I went around to the five occupied apartments to see who needed anything.

Sally wanted canned peaches if they had any. Mrs. Daily had an armload of orders, shirts she'd sewn. I stuffed my pockets with vouchers and lists.

I loaded up the truck with baskets of salmon to trade. It was not fit for human consumption, of course, but as a cheap feed for livestock it would be worth some vouchers. Beyond that, we had smoked trout and squash and peppers from the garden, along with comfrey.

It's not a long ride over to the market. The usual stores were open—the market occupied the old Redmond Town Center mall, anchored in the middle with a waterless fountain of a bear and cubs. There used to be a Starbucks there. And everywhere.

Nowadays, ever since It happened, there's not so many. There's not so many of anything.

We only know a few facts, although there are many speculations:

1.  On November 14, 2017, at 7:07 pm PST, the majority of the world's inhabitants vanished, leaving a very small number (some estimate 1 in 10000, others even smaller figures). A few people wanted to claim it was the Rapture, but when it became evident every religious sect, Christian or otherwise, was represented in those left behind, that theory died away.

2.  No children have been born since then.

3.  In the following years, society collapsed, not with a bang, but a whimper. The East Coast broke out into assorted kingdoms which battled each other, but few people wanted to work hard enough to build an empire. Here on the West Coast, most felt content to live out their remaining years. They clustered in the larger cities, although a few chose to live in isolation, vanishing into national parks or other deserted stretches.

4.  No one in politics survived, even those with the most tenuous connections.

Other leadership, more reluctant but more thoughtful, arose in the politicians' place. Here in Redmond, a market formed through the work of two men who said they were brothers, even though that seemed unlikely. Their store sold scavenged goods, bartering them for fresh food or long-hoarded treasures. We moved the library down to the old Borders and everyone brought books as they found them. Caroline Livegood lived in the back there, and spent her days cataloging and sorting books, subsisting on the food the market brought her. Perhaps a hundred of us lived around the market. Another thousand or so over in Seattle; smaller groups in other towns.

A self-appointed committee tried to keep water and power running at first, but as people grouped up, they formed small enclaves dependent on their own water and power. Villa Marina edged Lake Sammamish as well as the park, so we turned to growing vegetables in the old Pea Patch Community Sites, thick with rapacious comfrey that Sally chopped and boiled for medicinal tonic. Haphazard travelers carried mail for pay. Some, rumors said, just went through the mail for valuables once they left town, throwing the rest away.

At any rate, the market is the closest thing we have to a town hall. There's a computer network in the old Starbucks, which another woman runs off wind and solar cells and scavenged batteries, and sometimes people bring mp3s or software to the market to test them on the system there.

The other stores have been sorted through for the useful and distributed through the market or the companion stores flanking it, selling clothing and technology.

# NEAR +

I found three boxes of old-time candles at the Market. The label said T.J.Maxx. 12.99 each, but I got all three for a half-bushel of peppers, which was a good deal. I swapped the fish around back near REI –no humans would want to eat the salmon, swollen and ghost white, but as I said, they make good animal food. The Home Depot rep was there this week; next week he'd be down in Bellevue, so I traded him squash for some rope and screws, as well as several seed packets: sunflowers, hot peppers, tomatillos. No need to look through the envelopes of winter vegetables. Our lives will fall away in heat and growing silence.

I was sorting through canned vegetables and fruit when I caught sight of Celeste.

She wore black as always. She says she is in mourning for the human race and manages to say it sincerely. Most of us sound insincere when we say anything like that, I've noticed. We smirk too, unable to avoid the irony in the phrases. The Last Days. The Final Years. The End of Civilization. Or we mark it by the happening: the Vanishing, the Disappearing, the Gone.

Celeste and I met two years after it. She used to go sit beside the Sammamish River late at night, light candles and float them down the silent, black water in origami boats. I walked a lot in those first frightening days and stood there watching, when she turned and looked at me.

I spoke, wanting to reassure her I meant no harm. "The boats are pretty," I said. "What are they for?"

"They're to carry lost souls to the afterlife."

"Think there's many lost souls around?" Further down the river, the frogs sang frenzies. It was one of those moist, damp springs we used to get, when everything was growing and alive at once.

"Aren't we all lost souls?" she said. She rose from where she squatted on the bank and walked forward to shake my hand. "Two lost souls, swimming in a fish bowl ... "

I chuckled. "Do you live around here?" I asked, and blushed with the inanity.

"Down in Bear Creek, near Redmond Town Center. Where the herons are."

"I'm over at Villa Marina. Past Marymoor."

She nodded.

"Well, it was a pleasure meeting you," I said awkwardly. The only light was that of the full moon above, obscured by wispy clouds like curdled milk.

"Do you want to light a ship?" she asked.

"I do."

I stayed and lit a candle and sent it bobbing down the river, off into the darkness. We were friends after that, and nodded to each other at the market and library, and little by little, over the intervening eighteen years, we became lovers. She sent those ships out every week. In all the time Celeste has done this, I've never found any of those boats washed up on the lake shore.

"Bill," Celeste said, spotting me through the small crowd. "I have bread and goat cheese. Will you come for dinner tonight?"

"Let me give you a couple squash," I said, nodding in agreement. I stuffed a brown paper bag with red and yellow peppers as well. She gave me a half smile. She is tall and skinny, and keeps her hair cut short to her shoulders. She doesn't bother with make-up. Few women do anymore.

"Cheer up." I motioned at the sunbaked concrete outside. "Nice sunny day."

She rolled her eyes at me.

"At home, I found Gaston Le Deux dead. Its red-clothed skeleton lay half under a dessicated bush, mouth open and flies colliding on the soft flesh.

I didn't want Joe to see it, so I wrapped the cat in a gunny sack and put it in the back of my truck. It would be safe enough there. Celeste lives up the hill, within easy walking distance, but closer to Redmond Town Center. No one else lives in her apartment complex, but she says she likes it that way.

Celeste baked the squash out on her balcony in a solar oven to avoid heat inside. Like most of us she has taken an apartment and expanded it outward, claiming two or three in order to have the space to stockpile and hoard.

Celeste has three extra apartments, one filled entirely with goods scavenged from the Kirkland Costco.

"As soon as I heard what had happened," she said. "I drove down to the U-Haul place, and then broke into Costco. All the power was still on at that point. I took three cheesecakes and ate them in a week."

She's held onto it, too, doling out only what she needs to subsist on. Other apartments are filled with goods from other stores; she must have spent weeks methodically looting. She has pharmaceuticals, guns, survival gear, batteries, water filters, fishing gear, kayaks. For all that, she rarely goes beyond our small world's boundaries. She is a painter—she brought a truckload of art supplies from the Daniel Smith store to the downstairs apartment. I consider her images morbid, scenes of zombies staggering together, flesh falling from their limbs, pallid overripe skin sagging. Every time I go to eat there, she shows me new paintings and I make noncommittal noises she takes for approval.

This time she had a series called Legends of the Gone to show me: a zombie's transition to skeleton over a month's course, a thirty one-part set.

"You don't like it," she said, watching me, and I shrugged.

"It's the world," she said.

"It's a vision of the world. There are others."

She took a deep breath, avoiding my eyes. "I'm thinking about moving on."

At first I thought she meant leave Redmond, but that's not it. Other people have made this choice, to move on. Some have used drugs or guns. One sweet old woman starved to death by choice, spending her last days with friends nearby watching her die in apparent total peace. I was one. I touched her hand in the last hour and she smiled at me, but impatience lurked in her eyes as though she'd said all her goodbyes and was ready now to leave the station and embark.

"How would you do it?" I said carefully.

"Pills, probably. Would you miss me, Bill?"

"Of course I would. How can you even ask that?"

"It's that or watch the world wind down," she said.

I knew what she meant that time. I've thought it myself; we all have. I decided a while back how I'd go: climb to the Space Needle's top and jump.

"You're still deciding?" I asked.

She nodded.

"What things make you feel like staying?"

"You," she said with frank warmth. "A few other friends."

"That's it?"

She nodded again.

"When would you go?"

"I'll be out of candles in a month and a half."

"We can find you more candles."

"That's not the point. The point is that the human race is dying off and I see no reason to prolong it."

I had no idea what to say. I fell into silence as we sat there, looking at each other.

Back home, I sit out by the lake. Water lilies cover most of the surface; people used to cut them back, but fewer people have gasoline for their boats, nowadays. You can't just go along through a neighborhood, siphoning cans, the way you used to be able to. The eagles swooped out over the lake and the frogs sang. We're lucky here—most pollution was reversible, given time, and it's been twenty years.

Something splashes far out in the dark water, a fish, most probably. A long time ago, this lake housed perch and bass as well, but now we only have the fish pens and our mutant, ghostly salmon, which drift ashore to be eaten by Joe's robot cats.

In fifty or sixty years' time, only the last of us will be surviving, the ones that were children in 2017. They will be living entirely off the earth by then. One by one, the last will die, alone perhaps, or in small groups, as we are now. Some people will strive to leave a message behind, in case someone comes after them, like Celeste's paintings, but most will be content to slip into obscurity.

I see the reeds rustling near the fish pens, and investigation discloses Pierre and Heracles, working their way close. I shoo them off. Leaning over to stare into the fish pen, I see a light deep in the water.

It is elusive, escapes the long handled net I try to catch it with again and again, but I am experienced at this from years of fish breeding. Finally I net it, bring it up to look closer.

Coiling and writhing in the net is a tiny fish, phosphorescent green from head to tail. I know what this is. We've heard news of infestations in other waters.

They were originally ornamental. Bred for decoration. Rendered sterile with radiation before being sold to the public. But life is stubborn, and it will come out, somehow. They became so popular it was inevitable one or two, or ten or fifteen, would slip by. Some were released in lakes.

It's not as bad as the snakehead along the East Coast. Those things invade gardens and fields and eat them bare. But these little glowing fish will eventually fill the lake, eating what our fish live on, the plants and the insects. It will take a while. Years. Decades. Perhaps none of us will live to see the lake's death.

I stare out into the darkness. Should I go with Celeste? What holds me here? I spend my days caring for the others at Villa Marina, bringing in fish, tending the garden, trading at the market for the things we need to stay alive. I had been the director, the one coordinating what we did where and when. I planned the fish pens, and the windmill turbine, after spending days at the library and then Home Depot. It was tiring. Was there a point to it?

The clack of Pierre's steel claws floats from the parking lot, and then there is a screech as he jumps atop a rusting car. Everything is so quiet, so still, that I am forced to pause, as though held there, waiting for something to speak.

The air hoots near my face and a giant barn owl swoops past in the darkness, its ghost valentine-shaped face turned to mine as though questioning. A chill runs down my spine as it vanishes into the night, leaving a whisper of wings in its trail. It is a perfect moment.

As I cross the asphalt, headed towards my apartment, Pierre leaps from the car and assaults my ankles with a sudden friendly surge, purrs shaking his frame. The night is warm, but not as bad as the unrelenting, sunlit days.

In the morning, I'll talk Celeste into moving over here; interacting with the others will end her slump. She can help out with the garden, the fish. We'll learn how to make candles; I don't think the hobby stores have been scavenged heavily. We'll construct a wooden boat to hold Gaston Le Deux; ablaze, it will move slowly out into the lake, a

Viking funeral fit for the king of cats. I feel a wash of cheer that is, I know in my heart of hearts, as artificial as a fan's breeze.

I have a few years left in me, a few years to wait for the night when the lake will be full of stars, ghostly salmon floating among them, neighboring phosphorescence lighting the pallid bodies. There are still perfect moments yet to come.

## Afternotes

*This story is set in the condo complex I live in, and part of the enjoyment of writing it was taking that landscape and transforming it. This story was one of my Clarion West application stories, and I can hear Octavia's Butler's voice in my head, saying, "Well, it's a very peculiar story." I left the question of what had happened very much up in the air, because that wasn't the point for me. The point was what happened to the ones left behind. At the same time, I couldn't resist doing away with all the politicians.*

*Author photo by On Focus Photography.*

CPSIA information can be obtained at www.ICGtesting.com
Printed in the USA
LVOW122148210912

299863LV00001B/186/P

# NEAR + FAR

## STORIES *of the*
## NEAR FUTURE *and the* FAR

## Cat Rambo

Hydra HH House

# NEAR + FAR

Copyright © 2012 by Cat Rambo

978-0-9848301-4-5 (print)
978-0-9848301-5-2 (ebook)
Library of Congress Control Number:  2012943112

Hydra House
1122 E Pike St. #1451
Seattle, WA 98122
*http://www.hydrahousebooks.com/*

Cover art by Sean Counley
*http://www.seancounley.com/*

Cover design by Tod McCoy

Illustrations by Mark Tripp
*http://www.spiderpig.com/*

Text design by Vicki Saunders

# Praise for Near + Far

Five reasons to read Cat Rambo:
#1: If you like stories about strange places and strange creatures
#2: If you like stories that leave you yourself feeling a little strange
#3: If you like a good love story
#4: especially one with talking cats, deadly mermaids, mind-altering technologies, live coats, detachable limbs, gorgeous descriptions and great leaps of imagination, wit and power
#5: plus travel through space and time
Then this is the book for you.

*Karen Joy Fowler*

⊙▪▪▪▬▬

Cat Rambo's futures are complex, and often dissonant and eerie—they evoke the familiar in their careful world-building, intricate detail and recognizable characters, while simultaneously constructing futures flavored with the strange. Her futures are often unsettling, but never so simple as to be dystopic; her stories inhabit complex, ambiguous worlds. Her simultaneously familiar and unfamiliar settings sharpen her portrayals of human relationships. By recasting core experiences against disjunctive backgrounds, she causes the reader to appreciate them anew. People are always at the center: they fall away from each other, cope with betrayals, seek connections. While the inner eye marvels at her immersive images, the body resonates with the subtle, deft emotions imbued in her characters. Cat Rambo's finest stories shimmer in the memory like the lights of the Aurora Borealis: vivid and eerily illuminating.

*Rachel Swirsky*

Cat Rambo's stories never go where you expect them to. They twist and turn and end up in strange places—sometimes very strange indeed. Both the stories set on the Earth we know (or think we know) and those set far away will surprise and delight you.

*Nancy Kress*

Cat Rambo's newest collection shows two sides of her fiction. Powerful prose, coupled with telling details. Not only does the collection flip, physically, it will also turn you on your head. Read with caution: these stories are only safe in small doses.

*Mary Robinette Kowal*

Near + Far is a survey of the terrain of Cat Rambo's imagination, ranging from small fantasies of the moment to vest pocket planetary romances. She tends to the quiet, internal, disturbing reflection, far more Bradbury than Heinlein. Moving, thought-provoking literature in nicely comestible chunks.

*Jay Lake*

An exemplary short story collection in both senses of the term— excellent and also a model of what the range of the career of a speculative short story writer should be, and these days unfortunately so rarely is. Wide in its subject matter from the immediate future to the wide open spaces, deep in its psychological characterization when that is the central point, speculatively amusing when it isn't, well-realized almost all of the time, and always entertaining.

*Norman Spinrad*

## + Far Contents

# Introduction

I F YOU'RE HOLDING THE PHYSICAL COPY OF THIS BOOK, YOU'RE
seeing the outgrowth of my theory regarding how electronic
publishing will affect books. The book is more than a delivery
mechanism for text: it should feel nice in your hands if we've done
everything right. You can flip it to find a second set of stories,
which I find downright cool. Attention's been paid to the art, both
exterior and interior, and we've proofread the heck out of it, so
there should be very few typos to distract the reader. It's an object
that can be prized in its own right.

This is how, I think, physical books may survive, as objects that are
aesthetically pleasing or entertaining in their own right, and which
add something to the text they hold. Look at Subterranean Press'
strategy of making beautiful, collectible books: I've got more than a
few of those on my shelves and I'll keep buying them periodically,
despite the fact that I do most of my reading now on the Kindle. That's
the kind of book we've tried to put together.

If you're reading this electronically, we've tried to make the most of
that as well. You'll find there's an accompanying iPhone app (or will
be, Goddess willing, by the time this comes out) that lets you access
extra material, including audio recordings of several stories.

I am incredibly pleased with this book. It's allowed me to work with
some of my very favorite people, and particular shouts should go out
to: Tod McCoy, without whom this book would not have been possible;
Vicki Saunders, for incredible design skills and meticulous work; Mark
Tripp, for allowing me to use some of the art he's been showing me for
over a decade; Sean Counley, for his gorgeous cover art; Jo Molnar,
who kindly pruned typos and corrected embarrassing misspellings;
and Wayne Rambo, who provided support, encouragement, and
occasional nagging. You guys rock, and you rock hard.

The stories themselves come from close to a decade of writing.
Sometimes when you're writing, you feel you're leveled up, that you've
moved through some plateau and jumped to a new degree of skill.
Some of these stories are ones that let me know I'd leveled up. I hope
you enjoy them all.

# FUTURES

IN THAT FUTURE, WE LEARNED TO SEE ALL THE other futures. The one where we found out the world really was only 4000 years old. The one where the dinosaurs invented the abacus, the one where Deinonychi fought in cock-fights, bright feathers scattering like disintegrating fans. The future where cold-eyed aliens bought Manhattan for a handful of radioactive beads. A future of emotion and glass sculpture, where something danced like a quivering bird on the steps of a cloud coliseum for the en-couched, plugged-in ranks.

When we slept we dreamed more futures. Worlds where everyone was a superhero, worlds where nothing died but lived on in clanking golem form. A world of floating cities in the sky and the kite warriors that defended them. Worlds of darkness and peril as well as ones filled with sunshine and marvels.

We talked about them on the subway, online, face to face and mind to mind. I loved the one where mermaids taught us harmony; you preferred the future of textured light, where sorrow slanted sideways, slipping away along the grain like rain on nylon.

The unjust futures haunted many of us, the ones where the corporations sold us our jobs, where we lived on rotting beaches, walked among pine stakes tipped with black mold. Futures of plague and zombies. Realities of saliva and hunger and the arrogance of existence. So many of them that they eclipsed all the rest, obliterated the more whimsical, the futures of tiny elephants and

1

limerick-composing umbrellas. But we would have had to alter the past to prevent these grim-shaded dooms. It was too late.

Or was it? Time travel had been glimpsed before. We turned the minds, the machines, long caffeinated nights and scrolling whiteboards to finding ways to repair long gone decisions.

Gate after gate; every traveler vanished. Never seen again.

Are they elsewhere, did they escape?

Our choice now: follow them and disappear through the dreaming gate, or stay here, caught in nightmare, where all the futures but one are gone. Take my hand—or decide not to decide.

## *Afternotes*

*This was originally written for a flash fiction contest sponsored by* New Scientist. *(It did not win.) It later appeared in* Dream People, *under the editorship of Betty Lomax and D. Harlan Wilson.*

*My philosophy with theme contests and anthologies is this: if when you read one, an idea springs to mind, go for it. Otherwise I don't know that I would push too hard on a specific theme, particularly one of the very precise ones that our genre sometimes comes up with,* Carmen Miranda's Ghost is Haunting Space Station 3 *being a prime example. Also pirates, which I grew arrrr-tily tired of during my stint at* Fantasy Magazine.

*But this one was broad enough to inspire this piece, which is a type I'm fond of, a list with sundry commentary. (See also: "10 New Metaphors for Cyberspace" in* Near.*) The Deinonychi is a nod to a story by Ann Leckie, produced while we were at Clarion West, while the quivering bird dancing references Cordwainer Smith's marvelous story, "Golden the Ship Was—Oh! Oh! Oh!", a story that blew me away as an SF-devouring teen and which still amazes me with its beauty. I like the second person plural and the way it addresses itself while pulling the reader into that position; it's a neat little origami of an end that pleases me.*

*I used this collection in my editing class and challenged the students to put together their ordering of the stories and then defend it. This story appeared first on more than one list, and I had to agree that it's a good one to start off this collection.*

2

# KALLAKAK'S COUSINS

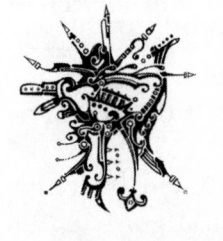

THE MORE ANNOYED KALLAKAK GOT, THE sleepier he became. By the time he found himself in the small trapezoidal office that served the Undersecretary of Spaces as a waiting room, weariness washed over him in waves threatening to carry him away into sleep. His mid-hands, which he usually employed for fine work, were shaking with fatigue. He slapped open a pouch and took out a syringe with an upper hand to jab into the opposite arm's pit, preferring that to the soft underside of his stumpy tail's base. He grunted once as the needle pierced the thick skin, and felt the chrome-edged wake-up shock through his nervous system.

The rustle of the space station's ventilating fans sharpened to a whine as the wake-up's second component jolted his metabolism. The only bad side-effect was his bladder's tightening, a yank on his nerves that made him wonder how far away the nearest eliminatory was. He allowed himself to feel gratitude for the lack of caff as his breathing and heartbeat slowed from the initial jolt.

The light was set to an annoying wavelength that scraped angrily at his eyes. Somewhere down the corridor someone kept walking back and forth, a metallic echo of footsteps. Three or four rooms away, he thought, and wondered whose waiting area they had been put in.

"Mr. Kallakak?" a woman said from the doorway, her voice officious and too loud to his tender ears. He flattened the frills atop his head, a rude gesture, but it dampened the noise's edge. She probably didn't know Ballabel etiquette anyway.

3

Unfortunately, her expression said she did. She said nothing, just turned and gestured him to follow. They traversed a winding corridor up several floors and into the Undersecretary of Spaces' office, where the Undersecretary and two other humanoids awaited him.

"Mr. Kallakak, is it?" the Undersecretary asked, glancing at the pad on his desk for confirmation before Kallakak could reply.

"It's a great pleasure," Kallakak said, preparing to launch into the speech he'd prepared, but the man simply pointed him to a stool.

The Undersecretary wore no uniform, which made Kallakak hope for a moment that he was a long-timer, someone whose position in things as far as the government was concerned remained the same, and didn't shift with every change of the government. But the official's hair was growing out of a military crew-cut, about two weeks worth. Kallakak resigned himself to another iteration of the negotiation for his shop's location that he had undergone, by his count, thirteen times so far.

The room's two other occupants sat quietly. Both were burly and broad-shouldered, with the look of people who had grown up in substantial gravity. Their augmentations were utilitarian, with no pretense towards naturalness: thick metal ridges protected their eyes and laser lenses set over the eyes shifted with the light as they moved. Dark blue plating layered over their arms. Kallakak did not doubt that there were other, more dangerous additions to their forms.

"The Jellidoos here say that they have a prior claim to the space where your shop is located," the Undersecretary said.

Startled by the bluntness, Kallakak looked to the pair. They stared back, expressionless. He had prided himself on his ability to understand shifts in human expression—it was of great value to him in negotiations with customers—but these two were unreadable to him. A wave of torpor washed over him, but he would not inject himself here and give them information about the angry terror their assertion had inspired.

"I have been there three standard years," he said. "What is the prior claim?"

"They have been off station and thought that their representative was occupying the space," the Undersecretary said. "Their claim dates back four standard years."

"They had no way of checking on their claim?" he said politely.

"Our representative deceived us," the woman said. "Now we have returned in person to take up our merchandising effort again."

"It is a very small and oddly shaped space," Kallakak said. "Surely fine beings like yourselves have access to significantly grander locations?" He looked to the Undersecretary. "Or perhaps such might be found?" He wished the Undersecretary had met him alone; it would be easier to find out how much bribe was needed.

"Despite spatial difficulties, it is a premium location," the woman said. "Just above the Midnight Stair and across from the Convention Hall."

Kallakak nodded to assert his command of human gestures. "May I ask what type of merchandise you intend to sell?"

"Much the same merchandise that you currently sell," she said. She permitted a smile to cross her lips. "We would be glad to give you a good price on your current stock."

He let his eyes slit to demonstrate annoyance while he thought frantically. Would it be best—or even possible—to take his loss and see about finding another location, build up merchandise stocks again?

It would be laborious to clear his things out and re-establish a new shop: across from the Convention Hall was, as he and the other merchants knew full well, a location rivaled only by the entrance to the University or the booths immediately by the port, where every sailor and traveler had to pass. He did not think any other location he could afford would let him stay afloat. Sooner or later, his capital would dwindle bit by bit and destitution would come knocking at his door.

"Will the matter be examined before a court?" he asked, and caught the twitch that might signify the Undersecretary's hope to have avoided the formalities. But the official only said, "Yes, of course." Pulling open a window on his desk, he studied it. "The next opening is ... "

"We would prefer to have it done quickly," the female Jellidoo said, and the official continued on as though he had not heard her, "five days from now."

That was astonishingly quick, and Kallakak wondered if the two realized it. They stood and Kallakak remained in his chair, hoping

5

to speak to the Undersecretary alone. But they continued standing looking at him until at last he resigned himself to exiting with them and rose to his feet in turn. All three bowed to the Undersecretary before leaving.

Outside, the Jellidoos fell in step with him, one on either side, as he walked towards the lift.

"We realize this is an inconvenience for you," the woman said. "We are prepared to offer you compensation for the trouble it causes."

"How much?" he said, tapping the lift call.

"Five thousand standard credits," she said.

While substantial, it was not enough to make up for the space's loss, which netted him that much again every few months. He grunted noncommittally.

"Sometimes we don't realize that what we want isn't good for us," the man said, speaking for the first time. He stared intently at Kallakak.

"Dominance rituals do not work well on me," Kallakak said, roughening his voice to rudeness. "I will see you in five days in the court." He decided not to burn his bridges too far. "I will tally up the cost of my goods by then and will have a definite figure." Let them think him acquiescent while he tried to find another way to save his shop. He stepped into the lift, but they did not follow him, simply watched as the doors slid closed and he was carried away.

Making his way back to his quarters, he saw three figures standing before it. He paused, wondering if the Jellidoos had decided to lean on him further. The trio turned in unison to face him, and he recognized them with a sinking heart. The cousins.

⊙▪▪▫▫▬▬

Kallakak had come to TwiceFar space station ten standards earlier with his wife, Akla. Both were Balabels of good family; their births had been normal and each's twin had gone on to a respectable mate and business of their own.

But Akla had a set of cousins who had been born not in a pair but a disreputable and unlucky triad. Moreover, they had continued to stay together long past their adolescence and therefore never matured into sexuality. Not unheard of, certainly, but unusual.

They had not been successful in business and Kallakak had grown

used to hearing Akla's stories about their efforts. At times she had been quite witty about it but without her presence to remind him of their existence, he realized he had lost track of them. He had not seen them since he and Akla had joined together, back on Balabel, but he recognized them: they were oddly graduated in size, not the same height, and had a peculiar slump-shouldered appearance.

The tallest—what was its name?—approached Kallakak.

"You may not remember me, sir," it fluted at him, its voice uncertain. "I am Tedesla, and these are my siblings, Desla and Sla. We are related to your wife, Akla."

"She's gone," he said roughly. The corridor lights buzzed brittly behind his head. He could feel a continuing push at his bladder, despite the several eliminatories he'd visited on the way home.

The cousins exchanged glances and conferred in whispers as he waited. He heard the smallest, Sla, say, "But we have nowhere else to go!" and reluctantly took pity on them.

"Come inside," he said.

They followed after him, crowding the narrow room that served him as eating and sleeping quarters as well as a warehouse of sorts. Double layers of mesh crates were stacked up against one wall and others had been assembled to create the furniture.

A bed made from a pallet of rugs covered with film plastic sat near two metal boxes pushed together to make a table. He pulled a tab on a caff box, setting it to Heat and put it on the table before rummaging for cups in a box of chipped mugs showing the station's logo. Glancing at the cousins, he grabbed for dried meat as well and opened it.

Two cousins sat on the floor, interspersing rapid bites of meat with gulps of caff, while Sla did the same, cross-legged on the bed, its bones still adolescent soft and flexible. Kallakak averted his eyes and focused on Tedesla.

"We won a prize," Tedesla said. "A ticket for all three of us to the station."

"A prize?"

"For our shopping, for being the 1,000,000th customer at the new grocer's."

"A prize for shopping?" Kallakak considered the idea. It would be easy enough to do something similar with his shop—if he still had it after

five days, he thought sourly. He bit into a meat stick, looking at Tedesla.

"How much money is left?" he said.

Tedesla shrugged. "That's all it was, a ticket."

"And one to go back on?"

"No." Tedesla hesitated. "It was supposed to be round trip for two but there were three of us. So there is a trip back for one."

"Which one?"

They shrugged in perfect unison. As though evoked by the gesture, he felt the day come crashing down on him, sleep crawling over his skin like an insect swarm.

"You can stay until we get things settled," he grunted. Setting his cup down, he moved over to the bed, Sla scrambling out of his way. He laid down with his back to them and fell downwards into sleep.

In the morning, he saw they had tidied away the food from the night before. He thought they might have gone exploring, but when he pushed the corridor door open, he found them sitting outside in the hallway. They rose to their feet.

"I am going to the store," he said. "Have you seen it already?" They shook their heads and followed him.

"I named it 'Akla's Wares,'" he told them as he walked along. "I stock the things she liked: Corrinti bubbles and other sparkles, things tourists buy."

"She liked such things?" Sla asked.

"She does," he said.

They turned the corridor and headed up the Midnight Stair, moving along handholds rather than taking the stairs, the gravity feather light around them. Kallakak's muscular arms moved him along more rapidly than the majority of pedestrians along the hundred meter wide tunnel, its sides lined with black stairs that showed no sign of scuff or wear.

"It wasn't smooth going at first," Kallakak said. "Twice I got robbed during sleep periods, so I hired a mechanical to run it while I wasn't there."

"A mechanical?" Tedesla asked.

"A robot," Kallakak said. "Most of them are trying to buy themselves or others free, they take on whatever labor they can manage. Alo2 is a good sort. Funny sense of humor, but a good sort."

"We could watch over the shop," Sla said. "With us here, you wouldn't need anyone else."

He didn't answer, but paused in the doorway of the pharmacist. "The usual," he snapped at Ercutio.

The pharmacist said as he passed over the pack of juice bulbs, "If you wouldn't retain your fluids in your body so much, they would not cause the infection."

He ran his card through the reader to pay. "I know, I know," he said.

"Who are those with you?" Ercutio nodded at the cousins, who stood backing Kallakak in a little ring.

"Cousins," he said. He toothed through the seal of a juice bulb and sucked down the salty-sweet fluid, mixed with antibiotics.

"I heard there's some trouble with your space," Ercutio said and Kallakak paused before hurrying out of the doorway.

"Some," he said. "I'll know more in a day or so, need to size things up."

They moved along towards the shop. The name "Akla's Wares", written in standard and red Balabel script rode the wall above the doorway, which Kallakak had widened at his own expense in order to make it easier for customers to enter.

Alo2 looked at them from where he sat beside the counter.

"We are Kallakak's cousins. You will no longer be needed," Sla told the mechanical in an officious tone.

Kallakak hastened to say, "Don't listen to it. Visitors from home. Go look at the merchandise, you three, while I catch up."

Alo2 registered the knowledge with a flicker of the blue lenses that served it as eyes. Its surface was matte steel, marred in places with dents from years at dock labor. "The shop took in 541 standards," it said. "A party of six sailors bought twelve souvenir items at 2:11. Two Jellidoos came by but bought nothing."

"Did they say anything to you?" he asked.

"They wanted to know the sum of my wages," Alo2 said. "I misrepresented them as considerably more than I make."

"Good," Kallakak said enviously. He was incapable of lying; the effort of it caused a purpling of the ear frills that was unmistakable to anyone knowing much of Balabel physiology. While a master of understatement and misdirection, he envied Alo2's ability to overtly misstate things.

"Jellidoos are tough to deal with," Alo2 said in a statement of absolute

truth and Kallakak nodded in glum agreement.

"They used to use a lot of mechanicals," Alo2 said.

"Used to?"

"They're superstitious. We spread a rumor that mechanicals hold souls that have been displaced from bodies—ghosts. Not all of us, mind you, just a few. They're terrified of ghosts and death."

"Too bad we can't convince them this place was once a body repository or something," Kallakak said. He looked around at the walls, which were a dull layer of cloudy plastic over gray metal.

It was unclear what use the station's creators had meant to put the space to centuries ago. Finding it unused except for storage, Kallakak had submitted petitions to three versions of TwiceFar's constantly changing government, achieving success on the fourth try. He touched the counter, a silvery glass slab he'd found in a cast-off sale at the University and swore.

"What?" Alo2 asked.

"I've put too much work into this to see it taken away," he said, feeling tired. "It is the only thing I have to remember Akla by. It is her past—my future."

He turned to the cousins. "All right. Desla, sweep the back aisles, Sla, wash the wall—you'll want to unpin those scarves first and then put them back up. Tedesla, sort that box of mail cards, and make sure they're grouped together by language. Alo2, can you stay a few more hours and show Tedesla how to operate the credit reader?"

"Where are you going?" Sla asked.

"To do some research."

⊙▪▪▪▬▬

"Huh," Bo said after he'd listened to the whole long saga. "Jellidoos are bad news; they know law inside and out."

"You'd think that they wouldn't know TwiceFar law," Kallakak said bitterly. He took a sip from the fragrant tea Bo had served him, redolent with yellow, straw-like flowers that smelled like honey and apple.

"They've probably been waiting for a turn that would allow them to do this," Bo said. His height had been augmented to over two meters and that, coupled with his ferocious black eyes, helped him keep his own establishment orderly. "A lot of people watch the station to see how things change, watching for opportunities. But how can they

claim your space? I thought it was unoccupied until you moved in there."

"It was," Kallakak said. "But there was a caff cart stored there for three days at one point, a temporary measure. They are claiming occupation based on having owned most of the cart."

"Feh," Bo said. "So you can make it too expensive for them to force you out, I suppose ... "

"Hard to do. In that location, they can recoup a very large sum quickly. Larger than I can raise against them."

"You can wait them out and see what happens next time the government shifts."

Kallakak shook his head. "Then they'll have been the most recent occupants—most law will lie in their favor."

"It's a shame," Bo said. "I remember when you arrived—took you a year to save up enough to buy citizenship, let alone start to make claim to that space. When you and your wife first came ... " The sentence trailed off in awkward silence.

"All done and gone," Kallakak said. He drank the last of his tea, now cool.

⊙••••▬▬

Back at the shop, he swore when he saw the mess Sla had created. The scarves, draped against a wall still damp from washing, had bled mottled dyes onto the wall's plastic.

"I didn't mean to," it said, shrinking unhappily into itself. Tedesla came up behind it and touched its shoulder, giving Kallakak a look that reminded him of Akla. By the end, she had learned to play his guilt-strings like a musical instrument. The emotion glittered in his mind like Sla's unhappy eyes.

"It doesn't matter," he sighed. "Take those down and fold them. We'll sell them to the Jellidoos for a decent sum, I'm sure." He frowned at the colored wall; the pink and green dye had left pale, feathery patterns like fern leaves.

Late that night, he heard them whispering together, admonishing Sla. After they finished, he heard the smallest cousin weeping and then the other two comforting it.

"Of course it is strange here," Desla said. "But tomorrow we will go and get the little cream pastries from the Food Court that the woman

was talking about. Sweet and light as air, she said."

"We'll bring some back," Desla murmured. "He deserves to be taken care of, now that he no longer has his wife."

"He never speaks of her," observed Tedesla.

"Never," said Sla. "Do you think she died of something gruesome?" The other two shushed it and lapsed into murmurs that he couldn't make out.

When the hallway lights brightened to morning shift white, he let the increased angstroms tug his eyelids awake and drank another of the sour bulbs. His bladder felt much the same as it had the day before, irritated and a little sore, but at least it was no worse.

Sla was cheerful. Kallakak gave the three the day free, with a handful of coupons and vouchers he had gathered through exchanges with other merchants.

Alo2 was sweeping out the aisles as he entered.

"Where's your entourage?" it asked. He shook his head. "Sent the pack of them off to the Food Court."

"Good. What are you going to do about the Jellidoos?"

"There's not much I *can* do," he said. Moving over to the card-reader, he tapped at it, checking the totals. "I'm going to see the Undersecretary today. Can you watch over the shop again?"

"And the cousins?" the mechanical said.

He shook his head. "I told them they were off today and to meet me at evening to eat together."

"They tried to ask me questions about Akla yesterday."

"What did you say?"

"That I didn't know anything. I think they don't understand that non-Ballabel can lie yet. Not that I'm complaining. I had the middle one fetching and carrying for me yesterday when I described the pain that sudden movements caused to my resistors."

He laughed. "They'll learn soon enough, I'm sure." He drank another juice bulb, feeling his outlook improving. His cheer was confirmed when the Undersecretary saw him with surprising promptness, but the emotion fled when the official bluntly mentioned the sum the Jellidoos had already provided.

"I can't match that in the short term," Kallakak ventured. "But perhaps over the course of time ... "

The official shook his head. "Things change too quick around here. There hasn't been a government that's lasted more than six months in over a decade," he said. "Who's to say what could happen? Better to grab what I can while I can."

"All right," Kallakak said.

Bo was similarly discouraging. "Chimp down in the Click Bar said the Undersecretary picks up lonely sailors every once in a while, treats them to a good meal and usually breakfast too, isn't too picky about looks. I don't have anyone that could lean on him."

"And the Jellidoos are better at brute force anyhow," Kallakak said. He sighed. "Thanks anyway."

Coming home through the Food Court, he came across a noodle vendor screaming at the cousins, who stood in a line before the livid, red-faced man, their upper and midhands clasped together in embarrassment.

"What's happened here?" he asked, hurrying up.

"They pick up soup unit, get it all mixed around, bad programming!" the man yelled, his voice grating across Kallakak's ears. "Expensive machine!"

"We were just looking at it," Sla said sullenly, its tail lashing.

"We thought that you might get one for the shop," Desla said.

"How much to fix?" Kallakak said to the merchant. He wished he could lie, wished he could pretend this trio, so clearly linked to him, were of no relation, no consequence. But their every movement proclaimed them his.

"Fifty credits."

"Give you ten here and now or twenty store credit."

"Fifteen here and now." The merchant swiped Kallakak's card through his reader, punching in the numbers as he eyed the cousins. As though his money wasn't flowing away rapidly enough, he thought.

"You're not paying him, are you?" Sla asked. "We were just looking!"

"Apparently you punched a few buttons," Kallakak said tiredly. They followed him as he circled around the entrance of the Midnight Stair, towards the shop.

"You could sell a lot of food in your shop," Sla said.

"We aren't zoned to sell food."

"But you sell the chocolate and fruit boxes."

"Those are sealed."

"Oh," Sla said.

"Tonight you can watch over the store with Alo2," he said. "First two of you in a five hour shift, then Desla by itself."

"All right," Tedesla said agreeably.

"What will I do by myself?" Desla asked, alarmed.

"You can go sit in the shop with them. You just won't be working. Although if you get bored, Alo2 can show you how to weave hiber baskets. We sell a lot of those."

"And what will we do when Desla is working?" Tedesla asked. "Sit and weave baskets as well?"

"You may also wish to go and fetch yourselves some food at that point, and perhaps bring some back for Desla. In such a case, do not look at or touch any machines, but allow the vendor to hand you the food," he said. "At any rate, I will see you in the morning."

But in the solitude of the room, things felt empty. Much as they had after Akla's departure, full of strange echoes and spaces that could not be filled with boxes of Corrinti jellies and bioluminescent inks. He drank another bulb of medicinal juice and chewed his way through a pack of dried protein flakes, washing them down with swallows of meaty, buttery tea, while his midhands spread lotion on each other, brushing away bits of accumulated, overgrown skin and picking away the cuticle in order to burnish each sharp, curved claw.

"I do miss you," he said aloud to the empty air. "I do."

⊙▪▪━━

The next day, Desla managed to flood the shop. All three had had digestive problems due to an excess of cream pastries and the eliminatory near the shop had overloaded and backed up. He waded through an expanse of dirty water, opening the shop door to see more water pooling in the aisles, bearing on its surface a film of dust, lint, and scraps of packing material. He turned the water off at its source and sent for a registered plumber before setting the trio to mopping. They carried the water, four dirty buckets at a time, to the recycler so he could reclaim at least some of the fee.

"Look," he said to Tedesla. "The three of you might search around for another job. I will lose the shop in three days to others with a prior

14

claim, and I will not have anything for you to do."

"We can do that," Tedesla said. It patted his arm. "Do not worry, Akla's husband. We will help provide for the household, and keep you in the style which she would have wished."

"That's not what I meant," he said. "I mean, I will have an excess of goods and no place to put them while I look for more shop space. The room will be quite full."

Tedesla's ear frills quivered eloquently with disappointment, but all it said was "I see" before going back to helping mop the water from the floor.

In between researching ways to save the shop, he tried to find them living space, but there was an influx of visitors—a trade market was being held within the next three days and so he resigned himself to another week of their presence. He kept them on a schedule opposite his own, pointing out its efficiency in keeping the store constantly open, and paid Alo2 double the usual wages to keep an eye on them.

Meanwhile he found a private access unit and searched through endless datanets, trying to find a legal loophole in between constant trips to the eliminatory to soothe the burning in his groin. He stopped on the way home for more bulbs and ignored Ercutio's questions. Every search had closed another door. When he got to the store, he found Bo waiting with advice.

"One of the new employees came from a Jellidoo background so I asked them about the culture," he said to Kallakak. "You need to be careful of what you say to them. Their specialty is libel and slander, and they'll provoke you into saying anything that you can possibly be sued for."

"As though taking the store were not bad enough?" Kallakak grumbled.

"Rumor says we might be in for a governmental tumble," Bo said.

"So soon?"

"This has been a pretty apathetic government; a lot of old-timers aren't too happy with it."

"But still, if it were to change within two days, that would be a quicker change than any I've seen here," Kallakak said.

"True," Bo said, "But I thought the mention of it might cheer you up.

How are your new additions doing?"

"They haven't done much so far today," Kallakak said. "Sla tried to eat a tourist's pet last night, apparently, but Alo2 stopped it in time."

Bo snorted.

"They're coming for dinner anytime now," Kallakak said, glancing at the light level in the corridor.

But the next people to come in the door were not the cousins, but rather the pair of Jellidoos. Kallakak smiled politely at them and signaled unobtrusively with a midhand to Bo, who drifted nearer, staring at them.

"We have heard that there have been acts of sabotage in the shop," the man said. The woman pointed at the colors on the back wall. "And water," the man added. "There has been a broken pipe?"

"A small problem, quickly solved," Kallakak said. Sla and the others came through the door just in time to catch the last.

"Is there a problem?" Sla asked. The three came to look at the Jellidoos as well.

"We do not want any more damage to our property," the man said. "We are prepared to offer a sum for immediate vacancy. Or else we will begin charging for damages to what will be our property."

"Never!" Sla said indignantly and behind him, Bo rolled his eyes at Kallakak, mouthing the words "libel and slander."

"You have no right to oust Kallakak! You are very bad people to do so!" Desla added.

"Tell me more," the woman said, listening avidly. "Why should we not oust him?"

"He named this shop after his wife and she remains to watch over it, with love and affection!" Tedesla said despite Kallakak's frantic signal.

Kallakak opened his mouth to correct it, then shrugged and remained silent.

"How so?" the man demanded. "Do you mean she still lives here?"

"In her death, as in her life, she remains by his side!" Sla declaimed. "Looking after him with eternal devotion."

"A ghost!" the woman exclaimed, paling. She and her compatriot exchanged glances.

"It is a trick," he said, but she shook her head. "Ballabels cannot lie," she said. "See his ear frills?"

Although they could, Kallakak thought, neglect to correct mistaken impressions. Akla had left aboard a freighter, saying that she wanted to "find herself" and had never come back. No sane Ballabel chose a life of solitude, and he had not wanted to correct the cousins in thinking her dead. She would have, he thought, preferred that.

"Will you be withdrawing the claim?" he said to the man as the Jellidoos pushed their way through the cousins towards the door. The woman spat and made a gesture he did not recognize as his only reply.

"Nicely done," Bo said as she exited.

Kallakak beamed at the cousins with effulgent satisfaction. Fumbling behind the counter, he took out an unopened decanter of spirits and fumbled at the stopper.

"So the shop is safe?" Tedesla said.

"Yes," Kallakak said, pouring drams into mugs patterned with glittering stars.

"We don't need to get jobs after all! We can keep working in the shop!" Sla said.

"Well," said Kallakak. "I don't know if I'd go that far."

## Afternotes

*While at Clarion West, I wrote two stories ("Amid the Words of War" and "I Come From the Dark Universe") set aboard a space station named TwiceFar. "Kallakak's Cousins" is the third story I set there, and was the first to sell, to Sheila Williams at Asimov's. In it, I deliberately used physical elements to force reader identification with the beleaguered Kallakak, and then followed up by heaping problem after problem on him. I'm also fond of the cousins, as well as the Ballabel social structure's intricacies. Akla will surely get her own story at some point.*

*My vision for TwiceFar is that it's a station prone to revolution as well as frequent hostile takeovers, in a constant state of economic and political flux, a theme that I tried to explore in a fourth story, "On TwiceFar, As the Ships Come and Go." A fifth story has been hovering for a while in the back of my mind and hopefully will make its way out by the end of this year.*

*The story was reprinted in several places, including Russian magazine Esli, and appeared in audio form on the most excellent podcast, Escape Pod.*

17

# AMID THE WORDS OF WAR

E VERY FEW DAY-CYCLES, IT RECEIVES hate-scented lace in anonymous packages. It opens the bland plastic envelope to pull one out, holding the delicate fragment between two forelimbs. Contemplating it before folding it again to put away in a drawer. Four drawers filled so far; the fifth is halfway there.

"Traitor," say some of the smells, rotting fruit and acid. "Betrayer. Turncoat. One who eats their own young." Others are simply soaked in emotion: hate and anger, and underneath the odor of fear. It lets the thoughts, the smells, the tastes fill it, set its own thoughts in motion. Then it goes downstairs and sits with the other whores, who make room uneasily for it.

It is an anomaly in this House. Most of the employees are humanoid and service others like themselves. It is here for those seeking the exotic, the ones who want to be caressed by twelve segmented limbs even though it is only the size of their two hands put together. They want to feel chitin against their soft skin, to look into the whirl of multicolored eyes and be afraid. For some, it only has to be there while they touch themselves to bring them to the flap and spasm of mammalian orgasm.

Others require its physical assistance, or its whispered obscenities telling them what they want to hear. It has learned what words to say.

It has never seen others of its race in this port. If it did, it would know that this place, far away from that distant front and its fighters,

had been invaded by one side or the other, that soon the bombs, the fires, the killings would begin.

⊙▪▪▪▬▬

It was raised a soldier. Its clutch-mates and it were tended until old enough to have minds, and then trained. It was one of six—a small clutch, but prized for its quickness and agility. They learned the art of killing with needle throwers, and once they had mastered that, they were given different needles: fragments that exploded, or shot out acid, or whistled until the ears of the soft-fleshed creatures who called themselves the Espen, their enemies, exploded.

Over the course of their training, they were provided with hundreds of Espen. They were allowed to select their favorites. Some of them played unauthorized games. They told the prey they would be freed if they killed a hunter or if they killed each other, because it made them fight harder.

When they were dead the clutch-mates were allowed to take fluid from their bodies. It liked the taste of their spinal liquid: salty plasma tinged with panic, complicated enzymes that identified where they came from. It became a connoisseur; it could name each of their three continents and tell you on which its victim had been spawned. None of its siblings could do the same.

The names such creatures call their clutch-mates differs according to many factors: the social position both hold, the spatial relationship, the degree of affection in which they are held that day. For the sake of simplicity, call them One through Five, and reserve the name Six for it. One was simple-minded but direct, and never lied, in contrast to Two, who loved to talk and tell stories. Three was jealous of everyone; anytime the others were talking, it would intervene. Four was kind-hearted, and had to be prodded before it killed for the first time. Even after that it would hesitate, and often one of the others would perform the final stroke. Five and Six were often indistinguishable, the others said, but they thought themselves quite separate.

In those early days they lived together. They groomed the soft sensory hairs clustered around each other's thoraxes, and stroked the burnished chitin of carapaces. It did not matter if what they touched was themselves or another. They sang to each other in symphonies of

caress, passing thoughts back and forth to see how they unfolded in each other's heads.

They were not a true hive mind. They depended on each other, and one alone would die within the year lacking the stimulation of the others' scent, the taste of their thoughts, to stir their own. But they were their own minds; it acted by itself always, and no other mind prompted its actions. It insisted that until the end to the Interrogator.

They were like any clutch; they quarreled when opinions differed, but when others intruded, they held themselves like a single organism, prepared to defend the clutch against outsiders. At sleep time, they spun a common web and crawled within its silky, tent-like confines to jostle against each other, interlocking forelimbs and feeling the twitches of each others' dreams. Five and Six had the most in common, and so they quarreled most often. Everything Six disliked about itself, the fact that it was not always the quickest to act and sometimes thought too long, it saw in Five, and the same was true for the other. But there was no fighting for position of the sort that happens with a clutch that may produce a queen or priest. They knew they were ordinary soldiers, raised to defend the gray stone corridors in which they had been born. And beyond that—raised to go to war.

There is a garden in the center of this house, which is called The Little Teacup of the Soul. Small, but green and wet. Everything is enjoyment and pleasure here—to keep the staff happy, to keep them well. This spaceport is large, and there are many Houses of this kind, but this one, Bo the manager says, is the best. The most varied. We'll fulfill any need, Bo says, baring his teeth in a smile, or die trying.

The staff's rooms are larger than any spacer's and are furnished as each desire. Its cell is plain, but it has covered the walls with scent marks. It has filled them with this story, the story of how it came here, which no one in this house but it can read. It sits in its room and dreams of the taste of hot fluid, of the way the training creatures struggled like rodents caught in a snare.

One of the visitors pretends that it is something else. Tell me that you are laying eggs in my flesh, he says, and it crawls over him and says the words, but it is not a queen, and its race does not lay eggs in the

living. It holds his skin between two pincers and tears it, just a little, so he will feel the pain and think it is an egg. He lies back without moving, his eyes closed. My children will hatch out of you, it says, and makes its voice threatening. Yes, he says, yes. The pleasure shakes him like a blossom in the garden, burdened by the flying insects that pollinate it.

◎▪▪▪▪▬

Everything was war, every minute of every day. The corridors were painted with the scent of territoriality—the priests prayed anger and defense, and the sound of their voices shook the clutch-mates to the core. They were told of the interlopers, despoilers, clutch-robbers, who would destroy their race with no thought, who hated them simply because of what they were. They massed in the caverns, the great vast caverns that lie like lungs beneath the bodies of the Espen cities, and touched each other to pass on the madness.

They were smaller than the Enemy, the soft fleshed. With limbs tucked in, they were the size of an Enemy's head at most, and every day the Espen people carried packages, bags, that size. So they sent ships laden with those willing to give their lives for the Race, willing to crawl through their stinking sewer tunnels or fold themselves beneath the seats of their transports, blood changed to chemicals that would consume them—and the Enemy—in undying flame, flames that could not be quenched but burned until they met other flames. They watched broadcasts of their cities, their homes, their young, burning, and rejoiced.

They put One, Three and Six in armor of silver globules, each one a bomb, triggered by a thought when they were ready. They flew at night, a biological plane with no trace of metal or fuel, so it could elude detection, and entered their city. Dropped at a central point, they clung to the darkness and separated, spreading outward like a flower.

Six found a café, full of the Enemy, drinking bitter brews that frothed like poison. They had no idea it was so close. The little ones ran around the tables and the adults patted them indulgently. They did not resemble the hatchlings Six knew, and each one was different in its colors. On the walls were pictures that did not show war: they showed clouds, and sun, and birds flying. It could smell the liquid in their bodies and knew it was on the third continent. It had tasted them before.

A child saw Six where it lurked, up near the eaves, and screamed.

Some force took over its limbs and it could no longer move. The area emptied, and it watched the death numbers tick downward as the blast radius cleared, trying to figure out what to do. Their soldiers shot it with a ray like crystal, a ray that made the world go away.

When it awoke, its armor was gone, and it could destroy no one, not even itself. Even the little bomb that would have shattered its body and freed it was gone, an aching, oozing cavity where it had rested so long inside its body the only trace.

The Espen talked to it. They said they were its friends, they said they were its enemies. They said it would be spared, that it would be killed. They cut away two of its limbs but ceased when they saw it did not hurt. They burned it with fire and acid, and laughed when it made sounds of pain. They mocked it. They said it would be alone forever, that its race had been killed. They said they would kill it too, if it did not communicate, if it did not tell them what they wanted to know, even though it had no knowledge and did not know what the priests at home would do next.

And when it could make sounds no longer, they made it into a trade. They gained three of their own in exchange. And when it was back among its own kind, the questioning began again, although this time it was by the priests. The Interrogator was a large, dark-chitined creature; the assistants said that the Interrogator's clutch-mates had all died in the war.

The first day the Interrogator came and asked questions: What had it said to the Espen? What had it revealed about their own armies and weapons? Why had they kept it alive?

Why indeed? It did not know and said as much. The Interrogator looked at its mutilated body, at the stumps of limbs, at the raw places where they had pried away the carapace and burned the soft exposed patches, and went away without another question, trailed by two assistants.

The next day, the questions came again. What had Six said? What had it revealed? Why was it alive? Six said it did not know and the Interrogator came closer to where it crouched, favoring its injuries. It reached out a forelimb and rested it lightly on a pain point. The touch was like fire all over again.

I don't know, Six said. Torture me if you like, as they did, and I will

tell you everything I told them, which was nothing.

The Interrogator leaned still further in, pressing harder, smelling the scents it gave off while sunk deep in pain. Finally the touch pulled back, and Six was alone again.

The act was repeated every few hours. In the dim light of the cell, as the cycles passed, as it came again and again, severed limbs began to regrow, and the places where they had pried away pieces of carapace healed and thickened, except for the tormented spot the Interrogator had chosen, ulcerated and sore, not healing.

Long after Six's regenerated limbs could flex as their predecessors once had, Five was allowed to see it. It stood well away, flanked by guards, so Six could not touch it from where it lay bound, no matter how it yearned toward its clutch-mate.

It asked the same question the Interrogator had. Why was Six still alive? One and Three had accomplished their mission, it said, and Four had died in a similar operation. Only Two and Five were left. But now they were suspect, clutch-mates of a renegade and no longer trusted soldiers. They had found work as cleaners, and subsisted on the gruel fed to drones, barely enough to keep their specialized frames alive. Five's eyes were dull, its delicate claws blunted from rough work. It did not think Two could survive much longer.

What can I do? Six asked. It felt itself dying inside, untouched. The Interrogator stood to one side, watching the interaction, sniffing the chemicals released into the air as they talked.

We are suspect, because no one knows what you have done, Five said. Tell them what you have done, and that we are not involved.

I do not understand, Six said. It was slower in those days. Its mind talked to itself but no one else, and it had grown lonely and unaccustomed to thinking. I have done nothing, Six said.

Then Two and I will work until we die, Five said.

Six could feel the thoughts pressing against its own, trying to shape it. I understand, it said finally. And Five went away without another word.

And so Six confessed to the Interrogator an hour later that it had told the Espen of their tactics, of the caverns full of training captives, of the plans it knew. It said its clutch-mates knew nothing. The Interrogator stood watching it talk. Six could not tell what it thought of the lie, but

after that it came no longer.

A few days later, they placed Six in a cage, hung high in the air, and the armies marched past to look at it.

Two and Five passed below, reinstated, but they would not look at it with their faceted, gleaming eyes. It looked at them, touching them with its sight, hoping that they would be well, that they would remember it.

It thought the priests would kill it then, but they sent it back to the Espen, with the message, here is your spy. And they sent it to another planet and then another, until finally someone opened the cage's door and said, we will provide for you no longer, you're on your own.

It lived as it could for a while, hiring itself out for high-altitude or delicate work that clumsy fingers could not perform. But there are many drifters on a space station like this one, TwiceFar, and people hire their own kind. It was not until it met the manager here that it realized uniqueness could be an asset.

The Universe is large, and the war of its people and that race of soft-fleshed is very far away now. But Six's race remembers its missing member, the one who they believe sold them all for life. Its image hangs on their corridors amid the words of war and tangles of foul scent adorn it.

Without the touch of its clutch-mates, it feels its intelligence fading, but each time the webs rouse it for a moment, and remind it who it is, who it was. And then it goes downstairs and finds a patron who wishes it to bring them pleasure, to torture them, or be tortured, or who will pay it to say what they wish, and earn enough to keep it alive another day.

Six drawers in its room hold the emotions that keep it alive—the thoughts of those who would see it dead. Six drawers. Soon they will all be full.

## Afternotes

*The first TwiceFar story that I wrote, this piece was inspired by Octavia Butler's series, Lilith's Brood and the idea of someone taken and tortured by an enemy who, when released, is treated just as badly by their own kind. Pondering the subject led to Six, a creature sustained by contact, forced to rely on hate to keep itself alive since it's the only sort of contact its fellows will give it.*

*The brothel in the story is named The Little Teacup of the Soul, which is a name I really like, and in my original vision for the series, the Teacup was the center of all the stories. However, when it appeared only peripherally in "Kallakak's Cousins," I ended up revisiting that decision. Still, the idea of what an establishment providing sexual services would look like in a multi-species setting is one that is interesting to explore, and certainly it's an establishment heavily affected by the station's economic flux.*

*The story was originally written in first person. It was purchased by Sean Wallace for Lightspeed, where it appeared in 2010.*

# Timesnip

I DIDN'T HOPE FOR MUCH WHEN I WENT AROUND to Roderico's office. Maybe a chance to record some new tapes, at least, get a little spending cash. The Institute covers room and board, but not much else. And lately, they've proven less willing to fund me on sales missions, visiting system to system to pitch their services—my success rate has been bad.

I don't know if Roderico's a timesnip like me or not. His office doesn't have the usual retro-detritus as décor that many do. Lots of the timesnippers take sidetrips and grab things they like. As long as they don't fall into the category of Artifacts, no one calls them on it. I'd have volunteered for the job if I could have, but timesnips can't become snippers, because of the physics of it all. They yank us out of the timeline, there's a buzz and whirl of interviews, and then when the dust settles, there you are, trapped in the future while the person you used to be labors on in the past.

Roderico was napping in his office when I went in. I tapped on the desk and he jerked awake, relaxing when he saw it was me.

"Greetings, Victoria," he said, yawning and stretching. "Did you have an appointment?"

"No," I said. "But I'm low on cash, Roderico. Any projects up for grabs?"

"Let me run a query." He tugged a data window open in the air before him and began to scroll through it. I settled onto a chair to watch him.

His face is lean and dark, Mediterranean blood somewhere in his

background—or tweaked into it, I reminded myself—and eyes glittering like a dark war.

His eyebrows rose. "You're in luck. This has been in the system about thirty seconds so far if you want to jump on it. We've got an Initial Pitch ... "

"Put my name in," I said.

"No details?"

Initial Pitches are major money. "Just put my name in," I said. In a few minutes the outside records would update and every saleslancer in the system would be aware of it. I wanted it.

He keyed my name in and sent it. It would take a few minutes for the system to confirm that I had the job, and there was no guarantee someone hadn't already spotted it and earned a tipoff fee. But the window chimed and we both smiled.

"All right," said Roderico. He glanced over the details. "You'll leave in a day—here's a datasheet." He gave me a silvery coin and I tucked it away.

⊙••••▬▬

I set a tea cube steeping and wandered through the pages of the datasheet. I didn't have the air interface that Roderico boasted in his office, so I unrolled my own square of black shiny fabric, no sign of its weave, and slotted the disk into its pocket.

The Tedum were a patriarchal, polygamous society, one of the many spread out human colonists. I rolled my eyes at that—I've never been fond of patriarchies. It's my greatest disappointment in the future, that the men's nonsense hadn't been eradicated. Instead, you had every possible variety of it, and only a handful of female dominant or egalitarian populations. Luckily, the largest of the gender neutral systems was Galactic Citizenship, and I'd bought my way into that as soon as I could.

Still, an Initial Pitch was major money. I kept reading.

The Tedum had harems. Younger men tended to be enlisted in the armies—three rival nations kept up ongoing, bloody conflicts that kept the number of males who reached thirty, the age for marriage, relatively low.

The documents had been badly translated—I suspected that no program had been available and some non-Standard language

speaker had taken a stab at it.

I didn't have much time and I'd never been a fast reader. They say they can input data into your head faster than you can think, but I still need to go over it piece by piece and worry it into the right shape in my mind. So I picked the following to read on the three-day trip:

The geographical overview: A mountainous planet whose largest predator was a six legged ursine-type that stood two meters tall and blended with the rocky cliffs. Two major cities, with trade flowing between them. I would be staying in Tabor, the larger of the two, which focused on textile manufacturing. The smaller was called Luxat.

The economic overview: A small trade in handicrafts and high end goods, including furs from the ursines, which were called Rawrs. Minerals used in manufacturing glass. Dried fish that were consumed by several species. A thick woven wool cloth.

I read through several months backlog of their primary mediapubs as well. There were men's and women's sections, with the men's devoted to trade agreements, finances, military skirmishes, exchanges with the bandit tribes living in the hills, sports, which focused on a sport called Pummel, a sort of team-based wrestling/boxing.

The women's section held weather, housekeeping, and a surprisingly rich literary scene. Five of the eight pages were reviews of literary magazines and poetry, rhyme schemes patterned like jeweled bracelets, intricate and rich with formal strictures.

At the spaceport near the Ardus System, I left the larger cruiser for a shuttle down to the planet. The spaceport was loud and busy, lines of people crossing other lines, the floors marked with thickly textured symbols designating different companies.

A Tedum, dressed in a briskly formal uniform with golden rickrack along the pockets, checked my ID disk, sliding it through the boxy reader he carried on a woven black wool strap. As he handed it back, looking politely over my shoulder to avoid meeting my gaze, he said, "A word of caution, ma'am. You'll want to dress more circumspectly on the planet."

I do hate patriarchies, so I'll admit I might have been spoiling for a fight. "What do you mean?" I said, staring at him.

"Our women wear dresses," he said.

"Your women don't conduct diplomatic missions, either," I said. "I'm

afraid that on this trip, you will have to treat me as an honorary male."

Standard policy, but I took relish in saying it.

"Yes, ma'am," he said, still looking over my shoulder. "Have a pleasant stay on Argus-3, ma'am."

⊙••••——

The shuttle was small—seven of us, counting the pilot, who was a borg-box. The other passengers were all male Tedum. One, Avi, was my guiding attendant, come to accompany me to Tabor. Like the other men, he would not look me in the face, but he chattered to me pleasantly enough.

"So how far in time have you come forward?" he said.

"Four hundred and thirty two years from the point where they took me," I said. "Humans had an average lifespan of approximately fifty years at that point."

"It must have been quite a shock for you!" he said. "What was the biggest change?"

"The food," I said. "We ate less processed food."

"You will like Tabor, then," he said. "The residence where you will be accommodated has a fine cook. Usually she serves the Ambassador from Luxat, but he has offered her up to your service to show that Luxat also wishes to welcome the Institute."

Sometimes the Institute is a hard sell to a population, but it was clear that this one already saw the advantages of being able to snip leaders from its past and bring them up to advance the current civilization. I relaxed in my seat. Despite the social structure, it would be an easy tour, and I'd go home with a split of the overall contract, enough to carry me through almost a year, maybe more, depending on how heavily the cities wanted to buy.

I had declined language training. My mind just isn't suited for it—it gives me migraines and still leaves me unable to assemble anything but the most rudimentary sentences. So Avi would be my interpreter.

He was fair-haired and pale, thick blonde hair falling to obscure the age lines marking the corners of his unfocused blue eyes. A line of thin garnets was set into the cartilage of his right ear, extending upward, graduated in size to become smaller and smaller until they were only dots against the pink skin. I would bet they weren't ornamental, but

I couldn't guess their purpose. As I watched, though, he absently fingered the edge of his ear, in a pattern that seemed deliberate. A covert communication device, then, I thought.

He was human, like myself, the descendent of the bio-modified settlers that had landed on the planet two hundred years ago. I had skimmed their history, which had presented that landing in bland, uninformative terms: a group of 5,000 from Earth, divided into the two settlements.

There were no mention of the names of those who had settled them, and the history seemed to start at approximately fifty years after the original settlement. It was an odd gap, and one I'd have to investigate.

"Have you visited many planets since you arrived here?" Avi asked.

"This will be my sixteenth."

"Ah, you are quite experienced, then."

Another passenger whispered something to the man by his side, and they chuckled, glancing at me before returning their gazes out the window.

"We will arrive in another two hours," Avi said, leaning forward and drawing my attention away from the pair. "I will take you to your accommodations, and let you refresh yourself. This evening there will be a celebration at General Nazra's estate and you will meet a great many people. The following day, you will present your company's offerings to a government assembly. Many of the attending will be the same at both events. I have prepared a list that may be of use to you."

I unrolled my interface and took the dataload in order to study it for the rest of the flight. Avi passed around juice bulbs to everyone and I sucked on the liquid as I scrolled through photographs and notes. The General was a grizzled, scarred man with piercing green eyes. Like Avi and every other man in the shuttle, his hair was luxuriant and long.

Sometimes I wondered if that was what had surprised me most when arriving in this century: everyone was so perfect. You didn't see rotting teeth, or eyeglasses, or bad breath, or any of the thousand other flaws that people had been riddled with in my century. Susan B. Anthony squinted, and Elizabeth Cady Stanton was overweight. It was an odd sensation, although I'd never been dissatisfied with my face or figure. Without the benefit of genetic manipulation, I'd lured in marks and stockbrokers, spoken before the United States Congress, and even

in my fifties, or so I was told, had enticed an English banker to defy his parents and marry me.

The planet wobbled towards us on the front screen: a brown and white marble rolling downhill. Avi smiled.

"About twenty minutes more," he said.

The quarters they had for me were luxurious by any standards: thick stone walls cushioned by woolen tapestries that showed chimeric monsters and soldiers with shoulder-mounted mortars.

"Those are rawr," Avi said.

"That's not how I pictured them," I said. "Do they really have three heads?"

"Yes, some of the ones furthest in the mountains," he said.

A thin man dressed in mauve corduroy and leather stood in the doorway, watching me. When I turned towards him, he looked away.

"This is Stentor," Avi said. "He will assist you with dressing and serve you at the table."

I was surprised and said so. "You cannot provide me with a woman to assist me?"

"It is not a thing a decent woman would do," Avi said, his tone unapologetic. "Stentor is without family and is well paid for his labors."

"Very well," I said.

Upstairs the bed was a mass of feather comforters. Before I could go to sleep, Stentor insisted on measuring me with a small paper tape.

"I don't intend to wear native clothing," I said in warning and he shrugged.

"I'm just doing my job, milady," he said. "I just give them the tapes and then you can tell them no, eh?" He chuckled drily.

I shrugged and let him circle my wrist, my arm, my waist, my neck, my bust, my hips. He wrote numbers on the tape. Then he walked me through the basics of the water closet and left. I took off my clothes and crawled into the bed. The linens were chilly at first, but warmed quickly. I could hear the wind howling against the fretted lines of the shuttered window, and a pane rattling at intervals.

I slept sporadically, falling in and out of sleep, dreaming of the last few moments of planetfall, the corrugated surface plummeting up at

us, and then catching myself as somewhere outside there was a crack of thunder. I opened my eyes to see lightning illuminate the room like a photographer's flash, a brilliant image that sprang out at you, then lingered in one's darkening vision. The monsters capered on the wall in afterthought, prancing in menace.

At dawn, oyster-colored light washed in through the shutters to paint slats of brilliance across the gray floor. I opened the shutters and leaned out.

The house was towards the upper end of a hill. The window looked out over a long sweep of stone houses and far far beyond, circular towers that sent soot-laden dark columns into the air. Overhead, two smoke-colored birds circled each other silently.

There was a knock at the door and Stentor entered. He had several dresses across his arm, and carried a bag in the other. I shook my head.

"My clothing will function," I said.

"This is a formal occasion." He laid the dresses on the bed: one was a cobwebby gray silk that managed to be concealing, for all its filminess. The other two were brown and black and made no bones about their respectability. I touched my blue jumpsuit and dialed the color down to black. Tweaking the cuffs lengthened them and made the shirt blousier. The neckline was equally easy to adjust. But Stentor still did not look happy.

"Respectable women ... " he said.

"Respectable women live in harems here," I said dryly. "Believe me, I have no desire to be a respectable woman."

He stood there, frowning at me.

"I let you take my measurements last night so you wouldn't get into trouble," I said. "But I warned you at the time, I wouldn't wear native dress."

He shrugged and gathered up the dresses. But rather than removing them from the room, he hung them in the wardrobe flanking the bed and set the shoes and undergarments on the appropriate shelves. He left the room.

The shower had multiple heads that protruded from three sides, spraying a hot, soft mist on my body, and the soap was soft and scented with some sort of spicy floral. I rinsed my jumpsuit at the same time to make sure it was fully charged and clean. Out of the shower, I touched

its electrostatic tag and let it dump its excess moisture in the sink.

I wore an everlasting white rose at my throat. I had packed it in my reticule along with necessities like my datapad and my fresher. The Institute had made it for me.

Avi was not impressed by the outfit, I could tell by the impatient hover of his eyebrows. But he handed me into the motorcar and followed me in.

We drove through dark, winding streets and outside of town, where the stars stretched overhead, up a long stretch of mountainside. We passed through several checkpoints along the way; each time the driver passed up his identification. At the third point, a soldier peered into the car, looking straight at me. He shouted something over his shoulder and was greeted with a burst of laughter. I folded my hands in my lap and looked out at the trees beside the road. Avi snapped something at the driver and we moved along.

We were high enough that snow fell outside the car on the shaggy, humped trees that clutched at the rocky hillside. Finally we drew up outside a high iron gate, capped with black arrows that pointed up into the snowy sky. A pair of soldiers checked the driver's identification and waved us through once the gates shuddered and opened.

The house was high-ceilinged and ablaze with lights. Off to one side several men sat in a circle with guitar and drums, sending out a light, easy melody. Several men danced with young girls near the players, but most of the women were clustered in the parlor, chattering with each other. Their high, light voices were like birds, but they stilled as we stepped into the main hallway and the outliers caught sight of me.

An elderly woman in steel gray caught my eye. She stood, looking at me, but before she could move forward, the General was there, bowing. He offered me his arm and swept me into another room, where a circle of men in uniforms and dress clothes waited to bow and shake my hand in turn.

They settled me onto a well-upholstered chair, and a liveried servant brought glasses of thin, bubbly wine and crackers spread with meat paste. Our talk was inconsequential—inquiries after my journey, or how I liked my accommodations.

I waited for a woman to be brought forward to meet me, but several hours passed with no such move. I drank my wine and nibbled on

the crackers. Finally I stood and asked my way to the necessary. A servant guided me halfway, then hovered an unobtrusive few steps away as I entered.

I waited fifteen minutes, but no other women came in. Finally there was a soft knock from the servant on the door. I washed my hands and exited. When I left, I did not make my way back to the room where I had been seated, but instead went to the parlor.

A hush fell on the room again as I entered. I stood there, looking around at them as they stared back. The elderly woman made her way over to me. She had a hawklike, craggy face and her eyes glittered at me in something like approval.

"I am Dame Ilias," she said. She curtsied and I mimicked the gesture, the two of us inclining our bodies to each other. She paused, glancing at the doorway, where the General had appeared. "Perhaps you will do me the courtesy of paying a visit in two days, in the afternoon? We will have an early supper. Tell Avi and he will bring you."

"Very well," I said. The General called to me and I returned to his side to be guided into the men's room again.

When the men finished dancing with the young girls, they escorted them back into the parlor and returned to the room where I was. One made his way over to me.

"You are enjoying the music?" he said. He leaned over and helped himself to a cracker from my plate. "May I bring you more wine?"

"Yes to the music, no to the wine," I said. "The latter is not necessary. Watch." I held out my glass and a steward moved forward from where he hovered and refilled it.

He chuckled. He was a pretty man, with dark black hair that matched his tilted, amused eyes. He had the handsomeness of youth, smooth skin and lips. I drank from my wine and looked at him as he looked back at me. The two of us stared at each other until the General said something from across the room and the other man suddenly dropped his eyes.

"I am reminded of my rudeness," he said. "But I thought perhaps where you come from, eye to eye contact is not the same as it is here?"

"It's not," I said. "I find it unsettling that no one will look me in the face, to tell the truth."

He smiled, and his gaze slipped across my face before returning to the carpet. "I am called Jorie, Victoria."

"Jorie," I said.

"Ah, never has it sounded as sweet as on your lips," he said, and looked surprised when I laughed at him, then laughed as well.

"Yes, I suppose that sounded foolish," he said.

"I'm not a thirteen year old to fall for that sort of flower," I said. "Speaking of which, your partner over there is trying to catch your attention."

He kept his back turned to the young girl he had been dancing with, his eyes moving from thing to thing, touching my face for the briefest of moments on each pass, before it slipped away to the carpet, the punch bowl on the table, the wide windows that showed the swirl of snow past the darkness outside. She was thin and pale, dark-haired. She bit her lip as she saw me looking at her and turned to speak to her companion.

"Go pay her a little attention," I said. I let my eyes touch his chest, his neck, his cheeks, before I dropped my voice. "Then come back to me and speak more extravagance."

A spark of silent delight touched his eyes before he turned to do my bidding. I smiled to myself and watched the room.

The bell rang, and the General offered me his arm to take me into dinner. To my disappointment, I was flanked by the General and Avi. Jorie was some twenty people down the vast wooden table from me.

The table was littered with slaughtered animals, like the gustatory aftermath of some woodland battle. Most of the animals had six limbs; their mouths were invariably stretched around pieces of fruit that had been roasted.

I ate sparingly for the most part, but found a cheese and smoked fish dish that I liked.

"Ah, that's one of my favorites," Avi said, helping himself and me. "My mother used to make it on my birthday, because I loved it so. It's called Rimmoah. It looks as though they made this just for you, but we will share it."

There was a smokey tang and richness to the dish that I relished. I ate, listening to the General to my right, discoursing

on a battle with the hill tribes.

"They left decent civilization behind a century and a half ago," the other man said. "They deserve no consideration, but you act as though they had equal diplomatic weight as real countries and intercede on their behalf, making peace between them."

"Their councils are invariably naïve," the General said. "We do them a kindness by offering them shelter. And as they deal with us more and more, they will take on our customs and be assimilated."

"If they do not end up influencing us," the man grumbled. "My daughter studies with a tribesman's daughter in her schooling, and comes home with strange ideas."

"You will be speaking before the Mayor and the Council," Avi said in my ear.

I nodded irritably, wanting to hear more of what the General was saying. "Yes, yes, I know." I tried to turn my attention back, but Avi pulled at my arm.

"Don't ... feel...well," he gasped, breathing hard. His breath smelled like cheese and rotten peaches. Two servants hurried over just in time to catch him as he writhed backward, falling off the upholstered, high-backed chair. His groans echoed across the room over the clatter of dishes.

A servant knelt beside him even as one of the other guests hurried over, fumbling with the pouches at his belt.

"What has he eaten?" he said, looking up from Avi's agonized face.

"Mainly that," I said, and pointed at the cheese and fish just as the first convulsion of pain hit my stomach. The room whirled in dizzy waves and I tried to break my fall to the floor with my arms but failed.

<hr>

How much later it was when I awoke, I didn't know. There was sunlight shining in the window—late morning? As I stirred, a chime sounded. Seconds later, Stentor entered. He helped me sit up, and brought me a mug of steaming, licorice-smelling tea.

"What happened? How long have I been sick?" I asked.

"Two days," he said. "The doctors have been to see you several times. They said that if you made it through last night you would probably live."

"What about Avi?"

"He didn't make it."

"Do they know who did it?"

"Someone in the kitchens. They're still investigating, but the woman committed suicide in her cell. Some disgruntled servant, perhaps, with an imagined wrong."

"Is this common, people being poisoned?" It would have been nice if that had been mentioned in the datasheet.

"Sometimes people kill other people. This is an unfortunate, human thing. When we catch them, we punish them. Do you not have murders, in your advanced society?"

I looked at him. Purple tiredness bloomed underneath his sagging eyes. "You've been up all night."

"Two days running," he admitted.

I was touched. "Thank you."

He shrugged. "The doctors said you should rest this afternoon, but that (again, if you should live), you should be ready to give your presentation within three days. They have suggested that you spend the first two of those days in bed."

I leaned back, tired by the effort of talking. "All right. But bring me my datapad for when I wake again."

He nodded and complied, then went off to catch his own rest.

Jorie visited the next day and sat beside my bed, talking nonsense to me. Stentor hovered as a disapproving chaperone, ostensibly reading from the small book that he carried in his vest pocket.

Jorie had been in two skirmishes against the bandits. That was the sole extent of his military experience so far, he said.

"How old are you?" I asked.

"I believe the equivalent in old Earth years is twenty-three," he said.

"You looked it up?"

He blushed. "I was working at my desk and wondered."

"That's sweet," I said. Stentor cleared his throat and turned a page.

"How old are you?" Jorie said.

"I would be sixty-three now," I said, "but my physical development was halted at thirty-eight, which was when they snipped me."

"Snipped you?"

"Took me from my timeline."

There was a knock from downstairs. Stentor went to answer it, and

Jorie took advantage of the opportunity to take my hand and press a kiss on the knuckles.

"I'm glad you're all right," he said.

I felt pleasant warmth throughout my body and smiled at him. He released my hand as Stentor came through the door flanked by two doctors.

"You'll have to be on your way," Stentor informed Jorie, and Jorie nodded.

"I'll see you again soon, I'm sure, Victoria," he said, and exited.

The doctors listened to my lungs, my guts, flexed my elbows and palpated my chest, throat and ears before pronouncing me fit enough to rest for another day.

⊙▬▬▬▬▬

I'd hoped for Jorie again the next day, but instead I had someone almost as interesting: Dame Ilias. She came bearing a huge basket of spiced nuts and dried fruit and trailed by several younger woman. Stentor dragged chairs in from the parlor and they settled to embroider while the Dame talked to me.

"You seem to be much recovered," Ilias said as I helped myself to a handful of the nuts. They were covered in some sort of spicy, sweet crystals, like pepper and honey mingled. "Stentor, perhaps you will go and fix us all hot klah? It is chilly outside and the girls had thin cloaks."

"I am feeling much better," I said as he bowed and left. "I don't remember much of the night, though."

She shrugged, flicking a hand in a dismissive gesture. "Chaos and shouting. You are better off without the memories."

"I don't like gaps," I said.

She paused for a moment before speaking. "Are there other gaps you object to?"

"It seems as though the first fifty years of this planet's history are gaps," I said.

She glanced over at the two girls. Without speaking they both went to the door and knelt beside it, listening for Stentor's return.

Ilias's voice was low and urgent. "You do not know about the council that was overthrown?"

I shook my head.

"I thought you did," Ilias said. "I thought you knew what had been done and were coming to help them."

"I don't understand."

"When we first came to this planet, we did not have harems or customs for 'decent' women to follow," Ilias said. "The council was, in fact, through accident more than anything else, mainly women. We were not a society that ruled things out for one gender or another at that time. The council wanted peace for all the settlements overall, but they had children who were merchants and who preferred war because of the profits that might be made. They overthrew the council and set laws and traditions in place so women could no longer come to power, lest they speak of peace. Every woman was subjugated, forced to act as the slave of the men who had overthrown them, each one bowing down to her son, and the men who had served on the council were set to death for acting against the newly created 'tradition'."

There was bitterness in her tone.

"And that's how it's been for a hundred and fifty years? Haven't you tried to rebel?"

"Rebel? Many times. Each time the ringleaders are killed. But we keep trying. We resist where we can."

"Like killing the bearers of new technology. You poisoned me."

"What would you do in my place?" she said. "We have so little we can do. We live in our poetry, our literature, trying to shape a revolution in couplets and tapestry needles. Even in your benighted time, you were not as wretched as we are."

Silence stretched between us.

"I don't think I can help much," I said. "Perhaps smuggle a few women offplanet."

She shook her head. "We will not leave our world. We will change it back to what it once was."

The girls stood, moving back to their places just before Stentor entered with a tray of cups and a steaming pitcher. He sat and read while we spoke of inconsequential things: the best treatment for headache, and the flavors of fish coming into season.

When they left, I said to Stentor, "What is the little book that you read from?"

"It is poetry that my mother's mother wrote," he said. He held it out to me and I leafed through it, looking at the spiky, alien script.

"Will you read one to me?"

He shook his head. "Some things are private." Taking the book back, he gathered the empty cups and pitcher and withdrew.

⊙▪▪▪━━

I was furious to find my clothing gone and that I would have to wear one of the dresses for the presentation. Stentor claimed not to know where the jumpsuit had been sent to clean it, but promised to have it found by the time I returned.

I dressed in the brown. I hated it. It reminded me of the dresses of my time, the absurdity of bustle and corset, and thick heavy fabric on hot New York days. Women learned the art of swooning so when they were felled by their garments they would land gracefully. The boots were heavy but warm, awkwardly heeled.

I tottered on them in front of the eyes, explaining the advantages of the Institute. How our technology would allow them to harvest the best minds of their past, to bring them forward to enrich their culture.

They exchanged glances. "How much would it cost to bring a group forward from a century and a half ago?"

"An experienced agent could do it, depending on the size of the group, in a week or two," I said. "If you want to train your own people—which is the package we recommend to our customers—it will take them a week or so to get up to speed on the technicalities of timesnipping."

"So for a group of eight, a week," one said. He was an unpleasantly oleaginous man, his black hair worn in an elaborate, fussy style. "And another week for their women."

"Their women?" the General said.

"They'll need the cores of their harems if they're to function as part of our social system."

"But wouldn't that be dangerous?" another said. They started to lean together and argue but the General and the Mayor made gestures for silence before the General turned to me.

"Madam, I have arranged for company for you, while we discuss

our questions and come to a decision." He ushered me into a small antechamber, where Jorie sat waiting with khav and sweet biscuits.

The two of us curled together. "They'll take hours," Jorie whispered into my ear. He kissed me, fumbling with the laces at my neck.

Afterwards, we drank the cooling khav and ate the biscuits.

"Do you have a harem?" I asked Jorie.

"You cannot be a functioning member of society without one," he said. "Without it, you are haraf, a motherless man. The harafs serve as soldiers in the wars."

"Is your harem very large?"

"It is only one woman right now," he admitted. "Leandra. The two of you should meet. You would both enjoy it, I think."

The General knocked at the door. At my invitation, he opened it and looked inside.

"We wish to debate another night," he said to me. "You may as well return to your lodgings and rest. In the morning, I think we will have a substantial contract for you."

"Perhaps Jorie might see me home," I said.

The General shook his head. "No, it would not be seemly. I will take you in my car."

Despite my disappointment, I appreciated the car's luxury.

"Please thank Ilias for her kindness during my illness," I said to the General.

He turned his attention back from the slick streets outside. "Ah, she has always been very kind. Did she bring you her fish tea? That always made me better when I was a child."

"You knew your wife when you were a child?"

"She was my mother then."

I blinked, agape.

"You have not done your homework," he said. "Our social structure is unique, I admit. I would have thought they'd include that in your reading."

"I focused on the trade and history," I said.

"Our harems have cores, which are our mothers. Only the oldest son may go on in that way; the rest are haraf."

The air in the car was stifling. My stomach roiled as though the poison had been stirred up again.

"I'm sorry, I don't feel well," I said.

He patted my hand. "I understand. Sleep until we get there, if you prefer."

I leaned my forehead against the window's cold glass and closed my eyes, my thoughts a dizzy whirl. The women, overthrown. Each son responsible for his mother's subjugation. Taking her into his harem—surely a position in name alone? Mothers, watching the next generation of leaders, knowing themselves helpless in the harem, the only space left to them. What would it be like, bearing a son here and knowing that he would be your eventual master?

⊙▬▬▬

I did not see Ilias again until the morning of my departure. She came into the room and I sent Stentor for hot klah for the two of us. That gave me enough time to give her the sample timebelt from my kit, and tell her the basics of its use.

"You'll want to take the council members unobtrusively. The originals will stay in the time line, but you'll have the copies," I said. "And at some point you'll have to tell them that they have counterparts, living in their sons' harems. I don't know how they'll react to that. But if anyone can help you plot a rebellion, they can."

Her eyes were dark with tears. "Thank you."

She hid the belt away before Stentor returned. We drank the klah together. She gave me the present she had brought: an intricate tapestry of rawrs, dancing or fighting, I couldn't tell which.

"That reminds me of one of my grandmother's poems," Stentor said from where he sat. He opened the pages and read.

"Monsters hatched within our breasts,
Twine and tangle, rawrs devouring each others' hearts,
Before turning to tear our own."

He closed the book.

"Gruesome," I said. I touched the tapestry's rough wool, brushing my fingers over brown and black and shaggy cream strands.

I lifted my cup to Ilias.

"May you live in interesting times," I said to her. "May you live in times as interesting as my own."

## *Afternotes*

Victoria Woodhull is an actual historical figure, and she's an awesome one. Someday I'm going to write a historical fantasy about her. She was an advocate of free love, a spiritualist, and a fierce advocate of women's suffrage, becoming one of the first female stockbrokers and then the first woman to run for the office of President of the United States, with Frederick B. Douglass as her Vice President. (She lost.) She also appears in "On TwiceFar, As the Ships Come and Go," which predates this story.

I'm hesitant to say much else about the story, lest I be forced to confess that to me on one level it boils down to an exploration of an expletive.

The story originally appeared in Basement Stories, *under the editorship of James Dent and Carol Kirkman.*

# Angry Rose's Lament

*What has happened, I cannot change ... what will happen, I cannot
decide. I am only responsible for the here and now. I will be honest
in my dealings; I will acknowledge the pain I have caused. I can
offer amends; I cannot demand that they be accepted. I can ask for
forgiveness; I cannot demand that I be forgiven.*

—Litany for the Recovering

 ALL HIS LIFE, PAUL RUTTER HAD HATED
dirt. He'd been raised in a decrepit
Project by a foster mother, along with six
other children. Those early years had left him
memories of stained sheets, maggots in the sink, and grime you
couldn't scrub away.

It was the main reason he'd worked to become a Spacer. When
he reached his first station, smelled the tang of recycled air and
water, and saw a metal hallway corroded with the effluvium that
humans inevitably deposit everywhere they touch, it was a vast
disappointment. But better, even so, than the roots from which he'd
come. And now his career, such as it was, had brought him back to a
place as dirty as he'd ever seen.

The main feature of Linko Port was grease. Greasy dirt, black as
tar, lay underfoot, grinding under the boot heels of the Fleet soldiers
keeping order. The smell of machinists' grease from the yard that
maintained the ferries coming down from its counterpart satellite
far above, circling in unison with the slime green moons, was heavy
in the air. Grease and black grime coated the walls of the buildings,
assembled from Alliance plastics and weatherworn native woods. Of
the dozens of races using this common rendezvous point, all seemed
shabby and grubby, particularly the humans.

"Welcome to Linko. First assignment planet side in a while?" his
attendant asked, thumbing through Paul's records.

"How can you tell?"

"It's in the walk. Spacers move their feet different, come down

flatfooted like they're not used to the pull."

Rutter grunted acknowledgement. "What do I need to carry here?" he asked.

"Some form of ID; best not to leave your docco at home. No guns. Credit chits for tipping, if you plan on being out doing much. Your guild marque if you're dealing as a rep."

"I'm rep to the Solins."

The man's smile faded. "Yeah?" he said noncommittally. "For what company?"

"Little outfit, doubt you've heard of it." Rutter preferred to keep his cards close to his chest. Besides, RecoveryCo's humble beginnings, compared to the larger corporations, were a little embarassing. *No matter*, he thought. They'd done well taking a small company and turning it into an active corp, capable of interstellar negotiations. The resources provided by Solin might be the company's big strike, help them struggle their way to a respectable third tier status as an all-out, multi-market corporation.

"Not one of the Big Three? Thought CocaCorp would want a piece of that."

Rutter had wondered that himself. By all accounts, Solin was a plum piece of real estate, the kind a big company like General M or Bushink would snatch up as an asset. Across the galaxies, they'd grabbed small systems every chance they got. Solin did have a native intelligent race to be wooed, but there was a surplus of impoverished races deep in debt to the Companies. Very few, the ones who knew to hire themselves savvy (and expensive) legal counsel, managed to keep themselves free.

There was, Rutter figured, something out of the ordinary about Solin. Not out of the ordinary in a valuable way, but something tricky, something slippery or scandalous, some taint the Big Three wanted to avoid. He'd find out soon enough, he guessed.

"What about hotels here?" he asked.

"There's a few. Carnival's a bit swanker—most of the visiting dignitaries stay there. The regulars go for the Jewel or the Home House, which is the cleanest. Not so pricey. Only real difference is that the Jewel's closer to the bars. They're all on the main drag."

The Home House quarters were simple but clean as promised. A

holo on the wall offered him his choice of space-scape or uploading his own images. Unlike most, he didn't carry such amenities. He flipped through the settings on the bed and chose the firmest, then settled himself to look through the docco again.

The Solins resembled nothing so much as giant wasps. Colored in dull reds and browns, they had the habits of hive insects, although the details were sketchy. Morgan had promised him more information soon, but when he checked his mail, it wasn't there yet. He fired off a reminder; Morgan was increasingly forgetful lately. "Slipped back?" he wondered, and sighed, rubbing his long fingers down the bridge of his nose.

Going into the fresher to splash his tired eyes with cold water, he looked into the mirrored wall. He saw an unremarkable face, although older looking than his fifty years. Ten years of addiction to stardrift had left him there, crevices worn irreparably into his brow and the skin surrounding his mouth, broken veins lacing the sagging skin of his cheeks. But unlike most addicts, he'd broken free, formed a company with five of the men he'd met in Rehab. Now he wondered if that had been the smartest idea; 90% slipped back into the drift, although they'd all sworn they were part of the lucky 10%.

He slipped into the Litany, murmuring it under his breath. "What has happened, I cannot change ... what will happen, I cannot decide. I am only responsible for the here and now." Muttering the familiar words, he went back to study the information he had.

⊙▪▪▪▬▬

The Representative building lay on the outskirts of town, a blocky tower misshapen by the demands of accommodating hundreds of different species. Blue bubbles held the distinctive toxic atmosphere of the Anjelis, and a tank near the ground floor showed swirls of blue and green liquid. Windows were tinted in shades ranging from bloody rust to bilious chartreuse, filtering Linko's dull and watery sunlight into more palatable shades. *Lucky me*, Rutter thought. Solins and humans were capable of breathing the same atmosphere, although the compromise was unpleasant to both.

The meeting room lay on the fifth floor. As he paused outside the

airlock, a voice hailed him.

"You rep Rutter?"

He turned. A slight figure in Pilot's Guild green coveralls stood there. "Yes. Do you have some question?"

"Just scoping you out," the woman said. She was small, dark-haired and olive-skinned. "I flew the initial mission exploring the Solin system. Look me up afterwards and I'll buy you a drink—I'm curious about your impressions." She flipped him an ID chip and turned.

He closed his fingers over the chip, gazing after her, then turned and pressed his code into the airlock.

Inside the room the air was unpleasantly acrid, stinging his nose with its vinegar reek. At one end of the room the Solin clung to the wall, watching him with its faceted eyes. A small table and chair had been placed in the middle of the room for his convenience.

Up close, the impression of a wasp diminished but the Solin still sported two sets of paired, pale rose wings. It was unexpectedly beautiful, a creature spun of crystal or sugar, edges sharp and defined as jewels, undulled by time or dirt. A stinger ending its abdomen dripped with a clear ichor that splattered on the floor. A small pool had collected beneath it. He wondered how long it had been waiting for him.

Its eyes were equally beautiful. Malachite and lapis lazuli warred for the surface of the bulbous orbs, swirling and coalescing like gaseous clouds. Two business-like mandibles sat on either side of its tiny mouth. Segmented, they flexed at intervals as though impatient to be used.

The voice emanating from the waxy collar around its thorax, though, was disconcertingly human, down to a slight, indefinable accent. "You are the Representative?"

"Yes," he said, setting his docco tablet on the table between them.

"I am called Kizel. You may begin recording," the Solin said.

He raised an eyebrow. "You have no questions? You are aware what this contract will mean?"

"Your company will offer certain amenities, payments, and legal agreements in return for rights to planetary resources within our solar system. This negotiation will be recorded, and when

it is complete, which may be a lengthy process, the record will be published publicly. Our race will achieve legal status as a result of participating, and we will no longer be vulnerable to those who wish to exploit our planet."

He nodded. "I'm impressed by your command of Galactic Custom. Not all races come to the bargaining table knowing how it is structured."

Kizel buzzed, in irritation or amusement, he couldn't tell which.

"We have accumulated necessary information," it said. "Assume that we have sufficient knowledge of humans that you do not need to explain each amenity."

A worm of confusion crawled its way through his head. Most native races weren't even close to this savvy. He took out his list and began. "Item 1: In exchange for the right to extract 500 kilograms of aurium each solar year, one energy replicator unit, no older than one year from the signing of this contract ... "

As the session wore on, he was increasingly puzzled by the intimate knowledge of galactic customs that the Solin displayed. At one point he made a slight witticism that he thought only a human would have caught. The Solin buzzed.

"What is the significance of that sound?" he asked.

"Your joke pleased me."

After a few hours, his throat dry and rasping from reciting the lists of what RecoveryCo was prepared to offer for the long, exhaustive list of the Solin system's resources, he signaled the end.

"We can resume tomorrow," the Solin said. Traditionally, a trade agreement took three sessions. Even when both parties knew exactly what they wanted—usually not the case—the Negotiation must be acted out.

The pilot was waiting outside the door.

"I didn't want to wait to talk to you. Hungry?" she said.

"Starving."

"There's a place near Jewel that makes a mean bowl of noodles."

He followed her to the restaurant. She walked with the swagger that he'd learned to expect from pilots, an insouciance sprung from their inviolability; harming a pilot could lead to a planet or system being put into Exile, trade withering away.

48

As they slid into the plastic booth, she signaled the server, a gray-skinned, four-armed Doolah, who brought them menu cards. Rutter fingered the sticky edges with distaste, but the pilot cast a practiced eye down the card. She said "Number 3 if you like spicy, number 5 if you like sweet, number 12 if you like bland. The beer's crap but does the trick. My name's Angry Rose."

"Sounds like a Harmonistic name."

She shook her head. "Self picked, I liked the sound of it. Harmonistics start with the noun, anyhow."

He studied her. Scarlet threads worked their way through her dark hair, and her right arm wore a sleeve of faded floral tattoos. Her outfit had the slapdash look of someone who preferred no clothes when on ship.

She studied him back, her look curious but non-sexual. "What did you think of the Solin?"

He used his napkin to wipe at the table in front of him, polishing away a smear of grease as he thought about it.

"I haven't dealt with that many alien races," he admitted. "Just in training, mainly. I didn't expect them to seem so human in their thinking."

Her lips twitched. "Wanna know why that is?"

"Huh?"

She leaned across the table towards him, lowering her voice. "They're brain eaters."

He snorted but she pressed on, her voice edged with urgency. "No, it's true. That Solin you're dealing with has at least one human mind in its own. I should know, he was a friend of mine. Luke Parse."

The Doolah slid a plate of Number 12 noodles in front of him, along with his water. Angry Rose took up her chopsticks, starting on her own plate as she watched him.

"Explain."

She claimed her friend had been the first explorer to make contact with the Solins. "Then they got to him, I dunno how. They left his body there, sitting, drooling ... smiling. Smiling like he was at his momma's tit. I was on the ship that recovered him. The Solin talked to me, said he had Luke inside him now, and that Luke didn't want me to worry about him. We took the body off planet to a medfactory, but he died a

month or so afterwards. Still smiling."

"How did the Solin absorb him? Did you test to see if it was really him?"

She shook her head. "I dunno much. Went a little crazy when I heard his voice coming out of it." She gave him a lopsided, halfhearted grin. "They just put me off the world, said don't come back. Not supposed to go near any of the Solins now."

He chased a noodle around his plate before his chopsticks seized it. "Why are you telling me all this?"

Her face took on a hostile gleam. "Seemed like the decent thing to do, warn folks before they met the same fate."

"I appreciate it," he said, his voice sincere. She untensed.

"Look," she said. "If you decide to ... do anything, lemme know."

"Do anything?"

"There's at least one human mind in there," she said. "Trapped in a body they never wanted to be in."

She slid enough chits onto the table to pay for both meals. "You got my contact info. Call me."

After she left, he chewed each noodle and washed it down with sips of water. He'd learned over the years that his body would falter if he didn't fuel it, although the drift had affected his taste buds to the point where any number on the menu would have been the same to him. Angry Rose had some agenda, but he wouldn't let it compromise RecoveryCo's dealing. Too many of his fellows were depending on the company's success; let this deal fail and half of them—if not all—would let it be an excuse to go back to their old ways. Even he'd be tempted.

The thought ached at him, reaching every corner of his being. The main thing stardrift did was make you feel connected. A warm, golden glow in which all the minds around you were tied together. No loneliness, no isolation. Knowing that you were just where you needed to be, as though the universe held you in her arms, held you close and warm and loved.

He pulled his jacket around himself, added a few chits for the tip, and left.

Back at the Home, he succeeded in reaching Morgan. Pages of information spilled from the wall printer.

"Thanks," he said gratefully to the screen where his partner's face hovered, looking much the same as always. "Hey, do me a favor ... look up a name and tell me if it's got any connection with the Solins?"

"What's the name?" Morgan said.

"Luke Parse."

Morgan grinned. "Ask and ye shall receive. That's already in the docco I just gave you. Three explorers made first contact: Conchetta Alo, Tresy Cooke, and Luke Parse. Parse had some sort of accident, and died a month or two later."

"Are his med records in there?"

"You're crazy, man. You know how much it costs, getting something like that? No, they're not."

"All right," he said. "Thanks, Morgan."

They finished as they always did, saying the Litany together. "I am only responsible for the here and now."

Parse's fate nagged at him all through the negotiations. Kizel clung to its wall, head downwards, supplying details to match his own. As the dialogue grew towards that day's end, he found himself asking, against every stricture of his training, "Are you Luke Parse?"

Kizel's wings stilled before it answered. "Luke Parse is part of us, yes."

"How big a part?"

"We currently hold four minds. An elder, by Solin standards."

He frowned, trying to pick meaning out of the words. "Hold the minds?"

The greens and blues of its eyes swirled. "Like all Solins, I am made up of the minds I have absorbed. Three Solin and one human. Luke Parse."

"Can you start from the beginning?"

This time he did detect amusement in the synthetic voice.

"The beginning of time, or of my life?"

He didn't find the joke as funny as it apparently did. "Your life," he said flatly.

"When we are born, we are mindless grubs. Or consciousness-less, to be more exact. The grubs are tended with care until they

metamorphose into something closer to my current form, and the best physical specimens chosen. When an elder is ready to die, they go to the nursery. The infant Solin gives them the Kiss for the Dying." Its stinger twitched. "Their consciousness fades and is absorbed by the new host, who then holds their memories. Throughout an individual's life, they may be given the opportunity to absorb more minds."

"Of the dying?"

"Not usually. Older Solins like to choose their mind partner. Someone they feel compatible with."

"If they hold more than one mind in turn, don't you end up with hundreds of minds in one individual?"

"The minds are consolidated into a single personality in the process of transfer."

"I don't understand why you hold Luke Parse," he said.

"We needed to understand how to deal with the creatures that had appeared on our world."

Panic gripped his throat. "So you just killed him?"

Kizel uttered a shrill buzz of negation. "No. He requested the Kiss."

"Why?"

"It was immortality," Kizel said. "I had been diagnosed with Pax two weeks earlier. I hadn't told my co-workers—was still figuring out how to deal with it. So when the process was explained to me, I asked for it."

"To become an enormous wasp?" He caught himself. "My apologies ... I didn't mean to imply ... "

"Understandable," Kizel said. "But life is life. And I knew I'd be here forever, with a mind that I found ... compatible. I don't know if I'm explaining it well, but you don't understand the lure."

*Oh, I understand lures*, he thought. "What about Angry Rose?"

The noise Kizel made was close to a human sigh. "Rose ... I tried to explain after the transformation, but she wouldn't listen. She thought I didn't exist any more."

Silence hung in the room between them like a web, torn only by the shrill whine of Kizel's wings.

At length, it said, "Perhaps we should end this negotiation here for the day."

He felt absurdly grateful.

Back at the hotel, he studied his lists. No outrageous demands had been made yet, but usually the third day was the time for tacking on the true bargaining chips. He had hoped that by being straightforward with the Solins, he might persuade them not to engage in this last minute dance, which sometimes became absurd and killed the whole deal.

He called Morgan.

"Sah went back," Morgan said without preamble.

"Shit." He rubbed at his face, feeling accumulated grime and stubble on his face. Sah was not the man he had expected. Morgan looked drawn and weary. "Well. Not like we can control anyone but ourselves."

"I'm starting to have some doubts," Morgan admitted. "I keep thinking how easy it would be to go around the corner and just keep walking till I find someone with drift."

Rutter laid his palm flat against the screen. "Don't do it, man."

Morgan's hand mirrored his. "Thanks." But the words were uneven and strained.

"Hey, once we get a good deal with the Solins, we'll be sitting pretty," he said.

Morgan ignored him. "It's just that I feel so alone," he said. "Remember being in the Drift? I never felt that way there."

"I know," he said. Like his fellow ex-addicts, the absence of the artificial connections provided by the drug ate at him with a constant ache. "But we're doing well, Morgan. RecoveryCo will succeed."

"Yeah," Morgan said dully.

After he got off the screen, he slammed his fist into the wall in frustration. Every time one of them went back, they knew it dragged the rest of them a little closer. In the fresher, he stood under the cycling water for an hour, soaping and rinsing every inch of skin until he no longer felt Linko Port clinging to him like a garment.

He'd never felt that way with drift, either. It was as though the drug removed all his anxieties, and what he would have considered filth in any other state seemed like just part of the chain of life. He thought it was the connectedness that did it—it was hard to object to something when you felt yourself so thoroughly a part of it. As though you belonged.

At the same noodle shop he had gone to the night before, he ordered the same tasteless meal. Angry Rose slid into the seat across from

him, her eyes expectant. "Didn't hear from you today," she said.

He sucked in a long strand, greasy with fat. "It said he's still your friend," he said without preamble.

"Shit. That's a thing. It knows what to say because it ate his mind."

"Why are you so sure of that?"

"Luke would have never agreed to something like that."

"He had Pax, he said. Two weeks diagnosed. That would have meant he had at most half a year to live."

She shook her head, dark hair falling to obscure her face. "He didn't."

"How do you know?"

"Because it's not possible. He kept clean. Look, it's just not."

"I know it's sad to lose a friend, but it's sadder still to do it when you don't have to."

"Fuck you," she said, loud enough to rouse several other people in the shop. The Doolah glanced over, but did not stir as he took another chopstickful of the noodles.

"Fuck you," she said again. "That thing isn't Luke." Sliding from the seat, she moved out of the shop with furious grace.

He felt tired to his bones. He didn't need this crap disrupting his first big Negotiation. He didn't need this crap driving him back towards the drift. So much depended on this deal. If it failed, all the money the company had spent on training him would be wasted and the company would go down the tubes. Taking all of them with it.

◎▰▰▰▰▬▬▬

Day three of the Negotiation. List after list of trades, the result of long research on his part, and consultation with his partners regarding what Recovery could and couldn't afford. The Solin hung motionless on the wall, speaking its assent when necessary. He'd been warned that his voice would go; the previous night he'd spent sucking on restorative lozenges and started the day wintergreen strong, but wavered as the hours progressed. Finally he was ready to hear the additional items that Kizel would demand.

"Your turn," he said.

"Ah," the Solin said. Again, Rutter wondered at the humanity implicit in that slight hesitation. How could Angry Rose doubt this was her friend?

"We require one thing only," Kizel said.

He shuddered inwardly. Single items were usually big ticket items. A spaceship? A station? Bleeding edge technology?

Again, the hesitation before the Solin spoke.

"We require a human mind to join with us. One trained in intergalactic trade negotiations."

Cold coiled heavy in his bowels as his mouth went dry.

"Mine, in other words," he said.

"If no substitute can be found. We are willing to give up other items in return for the fulfillment of this request."

"What other items?"

"Any ten from your list."

It was a magnificent concession. The sort corporations spent their existences pursuing, hoping for the odd superstitious race that would give up more than they should due to vagaries of numbers, moon cycles, or the whimsy of their gods.

"We realize you may see this as a sacrifice," Kizel said. "But be aware of what you are being offered. Immortality within a group consciousness that will always be with you. Knowing yourself safe and secure. All your anxieties gone."

They've read my files, he thought. They know how to appeal to me.

The Solin's voice took on the intonation he associated with Luke. "It's unbelievable," he said. "You feel connected to things. Like you're suspended in light, and can reach the stars. You have access to the memories of literally thousands of entities."

"Ever do Drift, Luke?" he said, his voice harsh. "Or are you taking that out of some junkie's description of what it's like?"

"I hoped to put it in terms that you would understand—so you can know what a marvelous chance this is."

The first word that came to his lips was an unconditional no, but thoughts of the others in the company caught him in the gut long enough to catch the word back.

"I'll have to think about this," he said.

The Solin seemed pleased. "We are prepared to meet again tomorrow, if you wish?"

"Very well," he said. Honesty forced him to say more. "I'm going to say no, you know."

"We are prepared for that," the Solin said. "Be aware that you would not just be benefiting your company but our race. We are unprepared for complex trade deals."

It was true that they had not challenged many of the items. He wondered again that none of the Big Three had approached them before suspicion seized him.

"You've proposed this deal to others?"

It buzzed briefly. "We have engaged in these negotiations forty-three previous times."

No wonder it had come down to RecoveryCo.

⊙▰▰▬▬

At first he sat in his room pretending that none of it had been said, but finally he acknowledged reality and called his partners.

"Shit on that deal," Morgan said immediately when consulted. The hopelessness in his voice gave way to anger. "Just stringing us along."

"They'd make good on it," Rutter said. "Just that ... well, it's a high price."

"It's out of the question," Morgan said.

Outside the window, the greasy smoke of the port roiled like a spreading contagion.

"Look," he said. "I'm going to try to talk them into the regular deal tomorrow. Maybe they'll take it."

"I'm sure the other forty-three guys felt the same." Morgan's shoulders slumped. "Dammit, Paul, I thought ... I really thought we had a chance at things. And here we are, all the work gone straight down the tube. Out more than we started with. My mother mortgaged her holdings to fund my share. She was that excited about me going off the Drift for good."

Others had made similar sacrifices. Rutter had been lucky; he'd stopped before the drift sucked everything away he'd owned. *All I lost were family and friends*, he thought wryly. He'd also been the one best suited to the training. The training that the Solins valued so highly.

"I'm going to grab a bite to eat," he said. "I'll call you tomorrow after the Negotiation and tell you how it went."

He paused, waiting for Morgan to begin the Litany, but the other man simply nodded and signed off.

Hunger had been gnawing at his gut like a parasite, but once outside he found his appetite had vanished. Instead he walked along the street, keeping to the more solid walkways and avoiding the dirty puddles that lay splattered across the roadway.

*I should have expected this*, he thought as he turned a corner and saw Angry Rose coming at him. *Perfect end to a crap day.*

"Well?" she said. She fell into pace alongside him. Her uniform was crumpled and worn, ringed with dirt around the neck.

"Well, what?"

"Found out what they want yet?"

"Is it common knowledge?"

"They've asked a whole lot of other reps the same thing."

"You could have warned me," he said.

"I tried to," she said. "Then you told me that I was wrong and Luke was still alive."

"I think he is. I think he's the luckiest man alive."

Her forehead furrowed in confusion. "What?"

He shrugged.

"So you're going to do it?"

"I don't know," he said. "It'd be giving in."

"You are one fucked-up individual," she said. "Look, you're kidding me, right?"

"Sure," he said. "Just kidding."

She thumbed a pocket open and took out a small cylinder. "This is a bio-bomb. Cost me a lot to get one that would kill a Solin and not affect any other species in the room. I want my friend avenged. But now I can't get close enough to use it. You can. You can free Luke."

"All right."

Suspicious, she glared at him. "You're going to use it, right?"

"I don't know."

"Shit," she said, but she pressed it into his palm anyway. "Tap the red button to set it going. Should take about three seconds, five tops, to work. Good tech."

He tucked it away without looking at her.

"Buy you some noodles?"

"No," he said. "I need to get some sleep for tomorrow."

"Surely there must be some room to negotiate here," he said to Kizel the next day.

"Not for this." It was regretful but firm.

He took the bio-bomb from his pocket. "See this?" he said. "Angry Rose gave it to me. She wanted me to kill you, and instead I'm giving it to you. Isn't that worth something?"

"It is appreciated," the Solin said. "We will change the number of items you may remove to twelve."

"I could just set it off right now."

"It is within the realm of possibility. I do not know what we would do then. It is most probable that we would try to start again before our system is stripped clean."

"God," he said. He leaned his forehead onto the surface of the table. *Maybe if I just don't move, nothing will happen. Maybe I'll wake up and find myself back in my old life.*

The Solin let him sit in silence until his cramping limbs forced him upright.

"We cannot survive without this," the Solin said.

"That's not my responsibility."

"No. It's not."

"I want to talk to Luke again."

"We contain Luke. You are speaking with him."

"What's it like?" he said. "What's it really like?"

"Like love," Luke said. "It's like love."

"How do I know you're not lying? Or that you're really there? Or that you haven't been altered by the minds with you?"

"You don't."

Tears ran down his face, washing away the traces of dirt left on the skin by his morning walk to the Representative Building. He thought about the others, of their hopes, of their dreams, of the losses they had already suffered to the drug. He thought about Angry Rose, and her refusal to forgive her friend for changing. And of stardrift itself, of surrendering himself to the drug, feeling that glow, feeling that connection, feeling loneliness slip away. He thought about all these things, the Litany a counterpoint behind them, before the word "Yes" echoed in the room, and the Solin moved forward, sting quivering and poised.

58

## *Afternotes*

*This story was written at Clarion West for Andy Duncan's week, where one classmate referred to it as the "Stick your head in this hole, there's cookies and kittens on the other side" story. It's an attempt to talk about issues of addiction, a theme that comes out of my own family history, and the Litany is a reference to the Serenity Prayer. It originally appeared in Abyss & Apex under the editorship of Wendy S. Delmater.*

*A rutter is a mariner's guide, used in the late medieval period through modern days.*

# SEEKING NOTHING

"REMEMBER THAT THEY'RE NOT LIKE you nor I, boy," Uncle Abraham said, his voice dusty as ash. "They're not human. Elder Samuel says the soul stays with the original body, and that's the real reason clones are classified Subhuman."

Sean buttoned his collar and adjusted its two ornamental pips. The uniform had come out of its package smelling of sharp chemicals and acrid plastic, cheap gear suitable for his low status occupation. The front hall mirror showed him pale and nervous, but ready to go on his first assignment. He'd hoped for better than working with clones. Jeb had made steward on a cruiser, Hank was going to be a tug pilot. He'd hadn't thought to surpass them, though he'd hoped it. Instead, here he was, ready to embark to Asiu, a planet cold and dark and ready for terraforming by the clone teams he'd be handling.

He ignored Abraham. What had the old man ever given him beside disapproval and grief? Now Sean was taking himself and his shameful activities away, leaving Abraham with nothing to disapprove of. Sean didn't look at Abraham as he said, "They're tools, Uncle. You don't need to worry. I'll be using them, not socializing with them.

Abraham grunted deep in his chest. "Just you wait," he said. "They were invented by the Red Hand, that's why we've never used them here on God's New Promise. How long is the trip again?"

"Three weeks."

"Three weeks for solitude and prayer, praise be," Abraham said.

"I'm going in cold sleep."

"Cold sleep! Why?"

"Maybe I don't think I have that much to pray about."

The elderly man grabbed the younger's shoulder, pulling him around so they stood face to face. "God sees into your heart, boy. You pray to him to keep you strong. To help you resist your foolish ways."

"Saint Francis said when we pray to God, we must be seeking nothing," he said.

Abraham said, "He was a Catholic. Here we know what prayer is for. We ask God for everything, and he gives it to us, including strength to resist temptation."

Sean's face burned. He hoped his uncle wouldn't guess at the evidence of those foolish ways in his duffel bag. Abraham had never approved of the hobby of perfumery, calling it weak and decadent. Evidence of civilization's soft taint.

But his uncle simply released him, stepped back, and shook his hand once, a single firm clasp and pump.

As Sean left, he could hear his uncle beginning to chant. He wanted to look back at the Church Elder that had raised him. Shaped him. But men didn't live for regret or sentimental farewells. That was best left to the women.

The pilot was a woman, which gave him a thrill. Her ship was built for durability, rather than speed. Sean had hoped for a courier transport. He must have had an awful lot of ill will stirred up before graduation. Or maybe this was what every new graduate got, to keep them in their place. He stood looking at it, duffel in hand.

Her name was Angry Rose, a space-scarred, olive-skinned woman. Cold eyed. When he boarded, she showed him where to put his gear. The air was full of the smell of oil and long habitation.

"I don't usually take a passenger," she said. "But I need to defray fuel costs this run. Bound for Asui, eh? Lots of ice there. Couple miners told me that they fish, but it means drilling tunnels down through the ice before they reach any place where they can drop a line. Said that the fish ain't so much fish as slugs, but that the fishing's good around the base, comes from having the sewage vents there."

He made a face and she laughed.

"You're funning me, aye?" Sean said. It can't be as bad as all that, he hoped. And the trip ... They'd flirt all the way to the edge of the atmosphere; she'd let him kiss her, maybe even go further, up to the forbidden. His schoolmates had said sin didn't exist between the planets, that in curlspace anything, everything was permitted.

But his balls crawled at the chill in her eyes as she said, "If anything, I'm glossing over the worst."

She gestured at him to follow her.

His quarters were broom-closet wide. Leaning in through the doorway, she showed him how to thumb the gravity button to make standing up lying down.

"Put what you don't want wet in the box," she said, opening and closing it by way of demonstration. "Then that button'll sluice you off, cycles water vapor through for two minutes, followed by air. Won't start with the door open like this. Water's recycled, but don't waste it. You stow in here while we're taking off."

"Wait," he said. "I'm supposed to be in cold sleep all the way."

"Yeah, about that." She rested her hand on her hip, jutting her chin out. "Coldsleeper's broken, won't be able to fix it till I swing by a Dockery. You're getting the better of the bargain, though, waking passage for the cost of sleep. Don't worry, I won't charge you for food and air. Water maybe."

He hadn't reckoned on being forced into wakeful days out in the blackness of space. The vertigo of the idea caught him up and he reached out to touch the wall. She pushed him towards the sleeper, and he reeled.

"I'll com when it's all right to come out."

But it was at least twenty minutes after the onset of the weightlessness of space that her voice spat from the intercom: "Out the door and follow the red line till you see yellow, and take that."

Snaking through a crawl of tunnels punctuated by one wider lockspace, the thumbwidth yellow line led him to the main room. Boxes and netted goods pressed inward, but there was enough space for Rose to sprawl on a couch, pointing him towards a lumpy chair.

"Exercise room in there with a runner and weights," she said, pointing. "You can fix yourself food in the galley—we're not a pleasure liner, and

I don't cook for passengers. Stay out of the red-taped drawer, that's my private stash." She gave him a level look. "And here's the thing—I don't want to hear your life story or tell you mine or sit around bonding. If I'm exercising, you stay out. You don't expect conversation from me and I don't expect any from you. There's plenty of tapevids and a shelf of printies."

That was the longest conversation he had with her for the rest of the voyage. He thought that every once in a while he caught her looking at him, but he wasn't sure. He hadn't interacted with an unchaperoned woman since days of childhood parties. He felt as though half his brain had been removed when he was around her—he wasn't sure what to say, what to do, even how to smile without it looking as though he were leering.

He would have liked to work with his hobby to pass the time. But the ship's air scrubbers were old and tottery as it was. He didn't want to bring Rose's wrath down on him for overstretching them. He went so far as to open his kit, trace his finger along the tiny bottles of fixatives and bases, the droppers, the synthesizer that had cost him three years of after-school extra chores.

Abraham had never been willing to give him money. Sean had worked where he could, anything for a slim credit, whenever and wherever. He'd read the Bible to Widow Jonas, sitting in her too hot parlor feeling her fawn over him. He'd worked in the fields, and one hot summer in a communal kitchen. And worse than that, on occasion.

He had learned about the perfumes from his mother. She had distilled scents where she could, trying to break the bleakness of the planet she'd been brought to as a paid bride. But she hadn't been able to hack it, and once her contract was up—three sons for Sean's father, she'd left. Not her fault that her husband and two of those boys died soon after in a fever summer. Not her fault that her oldest son, Sean, was left to Abraham at five, with only memories of her, her *fougere*, the smell of lavender and rosemary, the merest hint of tomato leaves... He'd spent years trying to replicate it. Unsuccessful years. He folded the case's lid back down.

In Asiu, he'd have his own quarters and leisure time to blend scents. He'd create the scents that the teams knew each other by. Only a nose

as delicate, as nuanced, as his could create something and then verify that the replicator had given the clones the right scent.

To pass the time, he read books on clone psychology, all of which seemed to contradict each other. *Use isolation as punishment*, one said, while another advised, *Never split clone families apart for more than a few days under any circumstances—the stress will undermine their sanity in an irreparable way.* He read about the genetic twist that effectively lobotomized them, removed their sense of selfness.

The cautions seemed excessive to him. After all, he'd endured weeks of isolation as a child, sent away to Exalted. It had been worst for him there than most. He'd wet the bed each night and laid awake, shivering and cold in the stink of it. He'd prayed all through those nights. But his sanity was intact, and God had sustained him, even though he would have never admitted that to Abraham.

But did God watch over clones? The Writings said not—clones were the same as animals, and God had not granted them souls.

He put down the reader and stared at the window screen. It displayed the mist and cold of curlspace, curdled amniotic fluid. Was he being reborn, in God's eyes? Was he being sent forth—to witness, to question, to preach?

Asui was the smell of steel and ozone, the air so cold that it bit at the inside of his nose, stiffening the sensitive tissue there. He made his way from the ship, head lowered, trying to blink away ice, in a flurry of wind and particles so thick and hard that it couldn't be called snow, rather a barrage of pea-sized hail. He followed the orange cord someone had strung along the ground and found himself in a plascrete Quonset hut where a column-shaped heater battled to put out heat, managing to keep a meter-wide space livable.

A parka-ed clerk checked Sean's billet. "Your shuttle's been waiting an hour," she snapped, and shoved him back out the door into the wind. He stumbled, bewildered, along another orange line until he found the shuttle and banged on the side to be allowed in. He clambered up the ladder barely in time; it folded in after him with malicious speed.

Inside the shuttle there was the smell of coffee and two men playing cards. They both looked up and grunted, almost in unison,

but not quite. For a moment the similarity threw him—were clones driving the shuttle? Surely that was too much responsibility for them. Then he noted the difference in features and realized the two were not so identical—brothers, perhaps, or cousins.

They didn't say anything, just gestured him to a seat. The shuttle was mostly unoccupied seats, twenty in five rows of four, the center set facing inward as though quizzing each other, an oval window set between each pair. He settled into one of those and stared at the unpersoned window across the aisle from him. Towards the front, a couple of heads sat. He couldn't tell anything about them. They bent together as though conferring, and then one rose slightly, turned in their seat to look back.

Their face was the same as the card-players, and the mirroring effect was disorienting somehow. They glanced at him, gaze skittering across his face, then flushed, slid back into their seat, leaned over to speak with their partner again.

He leaned back against the paper-thin cushions and tried to relax. His kit was tucked under his feet. He braced them against it as the shuttle jolted into motion and the snowy vista outside was replaced with more snowy vista.

☉▪▪▪▪▬▬

The station was just an impression of more snow before he was bundled into a squat building, its walls a pistachio green intended to be soothing. He followed the shuttle crew through a green hallway into a green room.

The woman in front of him was burly and muscular, broad shoulders suggesting life in heavy gravity, hair cut short and sensible. Broken capillaries scattered her face with fretwork as she said, "Sean Marksman?"

He nodded, setting his case down and rising again. He felt an absurd desire to stoop, reduce the difference in their heights.

She didn't seem to notice. "I'm Ghira Connell. Company rep on base. I'll give you the tour, show you where to drop your gear."

At least he had his own room, twice the size of his ship berth, a cot bumping into a small metal dresser, a fold-down two-in-one desk/com unit, a window the size of his fists pressed together, cloudy glass showing more snow.

He shoved his things under the cot, followed Ghira through more hallways.

"The clone bunks." She tapped the glass window of a door. He peered through the slit to see a space barely bigger than his own, six chest-wide bunks.

"They're all working now."

"Laying the tunnels?"

"That's the section of the project we're on right now, yeah. You've done your homework, Marksman." She studied him like a specimen, then turned. "C'mon, I'll take you to the canteen."

"How many personnel on base?" he asked, following her.

"Sixteen of us, eight hundred clones. They're not really clones, per se, of course. Created beings, straight from the pump and chump machines."

He blinked. "Is that the usual ratio?"

"No. We're worker-stressed. So we want to get you up to speed as soon as possible." She paused. He almost bumped into her.

"Look," she said. "I need to warn you, no preachy stuff."

"Huh?" he managed.

"Last guy we had from one of the fundie planets, he pissed everyone off, trying to convert them. He kept printing out lists of helpful suggestions on how they could find God, pinning them up. People didn't mind too much at first, but it got tiresome when he got to talking as well."

"Oh," he said. "That's not my sort of thing at all. I don't really believe, it's why I left." Still, it was hopeful people had tolerated difference, up to a point. They'd be patient with him as he adjusted. "You said people didn't mind too much, though?"

"Course not," she said. "Always need new toilet paper, good to have extra handy."

◎▬▬▬▬

Before the canteen, they visited the green infirmary. All of the clones there had the features he'd noticed on the shuttle.

Something odd with one on a table towards the back. He went over to it, pulled the sheet down over the face—they left their dead in the open here?—and was appalled.

"This man has four arms!"

The chest swelled unnaturally with extra muscles. The flesh around

the lower limbs looked diseased, raddled. He noted that only the upper pair had patches of hair underneath them.

"Some of the handlers experiment—they call it sculpting," Ghira said. "Most of the staff don't do it. It's a complex, time-consuming process. Most often the results aren't viable, like this one."

He stared at the body, repulsed and fascinated.

Ghira went up to a cot that held a live clone.

"How are you doing?" she said to it.

The face stared up at her. "Where are the rest?" it asked. "Are we broken?"

"You will be all right," she said, and patted its shoulder. She beckoned and Sean followed her out into the green hallway.

"What did it mean, broken?" he asked.

"Teams break when they don't have a full complement. We have to add substitutes, but it's tricky. That's one of the reasons we requested you. Your doc file says you have experience with pheromones, scent alteration? That's how we get them to accept each other."

"It's only a hobby," he said.

"We're giving you a full team, just one to start with, but you can help with the other teams, fixing them. We supply two other bases with clones—new teams go out each week."

They entered the canteen. He faced a phalanx of hostile stares. Whoever he was replacing had not been liked, and they expected the same of him. So he sat in a corner and watched for now. Should he try to make friends? Ghira seemed congenial enough, but everyone seemed to like her. Perhaps she'd be his passport to acceptance.

◉▬▬▬

In the days that came, though, he didn't find himself making friends. It was his background. They all assumed he'd disapprove of their words and actions, pre-emptively dismissed him. At night he tried to replicate the scents of home, cleanser and Abraham's slightly sweet, old-man smell but none of them were right.

His clones, oddly enough, were the closest he had to friends. They called him sir, and did whatever he asked, cheerfully, uncomplainingly, six identical faces. He tried to give them names, but the concept seemed unfamiliar to them. Come evening, they ate and changed, and then piled into their tiny room. Sometimes they shared bunks, not so much

for sex, as far as he could tell, but for the sake of skin against skin, like puppies in a pile. It seemed a human urge to him, but he knew they were not human. Just things, things that mimicked humanity.

After a week, he found himself slightly more accepted by the four men who called themselves Sculptors, themselves regarded as odd by the others. Social misfits together. Their leader, Pat Brig, showed him creations as though daring him to protest, things worked in flesh that were not human so much as furniture. He steeled his face, did not recoil, even when Pat showed him what he called "a sleeve." The machine could be used to create the humanoid clones or it could create beings like this, all flesh and no soul.

"Use that to satisfy yourself," Pat said. "Self lubricating. Better than a woman, doesn't talk back."

He thrust it towards Sean, who took it reluctantly, a baby sized cylinder of flesh, its surface blood-warm.

"Absorbs light and a feeding mist," Pat said. "You can have that one. I'm working on a better." He patted the machine beside him. "Put in a clone and the right instructions, and you can make them into whatever you want. You don't need to worry, I took all the brain out of that one, left only the autonomous functions."

Sean searched for excuses, finally said, "I want to keep my quarters sterile, when I'm working on scents. Thanks though."

He passed it back to Pat, who stood looking at it. Sean could tell he'd failed some test.

"Man needs satisfaction some way," Pat said. "Everyone here's paired or hooked up that's going to be."

It was true that he was frustrated. At night when he was showering, he touched himself and let his fantasies play out. The spaceship pilot, yielding to him in curlspace. Ghira, showing him exactly how friendly she could be. Women back home, the few he'd known.

Sometimes, he thought about the clones. Their skin, vat fresh and taut. Muscular and lithe. He thought some of the others might use them that way, but if so, it was kept secret. Something everyone knew but didn't talk about. Or maybe they talked about it, but not to him. The outcast. The religious. They thought he'd disapprove.

He had weekly letters from Abraham, hand-written, although printed out on plas. They always started with a Bible text, then related it to what had been happening at home. Crops failed because God was

testing them. A girl was stoned because she was suspected of being a witch. At Exalted, a cabin of boys caught fire and they all died. More of God's tests. Always ending with an exhortation to pray, to ask God what He wanted of Sean.

He tried, he really did. He would sit down at a canteen table and make conversation, but it was always stilted. They talked about recent vids, but he had no vid unit—they were forbidden on God's New Promise, and he had never acquired the habit. He watched some in the common area, and they just bewildered him. A wealth of flesh seemed to be the only coherent theme.

He talked to Pat, not about the vid, but the sculptures. "Why do you make them into new things?"

"It's a way to pass the time," Pat said. "I make ... well, you've seen the sort of things I like to make, conveniences. Vonda tries to make them beautiful. Avram wants to see if different shapes are better adapted to this place. And Lilo, he just likes to play."

So he spent time working on the scent work. It was solitary, but it was useful, and the others approved when he succeeded on fixing a team, making a clone smell right to the others, letting them accept it as part of them. He was good at it, in a way the others were not—he could smell an individual and then replicate the scent.

Pat liked it; he made two flesh sleeves that would interact with each other, drawn by the scent.

"It's as though the team bond was instinctual," he said, watching them bump into each other. "Maybe that's part of the make-up. What do you think?"

But Sean didn't reply. He was thinking about last night. He had stopped one of his clones before it went into the chamber.

"Would you like to sleep in my quarters tonight?" he had whispered, feeling shame burn along his cheekbones. When he was a boy, he'd made money doing this for older men. Abraham would have killed him if he'd known. But he'd needed components for his perfumes, and the men paid well.

And they had loved him, he thought, at least for a little while. And now the clone would love him for a little while, and he would touch it as they had him.

But it only looked at him with a pleasant, uncomprehending smile,

and went into the chamber where its brothers awaited. By now he was sure they shared sex, but not in pairs. All together. It ran through his veins, the realization.

"I said, what do you think?" Pat repeated, and Sean pulled himself back.

"I don't know," he said. "They guard the tech pretty carefully."

Pat snorted. "Course the company does. Wouldn't want one of us escaping with trade secrets, taking them to some other corp."

Sean looked at the machine.

"Want to take a test spin?" Pat asked with a leer. "Works reshaping humans too. Give yourself a new package."

He chuckled nervously. "People really do that?"

"Sheila fixes her face in it all the time," Pat said cheerfully. "Watch her. One day blue eyes, the next green."

He glanced back when they left the lab. The machine sat humming to itself. The sleeves were on the floor, nuzzling each other, rippling with the pleasure of touch. That was all any of them wanted, he thought. To touch. To be touched in turn.

A company directive came around that they were supposed to refer to the clones as "units." Ghira read it aloud to them over dinner.

"Don't want us getting them confused with humans," Pat sneered.

There wasn't too much chance of that, Sean thought. But he wondered about the donors, the men or women whose genetic material had gone into developing the first units. Who were still being created, again and again.

"What happens to the soul, when you make it over and over?" he asked Pat. "Your creatures ... isn't it a kind of slavery? Even if they don't know it?"

Pat's face was angry.

"Should have figured you'd revert to form, sooner or later," he said, and spat on the floor. "Fundie planets are all the same, full of soo-perior types."

Sean gazed after Pat as he left, distressed. He hadn't meant to

say anything. He looked around and all he saw were hostile eyes, even though they were doing the courtesy of pretending they hadn't heard the argument.

Even Ghira looked away.

⊙▬▬▬

Abraham's letter read: *Elder Wilson came by to ask after you. You never told me you knew him, boy. I would have warned you off—his theology is shaky, his morals proven dubious. You remember the scandal, back when he was teaching. Even far away, you're causing me worry, Sean.*

Wilson's generosity had bought the tiny synthesizer that let him make pheronomes. Without that, he might have never gotten away from God's New Freedom.

But now that he was gone, he missed it. Everything was bewildering to him. Everything was different. Someone had put one of the flesh sleeves in his quarter. Threat? Hazing ritual? Message? *You're not like us,* it meant, perhaps. *You can't touch any of us, here's a substitute.*

He put it out in the hallway, watched it slither away. It had been pleasant to touch it, but he didn't want to keep it, didn't want them thinking they were right, he was an outcast who could only touch made things. Never other people.

Despite himself, he knelt in prayer beside the cot.

"I don't know what to do," he said. "Please tell me, God."

The door swung open and Pat was glaring at him. "You just threw it out in the hallway?" he shouted. "We have to account for materials, you know! It got outside, froze!"

The mound of flesh in Pat's arms dripped with melting ice.

Sean lurched to his feet.

"No, no, you stay there and pray," Pat said sarcastically. The door swung shut behind him. Sean could only imagine the stories that would circulate. They'd think he'd reverted to form, that he'd be forcing his beliefs on them like the last one, who had vanished under slightly suspicious circumstances, from all he'd been able to tell.

What was it about his faith that made them think he was sanctimonious? What was it about his faith that drove them away? He had never tried to spread the word, but he had still bowed his head

in grace the first few meals until he had caught them staring. It had never occurred to him that some just began eating, without thinking about the meal, where it came from, how lucky they were to have it.

He groaned aloud.

No one spoke to him anymore, except to ask him to match a scent. He was useful for the moment. But useful could still mean untouchable.

A black bordered envelope tucked in his mail slot. "We regret to inform you ... " He put it down. Uncle Abraham dead. All his ties to the past broken, and no new ones to tie him down, to keep him from flying into the future.

There was a broken team that had lost a member. It was easy to program the machine. Easier yet to create the right scent. And then to enter the crowded room, not knowing if they would accept him.

Hands were on him. They drew him down into the pile. Tears rolled down his face. Someone licked them away. Someone hugged him. He put his hands out and touched them, and was touched, and something in his soul relaxed with a shudder, even as something else howled and was cast out into the darkness.

For a while Ghira wondered where Sean Marksman had gone. Speculation maintained that he had gone mad (if he wasn't already, bearing in mind his origin), gone out to freeze in the darkness, after fixing one last team. Rumor said Pat had killed him, recreated him. She didn't believe that. Pat would have known he couldn't get away with it again.

But even as Ghira was dispatching the load of clones to another base, even when she passed close enough that he could have touched her sleeve, she did not look at them, and so he left, his clone brothers and he, and he never prayed again, as long as he lived.

## Afternotes

*Angry Rose reappears in this story, but isn't the focus. Having grown up in Indiana, I am both fascinated and repelled by fundamentalist Christianity, and the idea of a planet governed by such a group is a little scary. Touch is, to me, one of the basic human needs and so I wanted to write about being isolated from those around you, and how it's possible to be lonely even among a crowd.*

*I wanted my hero to have an interesting hobby, and perfumery is something that's fascinated me ever since reading Patrick Suskind's novel,* Perfume.

*This originally appeared in* Daily Science Fiction, *where it was selected by publication by editors Michele Barasso and Jonathan Laden.*

# A Querulous Flute
# of Bone

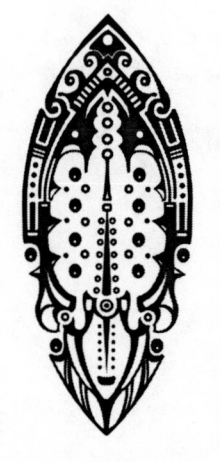 THERE ARE, WHEREVER WEALTH HAS accumulated enough to create the idle, those who collect things. Such collections may vary from those who catalog every cast off bit of flesh or chitin they shed to those who look outside themselves for art, or titillation, or an oblivion in which they might forget everyday life. They may consist of the most mundane objects: string, or chewed up paper, or broken teacups, for example—or take on outré forms: dioramas made of nihlex bone (death to be found with in certain areas), or squares of cloth exposed to the Smog, prized for the oracular patterns of dirt left deposited on the fabric, or the tiny snowflakes of metal that are said to have fallen into the world during an Opening over a century ago.

Ector was such a collector. S/he was one of the Geniod, whose gender varies according to mood, and location, and other private considerations, and who are known, in the face of great trauma, to forget who they are and become entirely different personalities, their old selves never to be resumed or spoken of. Some races adulate them for this, others mock them, and such excess has driven the Geniod to be a race that keeps to itself, not by law, but by choice.

Ector was an oddity in its own preferences, for it was willing to travel, to go farther than the rest of its race, driven by the desire to augment its collection, choosing to focus only on its quest.

The items it sought, ranging up and down the Tube in expeditions

funded by two sets of indulgent grandparents and a much less indulgent set of parents, were things that could be considered metaphors for the world and the state of those in it. In this pursuit, it followed the strictures of the philosopher-king Nackle, who described the emotions that such objects evoked in the beholder in one 500-page monograph and the intellectual effect of such exposure in a second, even longer, volume.

Ector had studied at the knee of an ancient Human who had himself been instructed by Nackle, and the teaching had impressed it with a gravity and depth of the sort that scores the soul and directs all its movements in later years. Its search was a tribute to Nackle's ideas, for it looked for the things that Nackle posited existed, which could only be discovered by matching the emotion they evoked with that described in Nackle's pages, a task that required the laborious memorization of all of the philosopher's works.

Nackle's theory, insofar as such a thing can be simplified, was this: twenty one types of emotion exist in the world. Certain artifacts create emotions in the viewer, emotions unaffected by the viewer's history or idiosyncrasies of personality, but which are basic to the existence of all intelligent creatures. There are literally hundreds of sub-emotions, ranging from a soul's regret when it wishes to sing but cannot, to the joy of carrying on one's ancestral line in the face of tremendous adversity. To find the artifacts that replicated the base emotion, the one from which all the smaller sub-emotions sprang, one must move through a progression of refinement of the senses, created by the search for and exposure to artifacts exemplifying the emotions Nackle described.

This simplification would be objected to by most of Nackle's followers, who would point to subtleties of one kind or another, but truth be told, the theory was uncomplicated. It was the lengthy cataloging of emotions that gave the philosophy density rather than any complex thought.

As such, it was relatively easy to follow and Ector intended to devote its life to the process. It demanded a certain purity of thought, a willingness not to mire oneself in the petty details of life that Ector was more than happy to embrace, even though at times it felt a little lonely in the superiority of its perceptions. It eschewed most pleasures, and had never moved beyond the simplest gender, the one that everyone

has, and had never thought of itself as he or she.

As is often the way in this world (or any other), Ector had a rival in its ambitions, Corint, another Geniod who had studied at the same philosopher's knee and delighted in challenging all of Ector's words in class, to the point where it sometimes feared to speak and would keep silent until the other's glee in pronouncements, often wrong, moved it to contradict what Corint said. The rivalry was bitter as tomb-wine, as bright as the sunstrip at its most fervid mid-day heat.

They thwarted each other whenever they could, until the action became second nature, unquestionable. Ector would search for the horn that had inspired melancholy for traditions that had faded into the past, only to find Corint there first, tucking it away in its pouch with a smile as greasy as the black oil that seeps near the rocks on which the iron and gears of the city of Indrus are perched. Or Corint would arrive at the Watershed shop rumored to hold the kaleidoscopic marble of joy in complexity of color and see Ector standing in the doorway, balancing it in his palm, watching hues roil in its depths.

They had chased each other downward this time, a journey through nest villages and bridge towns and basket farms. While in a cavern city's tavern chamber, Ector had overheard a scrap of conversation indicating it might have stumbled across a trail that would lead to an artifact falling in a category that had previously proved frustrating with its elusiveness: appreciation. This artifact might, Ector thought, actually lead its perception to spring along the ladder more than a few rungs; it was supposed to induce the appreciation of something's innate qualities. Rumor held that those capable of mastering it became able to make wonderful things: paper masks that spoke, stews that made the eater capable of dancing all day and night, or clothing that concealed a wearer's every defect until they were so noble and upright in appearance that populaces flocked to elect them mayor or ruler or demagogue or whatever form of leadership they practiced.

Paradoxically, the trail led Ector upward and back to a Geniod village, Halah, that it had not visited since a child so small that it had barely learned to walk on its own feet. The village was famed for its hot springs, and the baths that had been carved out of the rock in order to allow visitors to take the waters, some of which smelled of sulfur, others of copper, and others of harder to identify minerals. All that

Ector remembered of the place was the scented moisture of the air, and the trouble that its occupants had to take to scrub the black mold off their doorsteps and walls and other surfaces, lest it grow so shaggy and furry that it overran the place until it became one of the ghost towns that sometimes can be found along the Tube, places where one problem or another has ousted the inhabitants: plague or parasites or over-eager bandits.

It left in the time before dawn, trusting that Corint would still be sleeping and that when it woke, the rival would interrogate the innkeeper and be given the false story that Ector had planted, that Ector had taken the basket lift downward, headed to the savage tunnel jungle that was said to lurk only a few leagues on. It laughed to think of Corint, bewildered, searching in vain among fruitless dangers. It did not wish the other dead, but disaccomodated, perhaps even to a physical extent, was not unwelcome.

Then Ector thought that perhaps such vengeful contemplation was unworthy, would act to derange the perceptions, making them incapable of appreciating nuance. As it walked, taking the long spiraling trail that wound upward to the next settlement, it sorted through the objects that it carried about its person, the heart of its collection, twenty one objects, each representing advancement along a separate line of comprehension, towards perfect knowledge of the original emotion, and took each out in turn and looked at it, refreshing its knowledge of the object's essence and helping sway its soul away from any possible sullying of its evolving nature.

When Ector arrived at Halah, which was located inside a series of caverns, each with its own set of springs and a clever alignment of mirrors reflecting light from the sunstrip into its depths, the village smelled just as it remembered, a wet smell that crept inside the lungs and lingered there, moistly caressing the tissues until they burned. It was night so it took a room at an inn in the first cavern, thinking to go and look in the neighborhood where the artifact had been secreted, according to the overheard conversation. It occurred to him, a brief paranoid thought, that perhaps Corint had planted the conversation to divert its rival away from something else.

The inn, which took advantage of the direct light seeping in through the entrance, was built of stone, and unlike most, had several stories, due to the permissive height of the cavern. When Ector roused in the morning, from its room on the third floor, it could hear the sounds of the village and the inn, the sort of sounds that are pleasant when you're lingering in bed, conscious that you have no deadline. It drowsed, planning the day. The search would begin immediately after breakfast. What would the object look like? All Ector had to go on was the description of the emotions it evoked.

It was coming down the stairs. It saw her and became a him in an instant.

He stopped, dead still, on the third step, to the dismay of the servant following him, a Geniod with a load of linens in her arms, for she collided with him with a whoof, the force throwing the fabric up into the air until for a moment Ector was suspended as though in white clouds, able only to see the thing that had caught his attention.

It is of little use to describe what distinguishes a Geniod's sense of beauty when it comes to their own species: a certain evenness of features, a nose that slanted rather than curved, a particular curl to a fanged eyetooth.

Suffice it to say that she was beautiful to Ector, and he could feel changes deep in his body as he responded to her.

Ignoring the sputtering of the servant as she gathered up the cloth, he stared.

On her part, she took no notice, though it was unclear whether this was due to obliviousness or disdain, vanishing through a doorway that he thought might lead to the kitchen.

Once she had gone through that door, it was as though the spell that had imprisoned him, allowing him only to look and breath and hear the hammering of his heart, had been broken and he could move again. He knelt to help the maid with the last of the linens, but she only glowered, and did not thank him for it.

He took a Kihlain coin from his pocket and held it up, letting its light waver over her features, which smoothed into a mask as she eyed its promise and waited for him to speak.

"The person who just went through that door," he said, pointing. "Who is she?"

"That be the child of this household," the maid said. "The only heir

and well-loved. When you eat here, you be eating the food that comes from her pots. She's famous for it." She puffed a little with pride but said nothing more, eyes fixed on the coin in his hand.

He spun it in his fingers, let it roll over his knuckles and dance back into his hand. He felt the weight of the moment on his shoulders; slowly it squeezed the words out of him, "And her name?"

"Trice," the maid said, and snatched the coin before it fell, because the syllables echoed in his ears like singing bells until he could think of nothing else.

⊙▪▬▬▬

He did not go search for his artifact that day. Instead he lingered over his meal, trying to find traces of her in the excellent soup, the limpid beer, the sausages as fat and feisty as fighting pups. Sometimes she came out, bringing a dish to the sideboard, and he tried to be the first to reach it, to lay his fingers where hers had touched, as though he could absorb knowledge of her through his skin.

Finally they cleared away, and he kept sitting there in the common room, waiting. After near to an hour, she emerged, her apron put aside, and a basket on her arm.

Springing to his feet, he approached, asking if she were going forth to harvest fungi. When she nodded, he introduced himself and volunteered to carry her basket.

For a moment, he thought she would refuse him, and the shy blush that rode her cheeks only made her all the more entrancing, for it is a known thing that the entity which proves elusive is ever more alluring than that which comes readily to the hand. But in the end, she assented, and he followed at her heels, holding the basket.

Little conversation passed between them, and when he asked her questions, her answers were short and brief of detail. But he didn't mind, because every sound from her mouth made him tingle from his head to his toes.

When they returned, he was horrified to see Corint at the common fire, giving him a sardonic look as it noted his newly-donned masculinity. But he comforted himself with the thought that his rival would go after the artifact, rather than this new treasure that Ector had found. In fact, he decided, he would give the rival all the information he had, and let Corint have the joy of its discovery.

He took care, though, to give Trice the coldest of nods. There was no

sense in giving Corint any clue what was happening.

When he went upstairs, he took his pack out from under the bed and spread out its contents. He took up his most recent acquisition, a querulous flute of bone, its origin unknown, its surface spiderwebbed with fine cracks. Nackle said that one of the main emotions was fear, but that all fears came from a particular type, the fear of the world lest it hurt one. Ector put his lips to the mouthpiece and blew, so softly that it was less than a baby's first breath. The sound that emerged was sad and scared and resolute, but he could not narrow it down, because it was fear, he was sure of that, but the nuances in it were unfamiliar.

It occurred to him that if he fell in love, he would no doubt blunt his perceptions, undo all the careful work that he had undertaken to fine-tune his consciousness and make him the excellent artifact hunter he had become. But it didn't matter. He had a new purpose now.

He would write to his parents, tell them he had decided to settle in Halah. He would study to become a merchant, for what better way could there be to employ all the knowledge he had gathered in his wide-ranging quest? He was better traveled than the vast majority of his race, and he might as well use the fruits of that travel to earn a living that would make him a desirable partner. His parents would be bewildered but pleased; his grandparents less so of either, but equally ready to send him tokens of affectionate well-wishes in his new home: a blanket of knotted mushroom fiber and ceramic jars of fermented pickled cabbage.

He listened to the sounds of the inn all around. Someone in the room below him was walking back and forth, an impatient, thinking pace, and Ector wondered what might concern them. Downstairs was the noise of revelry and the beginnings of the dinner smells, wafts of scent that crept under his door curtain to speak to him of cinnamon and sage and browned butter with fragments of garlic sizzling in it.

He could scarcely wait for dinner, but he bided his time, went down only when he heard other footsteps descending.

The food was unimaginably good. Roots broke open to send up steam, their insides flecked with pepper, and a tangy, pickley sauce overlaid the fresh greens. The meat was unfamiliar, but another diner said it was a bird newly come to this level, migrated from somewhere down below.

"They say it means an Opening is coming soon," Ector's fellow diner

said, nodding wisely. "There are always signs and portents."

Ector forked another bite of meat and ate it. It was delicious, soaked in a sauce unexpectedly sweet and savory all in the same mouthful. The savor thrilled through him, and he closed his eyes, trying to pick out every nuance of the spices.

When he opened them, he saw Corint and Trice together, talking.

Fear clamped his legs and arms, a sense of panic that ran through him like electricity, made him as unable to move as an abandoned puppet. And even as he stared across the room, helpless, Corint's eyes met his and his rival smiled, letting Ector see his own newly-chosen gender, rivals even in this.

⊙▬▬▬▬

He did not want to talk to him, but he had to. Surely Corint could be warned off, or appealed to, or bought off? Trice was not an artifact, after all.

But, as it turned out, Corint had other suspicions regarding her and artifacts.

"The food's the clue," he said to Ector over too much wine, hearty swallows of it following slivers of cheese. "Is that how you found her too?"

Ector had learned, long ago, that silence often elicited more information than you thought it would. To other people, it often implied that you knew much much more than you were saying, and this proved the case with Corint. "Of course it was," he said before Ector could fill in anything else. "How could anyone produce such food unless they had learned to appreciate the ingredients, to gather them together in a jigsaw of tastes that fit so smoothly together that you cannot tell where one leaves off and the next begins?" He sighed, and his breath rippled across the surface of the carved stone cup in front of him. "Imagine that such a pretty young woman could hold the key to such a thing! She must have found it somewhere. Oh course I became male, it's clearly the best way to gain her trust."

Relief washed through Ector. Corint wanted the artifact he thought Trice must have, not Trice herself and now that Ector considered it, of course that would be why the food at the inn was so extraordinary. In contemplating the artifact, Trice must have absorbed its lesson well, in order to create such dishes.

Despite all their past difficulties, the happiness that surged through

him at this realization made him regard Corint, good old Corint, always reliable, always there, differently. He decided that honesty would be the best policy. He would be a new, changed being now, one who spoke the truth in a way worthy of the woman he adored.

"I will help you find the artifact," he said earnestly. "All I want is Trice." He felt a pang at the thought of an artifact in Corint's hands, he couldn't help that, it was old habit, but he pushed it aside. What he was seeking was much better.

Corint regarded him with a trace of suspicion that faded at the sincerity evident in Ector's face.

"Very well," he said. "Help me with that, and I will help you in turn."

⊙▪▪▪▬

True to his word, Ector broached the word of the artifact the next day while he and Trice were gathering pallid watercress from the river that spilled into the Tube near the village's entrance. He did so delicately. He didn't want her to think that he attributed her skill at cookery with some force outside herself; he must let her know that he acknowledged it as part of herself, intrinsic. She had cultivated the sensibility that allowed her to cook so through no-doubt unconscious contemplation of the artifact (for she had avowed no knowledge whatsoever of Nackle when Ector had brought up the topic the day before.)

But when he edged towards the subject, she skittered away, sought refuge in all manner of topics: the mating habits of crawdads, the sounds of dying unicorns, the secret name of the Nihilex Queen and whether that entity remained the same person from year to year.

At length he gave up. She seemed relieved.

⊙▪▪▪▬

That night in his room, listening to the sounds of the village through the open window, hearing distant snores and stony echoes, he thought about when all his heart had been given to artifact hunting, less than a week ago.

Those days seemed as distant as though they had fallen down the Tube like an addled suicide, leaving only their confused and water-colored ghosts behind. He remembered the fever of finding an object that completed a series, the glossy joy that could color days on end, at

least until the itch for some other part of the chain drove him elsewhere. Should he give what he had collected already, what he carried with him, to Corint? His fellow was one of the few who could appreciate the nuances of some of the objects; to do anything else was to waste them, surely, and if he kept his collection, wouldn't it just nag at him to go back to it, like the wine kept for sickness and cooking eats at an alcoholic through mere knowledge of its location?

He would wait. He would see.

He played his flute long into the night.

As the days wore on, he began to think Trice was some sort of Guardian; whatever artifact inspired her cooking was also her hereditary charge. Such things were not unknown; many of the artifacts that Nackle described had guardians of one kind or another.

If this were the case, to get the object and persuade his rival away, he must ask her to betray her order. He agonized over the ethics of the situation—what would Nackle have done, under what emotion would this worry have been placed, and what sort of artifact could possibly evoke it, other than the living one that was Trice, built of sinew and bone, of blood and hair and hands and eyes?

She knew he was wooing her, she acknowledged it, and let him speak of love and what he had to offer. But let the slightest syllable close to artifact cross his lips and she was on to other subjects, grown cold and distant one time, flurried and a mass of distraction the next.

He put on weight, eating deep of her dishes every morning, every evening. His pants were tight, and he discarded his belt entirely, then went to the tailor and ordered two new sets of clothes for everyday. He studied at the merchant's guild, working towards his license, and continued to stay at the village inn, despite the lack of economy the choice represented, since he could have (and was offered the chance to, more than once) rented a room in someone's house.

Corint also confessed himself unable to elicit any information from Trice about the artifact that allowed her to cook so well, despite his many conversations with her and his offers to assist her in the kitchen during the day, peeling roots, washing greens, and engaging in a myriad more chores that were, he told Ector, designed to find a chance

to snoop and discover where Trice had hidden the artifact.

It seemed to Ector that as time wore on, the girl's parents regarded him with a certain sympathy. Sometimes they waved aside the payment for an evening meal, saying it was on the house since he was such a faithful customer. It unnerved him, the look in their eyes, it made all will ooze from his veins.

He tried to stop playing the flute at night, but it soothed him. It let him sleep. Unless he played it, he found himself waking throughout the night, every time there was a footfall or a distant conversation. The inn was in the cavern closest to the Tube and sometimes he could even hear the wind rushing there, a sound almost as sad and lonely as the flute's.

☉▰▰▰▬

This had gone on for three weeks when he ran, by chance, into another artifact hunter, one who had not studied with the same tutor as Corint and Ector, thereby enabling an ease of interchange not always possible among fellow students. This was a human hunter, who lacked in senses but possessed the ability to make great leaps of logic. Indeed, after inviting him to a meal, she divined the circumstances in the space of time between appetizer and entrée and got him to admit to them in a series of pointed questions.

Her look, when the interrogation was over, was pitying in a way that reminded him of Trice's parents. The feeling sharpened when she tactfully steered away from discussion of his old obsession, as though it were a former lover whose new relationship might have saddened or infuriated him. The look was on his mind when he returned to the inn, determined to have it out once and for all with Trice. He would lay his heart bare, would explain all that he was thinking and feeling and hoping and perhaps in return she would embrace him or perhaps she would spurn him, but either would be better than this aimless existence, this void of not knowing what to do or say in order to gain what he so desperately wanted.

At the inn, Trice's parent stood feeding the little bats in the courtyard. The creatures flittered back and forth in unsteady flight, snatching morsels from their fingertips. The air was full of their squeaks, just on the edge of hearing, audible enough to be

annoying and yet still out of range.

Ector said, as he approached, "Is Trice in the kitchen? I must speak to her."

The parent blinked. "She's gone to be married," they said.

Ector gaped. "Married? To whom?"

"That fellow Corint."

Ector stood in silence for a moment, his lips parted but not breathing. His face twitched, just below the left eye, a persistent, maddened twitch of nerves pushed past their limit.

At length, he said, "Well. I suppose that's one way to gain her artifact."

The parent set the pan of grubs down and clasped him on the shoulder. "Ah, lad," they said. "Corint told us of your odd obsession."

"My odd obsession?" Ector said, not moving, his tone as bland as unsullied paper.

"These artifacts, the ones you seized on due to brain fever and too much studying. You must realize they are imaginary, my good fellow. Corint explained it all to us."

"Then Trice had no artifact," Ector said.

The parent gawped at him in turn. "Why would you believe such a thing?"

"Her food."

"You thought her cooking was due to some magical object?" The parent laughed, and somewhere inside there was an echo from the common room as someone there made their own joke. "Lad, she's been cooking since she was able to lift a wooden spoon, and cooking not just for her family, but for an innsworth of critics every time. It is a more demanding school for a cook than any academy."

"Corint told Trice of my ... odd obsession as well?"

"Ay, and she was hard pressed to keep you from the topic sometimes, she said. But she knew that if you were allowed to talk at length about them, you would fall prey to one of the fits that Corint described. Trice is a tender soul; she did not want to see you in such a circumstance."

Ector stood for a while longer as though absorbing all of these

things a morsel at a time, letting the meaning seep into him until he could comprehend it. His face gave nothing away, shuttered as a cliff-face window.

In later years he went back to artifact hunting, although never with the same relish that he had previously exhibited. He did not travel as far as he once had, and he never returned to the village where Trice and Corint lived.

He carried with him a packful of his artifacts. On the day that he had learned of Trice's marriage, he had returned to his room and smashed the querulous flute of bone. But then he reconstructed it, albeit in a different shape.

It was a heart-shaped thing now, with hollow tubes running through it until it was empty and as light as though it was a thought and not an actual object. Prone to turn in the hand, slicing bone-deep if you were not careful how you touched it. Sometimes he held it, because it evoked a set of emotions as deep and true as any he had ever experienced, a set that Nackle had described in the category of loss, which outweighed any fear of hurt. Indeed, that fear seemed as unimportant as the scars on his hands where the artifact had bitten time and time again, writing its own addendum to Nackle's final text.

### Afternotes

*This story was written for a shared world project created by Phillip Athans, and appeared in* Tales from the Fathomless Abyss. *The world premise is a giant tube, which opens up periodically on other worlds, sucking in beings and materials, and in which the inhabitants live on the sides in a variety of ways. I'm currently working on a novella set in the Fathomless Abyss world that draws on William S. Burroughs'* Junky *and H.P. Lovecraft's "Dreams in the Witch House," which is the scariest story I know.*

*When I sat down to write it, I knew I wanted to do something with gender, and I also wanted to model the piece on a favorite O.Henry story, "The Pimaloosa Pancakes". I found it extremely difficult to tinker with the genders in there, but it was an exceedingly interesting exercise as well.*

# ZEPPELIN FOLLIES

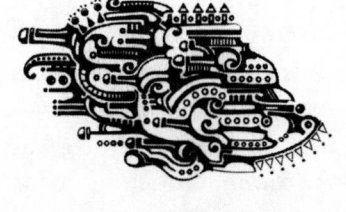

IT'S AN UNFORTUNATE FACT THAT Bodys break down with age. In this case, one of my heels was coming loose, and with two legs, that ended up being more destabilizing than if I'd opted for a model with four or six. Back before we'd split up, my girlfriend Sally had always been the one to remind me to get maintenance. We'd go together, two happy female lovers holding hands as they walked along, and sometimes people would smile when they'd see us, because we'd gotten matching Bodys in the Danish style that Sally favored.

Inside them, we were as different as night and day: Sally was dark and beautiful, and I was brown haired and ordinary, although pleasant looking, or so Sally always said, right up to the day she moved out.

So I got up early that Thursday morning and walked down the block to the Repair Shoppe to ask Laura, my mechanic, to take a look at it before work.

The shop was busy that day, and a phalanx of athletes was in, getting their stabilizers adjusted en masse and chatting about rugby scores. Like everyone else, I like to keep up on the ways to express my individuality, so I spent some time window shopping.

New models of Bodys hung along the walls: retro robotics in chrome and steel, adorned with blinking lights; the life-like human models, which I found a touch unsettling, towering like giant China dolls; and the latest line, shaped like Martian spiders, holding one's form in a

cylinder of glass, looking like collection specimens surrounded by flimsy, filamented legs. Laura insisted on taking the whole rig to run it through diagnostics—she was a Holistic Mechanic—so I took a rest booth amid the insipid strains of Stellar Music, and was preparing myself to flip through the channels on the holo screen, when someone knocked on the booth's door.

Those padded chairs are hard to shift around in for a reason. Body shops want to keep their customers down and not wandering around disturbing the other UnBodied. But I managed to get out of the bucket chair and open the door.

A Kali Suit, one of the more popular models in the Mythological series, stood there. Despite their cost, I've always thought they look tacky. There is an upper limit on the number of arms you need, which is six, in my opinion. And the wearer had twinked it out, the whole ten yards: red lacquer, a blue-skinned face mask, bindi, henna patterns on the arms, and an incense brazier in either shoulder. Only one was lit, but the blue curls of sandalwood smoke coming from it made me cough.

"Sorry," the Kali said and flicked a finger to set its internal fans into motion. The smoke swirled as it was sucked inside the suit and the set expression of the faceplate stared at me, its wearer rudely invisible behind it. Out of my Body, I was at eye level with its nipples, which were big and gold, and worked in ornate floral designs.

"I lost a screw when I was in here yesterday, and I was wondering if you'd found it," it said.

I shrugged. "Nope."

It hovered for an expectant moment until I reluctantly added, "But you're welcome to come in and take a look."

The booth wasn't very big for one person, let alone two, but I didn't want to be standing around in my UnderWear out in the shop, so I curled back up in the chair and watched the Kali. Stooping, it detached a set of fingers and sent them rummaging along the baseboards, to no avail.

"Look," I said, then decided to be polite and speak in perception-neutral forms. You never know. "Perceive," I said, "that your screw is not here and act accordingly."

The Kali's hair writhed as it considered my words.

88

Laura appeared in the doorway, my Body draped over an arm, and a flicker of disapproval visible through her faceplate as she saw the Kali.

"Miz Andrews, I think it's fixed, if you want to slip it on and check the gait," she said to me, and then, to the Kali, "I told you not to come around bothering my customers."

The Kali's faceplate cleared, and the wearer's face became apparent. Young, female, short blue hair and matching eyes, all combined in indignation.

"I'm not bothering her!" she said. "Am I bothering you?"

"Actually, I'd like to put my Body back on," I said with a touch of stiffness. I don't like standing around naked. While you expect some amount of that while you're at the mechanics, you never get used to it.

"Yeah, yeah," she said, and I felt a twinge of unmerited guilt at the hurt expressed in her voice. Reclaiming her fingers, she slipped out the booth door. "See you around."

Laura helped me back into my Body. At the ripe, mature age of 35, I'd found I preferred a classic model, suitable for business or everyday life—simple gray, plain lines, no flash or chassis augmentation, a touch of extra height so I can hit the standard two meters when Bodied. My one nod to style is a pair of butterfly vanes on the back. I don't know why I like them, but I do. On the inner surface they're shaded in vermilion and amethyst, almost metallic, almost jewel. Subtle but rich, suggesting that maybe inside the gray plastiflesh, there was something entirely different. Sometimes my job gets to me and I get carried away by my prose, but you get the picture.

I wriggled my way back into my Body, feeling its solidity settling around me, the augmented tendons and sinews adding strength to my limbs, and a new, if mechanical, grace to my movements. I ran the usual checks on my internal sensors, and then the Net hookup. One by one the icons shimmered into view at the edge of my vision: map, weather, bank, communications, news, analysis, medical, advertisements.

Laura checked the heel and nodded, satisfied.

"Need any augmentations, Miz Andrews?" she said.

"Not today."

"Got a sixth finger set on sale if you're musically inclined."

I shook my head. "I can't tell the difference between a patterdrum and a synpop. Wasted on me." My trade is words, not music, not

pictures. I paused, not sure why or what I was asking. "Hey, who was that Kali?"

Laura snorted, an odd and garbled sound as though her vocomotor had shorted out. "Mimsy? Mimsy Star. Knew her in college. Spoiled rich kid with nothing better to do than make trouble for other folks. She lives off her uncle's money—he's a big vid star on the cooking channel. Stay away from her, Miz Andrews. Nothing but trouble, I tell you."

I felt that irritation you feel when someone tells you something perfectly reasonable that you'd be doing on your own anyhow. Pressing my palm against the credit reader, I okayed the transaction with a nod and a blink, and headed out into the bleached light of the street.

It was one of those painfully bright spring days when visors shade to black and your cooling system kicks in the minute you hit the sidewalk carrier. My block's usually pretty uncomplicated, but some throwback must have been trying to raise its own luxuries again—there were bumbledrones all over the fake greenery, making futile attempts to extract pollen. Those were fine when I was a kid, but nowadays, real vegetation's a precious commodity. I eyed the bumbledrone corpses, neat pinhole laser burns through their nav systems, which marked the guard boundaries of the two real flowerboxes flanking one entrance. Even as I watched, one buzzed into range, then fell, emitting a single line of smoke, amid its dead fellows. I tried to extrapolate some new simile from it—you never know when you're going to come across something you can use, but ended up just snapshotting the image and storing it away. I was late for work as it was.

They cut us creative types slack as far as issues of late and early go, because the downstairs bunch had been bamboozled into believing that a certain amount of sitting around staring into space and waiting for the Muse to strike is part of the job. My office held three writers, one editor, and Daisy, the administrative assistant, who everyone feared.

Sure enough, as soon as I walked in, Daisy handed me a sheet of plastipaper with her latest batch of similes on it. Daisy wanted to be a

writer, and since the writers were always calling for fresh similes, she figured she'd break in that way.

"I thought of these while I was at the juice shop," she said. "Are you coming on Sunday, Addie?"

"Yeah, wouldn't miss it," I said. The annual office HyperBowl party scheduled for that weekend was one of the major perks of the job, and each year our publisher, Fitz, tries out a new batch of recipes on his team.

While that sounds as though there's not much going on in the office, it's actually the pleasantest place I've ever worked, and I've been a cog in some very big engines. Everyone gets along, mainly because Fitz jollies anyone who's in the doldrums back up and out of them, and we've got a certain amount of freedom as far as theme and structure goes. Within limits, of course—we are romance writers, after all.

I scanned down the plas, reading each of the similes. "His lips pruned like a lemon," was the most promising of them, although I did like the fruit theme that swirled like strawberry throughout them all. "Nope, nope, nope, possible with some tinkering, nope, nope, way no, and nope," I said. "You're getting better, though, kid."

Daisy took it on the chin, although I was pretty sure I saw a welling tear through the faceplate. She opaqued it as she turned away, but remembered to say, "Fitz is looking for you, Addie."

Every few weeks Fitz came through with an idea for a new line, usually from something he'd overheard in the pnematube. Plenty of time to talk to him later, I thought. I fired up my computer and started tinkering with a new script generator. We were working on a Viking line, and I'd figured out a new formula for dialogue that would eliminate the stilted tone of the last trial run they'd done, full of lines like, "Love for you festers in my soul."

But I hadn't even had the chance to get it to generate an opening scene when Fitz came in.

"Get this," he said, gesturing. "Time-traveling superhero romance."

"Baen tried that in the thirties," I said.

His face fell. Not literally, but one never knows with Fitz. He went with the Metaphorical for his suit, and it was full of quirks, like my favorite touch: shooting steam out of the ears when the emotional triggers went high enough. Right now, a swirl of clouds began to circle

over the shiny bald pate, and I kept a wary eye on them. If things got bad enough, the lightning could short a Body out for a few seconds. I hadn't gotten zapped by it yet, but some of the other writers had.

"Are you sure?" he said dubiously. "We need something new here, Addie. My inbox is full of nothing but invoices and credit-related spam. Besides, I don't know why you think you're so good at romances. I've never seen you with anyone—well, no, not since that cute little number you brought to the office party—what, a decade ago?"

"Nine years," I said. I'd thought Sally was the one. We showed up for the party in matching Bodys, ones Sally had chosen, with tasteful emerald laminate and blue piping. Usually matching suits were the step leading towards a Commitment Ceremony, but Sally had gotten cold feet three weeks later and run off to Chicago, telling me repeatedly, "It's not you, it's me", which has to be one of the lamest, most unsatisfying phrases known to humanity. Last I heard, Sally was living in a Triad with two men, so maybe there had been something to the explanation. Or maybe, as I frequently told myself, it had been a total lie.

I forced a smile and patted Fitz's shoulder. "Be ye of good cheer," I said. "I think I've got that dialogue problem I was having licked."

Fitz, as I well knew, hated getting drawn into the technicalities, so when I started to explain how reducing the adverbial modifier minimum downwards had tautened the syntactical delivery, he backed out pretty fast. I spent a few hours testing it out, and was pleased with the results. 90% of writing is putting together the formulas, so once I had this one, and a slight problem with the scenery equivalence parameters solved, I'd be sitting pretty, ready to generate a manuscript to hand over to Mikka the editor. Around three, I took a break and went out to sit in the Plaza.

Everyone and their extra suit had had the same idea, it seemed. Baby-faced Chubbo Safety Bodys chased each other through the crowds, playing tag, while a multi-armed dog-walker passed by. Tourists in rented Bodys furnished with city-specific adaptations milled by in crowds, each one led by a brightly colored Guide. A main flight path led over the Plaza, and flying Bodys in a variety of

colors and shapes ranging from Wasp to Balloon arched overhead, casting their oddly shaped shadows across the stone tiles. I set up a privacy field to signal I wasn't looking for conversation, and then sat enjoying the sunlight and recharging a few cells.

It was nice out on the Plaza, but crowded all the time. Which is why it took me a while to notice the Kali skulking around near the soya on a stick vendors. But no matter where I looked, the Kali seemed to be, its mechanical eyes coated in that half glaze that usually indicated they're set on binocular—and always pointed in my direction. I finally gave up and went over to where the Kali was pretending to pick through a recycling bin.

"What do you want?" I said.

The Kali turned, acting as though it had noticed me for the first time.

"Oh hey," she said. "Aren't you that woman from this morning?"

"Yeah. Addie Andrews. Ever find your mythical screw?"

Mimsy took me off guard by readily copping to the accusation. "Yeah, I wasn't looking for that," she said. "Honestly, I was looking for a servo."

"Your servo?"

"Sort of. It's my uncle's. It likes to hang around on that block a lot."

"And you thought it was in my booth?"

"Er, no," she said. "I just thought you looked interesting. Hey, is that a zeppelin?"

We both paused to watch the zeppelin float by overhead. Like the rest of the fleet circling the city in preparation for the Hyperbowl, its silvery flanks bore advertising insignias. This one was marked in scarlet and white, advertising Retro-New Old Coke, and by the time I turned back to look at her, the Kali was gone.

Back at the office, I increased the efficiency of my algorithm by another ten hearsts. The editor, Mikka, kept hovering over my shoulder and asking when I expected to be able to deliver, until I finally turned around and snapped, "You're not speeding things up any by asking every five minutes!"

Mikka's faceplate projected his hurt facial expression, but on the rounded cylinder surrounding his head, with a grainy quality

reminiscent of an old-time black and white movie. It was a look that those labeling themselves "literary" seem drawn to. He blinked lugubriously at me.

"You seem touchy today, Addie," he said.

"You know goddamn well I won't be able to give you this manuscript until I get the last kinks worked out," I snarled. "And then I'll hand it to you, you'll rip the heart and soul out of it, and then it'll go out in four standard editions: male/female, female/male, male/male, and female/female, because Fitz still thinks we should stick to the classic markets, and refuses to believe that there are more than two sexes. I'll make an appearance at a few malls, and then it's back in the office, working on the next set of parameters."

I was pretty sure I had strayed away from the subject of my original rant, but I continued, going with the flow.

"And then on, and on, and at some point I'll switch either to the geriatric lines or kids' books, and then from there it's a long slow slide into a nursing Body, so I'll be capable of feeding myself and wiping my own ass. And then death, a small but tasteful funeral, and my ashes scattered illicitly in the San Juans."

He kept blinking at me. "You want your ashes scattered in the San Juans?"

"It's in my will," I said. "Hey, I'm tired and hungry, and ready to go home. You hear what I'm saying? Give me a few more days fiddling the numbers before you ask me again. Lila's got her Regency Robots almost ready; go breathe down her neck for a change."

Mikka blinked a final time, then nodded and lumbered away.

When I got home, there was a small and shabby servo huddled by my doorway. I don't like the trend of making robots look human, and so I was prepared to dislike this one, with its Emmett Kelly air of bedraggled dignity superimposed over a smiling cartoon face.

"Excuse me, ma'am," it said. "Would you be Adelaide Andrews?"

"Depends on who's asking," I said.

It didn't have much of a humor lobe, because it just looked at me. I relented.

"Yeah, I am," I told it. "What do you want?"

"I'm so pleased, ma'am, to meet the author of *Thor's Hammer* and *The Eight Legs of Sleipnir*. Your programming style is as lean and taut as the stomachs of your protagonists, and moves with the grace of a Valkyrie aloft."

"Uh," I said. I'd never had a fan appear at my house before, and this one was a servo, to boot. Then I thought of something. "Hey, you don't belong to a woman who wears a Kali suit, do you?"

It glanced up and down the street, antenna poised warily. "No, no, ma'am. Of course not. I belong to ... " There was a pause as it performed a search. "Mr. and Mrs. John Doe of ... " Another pause. "101 Pleasant Street."

"Ooookay," I said. "Look, I'm tired and hungry, and I'd like to go in."

"Let us go in at once, and I will prepare grilled cheese sandwiches."

"What?"

"Mr. and Mrs ... .John Doe have sent me to express their appreciation for your writing. I will cook, clean, and tend to your needs. So you may focus on writing."

"Hey, I'm not about to let a strange robot into my house," I said. "You could be programmed to do anything. Murder me in my sleep. Or steal my silverware."

The antenna drooped. "I assure you, ma'am, I mean you no harm."

"I listen to public service announcements," I said. "I know the score."

It must have analyzed my voice and found resolve there, because it didn't put up any argument after that—just trudged off down the street. I watched it till it was out of sight, then punched in my door code and went inside.

My apartment was one of the larger ones in the building: three rooms painted in a tasteful off-white, and photos on the walls from Sally's senior year trip to Paris. IKEA's "Kludge" line had furnished the blue sofa and chairs, along with a few shelves for readers and some replicas of seashells. A sisal-colored carpet that stopped a few centimeters short of the walls. And not much else.

The sour mood that had seized me when scolding Mikka still lingered in the corners of my mind as I looked around the place. What exactly had I done with my life? I'd had promising grades in school and teachers praising my talents, and then I'd used them to become just another gear in the machine pumping out dreck to keep the

masses who felt they were too cool for video amused. Was this what I really wanted?

Turning on the wall screen in the kitchen, I let my favorite cooking show, "Juan's Mesa", guide me through a meal. Juan Estrella, a vivacious, elderly chef, was sponsored by a coffee company, so every meal ended with a cup, but I ignored that and focused on the braised seitan and black-eyed peas that seemed to be a rehash of a show I'd seen last year. "I could have been a chef," I thought, watching him pour and mix and hold a steaming strip of seitan up to the camera so the audience could see its browned surface. "I could have been anything."

I took a sleeping pill and went to bed.

◉▬▬▬

The next morning seemed brighter in the way that only a good night's sleep can accomplish. Out on my doorstep was a small basket of freshly baked muffins and a double latte in my favorite proportions. The servo from yesterday was lurking near the mailboxes. I chose to ignore its hopeful looks and took the offerings inside.

A few minutes later, after tasting the muffin, I went back to the door and let the servo in. It bustled around with profuse thanks, lights flashing in what I assumed what the robotic equivalent of happiness. Growing up, I hadn't been around many robots, and down deep in my soul memories lingered of high school stories of robots gone wild, massacring baby sitters and poodles. But I wasn't going to look a gift horse that could bake a chocolate chip cream cheese muffin that melted away with every bite in the mouth.

I was halfway to work, a basket of muffins accompanying me, when the Kali swooped down, wings extended, and grabbed me under the arms in a carry maneuver. I freely admit, I react slowly—we were thirty meters up in the air in a highly illegal flight path, the muffins lying in a sad little trail below us, before I could think to start shouting.

"Kidnapper!" I yelled. "Abductor! Thief! Fraud! Litterer!"

"I just want to talk," the Kali said.

"Anarchist! Arsonist! Rapist! Pillagist!"

"Just ten minutes," she pleaded.

"Okay, but make it quick."

We landed on top of a zeppelin. Yeah, it's an odd detail, but I

remember it well because the city was full of them that week, getting ready for the HyperBowl. Landing on one was about as illegal as it gets.

"This isn't where I want to talk," I said. Over the slippery, rounded side of the zeppelin, I could see the city laid out in very distant strips of steel and concrete. It made me nervous.

The Kali advanced on me, shaking a finger on three different hands for emphasis. "You have my servo, Ticky."

"My name's not Ticky, it's Adelaide."

"The servo's name is Ticky. I hate you people who think just because you're all competent and professional, everything can make sense. All I want is my servo back."

"Listen, I don't have any control over your servo, which you already said wasn't yours, but your uncle's. It came up, said a few nice things, then started baking me muffins. Plus it says it belongs to Mr. and Mrs. John Doe."

"Ticky," the Kali sighed. "Ever since Grandfather tried reprogramming him, he's been odd. He has ... ambitions."

"Ambitions of being a cook?"

"Nothing as practical as that." Fumbling in her waist pack, she handed me a business card that read, in bright fuchsia letters, *Mimsy Star. Body and Web design.* "I guess you can keep him for a while if you like, but call me if he starts showing any further signs."

"Any further signs of what?" I demanded. But Mimsy had already executed a showy backwards flip off the zeppelin, leaving me standing there.

I didn't have wings built into my suit—just gliders, and it looked far enough down that I didn't want to trust them. Instead I waited for the cops to show, and then insisted I'd been abducted. They were willing to chalk it up to pre-HyperBowl hijinks, but dutifully dusted me and the zeppelin for fingerprints, and one was kind enough to give me a lift back down to the surface, sticking to the regular, approved flight paths.

The office was bustling with life. "What's happening?" I said to Daisy.

"Someone's coming through, and might be buying the place," Daisy said.

"Buying the office, or the business?"

"The business," Daisy said. "I'm hoping they'll want to expand."

Panicked and bewildered, I made my way into Fitz's office. "What's going on?"

Fitz was standing staring out the window. The sunlight that day was bright and brassy, painful to the eye, and gleamed on the back of the two zeppelins circling the HyperDome a few blocks away.

"I woke up this morning to a horde of credit collectors on my doorstep," he said. "I just can't do it any more, Addie. This outfit's offering 12 mill—not a lot, but enough to pay off my debts and hold my head up again. I had to sell my cookbook collection last month."

"You sold the collection?" I said, astonished. Fitz's collection of 20th century cookbooks, each signed by their respective author or chef, had been passed down to him by his grandfather, a noted gourmand, and had been his pride and joy. Every Christmas, everyone in the office went round to his place in order to drink strange punches from the old books and slightly illegal treats laden with contraband cane sugar.

"Most of them," Fitz admitted. "There's still a few that I couldn't bear to part with."

I looked out the doorway and saw a group of three men in gunmetal gray Bodys, each arm laden like a Swiss Army knife with the paraphernalia of office living, walking around the desks while Daisy looked on with a brightly bland smile.

"Who's trying to buy us?" I asked.

The skin of Fitz's helmet pinked. "General Emotions," he said.

"Fitz! I've heard of their takeovers! They'll get rid of all of us and outsource the production to Mars!"

"You're all bright and talented people," Fitz said. "Even if you had to find new jobs, which they've promised won't happen, you'd find new ones."

"Fitz, do you have to make a decision today?"

"No," he admitted. "I figured I'd ponder it a few days and announce it at the office party this Sunday at the HyperBowl. One of the reasons they want this place is our box, but I figured we'd make use of it one last time."

"Do me a favor, Fitz—don't sign anything until then. Give me two days to try to figure out some better alternative."

"I suppose," he said dubiously.

From the time I was a small child, I associated the HyperDome with problem solving. My great-uncle Roy took me to every game as a child and then as a teen, and I'd used the time, bored out of my skull, to sit and watch the patterns of the players and figure out mathematical equations in my head. It was during the 2039 HyperBowl, and Vinnie Testaverde's famous final touchdown, in fact, that I'd worked out the formula for what became my trademark story arc, which allowed one extra chapter for the aftermath.

So today I returned to the stadium, using my employee badge to access the box under the pretense of checking out dimensions for the party.

"How many balloon bouquets can you fit in one of those and still let people move around, that's what I need to know," I told the attendant.

Sitting up in the box, I looked out over the empty green sward stretching from goal to goal and tried to imagine the patterns that would emerge on Sunday, not just the elaborate loops of the players as the ball moved from one group to another, but the even more complex patterns of the patrons and vendors, the swarms going to and from the restrooms. On Sundays like this, dedicated football fans might pull out a Body with their team's markings, a paw-print marked chassis for the Cheetahs, rainbow paint for the Freedoms, glitter and tinsel and sparkle for whatever team you cared to name. Everyone would wear something flashy, particularly those who could afford dress-up Bodys; others would make do with decals and temporary paint. But it would be a festive, party atmosphere.

The air-conditioned cold of the box penetrated my Body and I tongued the thermostat to up it. Gloom edged my thoughts with darkness. Some party, I thought, if it ends with a gladhand and farewell, see you all on the flip side. I *liked* working for Fitz. I didn't want to become a cog again.

Someone knocked on the door, and I opened it to find the Kali.

"Stars and Stripes," I said, employing one of Roy's more colorful expressions. "Are you everywhere? Are you cloning yourself?"

"Too expensive," Mimsy said. She craned her neck to look behind

me. "Would you happen to have Ticky with you?"

"No," I said firmly.

"My uncle's going to kill me if I've lost him."

"What's your uncle's name?"

"My uncle Juan. He owns half the HyperBowl."

"Such problems you have," I said. "Look, I don't have any control over your servo, but I'll tell it tonight to go home."

Clearing her faceplate, Mimsy brightened. She was a surprisingly pretty girl for such a ditz, I reflected. Her hair was the precise shade of her dark blue eyes, and her chin was narrow and vulpine. She looked a little like Sally. But a lot weirder.

"Will you?" Mimsy said.

"Yeah, whatever."

"I'm sorry I said I hated people like you."

"I'd forgotten about that actually. It was the abandoning me on the zeppelin that you should be apologizing for."

"I'm not apologizing for anything!" Mimsy said. "I was trying to be nice!"

I sighed. "There's no winning with you."

"I should hope not!" Mimsy said. "When can I have my servo back?"

"If it won't go back on its own, I'll bring it with me here on Sunday, and you can come claim it."

"That works," Mimsy said.

"Of course it does," I replied. "What, you think we practical and competent people can't come up with working plans?"

"See, there you go again!"

"What? What?" But Mimsy had vanished, leaving me there at a loss. And smiling.

That night, as Ticky served gazpacho in a bowl crafted from freshly baked spelt bread, I said, "Ticky, why exactly did Mr. and Mrs John Doe send you, again?"

It set salt and pepper on the table and gazed at me with eyes whirligigged with synthethic emotion. "Why, because you're such a fine author."

"They've read all my books?"

"Every single one. Even *Helga's Tunic*."

"That was out of print almost as soon as it appeared," I said,

astonished. For a robot, Ticky had excellent taste.

It rearranged the condiments on the table with a careful mechahand. "They like your writing very much," it said. "Perhaps at some point you would like to talk about your writing process and I would record what you say for them."

A dire suspicion grew in my head. "They don't want to write, do they?"

"Of course not!"

"Whew."

"But they would like for you to instruct me in the art."

"Oh." Now I understood. A servo who wanted to be a writer. No wonder Mimsy had said it had gotten odd.

"Perhaps after dinner, you would care to discuss how you began writing while drinking a fine port that I have synthesized for you."

"Perhaps," I said. "Hey, I'm going to be at a party on Sunday with some of the other writers. Why don't you come along and that way you'll get a chance to listen to them?"

It gazed at me, enraptured.

"You could make some treats for the party," I slyly suggested.

"I will start preparing right now!" And with that it vanished into the kitchenette, from which the smells of citrus and mint began emanating.

"I'd still like that port," I called after it, but there was no answer. Sighing, I finished spooning up my gazpacho, and flipped on the computer. Trying to find ways that the press could earn more money was harder than I'd imagined it could be. No matter what avenue I scouted down, I found traces that Fitz had been there before me. I slept briefly, then set to it again on Saturday, fueled by freshly baked cinnamon doughnuts and Mexican hot chocolate. Nothing. Again and again, nothing. I worked through the day and into the next night until finally I pushed the screen away with a groan.

"I can't figure it out," I told the wall. From the kitchen, a waft of coconut and orange was my only answer.

◉▪▪▪▬▬

At the HyperBowl, I made my entrance, followed by the servo with its arms laden with containers of doughnuts, cookies, empanadas,

churros, and coconut ices. I pointed to the buffet table, already laden with Fitz's offerings, and a massive punch bowl brimming with a murky, pale brown liquid.

"Try the punch," Fitz said, appearing at my elbow. "I was going to save it for Christmas, but I figured might as well use it now. It's coffee based. A recipe from one of the cookbooks I kept."

I looked at him as he poured me a cupful. "You've made your decision, haven't you?" I said.

In the corner, Daisy was talking earnestly to Lila, yet another sheet of plas in her hand. Mikka was staring out the window at the field as though witnessing the four horsemen of the Apocalypse. The other two writers occupied themselves with their dates and the containers the servo was setting out. Rapturous noises came from that corner of the room; I didn't want to look closely enough to determine their source.

Fitz's shoulders slumped, assuming an exaggerated and awkward angle. "Yeah. I appreciate your position, Addie, but I just can't go it any longer."

"Well," I began, then glimpsed Mimsy's face at the door. "Just a minute, Fitz. I'll be back in a second."

I opened the door and Mimsy entered hastily, followed by an elderly man in an immaculate vanilla-shaded BodySuit.

"You have my servo!" he cried angrily at me. "I could have you arrested for theft!"

"Now just a minute," I said, looking between Mimsy and the man.

"This is my uncle," Mimsy said unhappily. "He realized Ticky was missing."

I glanced back over my shoulder and saw the servo trying to unobtrusively edge behind Daisy and Lila.

"Arrested!" the man shouted.

"Is there some problem?" Fitz appeared at my elbow.

"I am Juan Estrella and this woman has stolen my prize servo, laden with ten thousand secret recipes!"

"Addie?" Fitz said, his tone full of admiring wonder. "Did you really?"

"It followed me home and baked me muffins!" I said. "How was I supposed to know?"

"I'm Fitzroy Huggins," Fitz said. "Now, here, Mr. Estrella ... you're the chef Estrella, aren't you? Come and have some punch, and we'll discuss this all like civilized adults."

"Arrested!" Estrella said again, but his tone was lower, mollified and flattered at being recognized.

"I'm so sorry," Mimsy whispered in one of my external microphones. "He saw me leaving and decided he wanted to come too."

Overhead, two silvery zeppelins circled, filming the crowd, their shadows falling across the flanks of festive Bodys and noBodys alike. Fitz poured Estrella a cup of punch, and the old man gingerly poured a sip down an intake tube. His suit colored in surprise and delight, blossoming peacock blue and turquoise.

"What is this drink?"

"Coco-latte punch," Fitz said, pleased. "late twentieth century ... "

"I must have the recipe!"

◉▪▪▪▬

I'm fond of happy endings.

"Well," I said to Mimsy, as we stood watching the halftime show. Down on the field, cheerleader Bodys marched in tandem, spelling out "Victory for all!" in cursive lettering. "That seems to have turned out all right. Your uncle has a new source of recipes and Fitz has enough cash to keep the house alive for a while."

"And Ticky has a new friend," Mimsy said, nodding over at the corner where the servo and Daisy were comparing notes on plot twists. "But what did you and I get out of all of this?"

I trailed a finger along the inner curve of one of the Kali's elbows. It didn't seem as tacky as it used to. "Oh, I don't know," I said. "But I'm sure something will emerge."

# + FAR

## Afternotes

*This story was written for Clarion West, during the week that L. Timmel DuChamp was our instructor, and is my attempt at a screwball comedy, combined with the idea of the Bodys, which was inspired by a long walk in which my foot began to hurt and I was thinking about what it would be like to be able to switch out body parts easily.*

*The story appeared in the final issue of* Crossed Genres, *a magazine which I was pleased to support during its existence, and which went away far too quickly (although at the time I'm writing this, a Kickstarter project looks as though it may succeed in reviving the magazine). "Long Enough and Just So Long," which appears in the Near volume of this collection, was originally written for a contest of theirs, but got purchased before I could send it to them.*

# Space Elevator Music

OKAY, SO IT'S NOT REALLY AN ELEVATOR OR even a space elevator in the way anyone originally meant it. But it looks like an elevator, the transo-chrono-ecto-vasi-via. You get on, you punch a button, you go to your destination. Sometimes you stop along the way, people get off, get on. You get the picture. Transportation for the masses. Rich people don't have to stop for other people, they just go straight up to the top. The rest of us stand waiting and listening to the piped in entertainment and the commercial pause every five minutes.

It's always the same music. At first it's just muzak, aural wallpaper, and then a few notes pluck at your consciousness, and then some others, starting to unsettle you, until you realize, finally, it's a Led Zeppelin song, glossed and slicked in a way that should bring Jon Bonham's corpse staggering out of the grave like a zombie dervish, spinning out protest.

Why do we have to turn our cell phones off until we reach the stratopause? What's the point?

Sometimes people leave posters or pamphlets in the elevator, crumpled on the floor or taped to the side with illicit magnetic tape, suggesting alternate transportation or hijacking, TAKE THIS CAR

# + Far

SIDEWAYS or EJECT THE RICH. You have to read them at some point, because you end up looking at every available inch as it is, counting the rivets lining the corner or the number of teeth in a fellow passenger's mouth. You find yourself humming the music, or tapping your foot in time maybe, the fourteenth or fifteenth time it comes up, not realizing that by the end of this trip you'll never be able to listen to that music again.

Every time someone gets on, there's these new configurations, an inch to the left, a step to the right. Everyone's line of sight adjusts, never colliding with anyone else's like laser beams guarding a security vault, never meeting anyone else's eyes as though to do so would be to cross the beams and risk the universe's implosion.

Someone thought glass sides would be a good idea. They were wrong. It's spooky, as though space were reaching into the elevator, the stars fingering at the edge of your consciousness. Unsettling as standing on Alice's mushroom for some unstable souls. You always have to watch for that.

Everyone's there, but you're in an iron tank of solitude if you don't know your fellow travelers. Those people can look each other straight in the face, maybe even lean together, while all you can touch is the chilly glass in front of you, watching their reflections. Maybe you listen to them talking about last year's turkey-plasma or bitching about the music.

At what point did you realize—this trip will never end?

## Afternotes

*A conversation at Confusion led to this flash piece, which has not previously appeared in print. It has some similarities to "Bus Ride To Mars," a slipstream story produced before this piece.*

# SURROGATES

**F**LOOR 13: GOVERNMENT OFFICES

They were married on a Monday in the Matrimony office. A poster on the wall said, "Welcome to your new life!" Belinda signed the forms in her careful penmanship, but Bingo simply spit-signed, letting his DNA testify to his presence. There were three rooms processing couples and triads—larger family structures required even more complicated licenses than the one they had secured. This room was painted blue, and one wall was an enormous fish tank.

Three fish spoke to Belinda, but she ignored them. She wished she'd remembered to have the Insanity Chip nullified for the ceremony, but it had been a busy week. The fish pressed their mouths to the plastic separating them from her world. Word pearls rose from their lips, seeped upward, through the barrier, and whispered in the room.

After the computer had pronounced them spouses, Belinda and Bingo stood there grinning at each other while behind them silver fish swam back and forth, back and forth, as though imitating the waves they'd never known. A wall camera took their picture.

In a few moments, a wall slot spat out a plastic bag containing two chipkeys, a silver-colored frame around their wedding picture, and a checklist of Entitlements on a slip of dissolvable paper, already graying around the edges.

The clerk handed over the items. "This is where I tell you that you should treat everything as though it's new," she said. "Studies have shown that the marriages which survive the longest are the ones where the newlyweds begin to build their new life together."

"Thanks!" Bingo said with a bright smile. Belinda could tell how happy he was, like he couldn't stop grinning. He looked at her, and the fish tried even more frantically to say something, battering themselves against the plastic until they were just blood and silver scraps drifting in the water, but she ignored them and focused on Bingo and thoughts of butterflies.

## FLOOR 22: SURROGATES

"Preferences haven't changed?" the technician asked as he strapped Belinda into the configuring bed. The straps turned into flowers, tiny lilac-colored bells that smelled like uncertainty.

"No," Belinda said. The question surprised her. They had filled out the forms for marriage only two weeks ago, including the list of preferences for her latest surrogate. It was something she'd thought about for a long time. Her old surrogate had been given to her when she first started having sexual feelings, and she had put it away for good a few years ago, when she'd met Bingo.

"Do people really change their preferences at the last minute?" she asked.

"It's not that their preferences really change, so much," the tech said. "But sometimes after they've spent a little time thinking about it, they realize things that they didn't realize they wanted at first."

He checked his data pad. "Blue eyes, blonde hair, skin pigment pale brown, no scars, no disfigurements, face model Adam?"

"That's it," Belinda said. She'd picked a generic face. She didn't believe in getting attached to surrogates. Her father had chosen to keep the one she'd used all through her teenage years rather than recycle it. The choice was vaguely illegal by virtue of a Statute that was rarely enforced. A person was entitled to one surrogate, which could be replaced whenever you changed status levels, as she and Bingo had done by marrying. But her father was a sentimental sort. She wondered how he would cope now that she was out of the apartment and he was living by himself.

The flower straps tickled her wrists. Perfume netted her, dragged her into sleep, content and dreamy as the machine went about its work, measuring her and calibrating the surrogate to her dimensions.

Afterwards they looked at the visuals of their surrogates. She was surprised by Bingo's choices: he had gone into much more detail than she had, as though designing a flower or piece of jewelry. Her face model was Maria and she wore elaborate blue tattoos like webbing over her arms and spreading across her nipples, half obscured by her long red hair.

Belinda liked the simpler look of her surrogate and she liked knowing that it was specifically designed for her, that it would smell and feel right, that it was *hers* in a way nothing else would ever be.

"They'll be delivered tomorrow, after we've done the final calibration," the clerk said. They signed data pads. "Congratulations," she said in a perfunctory tone and checked to make sure their names were spelled correctly.

<hr/>

## FLOOR 77: MENTAL SERVICES

On Floor 77, Belinda had her Insanity Chip reset so it would factor in her marriage. The Chips were subtle, she knew. They altered your perceptions, they showed the world in the way you wanted to see it. When she'd had a fight with her best friend Angie, she'd had the chip set so she couldn't see Angie for a week, even when the other girl was standing, shouting in her face. When she'd finally relented, missing Angie, though, she'd found the other had gone, moved away.

"I don't want the Chip to change Bingo," she told the doctor. "Let him stay constant."

The doctor fiddled with the machine, her stubby fingers recalibrating the keys. "Do you want hallucinations amped up or down?"

"What I want," Belinda said, "is for everything to seem more significant somehow. Can you do that?"

"Of course," the doctor said. She pressed a few more buttons and turned into a giant jellyfish that hung in the air, glistening greasily. "How is that?" Her voice was muffled, as though coming through water.

"Perfect," Belinda said.

Bingo was in the waiting room. He had worn his best for the wedding: gleaming black pants, a silver hoop in one ear, goatee trimmed to a

point. His feet were bare. He was talking to the child beside him but he broke off when Belinda came in. He smiled at her, rising.

"Ready to go home?" he asked.

Behind him the child wavered into a frog, a puddle, a big-eyed kitten.

"Perfect," Belinda said again.

***

### ELEVATOR 17-3

In the elevator between floors 45-75, Belinda said, "You never thought about having an Insanity Chip? Life is more interesting that way."

He kissed her despite the two other women in the elevator. "Life is already interesting."

The younger woman sniffed and stared at the wall; the older woman smiled at them before she got off on floor 82. Belinda saw stars in her eyes, promise in her smile, omens spilling out of the net bag she carried.

In the shop, they bought a new bedspread, dishes, cleaning liquids. They ordered an assortment of food and chose the color of their walls. Belinda liked a yellow and white diamond pattern because it seemed to her when she stared at it long enough, figures danced across it, harlequins in shoes with long pointed toes, kicking them up and down as they capered. She heard it in her head like a complicated marching tune.

Bingo gave her a dubious look. He liked a plain blue. But he let her pick the wall pattern and in return she let him pick a muted gray rug flecked with earth tones, like walking across fabric pebbles, a gentle hum underfoot in the key of C.

***

### FLOOR 689: GREEN LEAF LIVING QUARTERS

Floors 650-700 were Green Leaf Living Quarters. They would live on 689, in a studio that overlooked one of the four great hollow spaces contained inside the sector.

They kissed as they entered, dropping their bags in a cloud of butterflies beside the door. The curtains matched the walls, which had been prepared in the time they'd spent travelling on the elevator. It was as far in the Building as Belinda had ever travelled in one day. Bingo had been outside it to two other Buildings, but travel like that had never interested her. From what she'd seen on the holovids, every

place looked much the same. Belinda kissed the tip of Bingo's nose before she went to the window and looked out.

Portals marked the sides of the living unit walls, and zip lines led from one to another, letting people circumvent the space on hand held lines. Down below was a great green park, filled with grass carpets and plants in pots. Over it stretched the mesh that would catch those who slipped despite the safety straps, or the multitudes of young who delighted in falling, landing on the stretchy softness of the field.

Bingo started supper and she rearranged the pillows on the sofa, then unpacked her clothes into the wall drawers and shelves. Bingo came in smelling of spices and steam and kissed her again.

Bingo worked in advertising and Belinda was an assistant textile designer. That was how they had met. Belinda didn't think it very romantic, but Bingo always told the story as though he was writing an advertisement for it: I Saw her And Then Wham Be Still My Heart. It made Belinda smile when Bingo talked like that.

After dinner they fucked, and fucked again. Bingo nibbled her ears and she tickled his nipples and they gave themselves to each other and murmured sweet things until they fell asleep.

Before breakfast, they uncrated the surrogates and turned them on, flipping the knob on the back of their necks. The surrogates clicked to life, their wide eyes fastening on Bingo and Belinda's faces. After orders, both went to the kitchen and started breakfast, then Bingo's surrogate emerged and began putting their belongings away. While they ate breakfast, the surrogates worked.

An animal came out of the crate that Belinda's had been in, which lay dissolving on the floor with the other one. Belinda didn't know what it was. It had the usual animal shape. It turned cartwheels on the floor and made Belinda laugh.

"What?" Bingo said. He was watching her face, the movement of her eyes tracking the back and forth of the animal, which had purple fur and hair made out of noodles.

"The chip makes me see funny things sometimes," she said.

He reached out and took her hand in his. "Funnier than me?" he said. The animal was behind him, hanging from the ceiling. Its noodles dangled, limp and shiny. The surrogates came in; they were done, so they went into their closet, ignoring Belinda and Bingo.

"I don't think of you as funny," she said.

They fucked on the kitchen table. Flapping plywood tongues, the cupboards talked to Belinda while she jolted back and forth. They sang folksongs, oh my darling Clementine and green hills hop to my Lou and sweet sweet summer enviro-clime.

On Sundays they went to her father's for dinner with his parents, who were still married and her other father, who was not. This father, Father Bob, worked as a restaurant manager, and they ate well on last night's restaurant leftovers, fungus shaped into simulacrums of more expensive creatures, scallops and firm-fleshed shrimp and exquisite orange roe.

Father Anton worked in a news studio and would tell them about the Anchors, what they liked, what they said. He had a fervid adoration for one Morning Host, a perky blonde woman a quarter his age, and when he told stories about her, he did so in hushed tones, like a primitive talking about God.

They drank liters of home-made beer, which his mother distilled in her kitchen and always brought, and afterwards they played cards around the table while the holovision blared news of the Building.

Father Bob kept the surrogates, his and Belinda's, out for company much of the time. She went over a couple of times to pick up belongings she'd left behind and found the three sitting watching holovid. Hers was the size of a fourteen or fifteen year old boy; it was propped in an easy chair while the other surrogate leaned on the sofa beside Bob.

She had decorated this place herself, but since her departure, Bob had been pulling it slowly but inexorably into his own style. Restaurant containers filled the cooler. He had hung up several old pictures scavenged from the last remodel, which Belinda had designed the fabric for. The pictures showed leaves and golden light and flowers like great white cups drowning in blue water. They did not match the pink and orange carpet underfoot; they made it look old and shoddy. She did not like pictures of water. The tank in the Matrimony office had creeped her out.

She realized Father Bob was talking to her.

She said, "What?"

"Are you okay?" He got up from the sofa and peered at her. Behind him on the wall, the pictures undulated and swayed as though they

were windows to some vast, tide-drawn lake.

"Sure," she said. "I was just thinking about what it was like, growing up with you and Father Anton." She liked the new place better; she liked the tiny balcony, the view out onto the park. Here was quieter, certainly, a bit more privileged, but there was something to be said for the hubbub that surrounded them, the people swinging past on the zip lines, taking a short cut across the space rather than circle around the living area.

"You had a better childhood than I did," he said. It was a familiar refrain and she tuned out the details of how his family had worked maintenance for years and finally been given the chance to emigrate to this Building, far above the ruined, rotting planet. The food riots. The cold.

She knew Bob had begged on the street and he'd been rather good at it. The same charm and glibness that served him well running the restaurant had allowed him to cajole money, food, a couch to sleep on from people. He had lived a nomadic, room-to-curb existence for several years before becoming more established. He had moved in with Anton two years before they had decided to have Belinda. And life was good now for him. They could afford surrogates to do their daily work, let them concentrate on important things.

Belinda was a Creative type, always had been, and she did appreciate the chance at that which Anton and Bob's bloodlines had bought her, not having had to fight her way out of a less interesting job. She liked what she did and she was good at it.

Buzzing bees, colored violet and licorice and steel, swarmed through the air and she almost flinched.

"Why do you keep that chip?" Bob said. "You're not a child anymore, Belinda. You don't need constant entertainment."

"It makes me think of things differently," she said. "It keeps me on my toes."

She liked her unexpected world, hidden from most. She liked to know that she, and she alone, could see the faces in the wall work, the swords in the grass, the walking trees that paraded across the park every dark, late, when almost everyone was sleeping, the surrogates in the closet unless Bingo had taken his to bed already.

Sometimes Belinda wondered what life would be like without the

surrogates. Most of the time she didn't. The surrogates were there to do their work, but also in case one of them wanted sex when the other didn't. Two weeks after the marriage, Belinda didn't feel like it, so Bingo brought his surrogate in and fucked it there in the bed beside her.

After that she felt aroused. When Bingo just turned over, she went and got her own surrogate. Its rubbery cock stood up like a dildo, caramel colored. It went down on her, lips vibrating as she writhed, then fucked her. She thought that maybe Bingo would rouse again, that they'd fall into an endless sexual loop, but he kept snoring.

It surprised her how much she thought about that act afterwards. The surrogates were engineered deliberately so they didn't look like real people. Their eyes didn't track right and there was an odd translucency to their flesh. So it hadn't been as though it was another person Bingo had been focusing on, his eyes half-closed, looking somewhere inside himself. Had he been thinking about her? She felt oddly reluctant to ask, even though they were always frank with each other about what they liked and didn't like in bed.

On Bingo's birthday, Belinda made a cake by mixing the contents of one packet with another and letting it set inside a plastic shaping ring. She did it herself and frosted it, painting the white surface with green fish, pink flowers, yellow guitars. The cake sang to her as she painted it and later as she woke Bingo in the morning, singing his favorite song with the cake, "Baby baby flower baby."

She got home earlier than Bingo and she took to using the surrogate when she first did, then showering so she met him, freshly washed and ready, in the hallway, on the kitchen table, on the balcony. Today she fucked it and then showered while it and the other surrogate put up green and pink streamers that she'd pocketed from work.

Several of his friends and hers came over for dinner. She privately considered his friends brittle, and she'd heard him call hers vapid. Alfa and Veronika wrote musicals; Jonny and Leeza were clothing buyers. Veronika had an Insanity Chip too, but she made a point of saying that she did it for the sake of Creativity.

"It lets you drill down into the psyche of the really great artists," she enthused. "Van Gogh. Pound. Bacon. Doesn't it help you think up some really great designs, Belinda-baby?"

"Sure," Belinda said. She looked around. She had printed up some of the fabric swatches from work. They hung on the walls in odd trapezoidal shapes, angled in and out like blueprints of rocks. She wished she hadn't picked yellow for the curtains but she changed her mind when daffodil butterflies flew out of the fabric and spelled out words in the air: *Go Belinda you're great.*

Bingo flirted with Veronika; he asked her what her Chip made her see and gave her wide-eyed looks that were almost, but not quite, mocking. Veronika bit into it and wouldn't stop talking. Over her head, Bingo gave Belinda ironic glances until she got the hiccups from suppressing giggles.

They drank wine and ate and played cards. Belinda had a hard time focusing on the hands, and Bingo said, a little irritably, "Can't you manage to keep track of the simplest thing?"

It made her want to cry, and that made the cards even blurrier.

"Oh, baby," Bingo said, instantly contrite. He took her cards and put them face down on the table; he brought her hand to his lips, kissing at them. "Baby, I'm sorry, what's wrong?"

She lied. "It was something I saw. Something the chip showed me."

He frowned. Much later, after they'd gone to bed, he said, "Why do you keep the chip? You have me now."

"It makes the world less boring," she said.

"Don't I do enough of that for you?"

She faltered, not sure what to say. "But there are times when I'm not with you," she said.

He didn't say anything, there in the darkness, and after a while she said, "I could get the chip modified so it doesn't go off when you're around." The words came out of her mouth and swelled like glowing balloons, colored coral and amber and pumpkin and gold.

"All right," he said quickly.

The next day she had the modification made. It was easy. She rode home on the elevator on waves of blue, and her feet turned into fish, into birds, into kittens, and then Bingo was walking down the corridor towards her and everything was gone.

It was odd that evening, sitting across the table from him to eat food that stayed still and silent on the plate. She curled up next to him on the sofa and they held each other in the gray quiet, while the purple

diamonds stood statue-still on the wall.

When Bingo wasn't around, she could fuck the surrogate and ride silver rails of scent, could press her hands on his skin and feel centipedes coiling underneath, could see his eyes full of daffodils and roses.

Sometimes she hid from Bingo, stepped into the closet and closed her eyes. The clothing wrapped its arms around her and she sailed away into stars and fireworks. She could feel him outside the doorway like a leaden eye, a cloud of smoke. She wanted her surrogate to sneak up behind him and then ... she wasn't sure what. She wasn't sure what at all. And so she squeezed her eyes tighter and thought of light and its equations, like numbers on the inside of her head, and tried to dream even though she'd been forced awake.

It wasn't enough. She began to think she had agreed to things too quickly. She said to Bingo, "What if I had the chip gimmicked so it was just a little bleed through when you're around?"

His face darkened. "Why?"

"It helps me think," she said. She fussed with the food on the counter in front of her, making dinner. She laid a slice of bread on each plate, then a slice of cheese at an angle, so the food formed an eight-pointed star.

"Are you having trouble thinking?"

"Sometimes," she said.

"But only when you're with me."

"Never mind," she said. She poured white sauce over the cheese in a spiral and sprinkled it with green flakes. She could feel him watching her.

"I want you to be happy, Belinda, you know that," he said.

Then why do you want me to be something different than I am, she wondered. But she didn't speak the words aloud. It was the first time she'd ever censored herself for Bingo's sake and that night she lay awake, wondering what it meant. Bingo breathed beside her, the long slow sounds of sleep, and didn't stir when she got up and went into the other room.

There, without Bingo, an enormous golden figure eight hung in the air, blazing with a meaning she couldn't guess at. She sat down on the sofa. Her surrogate stirred in its closet, emerged, sat down beside her.

It was ready to do whatever she liked, but all she did was take its hand, flesh and plastic intertwining.

The next day Bingo said, "You could get rid of the Chip. It's silly. People laugh at you for having it."

That struck her to the quick. "Who's laughing at me?"

"Everyone," Bingo said. "Your friends and mine. Even Bob and Anton think it's funny."

She thought that might not be true. She thought of Bob, sitting with his own surrogate, her discarded one, a plastic family. She knew that it was wrong to think of them like that, she knew it was like befriending a toaster or a clock. But then Bingo left the room and their toaster smiled at her, chirped hello, and slid out two pieces of toast, perfect and brown, just the way she liked them, even though she hadn't planned on breakfast.

When she came home from work, Veronika was sitting on the couch.

"Bingo let me in," she said. "But he went to get some groceries. Belinda, darling, I've got to talk to you about something."

"The Chip," Belinda said. She looked at Veronika, at the glossy red hair, the wide eyes.

"Bingo thinks you want something else. That's why you won't give up the Chip."

Veronika's face was too solicitous. Belinda thought about the two of them discussing her, discussing the chip. Discussing Bingo's dissatisfaction. It felt like a terrible betrayal.

"Get out," she said.

She expected Bingo to bring it up again that night, but instead he said, "Have you ever thought we might change our marriage, make it a triad?"

"I don't want to marry Veronika," she said without preamble. He flushed at the accuracy of the guess. She said, "Isn't your surrogate enough?"

"I have a surrogate," he said. "I don't have you."

It made her sound like a possession, like a thing, like a toaster. She didn't know what to say, how to reassure him that he didn't *need* her.

His voice was tired. "Let's go to bed. Think about it. We'll talk more in the morning."

She left in the middle of the night as he slept. She travelled to the

77<sup>th</sup> Floor, to one of the many building offices that never closed. Riding in the elevator, the buttons sang to her, the carpet advised, the lights shed waves of warmth that settled on her like a feather cloak.

In the morning, he said, "Have you thought of it?" But she went on talking to the cabinets.

He said, "I thought you made it so the Chip doesn't work when I'm around!"

"It's a fine morning," Belinda said to the table, watching the wood grain melt and puddle. And then she turned and left without looking at him, because she didn't see him anymore and only a tickle of memory remained.

### *Afternotes*

*I read this story at the Wayward Coffeehouse here in Seattle with my mother in the audience. There's nothing like your mother's face in the border of your vision to make you notice words like "fuck" and "nipple" in a story. Afterwards—and this is one of the many reasons I love her so—all she said was, "That was a great story."*

*It originally appeared in* Clockwork Phoenix III, *edited by Mike Allen. It is in many ways an uncharacteristic story, but one that was a lot of fun to write, despite the seriousness of the theme, which is addiction and relationships. The names for the characters came to me early, as did the very first passage, and it set the tone for the rest of the story. The original title was "Sexual Surrogates."*

# FIVE WAYS TO FALL IN LOVE ON PLANET PORCELAIN

O VER THE YEARS, TIKKA'S JOB AS A MINOR Propagandist for the planet Porcelain's Bureau of Tourism had shaped her way of thinking. She dealt primarily in quintets of attractions, lists of five which were distributed through the Bureau's publications and information dollops: Five Major China Factories Where the Population of Porcelain Can Be Seen Being Created; Five Views of Porcelain's Clay Fields; Five Restaurants Serving Native Cuisine at Its Most Natural.

Today she was composing Five Signs of Spring in Eletak, her native city.

Here along the waterfront, she added chimmerees to her list as she watched the native creatures, cross between fish and flower, surface. Each chimmeree spreading its white petals as it rose, white clusters holding amber centers, tendrils of golden thread sending their scent into the air along with the most delicate whisper of sound, barely audible over the lapping of the water.

The urge towards love beat along every energy vein of her silica body, even down to her missing toes, but she resisted it. She would remain alone this spring, as she had every spring since she had made her vow and inscribed it in the notebook where she kept her personal lists, under "Life Resolutions," 4th under "Keep myself clean in thought and mind," "Devote myself to promoting Porcelain's tourism," and "Fall in love." The third item had been crossed off at the same time, in vehement black pen strokes.

119

Her first sign of spring had been the singing of the tree frogs, which had awoken her three nights ago, in the small hours when most of the citizens cracked, gave way to despair, and crumbled in the manner of the elderly.

She was afraid of cracking, examined herself with obsessive care in the sluice for any sign that her surface was giving in, allowing the forces of time to work at her. She'd lain awake in the darkness, checking her mind with the same care. Were there any sorrows, any passions that might lead her thoughts along the same groove till it gave, eroded into madness?

She knew of one, and she kept her thoughts away from it as though it were made of thorns. Pain surrounded its edges and she could not avoid brushing against them even as she avoided it, but she kept herself from touching its tender heart, when silica melted in emotion and loss. She clicked her eyelids shut and contemplated what the morning would bring: ablutions and prayers, and a walk to the stop where the balloon-tram would take her to work. The sides would be hung with flower-colored silks in honor of the season. That would be her second sign of spring.

⊙▪▪▪▬

At work, there was jostling going on over a corner, windowed office. A writer had given way to cracking, premature, as sometimes happened with those who lived carelessly. Tikka was keeping back; she liked to do her work outside, and didn't think herself enough in the offices to merit such a coveted space. Not that she would have been first in line for it; of the three Minor Propagandists, she was the most junior, with only six years to the others' respective ten and fifteen.

Attle met her with a list in hand.

"Not again," Tikka said. "I like doing my own, you know that."

Attle shrugged. She was tall and willowy to Tikka's squatter lines. "He says they're only suggestions."

Tikka took the list and studied it. "Suggestions that are heavily encouraged," she said. "If I don't take at least half of them, it'll affect my next review."

"No one really worries about reviews," Attle said. It was true; the small Bureau's turnover rate was glacial. Like most government jobs, it was steady and guaranteed work in a place where poverty was rampant.

"I do," Tikka retorted. She was all too conscious that she didn't resemble most of the other citizens in the office. She had won her post through a scholarship, was one of the tokens allowed positions so they could be held up to the lesser advantaged as what they could be if they kept their mouths shut and worked hard.

More tourists meant more money for everyone, even if it did have to trickle through the layer of upper citizens at first. She didn't think many of the topics were designed to attract tourists.

"'Five spots celebrated in the works of the poet Xochiti'? Who reads him? We need things that tourists are looking for, new experiences and new trinkets to buy. Five places where they serve fin in the manner of the Brutists is not going to do it."

"He believes in niches," Attle murmured in habitual response.

"Some niches are so small that no tourist would fit in them!" Tikka waved Attle off when she would have spoken again. "I know, I know, it's none of your doing."

She went to her desk, situated in a paper-walled cubicle. The patterns were from several years ago; the department's budget had been shrinking of late and even the plants that hung here and there were desiccated but unreplaced, delicate arrangements of withered ferns draped with dust that no one wanted to touch, lest they be mistaken for a lower-class servitor of the kind the Bureau could no longer afford.

Her fingers danced across the transparent surface of her datapad, which dimpled beneath her touch. She pulled up a master document and transferred the least objectionable of the Master Propagandist's "suggestions" into it, scoffing under her breath.

A clink of drummed fingers behind her snatched her attention. She turned so quickly she nearly collided with the author of the suggestions himself. "Sir!" She stepped back to a safer, more polite distance.

"Am I to believe you feel you have worthier candidates for your time than those I have advanced?" he said. Master Propagandist Blikik was made of smooth white clay, a material so fine that it gleamed under the office lights in a way Tikka's coarser, low-class surface could never match, even with disguising cosmetics. His colors would never fade, while hers would eventually succumb to

the sun, give way to pale, unfashionable hues.

She dropped her gaze to the felted carpet beneath his feet. "No, sir."

He waited.

"I'm sorry, sir." She met his eyes. "I thought perhaps we might consider some alternative ways of attracting tourists."

Clatter of halted movement behind her as others stopped to listen. She could feel the shockwave reverberate through the office as whispers of her boldness were hissed to outliers who hadn't heard.

Blikik's robes, swirled with gold and crimson, a style as outdated as the cubicle walls, rustled as indignation drew him upwards, made him tower over Tikka.

"You will do as you are told," he barked, so crisp his teeth snapped together with an unpleasant, brittle sound. "You are not paid to think. If you wish to think, other accommodations can be made for your employment. Is that what you wish?"

"No, sir, not at all, sir," she rushed to supply into the shocked void his words had left.

He nodded once, turned on his heel, and walked away.

⊙••••▬▬

After she'd drafted a couple of lists, Tikka escaped outside to the terraced gardens overlooking the sound garden (one of Eletak's five most impressive sites). Its massive steel structures were strung with cabling and wire that sang whenever the wind stopped sweeping across the water and came to investigate the inland. Shapes huddled on the sculptures, the winged monkeys that made them their nesting grounds, where they raised their thumb-sized offspring and lived the lives of one of Eletak's five most distinctive native species.

The air smelled of monkey shit, which, combined with the unpleasant sensation of the vibrations from the sound garden, drove most visitors away. Rumor held that the sound garden could set off interior echoes that might leave someone dust on a pathway, but she had never believed it. Childhood prittle prattle, don't do this or that or you'll fall afoul of unseen forces. Meaningless superstition.

She leaned on the wooden railing, using her jacket to cushion her arms. The wires sang a song she'd heard years ago, *love love careless love.*

# Five Ways to Fall in Love on Planet Porcelain

She could give way to it. She could go find a mate and the two of them could pose, take on the shape of love and freeze together in the most intimate contortion. She hated the helpless feeling afterward, where you were caught still mingled with the other person until the rigidity that came with orgasm, lasting hours, seeped away and you were your own unique person, rather than part of the larger construction, again.

How freakish, the ways of love on this planet, or anywhere else. The illusion that you had become something other than you were. The illusion that you could be something other than alone.

She would not succumb.

*Love, love careless love,* the wires complained. It was unseasonably cold. Two monkeys huddled together for warmth in a metal Y only a few feet down from her. Pathetic.

She would not love again.

Too many memories were in the way.

◉▪▪▬▬

It had happened the second spring that she had been working for the Bureau. She had traveled a lot the first year, taking pictures and conducting interviews of tourists in various areas to find out what had brought them there. She had written a private list: Five Things Tourists Dislike about Porcelain.

#1: The standoffish nature of its people.

#2: The unabashed attitude of greed towards tourist money.

#3: The slowness of the balloon transit center.

#4: The number of political uprisings.

#5: The number of native species prone to throwing shit at tourists.

The man had been trying to clean monkey shit off himself near the sound garden. She'd intervened, led him to a public sluice.

"No wonder all your people seem so clean," he'd said, washing himself off in the stream of heated water.

"Down here," she said. She didn't know why she said it. It was forbidden to speak to tourists with anything other than pleasantries. She'd had to go through weeks of training to do it.

"Other areas don't have these?" he said.

"Other areas don't have running water," she said. "Why waste technology on lesser clay?"

A monkey screamed behind him and he flinched. His eyes checked the badge on her chest. "You can deal with tourists, can't you? Not like most of these, forbidden to talk to us. Come and have lunch with me."

So few restaurants catered to both kinds, but she took him to a place near the Bureau, disks of aetheric energy which she slotted into her mouth, a salad for him, odd grainy lumps scattered through it.

Humans. The richest of all the multi-verse dwellers, at least many of their branches were. Was he from one? She rather thought so, given the cut of his clothing, the insouciant ease with which he leaned back to survey her and the restaurant. His was not a species accustomed to scraping or scrabbling.

He said, "I've never understood why more people don't come here. A world peopled by china figurines."

There were more interesting worlds in the multi-verse, she knew. Paper dolls, and talking purple griffons. Intelligent rainbows and everyone's favorite, the Chocolate Universe. She shrugged.

"I want you for my tour guide," he said, staring at her. "Can we do that?"

It was unorthodox. But he had unexpected pull. Blikik had been forced to allow it, although he heaped her with instructions and imprecations. Porcelain must preserve its public face for tourism, he had said. No talk of politics, no talk of clays or those who did not live in the cities.

She nodded until she thought her neck would give way from the motion.

⊙■■■—

Places to take tourists on Planet Porcelain:

#1: A birthing factory, where the citizenry are mass produced. The list is short; tourists are only taken to the upper class factories, where citizens are made of the highest quality porcelain, rather than one of the more sordid working class manufactories.

#2 The bridges of Etekeli, which run from building to building in a city more vertical than horizontal. There is a daring glee to the citizenry here; the ground is littered with the remains of those who came to this place, which has a suicide rate twenty times that of elsewhere on the planet.

#3 The Dedicatorium.

# Five Ways to Fall in Love on Planet Porcelain

The first sight of the Dedicatorium awed him. She understood how it must look: from afar a wall of thorny white. Then as one approached, it resolved itself into a pattern made of feet and hands, arms and legs.

"People leave these here?" he half-whispered, his voice roughened by the silence.

"They do it for several reasons," she told him. "Some in gratitude for some answered prayer. Others to leave a piece of themselves behind."

As they watched, a woman approached. She carried a bundle in her only hand. When she got close to the wall, she fumbled away the coverings to reveal the other hand. She searched along the wall until she found a place to fold it into a niche. It curled there, its fingers clustered as though to form a hollow where a secret might be whispered.

His face was flushed, but she could not read the emotion. "Your people can detach their own limbs?"

"It is easier to get someone else to do it," she said. "It is not without pain. The joints must be detached, and it usually breaks them to do so."

"I have seen no amputees on your streets," he said. His eyes searched the wall, taking in the delicate point of a toe, the rugged line of a calf's stilled muscles.

"It is an injury that often leads to cracking," she said. "Few survive unless they take great care of the point where the limb was severed."

"It's barbaric," he said, but she heard only love and appreciation in his voice.

"You spend too much time with him," Blikik complained.

She let his complaints wash over her like water, eroding irritation. Through his eyes, she was learning to craft lists tailored to humans, their petty desires for restrooms and food that tasted like the food they had at home. And their greed, which must be fed with lists of the cheapest markets, the most inexpensive hostelries, free performances.

Tourism had increased a very small percentage, but it was due to her efforts. She could not spend enough time with him. He was too full of valuable information, conversation, insight.

He was such good company, so interesting to listen to, so fascinating in his different viewpoint. She wrote lists specifically for him, five restaurants that served his favorite condiment, five places to view a sunset shaded with indigo and longing.

Five places to be alone with your native guide.

◉▪▪▪▃▃▂

Ways to fall in love on Planet Porcelain:

#1: Slowly, so slowly. At first just a hint of delight at his face when he heard the chimmeree singing.

#2: Like a revelation, a book opening as he told stories of his childhood, life under a different sun, where different songs held sway. He never talked of taking her there, but she was content. This was his story now, its happy ending on Planet Porcelain.

#3: Knowing that it was wrong, unheard of. And knowing that its forbidden nature gave it extra savor, gave it the allure of something that shouldn't be, overlying the touch of the exotic that it held for them both.

#4: In snatches and glances, moments seized outside the monitors. In a corridor, his fingers touched hers, warm against cool, and she felt a liquid warmth pervading her brain until she could barely think. Apart from him, she dreamed of him, and totted up list after list of the things she loved: the hairs on the back of his wrists, the way his teeth fit into the gum, the shape of his ankle, the burr his voice took on when tired or irritated, the flush that mounted to his cheek when he felt aroused.

#5: Verbally. Word after word, opening secrets. He asked her about coupling and she told him how it was, how the urge drove you together, touch and caress until the moment where you froze and fused, knowing yourself a single part of a larger thing. And how, afterwards, that feeling faded, until you could see the body that had been part of yours and think it something entirely different.

"Can we go to bed together, you think?" he asked her. At first she didn't understand what he meant. There was no reason they could not share a bed. But his words, the heat in his face, made her realize her mistake.

Could they? Lovemaking was mental as much as physical, she had always been told. As long as they took care, could they not touch each other to arousal and beyond?

She could find nothing about such moments in her research. Unthinkable that they could have invented a perversion new to the multi-verse. And yet perhaps they had.

He circled the topic, over and over. She could feel her resistance wearing away.

Wearing away.

It was the only flaw in their affair, his curiosity about her body. Everything else was so perfect.

Asked again. And again.

At some point she realized she would give in eventually. Her determination crumbled beneath that assault.

In his hotel room, she removed her clothes, let him stroke her.

"How would we do this, if we were the same?" he demanded.

"As we become aroused, our flesh softens," she said. "Can you feel how mine has changed?"

He touched it cautiously, as though afraid he might leave finger marks. "It's closer to my own now," he said.

"We soften and we come together, and merge," she said. "It is a very intimate and secret thing."

"And you harden again, together." His breath quickened as his fingers dragged across her skin.

"When the moment of the most pleasure comes and peaks, we harden," she said. "We become a single thing, melding where our skin touches."

"And you stay that way for hours?"

"Till the state gives way, and we can separate," she said. "Hours, yes."

"And you think I can bring you to the point where you come like that?" he asked.

Everyone made their own experiments in self-delight as a child. It was not the same, but it was similar, and hard to hide, although the motionless state was shorter. He could do that for her, at least.

She reached for him.

He entered her arms without hesitation.

He played with her as he would have a human woman, licking, spreading, opening. He did not penetrate her—they had both agreed it was too dangerous.

This was the only time most people could touch without fear of chipping, of breaking each other. Was that the draw he'd had for her all along, that she could touch him like that and know there was no danger of breaking him?

Her breath filled her, energy rushed along her like swallows fluttering in the wind, trying to break free of its grasp. Pleasure drowned her and she succumbed, feeling her flesh shudder and stiffen, frozen in the moment.

Where a Porcelain lover would have stayed with her, he drew away. She was aware of him circling her, his fingers straying over and over her surface.

Touching.

Testing.

He began with a toe. Pain surged through her as he broke it off. If she had been able to move, she would have screamed. As it was, all she could do was let it shine in her eyes. What sort of mistake was this? An accident, surely.

But then he began to detach the joints in her knee. He intended to take her foot. Anger and pain and agony surged through her and she fell unconscious, carrying with her the vision of him sitting on the side of the bed, examining the foot in his lap with an expression she'd never seen before on his face.

Tikka had never seen him again. She had never been able to guess if the moment had been there in his head all along or if the desire had seized him somewhere along the way, perhaps when she showed him the Dedicatorium.

In time, she did learn that the perversion was not new. In some channels, the severed limbs sold very well, particularly those unmarred in any other way.

She padded the stump with soft plastics, a cap that fit over the protrusion, the jagged bits of joint that had not fallen away. She limped, but not much, grown accustomed to the way she moved.

She paused to watch the sky. Clusters of limentia, like jellyfish floating on the wind, translucent tendrils tinting the light. They filled the air with their mating dance, drifted around her till she stood in

128

the center of a candy-colored cloud. Love surrounded her in a web of tendrils, unthinking action and reaction that drove life, all life, even hers.

She made a mental note of their presence, of the way they shone in the sunlight, of the acrid smell of their lovemaking, filing details away with clinical precision.

They were only another sign of spring on Planet Porcelain.

## Afternotes

*This is a retelling of Carson McCullers' "Good Country Folk," liberally mashed up with some thoughts derived from travel writing and a number of "Top 5" lists compiled while working for HelloSeattle.com.*

*This is a piece I consider slipstream, along with "Bus Ride to Mars." I hope it makes you feel very strange.*

*It is original to this collection.*

# Bus Ride to Mars

Day One
After Djuna had been ushered outside by the men in dark sunglasses, she realized it was cold, even though yesterday had been balmy. Spring's uncertain chill chased her up the steps into the bus's welcome heat. Even cold, though, it was spring, and she wavered on the very last step, suitcase in front of her like a wall. Then someone pushed at her from behind and she went in.

Wider than most, the bus took up one of the highway's double lanes. Inside two aisles ran between three banks of seats upholstered in royal blue, squares of clear plastic clamped onto each headrest. Shadows pocked the aluminum floor.

The bus shuddered away from the curb. Azaleas bloomed in each yard, mop-heads of purple and pink and crimson and the occasional yellow.

They left the neighborhood behind and passed through a wooded area on the town's edge. Fenced-off trees bore carvings featuring pluses and hearts and arrows and one mysterious biohazard marking. Was it warning her, confirming every misgiving about this journey? She could have stayed, somehow. Would have stayed, somehow, refused to remove herself from her house despite the polite gentle insistence of the spirits in black. Could she touch the cord, bring the bus to a stop, get off, walk back home? She flexed her hand, looking up, but made no move to rise.

When in doubt, eat. She'd packed a hamper. Two sandwiches, bacon

and crunchy peanut butter, four more peanut butter on whole wheat, a cooler with four strawberry yogurts and a gamepiece's worth of cheesecake among the ice packs, baby carrots, and a stalk of celery in a baggie. A dozen juice boxes. Tofu cubes marinated in sesame oil and soy sauce, and squishy avocado wrapped up in nori. That was lunch for today, in a few hours.

She had two carrots now, biting them off with angry snaps. She'd set off and now here she went, despite the fact that she'd rather stay home, to Mars, which was also the Afterlife, somehow.

The air smelled like old French fries and stale donuts. An unceasing fan blew down on Djuna, making her extract a sweater from her carry-on. She had never expected the Afterlife to have a temperature.

At the front the robot driver, tireless, drove without ceasing on its own behalf, although it would park every six to twelve hours for the benefit of its passengers. It wore an absurd blue plastic hat and no other illusion of clothes.

The windows with which the outermost seats were privileged featured mask-sized ovals with plastic shutters. Two-thirds of the way back in the bus, Djuna slid the shutter closed, leaving a slit of brilliance.

From her vantage point, she could see most of the bus and her fellow travelers. She'd treated it like any other journey. She'd hoisted her rollaway in the overhead shelf, dumped her shoulder bag and coat on the middle seat to discourage seat seekers, and shoved her paperback in the middle seat pocket. The book's cover showed a dolphin curved around a woman, titled *Forbidden Waters: A Real Life Odyssey into Inter-racial Passion*, blue and silver foil waves shimmering around the couple.

She hooked the Traveler's Marvelous Window Garden's suction cups below the window's lip. A silly souvenir bought at the station. She did not read the 8 point font descriptions on the seed packets, simply shook vermiculite particles like mica grit from their puffs of plastic into the windowbox. She planted and watered, and read the first two pages of her book and ate another carrot. She was in it for the long haul, the five day trip to Paradise, Mars.

Most of the other travelers were nondescript. A few stood out, particularly a young woman all in pink and gold, dark hair, a spiral unicorn horn—Djuna couldn't guess whether it was cosmeticked

there or some mark of Faerie. Her eyes were saltwater deep, blue as storms. She sat near the front, just behind the driver.

An elderly man in a slouchy cap stared at her briefly, like an arborist examining a tree, assessing her height and blossom schedule and composition, before going to the back of the bus and sitting down with a sulfur-scented huff.

A trio of identical blonde ... girls? Young women? Hovering on the edge of adulthood, maybe a little past. They were late getting on. They wavered near her row, clearly thinking three of us, one of you, but she buried her nose in her book and refused to look up. One cleared her throat, but the others tugged her over to a middle row, towards the back.

Triumphant, Djuna ate another carrot, more slowly this time. She looked out the window. Thunder Lanes Bowling. Lightning Shoes. Kang Acupuncture and Herbal Medicine. Fungi Fun-Go. Mi-go Me-go. Shoggoths-R-Us. Strip malls and lanes of traffic. Spirit houses beside the road, edged with gold and crimson paint. She thought of her little house, of the intricate banisters, the upstairs and downstairs she had furnished with her thoughts, her dreams, her china cupboards.

The red-haired kid a few seats up tried to explain his hand-held game to his mother again. "You can be animal, vegetable or mineral," he said.

"Yeah, yeah."

"I control my race's starting philosophy."

"Yeah, yeah."

"I'm warlike and spiritual."

She took her attention from the phone. "How can you be warlike and spiritual? Isn't that a contradiction?"

"Aztecs were warlike and spiritual. I was reading a book about them the other day. They had these sacred warriors, Jaguar warriors."

She snorted but said into the phone, "Will the house be ready? By ready, I mean completely ready. I want linens on the beds and groceries in the cupboards." Then with a shift of tone. "Yes, we'll be fine, the seats are big and he can sleep in them. Yes, I have all of his medication. Bye." She flipped the phone closed and stared at the concavities on the floor, pressing her hands together as though praying.

"Mom? Mom!"

"Jaguar warriors," she said wearily. "Listen, do you want to hear a story about Jaguar warriors?"

"Yeah," he said warily, as though unsure what he was agreeing to.

"Once upon a time, there was a king named Gil."

"Was he a Jaguar warrior?"

"He was a warrior king, fierce as a Jaguar. He ruled his kingdom with a fair and gentle hand, but every time he went out to speak to his people, the people he'd agreed to govern, to oversee, to be the head to, he'd get this sad look on his face. They'd ask him what was wrong, and he'd look away at the horizon with a sad and noble face and shake his head. This was infuriating."

"Infuriating?"

Djuna ate her nori lump by squishy avocado lump, chasing the melt around the roof of her mouth with a tongue tip as she listened. The Traveler's Garden sent out a hesitant smell of rain.

"Infuriating. Because, after all, what were his people supposed to say to that? He was clearly unhappy but he refused to say anything. And then, eventually, he put aside his crown and went walking down the road, and blamed it all on the unhappiness he never would explain to them."

There was a silence before the kid spoke again, voice like an uncertain snail's horns emerging. "Is this story really about Jaguar warriors?"

"It started out that way," she said. "Then it all went pear-shaped, and I don't know when."

Silence stretched between them. A few seats forward, a nerdy boy was interviewing the unicorn girl. She spoke in upper-class, almost accentless English.

"My name is Cristen Night," she said, blinking at the camera. "What should I say?"

"Talk about anything. Talk about what sort of TV you like to watch."

"I like to watch that new show, These. You know the one? It's been around for two seasons, just starting the third."

Nerdboy made a noncommittal sound, gestured at her to keep talking.

"There's the main character, King T, who's married the Queen of the Centaurs and brought her and her sister Emily to live in

his place. It's like a huge cloud castle, all misty white corridors and you know, atmosphere."

The plastic creaked as she shifted against it, getting more animated.

"The actor they have playing him is all-vid, latest gen algorithm. Kurt Destiny is the brand. So swank! Dublicious. Anyhow, he was getting married at the end of last season, and all these glims in black show up, laced and gothy. They're wailing and beating on these hand-held drums they wear around their necks. He asks who they are, and they turn out to be genetic constructs whose male counterparts, like their twins, have all died out due to a bad DNA twist. All bereft, widowed twins. They tell him they need him to wrestle this minotaur thing."

"Why?" Nerdboy adjusted his camera, brought the focus even closer in on her face, her perfect eyes, polished horn gleaming like mother of pearl in the bus's overhead lighting.

She shrugged. "Television." She continued on.

"There's these two PoWs, Palamon and Arcite. They are in this tower and look out, and see Em—that's the Queen's skanky sister—in the garden, her arms full of red and white roses, and more growing from her jacket. They're big bang crush right off on her, and they start fighting over who loves her the most. Then Arcite gets freed and they argue over who's better off, Palamon, who has the chance of glimpsing her every day, or Arcite, who can go home and raise an army to come and get her with."

The bus jerked to a stop. This close to the sea, salt water rode the wind.

After dinner, the smokers excused themselves as soon as possible from the meal to go outside and power through cigarettes or long thin cigars as fast as possible. The man in the suit didn't even pretend to eat, just ordered a large coffee, black. He took it outside. By the time Djuna came out of the burger taco squid joint, cigarette butts mounded by the heel of his black snakeskin shoe.

Later some riders watched the evening news on the bus TV screen, which hung down to the driver's right. The light was blue and soothing. With headphones in, all she saw was the flicker of faces. Later, she took the headphones out and leaned back. Someone behind her was telling this story:

"I knew this kid, he was a game developer, got snagged by a company fast out of college, bright kid, worked hard, played hard, did a lot of mountain climbing, kayaking, that sort of thing. Truth be told, he was stronger, had a bit more swagger, than the average geek at his company and he became a bully, lorded it over the other devs, and the company let him get away with it because he had the programming chops to back it up.

"He married the CEO's daughter, a bright young Wellesley grad, a geek's daughter, who loved online games as much as any solitary nerdy kid that had been raised on World of Warcraft.

"He was one of those weird, obsessive kids and he noticed his wife spending a lot of time playing online games. He'd go and make characters on whatever server his wife was playing on and go grief kill anyone she was flirting with. Over and over again.

"He kept on doing this, rather than working on the games he'd been hired for. He'd try to get his wife into the betas of the games, but she was on to him by that point, I think, wouldn't log into any virtual world he was in, said he was too intense, and of course that just made him more intense.

"When his manager talked to him about his job, he went nutso and accused the manager of having virtually seduced the wife. He'd noticed her playing this one online game, Paradise Garden, an adult encounter game, and when he'd tried to join it, he learned his IP was banned, and all of his credit cards. He said the manager ran the game and that was how the game knew to ban him.

"He went to some sort of halfway house for people that the Internet had damaged. And while he was there, he took up in an online relationship with some kid on Mars."

"And you know him, or you know this kid?"

"I'm him. I'm going to meet the kid."

Silence. Djuna wondered what he looked like. The other voice said, "I thought you said he was young."

"Sure. Twenty years ago, before he went into jail and then the house. He was young back then. I was young back then."

"How old is the kid you're going to meet?"

"She's 18. Cute and smart and funny, and wants someone to help her run the restaurant she inherited. Life's good." He drummed

restlessly on the back of the seat, and she wondered again who he was, which of the crowd he was, as he repeated himself. "Life's good."

⊙▪▬▬▬

## Day Two

In the rumble of early morning, the Traveler's Marvelous Window Garden was filled with silvery green shoots, soft as toothbrush bristles. Djuna ran her palm over the surface and stared outside. A construction site surrounded the highway, orange plastic, then yellow, then olive green, then concentration blue, and tangles of machines and signs that pointed forward and backward, up and down. The bus lurched, swaying from lane to lane.

Like everyone else, she conducted her morning wash in the bathroom, and was glad the bus wasn't more crowded. She stared at her too-pale face in the jerk-surfaced mirror as she brushed the flavor of last night from her mouth and washed her hands with vanilla ginseng bubble pearl soap. She didn't bruise herself changing into a fresh shirt from her bag, but it was close. She'd always bruised easily, banged into door frames and tripped on missing top stairs. She'd lost the ability to be bruised, though, somewhere along the way.

Was that how it went, were the dead unaffected by any events? Was that why they resorted to story after story, half-glimpsed or fragmentary or laboriously whole? They were all the same effort.

When she returned to her seat, she found that the bus had entered the Underwater Tunnel. Outside, she could see the rivets and glass holding back seawater, and the silvery slide of fish every once in a while. The children were glued to the window, and the three blondes stood near the forward luggage rack, taking turns to gaze out. One of them flicked their hair back, away from their flat smooth forehead, and within a few seconds, the others followed suit, made the same gesture.

Behind her—which was the Internet junkie, on his trip to meet a kid, a child? Was it the flat-faced, pleasant-haired man, or the one beside him, who looked surlier, bruised like a peach bounced down the road by life. Maybe that tubby middle-aged man wearing the Darth Vaderix Giz-Pop t-shirt or the very polite looking elderly man.

Two looked back at her then let their eyes slide away.

Later that day, around 2 bus time, or so the buzz went, they'd be stopping in Elfland as they passed through. Just as one of the blonde girls, who said her name was Magda, confided this to Djuna, the robot driver announced it over the intercom.

Its voice buzzed like a wasp: *At 2:35 PM, we will be stopping at the Elfland Border Park and Shop. You will have one hour, fifteen minutes for meal and recreational purposes. Please return to the bus promptly at the appointed time.* The announcement stopped with an admonitory pop and crackle of static and the robot continued staring forward, its metal claws buried in the steering column, maneuvering the bus along the twenty-lane highway.

Signs swooshed past, underwater settlements, sometimes just single homes clinging to the side of the tunnel like a barnacled bubble: Who-ville, Perelandra, Surf N' Turf, Dagon's Deeps, Bucket and Tub, Tile Place, Atlantis. Atlantis looked like a fancy resort. Buses and small, gimcrack cars with their tops down filled its parking lot to its attendant booth gills. Djuna counted cars and tried to convince herself that she wasn't really on the way to Mars. She was at home, snug in bed or on the couch with a cat curled on her stomach.

Who would be feeding her cats?

The red-haired boy told his mother that his civilization just completed the pyramids.

"Did you build the Sphinx too?" she asked, but he didn't know what that was. The mother returned to her phone conversation. They were arguing about interiors and paint and why she didn't just fly there. She said, voice pinched tight with anger, "You're always complaining about the cost of things. I thought you'd appreciate the gesture." The phone clicked as she turned it off.

Nerdboy was interviewing Bristle Woman, standing with his camera transfixed by her face.

"My name is Tulip Song," she said. Her face was lined as though by weather, but a chemical edge to the redness made Djuna think she was younger than originally estimated.

"Are you going to Paradise?" Nerdboy asked. He smirked, and Djuna sensed a tagline for the documentary in his head. Are you going to Paradise? Indeed.

She said, "I am."

"In order to ... "

"I'm going to visit my childhood servant."

Did she say servant or sweetheart? Djuna wasn't sure, and her following words didn't point her in either direction.

"A little girl name of Laura—I haven't seen her in over half a century! Oh, how I look forward to seeing her!"

In Djuna's book, the woman wondered if the dolphin really liked her while the dolphin wondered if she really liked him.

Tulip Song simpered but said nothing more about Laura. Djuna wondered what Laura thought, waiting for the child mistress. What would it be like to grow up with servants at hand? Who did that anymore?

Elfland was disappointing, too neon and clove scented, too ready to hawk jeweled bridles and flasks of love potions. The passengers ate a late lunch there, including fresh fruit from the little goblins hawking grapes and strawberries and apricots in the rest stop parking lot. Djuna sat among the ancient oaks, filled with gloom and doom and signs warning her not to go too far into the trees.

The cheap fruit was sweet, so delicious that she ate it all within an hour or two of having re-boarded the bus, which swayed its way up the Elfland Entrance Ramp, 77BAA. She licked her fingers clean long past the time when the savor had left them. This would have embarrassed her more if she hadn't noticed others doing the same. The children were uniformly asleep, drooling like opium smokers. The elderly man had bought a birdcage with three blue butterflies in it. They sang the same tiny shrill song, over and over again.

Mr. Suit had bought more than fruit—he drank from a little golden flask. Restless, he paced around the inside of the bus. Finally he leaned over the back of the seat in front of her and said, "Hey, you?"

She squinted at him.

He squinted back. "You look like a palm reader. You read palms?"

She shook her head.

His eyes squinted harder. Dirt lined his collar and stubble sprang out on his jawline like an untamed assertion.

"I knew a palm reader lived in a guy's house one time, upstairs in the spare bedroom, 500 socks a week including breakfast and Sunday

dinners. Real pig too, had piles and piles of books and noodle cartons.

"His landlord was a regular guy, a carpenter. Had just re-married after his wife died from being hit by a garbage truck. Sweet little thing, just barely legal, his dead wife's sister." He exhaled and she could smell the fairy brandy on his breath. "Puppet pretty."

"The carpenter's out one weekend, helping the guy next door build a miniature golf course. They've been working on it for a while, it's going to help fund their early retirements. She's doing laundry and cooking lunch and the palm reader catches her in the stairway, halfway between the first and second floor. He can see her husband next door, building something that looks like a wooden snowman."

He paused dreamily, closing his eyes and breathing out a second invasion of alcoholic air. Behind her, the caged butterflies began their song again.

"He takes her hands and leans in close, telling her he'll read her fate in her palms, turns them over like soft little doves to examine their bellies, releases one in order to trace the other with a fingertip, running his nail up from the wrist towards the fingers, along the life line, then strokes it from left to right, wavering between the fame and love lines."

Every word made her more uncomfortable. There was something about his face, as though he'd forgotten she was there, as though he was telling himself the story and had forgotten the punch line.

"He brings her wrists to his lips, still looking out at her husband and the pine skeleton of the snowman and browses along the skin there. But she manages to yank away, looking out the window herself. She pulls up the window, sticks her head out, shouts and waves to her husband while the palm reader shrinks back against the wall. She doesn't say anything like *Hey, the boarder is hitting on me*, though. Just says hi to her husband, and then pulls her head back in, shuts the window, and says to him, *My husband's the jealous type. Anything you're proposing to me, you better be factoring that in*."

Man in a Suit breathed out, breathed in, and out again. Djuna wondered whether he was falling asleep, but he opened his bloodshot eyes and said, "And he did. He factored that in quite adequately."

His voice was bleak as air-conditioning. He said the last part again, as though worried she might miss its meaning, "Quite adequately."

Djuna didn't answer and he went on. "The carpenter was going out of town to a meeting of his church. Had I mentioned he was a religious man, a deacon of the Fist of the Luminescent Salvation, a first-class deacon, no less?

"All that she wanted was to sleep in her lover's arms, and that was all he wanted too, he said, envisioning a night of this and that and the other thing. And the next day, the carpenter came home and his wife told him that the palm-reader, Nicholas by name, had been ill and had been staying in his room all this time. A day went by and another, and the carpenter grew uneasy that the palm-reader might have died. He went upstairs and used his master key to open the door and look inside.

"The room was crowded with books and tapestries showing hands and skulls and seas of the moon. Nicholas sat on his bed in lotus position gazing at a tapestry showing a mandala with lotuses blossoming outward.

"The carpenter went to him and shook his shoulder until Nicholas shuddered and came to himself. *Gracious*, he said, and then thanked the carpenter for waking him from his vision. *What was the vision of*, the carpenter asked in turn.

*Next Monday at a quarter past midnight, it will begin to rain, and rain so hard that it floods all this world*, the palm reader said."

The man's suit was the latest cut, but the cheap, shiny material showed threads clumped along one hem. Crumpled Kleenex protruded from his jacket pocket and it looked as though he had been crying. As though he might burst into tears again now unless he was humored.

"And he believed the palm reader?" she said. A dubious twinge tugged at her.

He looked earnest. "Sometimes we aren't raised to question things," he said. "Sometimes we just ... sometimes we're as shocked as anyone that things turn out to be different than what they say."

She licked the memory of goblin fruit from her fingers and felt his eyes on her. He was bending forward towards her, almost head to head.

"I need to sleep," she said, uncomfortable at his proximity. She leaned back in her seat and pulled the blanket over her like a shield. She could feel him standing there, staring at her for a few more moments and then he lurched off to the restroom. She heard him retching in there,

again and again. She held her fingers up to her nostrils, underneath the blanket, and smelled the apricot perfume on her skin as she licked them again, each finger in careful turn.

## DAY THREE

Today, the plants of the Traveler's Marvelous Window Garden had split into two kinds of plant: a set of heart-shaped, fuzzy leaves and fern fronds salad-suitable, tasting of thyme and lemon when she picked one and ate it.

The bus climbed, up and up, a slant that continued for an hour, maybe more, before they broke into sullen sunlight and saw the Space Needle glimmering, the gulls overhead. The bus stopped for a little while at the station there and everyone got out to stretch their legs. Three new passengers got on: a pair of tattooed kids, and an elderly woman with short gray hair and no nonsense running shoes. Within a few minutes of her arrival, the man in the slouched hat was next to her, talking. Waiting near the bathroom, Djuna overheard:

"You look at me and you don't see much, but once I was a sales guy, such a sales guy I could sell kittens to cats and the dry litter left over to a cactus. The home office loved me, they sent me to Boston, Bangkok, Berlin, one time to Baltimore, you name it."

"I used to sell things too," she said. "And trade. One time I started with an empty glass jar to trade and ended up with an entire house, and two ponies, and a basket full of mushrooms."

"One time I promised to sell the moon."

"I told a woman I'd give her fifty percent off on true love."

"I got a guy to approach me about buying his mother's name."

"I bought and sold genders, three for a buck."

"Every time I touch a Ouija board, I'm selling ad space in Hell."

There was a congratulation to their tones that made her look hard for horns amid the sparse gray hair, but they looked human enough.

She peed and washed her hands for the fifteenth time this journey, gloomily estimating the cleanliness level by the end of the trip. She made bargains with herself. If anyone complained about the rain, she'd just go home and skip Mars. If anyone said the word "fish" or "petunia". If the red-haired boy completed the Hanging Gardens. If

**141**

the blonde girls looked at her and smirked one more time. None of this happened.

The man in the suit got out here. Djuna was glad he wasn't continuing to Paradise. Something about the way that he looked at her made her think he would be fine here in Seattle.

Tulip Song was talking to Nerdboy again.

She said to the round-eyed camera: "I once knew this guy, a little rooster of a guy, named Perkins. A partyer, he'd run through your money faster than goose-snot."

"Yeah?" Was that a note of challenge in Nerdboy's reply? Tulip Song kept on like she didn't hear it. She started some long story full of cuff-links and bell jars and errors of circumstance.

But Djuna's attention was caught elsewhere: out on the street an old woman swept with a broom while another one, almost identical, with her skirts hiked up, pissed in the gutter. As she watched, the first woman saw the second, came running, belabored her with the broom while the second continued pissing before gathering herself and scrambling away, serene as salt, and heading down the hill where the glitter of sound's water awaited.

It was an hour and a half by the station clock. Then they were on the road again, rolling out over a lake, another lake. Mountains and more lakes and pines. As she watched, the landscape shifted. There were black and white magpies on the fence poles by the time true darkness overtook the bus.

⊙■■-━

## Day Four

The Traveler's Marvelous Window Garden gave Djuna tiny, perfect pears, sweet as melancholy, and stalks of pink-ribbed celery. Around the edges of the box, strawberries were ripening, but still not quite there. She ate a bite of pear, of peanut butter sandwich, of pear, peanut butter, pear as the road rolled past. It was flat here, all monotonous wheat fields and the great green circles of irrigation. The red haired boy's civilization was battling the upstart Persians.

A small town passed by in a succession of churches and garage sales and one monumental ball of twine. The road stretched like string, taut as heartache and goodbye, leading her into the future.

142

At evening, they pulled into Lawrence and the Burroughs Space Lift. People got out and milled around while waiting for the bus to be loaded into a transport. The station was vast, high-ceilinged. Some of the travelers passing through here were not human: mutants and tentacled Martians, gelatinous Ood and frond-waving Barbai like cinnamon-scented bushes. There were clones and steam-powered constructs and every kind of robot, from a retro, man-muscled brass and silver Adonis to tech robots as boxy and unadorned as vacuum cleaners.

The elderly woman and the man in the slouched hat sat outside in the humid air. Locusts sang in the surrounding cottonwood trees, still spindly new as though less than a decade had passed since their planting. The air smelled of exhaust and wheat and dying flies. Djuna sat near them and ordered a Tecate and listened. The sugar packets on the table showed a series of zeppelins, balloon bellied and intricate as flowers.

This time the woman was the one doing the talking. She said:

"Once I knew a woman who was a marvelous inventor, who built things of jackstraw and metal gears as thin as paper. She built herself a house that she lived in, like a hermit crab inside its shell, and she kept building inwards, until she grew as thin as a serpent, coiled among her books and magazines and old lanterns."

"What did you sell her?" The man sounded sullen as a chessboard, slouched in his seat as though set in cement. "Space?"

She took a drink of milky soda.

"Death," she said. "The ultimate closet." A shiver went down Djuna's spine as they looked at each other.

Later, much later, the driver came around, got everyone into the bus before it was loaded onto the transport.

The hamper was almost empty, but Djuna took out the cheesecake as she felt the shudder and grip of the Space Elevator, of the transport moving her up, inexorably, into the sky. She ate it, bite by careful bite, as though saying goodbye to its flavor. She thought about what she'd seen along the way, what she'd heard. Maybe any place was the same as any other. Still, she thought about the red dust of Mars. They said it got into the food, that there was an iron tang to the grit there that you couldn't get anywhere else, that had old Martians licking rust in their

retired days in too green places.

She thought about opening the window and crawling out, jumping off into space. What would happen then? It could be anything, really. Like a sit-com or a musical or a wonderful book. She'd always thought it would be pleasant to live in a world where people spontaneously broke into song.

If the window didn't open? She'd have to smash it, perhaps with the heel of her shoe. It would be so complicated and messy, though. Would it really be worth it?

Djuna fell asleep dreaming of the sad surge upwards. Of the struts and wickets of her ascent. Of depressed gremlins clinging to a plane's wing, of balloons at dusk over a prairie's red sweep, of the smell of rain-kissed earth. She dreamed of the life she'd left behind, and told it to herself, but the story was dull, like little pearls of days strung on knotted twine, uniformly even and bland as pudding. When did her story begin? Had it yet? Was it done before it had really begun?

☉■■■━━

## DAY FIVE

The bus was still moving, she could feel it, when she woke in the small hours of the morning. Almost everyone on the bus was. She could hear gentle snores and snorts and the humming of the ventilation system. Outside the stars hurtled past as they went up and up. Below them, the world was the size of a half-shadowed duckpond dwindling to a lilypad.

She contemplated the journey as the bus rose through the darkness. She thought about Point A and Point B and the distance in between. She thought about the impossibility of staying at Point A, of poltergeists and zombies and séances full of dust. When she exhaled, the fronds of her marvelous plant stirred and swayed as though they wanted to whisper something.

She read the last page of her book, and then the advertisements in the back, and then the back cover, and then the numbers of the UPC code. She added them up, and understood what they mean, what the bus represented, and why there was no way to go back. Her story was not done, had not yet experienced its Freitag's triangle, its rising action (though surely she was rising now?), its climax, its denouement like

the shuddering release before one curls into the seats knowing that the story is done and the lights will come up soon. Stories flowed around her, predicting and shaping her own, as though now were the moment of her birth, the moment she began to speak.

Red dust dunes pulled past, lazy armadillo shapes repeated over and over again. She looked for fellow characters out in the rusty sand, or even footsteps or a bit of discarded paper, its letters desiccated and spiderlike. But the landscape was an empty frame waiting to be occupied.

The other passengers were restless. The mother spent a solid hour on her phone, ignoring the boy asking her questions, tugging at her sleeve. The unicorn girl could not stare out the window easily; her horn tip collided with the plastic, had pocked it painfully once or twice when the bus had jolted. So she stood near a window, bracing herself with an arm, watching the horizon and the sun glaring censoriously overhead.

They pulled into Paradise at dusk. Djuna left her trash in the seat. Someone would come by and clean it after all, and her finished book would be a bonus prize for some lucky cleaner interested in dolphin sex.

The air smelled of iron as she pulled her rolling bag across the bus's pockmarked floor, exited and inhaled, curious. Glass stretched overhead in an enormous dome, etched with ravens and thunderbirds. Hope entered in at the soles of her feet and made her stand straighter. There was no turning back. This was Paradise, after all.

## *Afternotes*

*This story is my tribute to one of my favorite books, Chaucer's* The Canterbury Tales. *It appeared in a shorter form in* Daily Science Fiction, *where it was chosen by editors Michele Barasso and Jonathan Laden.*

*I opted to use the book's greater length as an excuse to bring back the earlier version.*

*I hope it's as much fun to read as it was to write. In fact, I hope you enjoyed all of these stories as much as I've had putting them together and writing these notes. It's a great gift to a writer when a reader gives them their time—there's plenty of other books out there after all—and it's appreciated.*

## About Cat Rambo

Raised in the wilds of Indiana, Cat bounced around for several decades before settling in the Pacific Northwest, where she began a prolific writing spree, publishing over a hundred short stories to date in venues that include *Asimov's*, *Weird Tales*, and Tor.com. Her work in the field of speculative fiction includes a stint as *Fantasy Magazine's* editor, numerous nonfiction articles and interviews, and volunteer time with Broad Universe and Clarion West. She has been shortlisted for the Endeavour Award, the Million Writers Award, the Locus Awards, and most recently a World Fantasy Award. This is her third collection.